HAVING THE TIME
OF HER LIFE...

D0951767

continued . . .

"A fun and sexy read."   —The Season for Romance

"A wonderful, lighthearted romantic romp as a kick-butt American Amazon and a hunky Greek find love. Filled with humor, fans will laugh with the zaniness of Harry meets Yacky."   —*Midwest Book Review*

"Katie MacAlister sizzles with this upbeat and funny summer romance.... MacAlister's dialogue is fast-paced and entertaining.... Her characters are interesting and her heroes are always attractive/intriguing...a good, fun, fast summer read."   —Books with Benefits

"Fabulous banter between the main characters.... Katie MacAlister's got a breezy, fun writing style that keeps me reading."   —Book Binge

Much Ado About Vampires
A Dark Ones Novel

"A humorous take on the dark and demonic."
        —*USA Today*

"Once again this author has done a wonderful job. I was sucked into the world of Dark Ones right from the start and was taken on a fantastic ride. This book is full of witty dialogue and great romance, making it one that should not be missed."   —Fresh Fiction

"An extremely appealing hero. If you enjoy a fast-paced paranormal romance laced with witty prose and dialogue, you might like to give *Much Ado About Vampires* a try."   —azcentral.com

"I cannot get enough of the warmth of Ms. MacAlister's books. They're the paranormal romance equivalent of soul food, deeply comforting because I can feel her love for her characters and their stories pouring off of the pages. Her sense of humor really can't be beaten.... Readers who enjoy snarky vampires and feisty vampires will also find plenty to love here, and there are plenty of giggles to be had as well. I'm eagerly awaiting her next book!" —Errant Dreams Reviews

"A lighthearted and humorous paranormal romance.... Sexy vampires, over-the-top bad guys, and other eccentric characters will have you in stitches."
—Smexy Books Romance Reviews

The Unbearable Lightness of Dragons
A Novel of the Light Dragons

"Had me laughing out loud.... This book is full of humor and romance, keeping the reader entertained all the way through ... a wondrous story full of magic.... I cannot wait to see what happens next in the lives of the dragons." —Fresh Fiction

"Katie MacAlister has always been a favorite of mine and her latest series again shows me why.... If you are a lover of dragons, MacAlister's new series will definitely keep you entertained!"
—The Romance Readers Connection

"Magic, mystery, and humor abound in this novel, making it a must read ... another stellar book."
—Night Owl Romance

"Entertaining." —*Midwest Book Review*

TIME THIEF

A TIME THIEF NOVEL

Katie MacAlister

A SIGNET BOOK

SIGNET
Published by the Penguin Group
Penguin Group (USA) Inc., 375 Hudson Street,
New York, New York 10014, USA

USA | Canada | UK | Ireland | Australia | New Zealand | India | South Africa | China

Penguin Books Ltd., Registered Offices: 80 Strand, London WC2R 0RL, England
For more information about the Penguin Group visit penguin.com.

First published by Signet, an imprint of New American Library,
a division of Penguin Group (USA) Inc.

First Printing, May 2013
10 9 8 7 6 5 4 3 2 1

Ⓟ REGISTERED TRADEMARK — MARCA REGISTRADA

ISBN 978-0-451-41742-8

Printed in the United States of America

PUBLISHER'S NOTE
This is a work of fiction. Names, characters, places, and incidents either are the
product of the author's imagination or are used fictitiously, and any resemblance
to actual persons, living or dead, business establishments, events, or locales is
entirely coincidental.
  The publisher does not have any control over and does not assume any responsibility for author or third-party Web sites or their content.

ALWAYS LEARNING   PEARSON

This book would never have seen completion without the support of my family, especially that of my mother, Shirley, and sister, Karen. Both were there when I needed their help coping with the unexpected death of my husband, and both unhesitatingly stepped in to deal with all the ramifications of the death so that I could grieve in peace, and ultimately finish writing this book. My love and gratitude to them is unbound.

I'd also like to thank my editor, Kate Seaver, publisher Kara Welsh, and the production team at NAL for their support in giving me the time I needed to finish the book. They made a very stressful situation much more bearable.

ONE

"You know that saying about lightning never strikes twice in the same place? Well, I'm the living proof that it's totally false."

"The lightning is false, or the saying? Aaaa . . . aaaa—"

"—choo," I finished for the man sitting across from me in the small reception area. I flinched in sympathy when he wiped an already red nose, his eyes just as angry-looking, and swollen to boot. But it was the really magnificent array of hives all over his face and what I could see of his chest through the neck of his shirt that had me adding, "Don't worry. I've heard from my friend Lily that the doctors here are awesome. I'm sure you'll be de-hived and de-puffed in no time."

"I truly hope so," the man said wearily, closing his eyes and leaning back in the waiting room chair, dabbing at both his streaming eyes and nose. "I'm used to pollen allergies, but the hives are new."

"I didn't know that you could get hives from anything but drug allergies," I said, absently mimicking his movement when he reached for his neck before he forcibly stopped himself. Just seeing all those angry red welts made me itchy all over.

"Evidently if you are hypersensitive to some plants,

you can. As I found out this morning when I ran into a large sagebrush next to the road."

I scratched my arm. "Huh. I see mountain sagebrush all the time. They've never bothered me."

"Stranger things, Horatio," he murmured, his hands fisted as they rested on his legs. Poor guy must have been miserable with all those hives. He looked nice enough, too, probably in his late fifties, with brown hair and eyes, and round little 1930s-style wire-rimmed glasses.

"You got that right."

His eyes popped open suddenly. "My apologies, Miss . . . Miss—"

"Mortenson. Kiya Mortenson."

"Kiya?"

"Yeah. It's kind of odd, huh?" I scratched my shoulder. "Mom and Dad were hippies. Smart hippies. They thought it would be fun to name me after some ancient Egyptian who people used to think was King Tut's mom, but I heard recently that she's not. So now I'm named after someone who isn't related to King Tut."

"There are worse people to be named after."

"True that. I could be Hitlerina." I smiled when he gave a rusty chuckle, then grimaced at his itchiness, his fingers twitching with the need to scratch. I scratched my wrist for him.

"I am Dalton."

"Just Dalton? Like a movie star one-name Dalton, or you're afraid to tell me your last name in case I covertly take a picture of you all puffy and hivish and post it on Facebook, where it'll embarrass you in front of all your friends and family?"

He opened his red, swollen eyes as wide as they could go. "Are you likely to take covert pictures of me?"

"No, but mostly because my cell phone is a dinosaur, technologically speaking, and doesn't take photos."

He chuckled again, more carefully this time. "Since my friends and family are safe from my gruesome visage at the moment, I shall risk your suddenly blooming into stalkerhood and will tell you my surname. It's McKay."

"Hi, Dalton McKay."

"Hello, Kiya. I'm sorry I interrupted you when you were telling me something about lightning. You said you were struck by it? That sounds like a major life event. I would think you would have gone to the emergency room rather than a walk-in clinic."

I shrugged. "I wasn't really hurt. Just kind of a bit woozy for a few seconds, but then that cleared up and I was fine. Though I figured I'd better check in to make sure that my heart was OK and that the lightning didn't screw up something in my head. That sort of thing. So here I am."

"Indeed, you are." He blinked owlishly behind his round lenses. "I don't believe I've ever met someone who has been struck by lightning."

"Twice. This was my second time. Hence the comment about the saying being false."

He blinked a few more times, dabbed at his eyes and nose again, and said with a little frown, "What were you doing when you were struck?"

"Helping a chipmunk." I gave a wry little smile. "Well, gasping and heaving and swearing that I was going to get back to jogging regularly is more accurate, but the reason I was doing all that is because I was trying to help a chipmunk that had his head stuck in a plastic milk container. Little bugger could sure run despite that handicap. I had to chase him all over a mountaintop before I caught up with him. I forgot that you're not supposed to hide under tall cedar trees when there's a storm. One minute I was fine, and the next, crack, zap, and sizzle."

"Sizzle?" Dalton looked appalled. "You actually sizzled?"

"Well . . ." My face screwed up as I tried to remember the event of that morning. " 'Sizzle' may not be the right word. There was kind of a scratchy noise when the lightning flower grew. At least I think that was it. Maybe the scratchy noise came from the chipmunk ripping the milk container off his head."

"I don't think . . . no, I'm sure I have not ever heard of a lightning flower. Is it a plant native to this part of Oregon?"

"No, no, it's not an actual flower." I moved over and plopped myself down on a saggy sofa next to his chair, pulling off the gauze overshirt I wore over a tank top. "It's a feathery pattern that sometimes shows up on people who are hit by lightning. See? Supposedly, it's from all the veins and arteries and stuff being lit up by the lightning, but because it's so delicate, it's called a lightning flower."

"That is just . . . amazing." Dalton leaned forward to examine my upper arm. "How very unique. And it doesn't hurt?"

"The lightning flower?" I gave a cursory glance to the feathery pattern of light tan that ran down from my bicep to my wrist. It wasn't like I hadn't seen the same pattern before. Well, assuming I was naked and looking over my shoulder at a mirror. "No. Getting hit by lightning is a bit like touching an electric fence, only more so. But this? Doesn't hurt at all."

"It's almost . . . feminine in its delicacy."

"Yeah, they are kind of pretty in a weird sort of way."

"Will it last long?"

"Well, that's where it gets a bit strange," I said, making myself comfy on the sofa. I couldn't quite say why, but I was content to while away the half an hour or so it would take to be seen by the clinic doctor by chatting with this man. "I looked it up online a few years ago, and they're not supposed to be permanent, but mine are. It's kind of like a scar."

"It doesn't look like a scar." He leaned in closer, touching the pattern with the tip of one forefinger. "It looks like a henna tattoo."

"It does, doesn't it? My foster mom says my other one looks like I drew it on with a tan felt pen, but really, it's just a case of me being in the wrong place at the wrong time. Again."

"You should definitely give trees a miss the next time a storm comes up," he agreed.

"I couldn't really help it. I was . . . er . . . kind of working a temp job. An unofficial one. I was helping out Lily, a friend who wanted to take a couple of days to go see her family, but she had to be up on top of a mountain watching for fires. So I said I'd help her out and take over her shift for her. We figured that this way she'd get to see her family at the same time that I'd make a few bucks, and no one would be the wiser. So, of course, what happens but I chase a chipmunk to kingdom come and back again and get struck by a freak bolt of lightning that I swear came right out of nowhere? And when I called 911 to see if there was someone who could drive me off the top of that mountain to the hospital, everyone had a major hissy fit, and they called the Forest Service, which meant Lily's boss found out that I was there instead of her, and . . . well, you can guess how that all turned out."

"Mmm," Dalton said noncommittally, returning his gaze to my arm. "You said this was the second time you were struck?"

"Yes." I examined his face for a few seconds. "Are you really so miserable that hearing my boring life story will distract you from all the itchiness?"

"Yes," he said frankly, then made a face. "I apologize; that was rude."

"Not in the least," I said, laughing and waving away his apology. "I know what it's like to try *not* to do something, so I'm happy to give you something else to think about. I was hit by lightning once before, when, according to my foster mom, I was about three years old. I don't really remember anything about the storm or the fire that followed it." I smoothed my hand down one leg of red Capri pants that made me feel very 1950s.

"And you weren't hurt? A little girl of three?"

"Nope. Evidently I was just struck by lightning on my butt. Which is odd enough, let me tell you. Carla—my foster mom—says that the lightning that hit me also started the forest fire that killed my folks and a couple of people who were with them in the campground, and that the firemen couldn't believe I hadn't been hurt other than having my clothes blown to shreds." I thought for a moment, then gave a shrug. "I've tried to remember what happened because I have absolutely no memories of my parents, but it's all just missing. Carla says my id and ego and superego are all blocking the events of that night because they were so horrific. Sounds kind of odd, since they don't block any other bad events I've lived through, but I guess Carla would know; she's a clinical psychologist."

Dalton peered at me through the thick lenses of his glasses, his liquid brown eyes full of empathy. "I lost my parents at a young age, as well. You are lucky not only to have survived but to have found a good home after the tragedy."

I smiled and curled my toes around the toe-grip on my sandals. "I've always been lucky that way. Well, I used to be lucky. It seems to have run out of late."

"Oh? In what way?"

"No job, no boyfriend, my apartment house is going to be torn down, and I've got too many fines at the library to do anything but sneak in and read books while hiding in one of the back study carrels."

"And then you were struck by lightning," he said with a little smile.

I answered the smile. "Yup. Kinda makes you glad that all you have are easily fixed hives, huh?"

The nurse behind the frosted glass window slid open one section and said loudly, "Dalton McKay? You may go into room two. The doctor will be with you shortly."

"Ah. Excellent." He stood up and started toward the door the nurse had gestured at, then turned around and offered me his hand. "Thank you for entertaining me, Kiya. I hope your luck changes soon."

"Thanks. Happy dehiving!"

I didn't see him again, since I was called into another room and had to repeat my story of the morning's adventures, which necessitated a number of tests, but after a couple of hours of giving up what felt like way too much blood, having an EKG, and explaining just what a lightning flower—officially known as a Lichtenberg figure— was, it wasn't until early afternoon that I was released from the clinic with a clean bill of health. I waved to the nurse as I headed out to where Eloise sat somewhat lop-sidedly on the side of the street.

"Right," I told the car as I climbed in through the window, not an easy task on a 1969 VW Bug, crawling over the passenger seat to the driver's side. I gave the dashboard a little pat. "I've given you gas and oil and water, Eloise. I cleaned your spark plugs. I washed your front window, and if you had a back one, I would have washed it, too. I even vacuumed, and found a piece of fresh rope to hold the driver's-side door tight. There is no earthly reason why you shouldn't start, so let's not go the prima donna route this afternoon, OK? We have a good two-hour drive to get home, and since there's no one here in town I can stay with, I really, really, *really* need you to be reliable today."

I took a deep breath and, bending down, fished out the ignition wires that I had to use to start the car because the ignition was shot. Literally. Stupid hunters thinking Eloise was a derelict when she clearly was in fine working order, if admittedly suffering from a few cosmetic insults.

"You're not the only one who's had a few years on her," I told the car while I touched the wires together.

A few sparks, a puff of acrid electrical smoke, and Eloise's engine coughed and sputtered to life.

I sang while I drove out of the southern Oregon town that nestled up against the Cascade mountains, interrupting myself periodically to swear at the logging trucks that barreled out of the wilderness, their swaying loads of freshly cut trees annoying me on many levels. Not only were the truckers arrogant with their "we're bigger than you and thus you have to give way to us" attitude, but I hated the clear-cutting that went on in the interior of the state, even if the lumber companies had a stringent replanting policy.

"The forest belongs to everyone, you road hog!" I bellowed at one truck when it came whipping around a curve, straddling the center line of the road, and causing me to jerk the wheel to the right, sending poor Eloise onto the shoulder, where the passenger side was forced to endure the savagery of a long stretch of wild blackberry bushes before the car came to a shuddering halt. "I've got your license plate number! I'm going to turn you . . . Well, drat, no, I didn't get the number. Bastage."

It took me a few minutes to get a grip on my jangled nerves, but at last I stopped shaking and tried to start the car.

Eloise gave a few oily coughs, backfired twice, and lapsed into an ominous silence. I swore to myself. "Great. Stupid logging trucks picking on innocent little Bugs. Well. Only thing for it is to get out and see if you're truly stuck or just being cranky."

I crawled over to the passenger seat, intending on exiting the car the same way I entered it (which was pretty much my only option), when I realized that in my haste to avoid being squashed flat by the logging truck, I'd run the car right off the tiny dirt shoulder and into a dense wall of blackberries. There was no conceivable way I was going to climb out of the window into that, even assuming I could shove the blackberry vines back enough to escape the car.

"Crap." I sat back down in the driver's seat and considered the door to my left. Due to the fact that the door itself didn't work, it was tied on tightly from the outside. Likewise, the window had been cemented into place, since the mechanism that managed it had long since given up the ghost. "Well, I guess I'll have to go out the back."

The little car shook as another logging truck whizzed past, the wind from its passage sending my shoulder-length hair whipping around my face when I peeled back the duct tape holding the thick, clear plastic that stood in place of my rear window.

I was halfway out the window, swearing to myself as I tried to reach behind me and disentangle the bit of my shirt that had somehow been caught on the twisted window frame, when a car passed me, slowed, stopped, then, with blithe disregard to both laws of the road and common safety, backed up until it was stopped behind me.

"Problem?" the man who got out of the car asked as I struggled with the tangled wad of shirt behind me. I was half in the car, half out of it, one hand braced on Eloise's sloped rear while my legs kicked around inside.

"Yeah, my shirt is caught on something and I can't . . . ow! Son of a bitch, Eloise!"

"My name is Gregory, not Eloise," the man said with a voice filled with humor. "Perhaps I can help."

"Sorry, I was swearing at my car, not you," I answered, releasing my hold on the twisted cloth, and leaning forward, sucking the blood off my punctured finger. "Be careful. The metal's jagged just around the top, and it's sharp."

The man reached in alongside my hip, sliding his hand up and onto my butt.

"Whoa, now!" I jerked to the side, my legs kicking again as I tried to escape both the caught shirt and the butt groper. "That is totally uncalled-for! What sort of a man takes advantage of a snagged woman to cop a quick grope?"

"Sorry," he said, quickly moving his hand. "I didn't mean to ... er ... grope. I'm just trying to locate ... Ah, this must be it. Hold still, or I won't be able to unhook the material."

I twisted around to glare suspiciously at the back of his head as he bent into the empty window, but he must have been telling the truth, because he didn't attempt any more unsolicited touching. The shirt gave way as he released it.

"Oh, thank you," I said in relief, intent on sliding forward down Eloise's rear. Two strong hands under my arms caught me instead, pulling me out until I was upright on the road. "Oh. Er. Thanks," I repeated.

"My pleasure. I don't mean in reference to touching your ass, although that was very nice. In a wholly accidental way."

"Yeah, well, it's not the way to make friends or influence people," I muttered, spinning around as I tried to see the damage to my favorite gauze blouse. I finally twisted it around, grimacing at the dirty hole now present in the back.

"Would it be rude of me to inquire why you were climbing out the back of your nonexistent rear window?" the man asked.

I sighed and released the shirt, then turned my attention to my butt-groping savior. One look at his curly blond hair, Californian surfer-dude good looks, and mischievous blue eyes had my mind going blank for a few seconds.

Gently, he reached out and pushed my chin upward until my mouth closed. I blushed, ashamed that I'd been gawking so brazenly.

"Sorry," I mumbled, wondering how the hell one man

could be so handsome and not have a harem of women traveling around with him. Maybe he was gay? No, in that case, the harem would be male. I shook my head. No matter what his sexual preference, this man was so handsome, it just wasn't possible that he was there at that moment, standing by the side of a little-used road in the backwoods of southern Oregon.

"Why are you shaking your head at me?"

"You're not real," I said. "You can't be real. Unless *America's Sexiest Male Models* is filming at Crater Lake, or something like that. Because otherwise? No. It's just not possible."

He laughed. He had a nice laugh, baritone with just a hint of huskiness. "I assure you that I am very real. Although I do thank you for the compliment. At least, I think it was a compliment."

"Oh, it was."

He laughed again, which relieved the awkwardness of the moment, then suddenly jerked me to the side as a large Land Rover with a boat in tow hurtled past us, far too close to the shoulder for safety. "Idiot American drivers."

"You're not American?" I asked in surprise. He certainly sounded West Coast to me.

"I was born in a very small town in what is now Romania, actually," he said with a little bow. "My name is Gregory Faa. And will you give me the pleasure of knowing your name?"

He had absolutely no accent, but the way he put words together did sound a bit foreign. Or at least, very upper-class. "Kiya Mortenson. Sorry I gawked just then. I wasn't expecting to be rescued from the depths of Eloise by a Romanian supermodel."

"I'm not a model," he said with another smile. "I take it that your car has broken down?"

"Well," I said slowly, following him when he went around to the front of the car. "With Eloise, it's not so much a case of breaking down as it is running on a hope and a prayer, but yes, we got run off the road, and she stopped and won't start again. Oh, the engine is in the back on a VW Bug. Are you good with cars?"

"Not particularly." We moved to the rear of the car. In silence, we both contemplated the workings of Eloise's motor. "I can give you a lift into town, though. I'm sure you can get someone to tow the car there."

"Ew. Tow truck." I bit my lip and tried to calculate how much money, if any, was left on my credit card. My bank account was sorely depleted due to Lily having to return to work, and thus not paying me for my covert fill-in job. "Um ... yeah. Maybe I'll just let her rest for a bit. Sometimes she will start up if she's had some time to recuperate from trauma."

A large RV lumbered past us, narrowly missing hitting Gregory's shiny red car. He cocked a light brown eyebrow at me. "I wouldn't risk leaving my car on this road, even if it was"—he glanced over my shoulder to where Eloise sat—"temperamental. It's not safe."

I eyed his sports car. "I don't suppose if we had a rope, you could tow me into the nearest town? Or maybe just to a pullout spot, if there is one on this road?"

"No," he said gently, taking me by the shoulders and pushing me toward his car. "Jaguars do not tow other cars. Get in, and I will take you down the road to the next town. It's not far, three or four miles at best."

"But, Eloise—"

"It will take us ten minutes at the most to get to town.

We must hope that your car will be safe for the time it takes for the tow truck to fetch it."

Limply, I allowed him to seat me in his car, all the while mentally chastising myself for not standing up to this handsome Good Samaritan. It wasn't like me to be a doormat for any man, but here I was sitting silently, guiltily enjoying the mingled (and heady) aroma of leather seats, expensive car, and sexy man as he whisked me away.

"Were you on your way to your workplace when you had car trouble?" Gregory asked politely a few minutes later. Fir trees that lined the narrow road whipped past us on the right side, leaving the impression of a green blur that was punctuated now and again by sharp, craggy rocks that jutted out of the earth and jabbed pointy fingers to the sky. To the left, off and on through the dense trees I caught a flash of silver light, indicating a stream or perhaps one of the lakes that dotted this area.

"I wish. I'm unemployed at the moment. I was helping out a friend, but that ended kind of badly; hence I'm on my way home. I live near the coast, so it's important that I be able to get Eloise started again." I gnawed my lower lip for a few seconds, not wanting to ask the question uppermost in my mind, but not seeing much of a way out of it. "Do you think a tow for Eloise would be much above fifty bucks? If it's only a couple of miles, that is?"

He glanced at me out of the corner of his eye. "I shouldn't think so. A bit on your uppers, are you?"

"Huh?"

"Sorry, that was a Briticism. I take it that you're a bit short of ready cash?"

"And unready cash, and cash that will never have a

chance to be ready because frankly, it doesn't exist, and probably never will." I sighed. "My unemployment ran out a few months ago. The job market is crap for someone who has no marketable skills other than the ability to coax a forty-five-year-old car into running long past its normal life span. You don't happen to know of anyone who's looking for a secretary or receptionist or something like that? I can type and answer phones and file if needed."

"I'm afraid I don't, no," he said, shooting me a sympathetic look as we headed into a tiny little town named, according to the decorative sign by the side of the road, Rose Hill.

"What do you do?" I asked, grimacing when the question came out somewhat accusatory. "Sorry, I didn't mean that like I expect you to give me a job. *Are* you a model?"

"Me?" He laughed again. "Hardly. I'm in acquisitions."

"What kind of acquisitions?"

He shrugged. "Whatever I find profitable at the time. Lately I've been working out of Los Angeles exporting artwork to affluent Asian technology companies who wish to make an entrance into the global marketplace."

"Sounds cool. What are you doing out here in the boonies of Oregon, if you don't mind me being nosy?"

"I don't mind at all. My family is here, and due to the work I just mentioned, I haven't been around much. My grandmother has been demanding I visit for the last six months, and this was the first opportunity I've had to drive up here. Ah. There is the garage I remember seeing on a visit earlier. Would you be terribly offended if I offered you a small loan to cover the cost of a tow?"

"Offended? Are you kidding? I'd be more likely to throw myself on you and kiss you in gratitude."

His eyes twinkled at me with a roguish glint that had me grinning. "I'm in a bit of a hurry right now; otherwise I would take you up on that offer."

"Hot art acquisition waiting for you?" I asked, climbing out of the car once he had stopped in front of a tiny gas station with an attached one-car service bay. On the far side of the building a shiny new tow truck sat in the shade of the ever-present pine trees.

"As you said, I wish. Unfortunately what awaits me is a visit to my grandmother and her nightmarish herd of five pugs. Hello? Is someone here able to help me?"

I followed him into the minuscule office, filled almost to capacity by a man in dirty blue overalls and, inexplicably, a knitted hat with antlers and deer ears.

"Whatcha need?" the large man asked as he shifted off a hard metal stool and gave us both the once-over. "Gas is self-service. Pay in advance at the pump."

"My friend here is in need of a tow."

I listened silently as Gregory described the location of Eloise, and tossed a hundred-dollar bill across the cluttered counter just as casually as I might flick a piece of lint off my shoulder.

The tow man grunted an acknowledgment, pocketed the money, and hoisted his bulk back onto the stool at the same time he bellowed out a name. "Norm!"

Another rotund man emerged from the depths of the service stall, wiping his filthy hands on a crusty rag. "Yeah?"

"Got a tow for you. 'Bout five miles out of town between here and Heron Creek Road. Old VW."

Norm hawked and spat, nodding as he trundled out to the tow truck.

I watched him nervously, and wondered aloud if I should go with him to ensure Eloise's safety.

"Can't. Against the law," the station owner said before picking up a hunting and fishing magazine, and burying his nose in it.

"Don't be such an automotive mother hen," Gregory said as he escorted me out of the confines of the small office, and steered me over to a bench that sat in the shade opposite the station. I eased myself down carefully, mindful of splinters, since the bench was made out of a roughly hewn split log. It marked the outer boundary of what was obviously a little picnic area, complete with two squirrels who were mating under a beat-up picnic table, and a trash can that—if odor was anything to go by—was housing the several-days-old corpse of a large mammal. Some of the mountain sagebrush that Dalton was so allergic to lay just beyond the area. "Your car will be fine. I hate to leave you by yourself, but if I don't get to my grandmother, she'll rip several strips off me."

"Sorry to delay you," I said, and I was, although not so much that I didn't add, "Enjoy the pugs."

He made a face. "I'm hardly likely to. They're little monsters."

"Aww, they're so cute and adorable, how can you say that? I love pugs. I've always wanted to have one, but just haven't been able to get enough saved to afford it. Do you have far to go?"

"You've never met my grandmother's beasts. She treats them like they are human, letting them in her caravan, and eating food she cooks. And no, she's staying about a mile from here. Are you familiar with the Appleton Mill in the Umpqua Forest?"

"Not really, no." I searched my memory for grains of information. "I know the forest is near here because I've seen a ton of signs for various camping facilities."

He nodded. "My family is residing in the forest at the present."

"Residing? I didn't think they let people build there."

"Not in houses. In caravans ... er ... RVs, you call them."

"Now, that's the way I've always felt camping should be done," I said with a smile of appreciation. "None of this sleeping out in a mildewed canvas tent that every animal stronger than a slug can get into. Is your family back-to-nature kind of people? I heard there's a fairly large contingent of nature lovers who hang out in this area."

"Something like that." He glanced at his watch and swore under his breath, then eyed me for a second. "It's too bad you live so far away. My grandmother said just this morning that she is feeling the strain of caring for her little monsters. If you were available ..."

He left the statement a half question. I shook my head with real regret. "I'd love a job taking care of dogs, especially adorable pugs, but I'm afraid the commute from my apartment to this area would kill Eloise. Not to mention would cost more in gas than any dog-care salary would cover."

"Alas." He took my hand and, to my surprise, bent over it, pressing my fingers to his mouth for one scorching hand kiss. I gawked at him again, amazed at the sensation, and unsure of how to react. Did one clasp the hand that held one's own? Shake it? Kiss his hand in response?

A giggle built up inside of me at the idea of me gravely bending over his hand and kissing his knuckles.

Oh, if only my phone could take pictures, my friends would all receive one of me doing just that.

"It was a pleasure to meet you, Kiya," he said, releasing my hand. I held it stiffly at my side, feeling horribly awkward.

"Likewise. And thanks for the tow loan. Do you ... er ... have a card or something with a mailing address so I can send it back to you when I get home?"

He hesitated for a few seconds. "I am between addresses at the moment, but a letter sent to me care of this address will reach me." He pulled a card out of his wallet and offered it.

I mouthed the name of the law firm printed on the card, then tucked it away, and thanked him again. He smiled and got into his car, leaving me alone with the two randy squirrels, the dead thing in the garbage bin, and a wish that, just once in my life, something would go right.

TWO

As it turned out, luck was with me for once. Norm the mechanic managed to get Eloise started, although her engine definitely sounded worse than normal.

"Thanks for all your work," I told him as I winced when she backfired.

"She's going to need a lot more if you want to make it back to the coast," he warned.

I thought of the repair amount he'd quoted me, and blanched. "I know, but she should at least get me to a potential job. Can you tell me how to get to the Appleton Lumber Mill?"

Norm spat at Eloise's tire and gave me an odd look. "You mean where those Gypsies are campin'? Buncha thieves. Old mill is about a mile outta town. Take the left at the crossroads. Can't miss the sign."

"Wow, that was unpleasant," I told Eloise as we drove out of town, turning off at the listing, faded, mud-splattered sign sprouted out of the sagebrush at the edge of the road to announce that I was in the vicinity of the Appleton Lumber Mill.

"Well, at least Norm was right in telling me where this mill was," I said, turning onto the private drive. It had once been paved, but was now more potholes and rocks than anything resembling an actual road. Crowding in on either side of the drive were fir trees, and dense tangles of sagebrush, the subsequent wall of green giving the drive a closed-in, almost eerie feeling. "Careful does it, Eloise. Ouch. Sorry. Didn't see that big hole. If we can just—what the hell?"

I had been creeping along the road, given its (and Eloise's) bad state, but as the drive curved to the right, a mossy chain with a battered and almost unreadable PRIVATE PROPERTY—NO TRESPASSING sign popped up and blocked the way.

"Well, crap. Um. Hmm." I shifted into park, grabbed my accelerator brick from where it sat on the passenger side of the car, slapped it over the gas pedal so as to keep the engine running, and climbed out to examine the chain. If it looked like it was a hard-core "keep folks out at all cost" sort of chain, then I'd simply park Eloise and continue on foot. But if it looked like no one paid any attention to it . . . "Ah, good, you come off easily. And since those tire tracks look fresh, and very much like they belong to a fancy British sports car driven by a potential male model, then I guess we can risk being arrested for trespassing, Eloise."

I unhooked one corner of the chain, allowing it to drop into the muddy potholes. Although it was summer, there had evidently been a heavy rain recently in this area, since most of the potholes were partially filled with chocolate brown water.

"And besides," I muttered to myself as I climbed back into the car and retrieved the accelerator brick, "it's not like a trespassing fine is going to do anything but add to an already mountainous amount of money that I need. Ouch. Oh man, that was a bad one. Hang in there, little car. It can't be much further."

And it wasn't. A few minutes of bouncing my slow way toward the mill, the drive turned sharply to the left, and the vista opened up. The lumber mill had evidently been on the small side, if the remains of the buildings were anything to go by. There must have been three originally, one large main building that was now nothing more than some broken concrete foundations with the odd bit of rebar jutting up into the air, flanked on either side by two smaller structures, one of which had only one scorched, black wall standing, while the other appeared to be mostly intact, if minus all the glass in its windows, and no doors in the doorframes.

Five shiny RVs were parked in horseshoe formation in the center area. Off to one side was a small green child's wading pool, and a collection of kids' tricycles and other summer-fun paraphernalia. There were no people visible, however, nor was there a bright red British sports car.

"Hmm." I pulled up to the right, and switched off Eloise with a whispered plea for her to start again when I needed to drive somewhere. After the noise of her asthmatic engine, the silence that followed seemed almost smothering until my ears acclimatized themselves to the sounds of the deep forest.

Birds chattered and sang in the trees that surrounded the derelict lumber mill. Bees droned softly as they flitted amongst a bright patch of purple and yellow wildflowers. Tree branches rustled as the wind gently lifted them, and every now and then a chipmunk or squirrel squeaked as it went about its daily business. But from the RVs there was no sound.

"Hmm," I said again as I climbed out of the window and stood considering the six vehicles. I bit my lip. I felt incredibly stupid standing there, not knowing if Gregory had been polite when he said he wished I could take on the task of dog nanny, or if his grandmother was really looking for someone for the job. I didn't even know her name.

I frowned as I tried to remember Gregory's surname. It was something odd, something vaguely foreign. Something that sounded like an exclamation made in one of the old upper-class novels by P. G. Wodehouse. "Faugh, that was it," I said softly, then gathering up my courage, marched over to the nearest RV and knocked on its door.

There was no response. I knocked again, then after a minute moved to the next RV and tried it. It wasn't until I was on the third one, the one in the center of the RV horseshoe, that my knocking got a response. An immediate yapping sounded forth, along with the sound of several small bodies thumping against the door.

"Clearly I've found the right—aieee!" The door opened just then and a wave of gray and tan and black furry bodies swept down the steps and flung themselves upon me, sending me falling backward. I lay on the ground stunned for a moment or two before I realized that the squirming bodies that had swarmed me were now licking me with enthusiasm. "Oh my god, you guys are so adorable," I said, laughing as I tried to sit up. "No, seriously, I do not need another bath. But thank you. Whoa, now, no getting frisky with my arm there, Romeo."

"My darlings!" a sharp voice called from the trailer, followed by a loud handclap. "Darlings, behave. Are you hurt, young woman? Terrance, that means you, too. Cease that action at once!"

I plucked the pug who was having his amorous way with my sleeve from myself, and patted him on his head before gently pushing off all the other small bodies that were dancing around on top of me. "I'm fine, just got the wind knocked out of me. Oh my gosh, they are so cute!"

"They are, aren't they?" The woman behind the voice came stiffly down the stairs of the RV, a small, thin figure, her posture showing that she suffered from a curvature of the spine as she carefully descended the steps, holding tight to a handrail. "They are all siblings, all but Terrance, who was a stray I found in Reno. Who are you?"

I straightened up from where I was trying to pet the five wiggling bodies, blowing my hair out of my eyes so I could see the woman whom I took to be Gregory's grandmother. "My name is Kiya. Are you Mrs. Faugh?"

"The name is Faa." She spelled it for me, waving one gaunt hand as she did so. She didn't look very grandmotherly to me—standing up straight, she probably was a few inches shorter than my five foot seven. Bent as she was, she reached my shoulders. Her salt-and-pepper hair was pulled back in a bun low on the back of her head, leaving the sunlight to catch on large dangling gold earrings, several gold chains around her neck, and the jangling gold bracelets with which she was bedecked.

Her face was as gaunt as her hands, the cords of her neck standing out starkly against flesh that had sagged with the passing of time. The rest of her might reflect her age, but her eyes were anything but vague. There was a sharpness to the gaze with which she raked me, enough so that I started babbling despite my intentions of presenting myself as a competent, collected person. "Really? That's so unusual. Is it Romanian? Gregory said something about being Romanian. That's Gregory your grandson, by the way. I met him earlier today, and he mentioned that you might be looking for some dog help.

I love dogs, and I'd be happy to . . . er . . . help," I finished lamely. "If you need me, that is. Although, I'm really only looking for temporary work. I need to pay for Eloise, you see. She's broken."

Mrs. Faa looked where I gestured at my car. "I see," she said after I had finally run down. She looked at me again, making me squirm a little; then her gaze dropped to the pugs, who were milling around my feet. "My darlings seem to approve of you. And if Gregory recommended you, then I see no harm in discussing the situation with you."

Rather than invite me inside her RV to chat, she came down the last step and herded me over to a steel picnic bench painted with *Property of Oregon State Parks* along one leg. The next ten minutes were spent answering questions about my job experience, my ability to care for a large number of dogs, and my willingness to work in the present location.

"Like I said, I don't have the money to get my car fixed, so I'm kind of stuck here until I can raise it. So if you don't mind me being temporary help, then I can have my foster mom check on my plants and feed my fish while I'm out here. Although I'm not sure where I'd sleep. I can't afford a hotel, and frankly, I don't think Eloise is up to much driving."

She waved away that concern. "I must have someone who can take my darlings for their daily swim in the lake, but it will not involve much driving. As for sleeping arrangements—" She picked up the nearest pug and smooched him on the top of his wrinkled little head. "My caravan has only one room, and I'm using that. However, one of my grandsons has camping equipment that you would be welcome to use, so long as you don't mind staying in a tent. You understand that I prefer that you be close by in case I need you."

I wasn't wild at the idea of being at her beck and call 24-7, but I reminded myself that beggars can't be choosers, and accepted the amount of pay she offhandedly mentioned. With luck, a couple of months of dog care and I'd have the amount to get Eloise fixed so I could make it home. "A tent is fine, and this area looks pretty, so no, I don't mind."

"I will introduce you; then you may start immediately. My darlings haven't had their walk today—my grandsons refuse to take them either to the lake or for their walk—so you may begin with that. I will show you where I keep their things, and then you may commence. But first, you must meet each one. Clothilde is the shy one. This is Jacques. He is not shy. Terrance you have already noticed. He is . . . yes. We are working on controlling our baser appetites, are we not, Terrance?"

As the pug was, at that moment, attempting to get busy with the leg of the picnic table, I doubted if Terrance had been working very hard on his issues.

"Maureen is the one chewing on your shoelace—nasty, Maureen! Leave it!—and to her right is Frau Blucher."

I looked up in surprise. Mrs. Faa shrugged. "It is a very long story, too long for today. My darlings are all very well behaved, and have nice manners. You will not allow them to become unruly. And now that you have met them, I will take you to where their leashes and collars are kept, and you may take them for a short walk."

Thus it was that approximately seven minutes later I stumbled out of the clearing and headed down a barely visible trail that Mrs. Faa had indicated, five pugs on five leashes, each equipped with its own small plastic grocery bag, the dogs leaping and barking and running in circles around me until my legs were so bound that I could only take baby steps.

"You guys do realize this is my test to see if I can handle you, right?" I told the dogs as I staggered down the trail. What with the lush vegetation of the forest, it wasn't a minute before I had lost sight of the clearing and RVs. I wondered if Mrs. Faa would really let a stranger—even someone so obviously honest and upright as myself—walk off with her precious dogs, or whether she was somehow keeping me under observation. I certainly had an itchy feeling between my shoulders that I equated with being watched. "So let's all be on our best behavior, OK? Jacques, that is not my idea of best behavior. Man. And you're such a little dog, too."

I looked around quickly, wondering if I could just pretend that I didn't see what the pug had just done on the trail, but decided with a sigh (and a double-bagged hand) that it was important to start off on the right foot.

"Not that I appreciate you doing that the second we set off. Now I get to carry this around for the entire— holy jebus!"

The last two words were uttered in a shriek as a man suddenly stepped out from behind a tree right into the path about a foot in front of me.

THREE

I jerked the dogs toward me when I jumped back in surprise, my body intent on running away from the startling danger while my mind was determined to protect the innocent little pugs. Unfortunately, not being the most coordinated person in the world, I snagged the back of my gauze overshirt on a prickly arm of a blackberry bush, which in turn caused me to lurch forward, forcing my arm out in an arc, which ended when the loaded grocery bag struck the man smack-dab in the face.

He said something in a language I didn't recognize as he recoiled from the bag, an almost comical look of disgust on his face. His nose wrinkled in a manner that I would have thought was adorable on someone less bent on scaring me half out of my life. "What the hell?" he finally said in English.

"That's what I say!" I shrugged myself out of the shirt still stuck to the blackberry vine, and gathered the pugs to me, all of whom were barking in high, brittle voices. My mind raced with the need to find some sort of weapon I could use to protect us from this stranger should I be called upon to do so.

"No, you said 'holy jebus,' which I assume means you have some sort of a speech impediment that makes it impossible for you to say the word 'Jesus' correctly. What do you have in that bag? It smells like shit."

"It is. Well, dog poop, that is. And I don't have a speech impediment." I straightened my shoulders, and clutched my bag of poop. Clearly, that would serve as a weapon. If not one to disable, then one to disgust my attacker into giving me time to escape. " 'Jebus' is a polite way of saying 'Jesus.' You say it when you don't want to offend someone, such as when you're in company with a person whom you don't know, but want to swear at nonetheless. I don't know you. I do want to swear at you. Hence, jebus."

The man's eyes narrowed. "I have done nothing to justify you attacking me with dog shit, or swearing at me. Who are you, and why do you have Lenore Faa's dogs?"

"Look, you annoying man, I am the victim here. I am the startlee, not you, and thus, I have the right to swear, and ask questions of you, not vice versa. Besides, it was just the bag that hit you in the face—not that I tried to punch you in the face with poop; my arm kind of flew out when I jumped back—and, I'd like to point out, not the actual dog poop itself. Clothilde, don't sniff his shoes. He is a clearly a bad person."

I swore the man ground his teeth at me. I took a moment to stop being irritated and look at him. Just in case I'd have to describe him to the police, you understand. The pugs had all stopped barking and were happily snuffling around his shoes—expensive-looking shoes, ones with a high-gloss finish that I bet wouldn't last too long in the woods. He already had a smoosh of mud on one side of his right shoe. He wore black jeans, and an olive green shirt with the sleeves rolled back to show nicely muscled forearms.

I liked his arms. They weren't too hairy, the way some

men's arms get, but not plucked-chicken naked, either. They looked like strong arms, competent arms. Arms you could trust.

"Well, that's it, I've lost my mind," I muttered as I dragged my gaze off his arms, and up to his chest, where it stopped, my brain just kind of grinding to a halt altogether.

Clothilde and Frau Blucher stood on their hind feet, their little paws on his legs, and whined to be picked up.

What were the odds, I asked myself, of meeting in one single day two men who were clearly displaced male models? The man before me had one of those chests that you want to touch, all manly bulges and swoops of muscle and tendon and warm, sleek flesh visible even through his nice, normal cotton shirt. I enjoyed watching those muscles move when he bent to pick up the two pugs, tucking then both into one arm, and fondling their respective ears with a large, masculine hand.

I liked his hand, too. It looked . . . sexy.

"If you continue to stare at my chest in that fashion, I will be forced to agree with you," the man's voice said, finally penetrating the haze of lustful bemusement that had me in its grip.

"Hmm?" I shot a look at his face. He was frowning. Dammit, he was even more gorgeous than Gregory. Although this man was as dark as Gregory was blond, he had eyes that I realized with a start were violet. "Just like Elizabeth Taylor."

His gaze raked over me. "You are a very pretty woman. No, more than pretty. And yet, you have red hair and green eyes. Thus, although you're quite attractive, you do *not* look like Elizabeth Taylor."

My face turned pink with mingled embarrassment

and pleasure at the compliment. "Thank you, but I have strawberry blond hair, not red. There's a difference. Besides, I never said I looked like—Terrance, down! We do not get busy with people we have just met, especially when said people jump out and try to scare us to death."

"I did nothing of the sort." I watched his mouth for a few seconds before forcing myself to look into his eyes, those smoky violet eyes ringed with the thickest black lashes I'd seen outside of a mascara commercial. He had high cheekbones, with sharp, angular planes to his face, a thin, autocratic nose, and lush lips that made my knees feel like they were made of water. "For the love of the gods, woman, will you stop staring at me like I'm the last piece of pot roast in the pan?"

"Oooh, pot roast," I said, my mouth watering. "Nice metaphor."

"It's a simile, actually."

"Damn. I always get those two confused. Regardless, it was a good one."

He made a little gesture with the arm holding the pug girls. They groaned in happiness. "I'm hungry. It was the first thing that came to mind. Also, I like pot roast."

"So do I. You don't find many people admitting that these days, what with everyone eating leaner and healthier cuts of meat, but I always say that you can't go wrong with a good piece of pot roast." The incongruity of discussing pot roast with a stranger in the middle of the woods didn't strike me until much later.

"Agreed."

Silence fell around us, at least so far as speaking went. He continued to stare at me, one hand absently fondling the pug girls' heads. I watched him with an avidness that I was hard put to explain, even to myself.

"You're looking at me that way again. You will cease doing so now."

I shook my head. "I can't. Sorry. You're the second male model I've seen in a couple of hours. I should go buy a lottery ticket, because clearly, my luck is riding high right now. Terrance, no means no! I don't care if he likes pugs, it's still rude to attempt to romance someone's ankle without their express permission."

"I do not like dogs," the man said sternly, glowering at Terrance when I tried tugging on the leash. It didn't work. I had to pry him off the man's ankle.

"Don't be ridiculous. Of course you do."

He sighed heavily, like it was just so much trouble to speak. "You might be a lovely woman who is clearly allowed to have her own way far more than is good for her, but that doesn't mean I'm going to allow you to dictate to me. I said I do not like dogs, and I don't, and telling me I'm ridiculous because of that is unacceptable."

I pursed my lips and looked pointedly at the girl pugs snuggled in his left arm, their faces turned up to his, expressions of adoration filling their bulgy little eyes.

He looked down at them, visibly startled. "How the hell did they get there?" Before I could answer, he glared at me. "You did this!"

"Huh?"

"You thrust them upon me when I wasn't looking!"

The girls wiggled in bliss, their back legs kicking as they tried to lick him.

"How on earth do you thrust pugs on someone when they're not looking? It's not like they're notes you can tape to someone's back!" Honestly, the man may have gorgeous eyes, and a model's body, and well-intentioned, trustworthy arms that I suddenly wanted to feel about me, pulling me tighter against his body while his wickedly delicious lips did erotic things to me . . . Drat. I lost my train of thought. Oh, he may be all that and a wedge of cheese, but that didn't mean he had the smarts of an Einstein.

His glare hitched up a notch. I noticed that his right hand, apparently unbeknownst to him, had moved up to scratch the girls under their chins. "You magicked them here."

"You are seriously off your rocker. Here." I set down Terrance and held out my arms. "If you're done petting the dogs, I will take them back."

He looked somewhat horrified to find he was still holding them, and quickly shoved them at me. "I've told you, I do not like dogs. I was not petting them. And I will thank you to keep your dog magic to yourself from here on out!"

The two girls sighed sadly when I put them back on the ground, and tightened the leashes to keep them from jumping him again.

"You just keep telling yourself that, buster."

"My name is not Buster." He cleared his throat, and pinned me back with a look that was all business. "I will ask you again—what are you doing with Lenore Faa's dogs?"

"Do you know Mrs. Faa?" A sudden realization smote me. The man must be one of her friends, or even her family, and was no doubt lurking in the shrubberies to watch how I did with the pugs. No wonder Mrs. Faa didn't feel compelled to follow me herself; she was counting on her handsome, if slightly annoying, friend to guard her dogs' well-being. I'd do the same thing if I were an elderly woman living out in the woods in an RV, and were trying out a potential dog nanny.

"Why are you refusing to answer my question? It's a simple one, and I've asked it twice. Are you abducting the dogs?"

"No! I'm just walking them, honest!" I said quickly, trying to focus on my job. If this man was a friend of Mrs. Faa, then I'd better watch my p's and q's. Which annoyed me because he was clearly not playing with a full deck. "She asked me to take them out so they could stretch their legs a bit."

His eyes narrowed again. "The grandsons had care of the dogs. Are you working for one of them?"

"Nope. I only know Mrs. Faa and Gregory."

"But you admit to knowing Gregory Faa?"

"I just said that, yes. You know him, too?"

I was surprised, but I suppose it made sense. Why wouldn't the two most gorgeous men I'd ever seen know each other? Maybe there was a "looks like a male model" club that they belonged to.

"Why do you insist on answering every question with another question?" he asked, looking as annoyed as he sounded. His lovely purple eyes raked me over with another look, pausing to focus on my now bared arm. "Do you have some dragon blood in you? Is that how you magicked those annoying furballs into my arms?"

"Right," I said, de-snagging my gauze shirt in order to put it back on. I gathered the dogs to me, and edged around the man. "I'm not going to say you're outright crazy—"

"You already have. You said I was off my rocker," he pointed out.

I took a deep breath and continued on. "I won't say it because that would be rude, and I really need this job, but you, sir, need to seek some sort of professional help.

I'm going to walk these dogs, and I will warn you if you try to hurt either them or me, I will scream my freaking head off, and I have a very big pair of lungs."

His gaze dropped momentarily to my chest. "Yes, you do."

"Those aren't my lungs, and you know it. Now, shoo. I have dog-walking to do, and I can't do it while your chest is right there tempting me."

He glanced down at his own chest in surprise, an act that allowed me to finish sidling past him and make my escape.

"If you are stealing the dogs, I am obligated by law to arrest you," he called after me.

"Are you a cop?" I asked, pausing to glance back at him.

"I am a member of the Watch."

"The what, now?"

"You're speaking in questions again." He was back to looking annoyed. "Stop that."

"Stop what?"

The words that followed were bellowed loud enough that nearby birds squawked and fluttered away. "Woman, you are trying my patience!"

I smiled. "Could you be any more obtuse?"

He took a deep breath, and much as I enjoyed how that action showcased his chest, I felt the time had come to move on from the clearly unbalanced—if hunky—man.

"So, he's a cop, huh?" I murmured to the dogs as we proceeded down the path. "A sexy male-model cop. Who'd have thought, eh, pugs?"

Jacques paused at a stick and piddled. Terrance flung himself onto a fern with a lusty grunt. Clothilde suddenly put both front paws on my legs, and clearly demanded to be carried.

"Oh my god, you are so incredibly cute," I told the little dog, and, unable to resist her bulging eyes, picked her up and tucked her under one arm. Immediately Maureen and Frau Blucher begged to be picked up, and before I knew it, I was staggering through the woods on a narrow path with three pugs tucked into the front of my tank top, while the other two were stuffed under my arms.

"Somehow," I told the pugs as I stopped by the side of a stream to catch my breath, "I imagined the phrase 'take the pugs for a walk' meant that you guys would be doing the actual walking. Oh, how beautiful!"

The trail I'd been on petered out into a black basalt bank along which a little stream ran. The rocky bank looked as if some giant potter had slapped down chunks of clay, roughly shaped, but beautiful against the clear, sparkling water. A few ferns clung desperately to the rocks, while a smattering of small white and yellow wildflowers poked up from the cracks in the rock. The sun beat down with mellow July warmth, taking from the air the bite of chill that was pronounced in the deep shade of the woods.

"This is so lovely. OK, everyone out! We're going to have a little romping fun here." I unloaded my shirt and herded my charges along the bank to where a tree had toppled into the water, leaving a long stretch of trunk lying out of the stream, at the perfect height for sitting. "Look, water! Who wants to go wading? I'll sit here and you guys can splash around and have some fun."

The pugs, unhappy to have been removed from their comfy transport, clustered around my feet and shivered pathetically.

"Pfft. You don't know what you're missing." I stepped

over the pugs and, pulling off a sandal, stuck my foot in the stream.

Immediately, I lost all feeling in my toes.

"OK, so it's a bit chilly. I would like to point out that you guys have fur coats on, and it probably wouldn't be that cold to you. Certainly a dip in the cold water would do your overactive libido some good, Terrance. Terrance? Where are—no! Bad pug! Clothilde does not want to do that with you, and besides, that's her head. Oh, for pity's sake . . ."

I plucked the randy pug from where he was annoying Clothilde and, a bit desperate to cool his ardor, stretched out along the length of the tree trunk so I could dangle him over the stream and let the water wash over his legs. If it seemed too cold for him, I'd forgo letting the pugs wade in the water. "Stop squirming or I'll drop you. Now, see, the water isn't really that cold, it just seems a bit chilly because we're in the nice warm sun—"

"If you're going to drown the little bastards, you're going to have to do more than get their feet wet," a masculine voice said from behind me.

It's hard to whirl around while you're lying prone on a mossy tree trunk that is reclined into a small but burbling stream, all the while dangling a pug over the water, but I managed to not only accomplish such a move but keep the amorous Terrance from falling into the water. I was rather proud of that last fact.

"Who the hell are you?" I snapped before thinking better of such a thing, clutching Terrance tightly to me as the other pugs stood in an unhappy mass on the bank. None of them paid any attention to the man who emerged from the way I'd just come, which told me either they were so annoyed at being near the stream that they didn't care if strange men popped out all over the forest, or they were familiar with him, and his presence wasn't an exciting event in their lives.

"My name is Andrew Faa." He stared at me like the name should have meant something to me. He wasn't bad looking—I assumed he must be related somehow to Gregory, since he bore a fair resemblance—but unlike the dashing, kind Gregory, this man's attitude prickled down my skin like nettles. "You must be the mahrime."

"My name is Kiya, not Mahrime." I struggled to slide down the tree trunk without getting any splinters in my butt. "Are you related to Mrs. Faa?"

"She's my grandmother." His cold blue eyes rested briefly on the dog on my arms. "Are you going to drown them or not?"

I gawked at him, outright gawked with my mouth hanging open (again). "You are kidding, right?"

He said nothing, just turned around and started down the path. "My grandmother is waiting for you. She doesn't like to wait on anyone. Stop playing with the little bastards and get back to her."

I bristled at both his tone and inhuman attitude toward the adorable pugs. "Puggies, heel," I said, snatching up the leashes from where I'd secured them on a bit of the tree's root. "I am so going to tell your mom what her grandson said. I don't care if tattlers never prosper, he was serious when he asked if I was going to . . . no. I can't even say it. What a jerk."

The pugs and I marched down the path (if you could call five pugs—joyous at having escaped wading in a stream—frolicking and leaping about one as "marching"), muttering to myself about the cruel man we'd just met. We got lost twice, paused to rescue a deceased raven from Terrance's advances, and had several exciting adventures with assorted leaves and sticks before we managed to burst free of the fir trees and arrive back at the old mill clearing. "If I could drown anyone, I know who I'd pick," I finished before stopping next to Mrs. Faa's RV to untangle the pugs from my legs.

I'm not an overly shy person, but when the group of people who were clustered around a picnic table in the center of the mill yard turned en masse and looked at me, I was overcome with a sudden desire to bolt.

There were four men—one the obnoxious Andrew Faa—and two women (both of whom held a child in their respective arms), and two toddlers playing quietly nearby.

"Go away," one of the men said loudly, turning a craggy face with an unbearably proud expression on it toward me, grandly gesturing toward Eloise as he did so. His voice was deep and rich with something it took me no time to identify as pure malice. "Your kind is not wanted here. Leave before we force you away!"

"That will be enough, Vilem." The razorlike voice of Mrs. Faa emerged from the group of people, followed shortly by the woman herself. The people—presumably her family members—parted like the Red Sea, an act I thought was due to respect for her until I saw her use a knobby cane to smack the legs of whoever was impeding her progress. "The girl is here on my authority."

"But, Mama!" The sallow-faced man named William turned to frown at her. "She is mahrime!"

"Actually, my foster mom is Presbyterian, but I don't see what that has to do with the price of tea in China," I said, allowing the pugs to pull me over to where Mrs. Faa had seated herself on a wooden lawn chair.

She cooed to them for a few seconds, her arthritic hands patting each dog as she asked them if they had a good time. "I have engaged Kiya to attend to my darlings for a few months, until we go to Scarboro," she finally said, leaning back in her chair. I unhooked all the leashes and, with a murmur, replaced them where they hung on a couple of pegs just inside her RV.

"But, Mama—"

"She will stay here with us, so that she may take care of my darlings as they deserve." Mrs. Faa cut across her son's protestations. She pursed her lips and added, "Unless you have changed your mind, and wish to take over that task yourself?"

William snarled something under his breath that I was willing to bet wasn't at all what one should say to one's elderly mother, and turned his glare to me. "Stay away from the women," he snarled, jabbing a finger toward the two women who were still clustered together, wary looks on their faces.

"I beg your pardon?" I gasped in surprise.

"You are mahrime. Unclean. I will not have the women and children tainted by your presence." He shot a fast, nasty glance at his mom before pinning me back with a look that should have stripped the hair from my head. "Remember what you are here to do, and stay out of our way."

Before I could respond to the not-so-thinly veiled threat in his voice, he turned and stormed off to the RV at the far end of the semicircle, Andrew following him.

I glanced at the women and men who remained behind. They stared back at me with hostility. "I am not unclean," I told them. "I shower every day. And I love long bubble baths. I might look a little grubby now, but that's because I had three pugs stuffed in my shirt, and was lying on a log, and Terrance kept trying to get it on with my ankle, and he has dirty paws. So that 'unclean' slur is just totally bull."

"My son is volatile," Mrs. Faa said, waving a dismissive hand toward William's RV. "You will not be distressed by him. I will now take my nap."

Immediately, one of the women handed her child to the woman next to her, and moved over to assist Mrs. Faa in rising. The old woman slapped at her hand before beckoning imperiously toward me. "Kiya will assist me. Piers, Arderne, you have work to do, yes?"

The two men—both dark-haired, and apparently twentysomethings—nodded.

"The women will attend to their duties, as well."

A hurt look flashed in the woman's dark eyes before she nodded and bowed her head, returning to claim her child before moving off to one of the RVs, the other woman herding the toddlers into another RV. The two men scattered, one grabbing a gas can and heading to a motorcycle, the other taking an ax and disappearing around behind the one standing building.

"Were those your sons and daughters?" I couldn't help but ask as the old woman grabbed my arm and used it to pull herself to her feet with a grunt.

"I have seven sons, and fourteen grandsons, but no daughters. Vilem is my oldest son but one. Andrew, Piers, and Arderne are my grandsons. The oldest of the women is Lorna, Piers's wife. The other is Rachel, Arderne's bride."

"Wow. Big family. And all boys, huh? Here, let me help you—"

She didn't need me to hoist her up onto the step of the

RV—she simply grasped my arm with one hand, and the handrail with the other, and more or less pulled herself up the steps. The dogs must have been trained well, because they stood back until she had climbed the three steps before clambering in after her. "Three of my grandsons are wed, and have eight children between them, so yes, we have a big family."

"Are they all here?" I asked, trying to remember how many RVs there were in the circle. Five, I thought.

"No. They will join up with us in August when we journey to the Scarboro gathering. Here. I will rest on the sofa."

She settled herself on a long butter-colored leather sofa that ran along one side of the RV. I used the time it took her to get settled with all five dogs around her to surreptitiously glance around the motor home. I may not be a connoisseur, but I recognized money when I saw it, and the interior of Mrs. Faa's home away from home screamed affluence. The couches (two) and chairs (four, not counting the driver's and passenger's seats up front) were all the same rich leather. Gleaming, highly polished oak was highlighted with brass fittings, and the kitchen area toward the rear had what looked like real marble on its tiny counters. "We will rest for two hours," Mrs. Faa said grandly, patting a pug (Jacques) with one hand while picking up a book with the other. "You may use this time to get yourself settled. You will tell Vilem to lend you the camping equipment that is stored in one of the caravans. You may also wish to go into town to purchase whatever else you need for your stay."

I stopped eyeballing the interior of the RV and tried to look attentive and highly reliable. "Oh, like a toothbrush and such? Yeah, I suppose I should get that."

"I will provide you with an advance on your salary since you are obliging me by staying on the mill grounds with us. Tell Vilem to put up your tent next to where you parked your car. That should provide you with the privacy you no doubt seek."

"Sure. But what about water? And bathroom facilities?" I adopted an expression that I hoped would demonstrate just how ill equipped I was to cope without basic amenities.

"Hmm? Oh, you've seen the stream. It is quite clear and suitable for washing, although I would not drink from it without first obtaining a water purification kit. As for the other—Vilem will instruct one of my grandsons to dig a latrine for you. Since we have limited running water here, we have set up similar facilities so as not to strain our resources. You will no doubt wish your own facilities."

"Yeah, that's probably going to work out better." I didn't want to think too much about using any pit toilet, but at least one dedicated solely to me would be less icky than using a communal one.

"Just tell Vilem what you need, and he will see to it."

I thought of the unpleasant William and blanched. Until that moment, I never fully understood the act of blanching, but just the idea that I'd march out and tell Mr. Anger Issues that he had to dig me a pit toilet left me with a very fine appreciation of all those Victorian heroines who blanched at the drop of a hat. "Um. He might not want to do that. He didn't seem to like me. . . ."

"It matters not." She pinned me back with a look that had me straightening my back and squaring my shoulders. I wondered if Mrs. Faa had ever been a drill sergeant. "He will do as he is told. Come back to me in . . .

It will take Vilem some time. . . . Four hours should be sufficient for you to go to town, do your shopping, and return here. By that time, Vilem should have your tent erected, and your facilities arranged. You will then take my darlings out for a drive. They will enjoy that. Do not let Maureen sit in the front seat, though. She gets carsick."

I all but saluted her as I left the RV, her snappy commands sealing the impression of a drill sergeant. "Just a couple of months, and I will have enough to get Eloise fixed up properly. I can do this," I muttered to myself as I crossed the mill yard over to the RV into which the cranky William had disappeared. I braced myself to knock, adding my foster mother's favorite motto depicting courage: "With your shield, or on it, Kiya. Although I really hope it's with my shield, because if it's on it, it means I'm dead. . . . Oh, hi. It's me again, the unclean one. Um. Mrs. Faa said that she'd like you to do a few things for me." I gave him the list of his mother's commands, and waited for the explosion.

I wasn't in the least bit disappointed. I spent ten minutes sitting next to Eloise, waiting while William had an argument with his mom, but in the end, Mrs. Faa had her way. A few minutes after that, I was driving down the long drive toward the main road, a salary advance nestled safely in my pocket—courtesy of a snarling, obscenity-laden William—and a fervent hope that maybe things would be all right.

FOUR

Peter Moore Faa was annoyed. It was becoming a normal state of mind, given his situation in life, but
nonetheless, he was annoyed that he seemed to be
annoyed so much of late. He thought briefly of being annoyed over the annoyance regarding his present state—
annoyed—but decided that down that path madness lay,
and if he didn't stop, he'd be caught up in some sort of
endless loop that would result in his brain exploding. Or
something of that ilk.

"Travellers," he snarled to himself.

"Yes?" the stuffy-sounding voice in his ear asked in a
mild tone that would have annoyed him, except he knew
he'd go stark, staring insane if he added any more shades
of irritation to his life. "Are you speaking of something
in general about them, or just making an observation
that there are Travellers near you?"

"Neither. Although they are here."

"What is that being ahead?" Peter didn't bother to
turn to look at the source of the slightly singsong Indian
voice. It wouldn't have mattered if he had—in the bright
sunlight that flooded the passenger seat, the speaker
would be all but invisible. "It is another tunnel? What a
lot of them this area has. I enjoyed the last one most

greatly. Peter-ji, if you would be so kind as to roll down the window of your expensive car, then I might chant loudly and hear my echo again. A wondrous thing this is, yes?"

"You've had enough yelling in tunnels for one day," Peter told the faintly visible blob of light that bounced excitely in the seat next to him.

"What's that?" the voice in his ear asked.

"Nothing. I was speaking to Sunil."

"Sunil? Oh, the animus that was bound to you. How's that going?"

"As can be expected." The predominant note in Peter's voice was resignation. He was momentarily pleased by that fact. It made a nice change from annoyance.

"Just so. Still, he's a cheerful fellow, and bound to be good company for you. And as for the Travellers you say are in the area, I'm glad at least that my journey out to this sagebrush hell hasn't been in vain. Have you seen them?" The voice faded out for a few seconds as Peter drove through a tunnel that curved around the side of a massive granite cliff, affording him a brief moment of respite from pain. Unfortunately, the Bluetooth device clipped to his dashboard indicated he was still connected with his boss. " — if they're not here as you thought, then we might try Portland. I've heard a rumor, a very nebulous rumor, that a group of Travellers was seen in the suburbs."

"You will please to give my compliments to the sahib-ji," the quarter-sized ball of golden light said when they emerged back into the sunshine. "I am hoping that he and his family are well and happy. Look, there is a sign ahead. It is being a different color from the other signs. How very curious that is. It must be a sign of most importance. I cannot read the lettering yet, Peter-ji, but I am fully confident that it will indicate something of great desire. I await with breath most bated our arrival at the sign."

"As do I, Sunil." Peter flinched at the resumption of the stabbing pain in his head when the connection was restored. "Sorry, Dalton, you cut out there for a minute. If you were asking if I was sure that Travellers were here, then yes, I am. I ran into one of them in the woods while I was out discovering where they were living."

"So it's true, then? It is this group that you've been looking for?"

"Yes. Considering the abuse that was hurled at me by the man who found me checking out their camp, they aren't happy to see me. I couldn't make any arrests without enough proof, naturally, but we had better do so soon before they decide to cut and run again."

"We'll have proof soon enough, assuming you managed to acquire the DNA from the mortal police."

"I've got the DNA, and yes, I'm certain it's this family that is involved. No one else was seen near the last mortal who was killed. I'm confident that an examination of the DNA traces the mortals found around the body will be enough to identify just which person killed the victim."

"The sign informs us that there is a falls of the great height of two hundred feet shortly to come before us," Sunil read as the local landmark sign became readable. "Fatalities have—ah, but we are driving too fast for me to finish reading about the most impressive sight. Ahead, however, appears to be a location where we can stop and view the deadly spectacle!"

The earpiece buzzed and crackled softly in Peter's ear

as he continued to drive through the mountains, indicating that Dalton was thinking about this news. Peter damned for a thousandth time the creator of the cellular phone.

"Peter-ji, are you concentrating so hard on the sahibji's conversation that you perhaps did not hear me?" Sunil asked, his light bobbing and weaving with excitement.

"I heard you. It's probably just another waterfall," Peter told the animus. "We've already stopped for three. I'd like to get to our destination before nightfall."

"It is probable that the fine government of this country would not go to all the considerable trouble of placing a sign notifying travelers of this most impressive sight if it wasn't a place of extreme importance and beauty," Sunil gently chided him. "I am thinking that it would be disrespectful of us to drive past it without at least looking for an hour or two."

Peter gave in to the censure. He didn't want to stop at yet another waterfall, but his conscience couldn't bear the note of sadness that would creep into Sunil's voice if he failed to indulge the animus's desire. He pulled over and used the master switch to lower the passenger window. Sunil bounced out of the car, his ball of light hovering briefly around a brown scenic-view sign before perching on the edge of the overlook.

The earpiece crackled again in his ear. Dalton's voice was hesitant when he spoke. "I'm sorry to hear that."

"Sorry to hear what? My conversation with Sunil? He's driving me insane on this trip, Dalton. He insists on stopping for every single tourist trap and natural-wonder sign he sees, and there are a lot of the latter in this area. I know he's young, and it's all new to him, and I am responsible for his happiness after the ... incident ... but there has got to be a limit! I don't know of anyone else who has a soul bound to them who hasn't yet gone insane, and I begin to understand why!"

"How many people do you know who have an animus bound to them?" Dalton asked.

"Other than me? None. But it has to be a common phenomenon."

"Sunil has been with you for how long now? A year? Two? How old was he when he died?"

"It's been three years, and he was seventeen then." Guilt swamped him at the memory of the tragic event three years past, making him feel like a living, breathing personification of Eeyore. Idly, he wondered if there was a black cloud hovering over the roof of his rental car.

"I'd have thought you would have worked out a bearable relationship by now."

"It hasn't been this bad before, but we've never been on the West Coast, and he seems to feel like we have to see every inch of it."

"And of course, you give in and let him see whatever it is he wants to see."

"If he wasn't so damned nice about everything, I could tell him no once in a while. But when I do, he just gets sad, and that makes me feel like a bigger monster than I already am."

"You're not a monster, Peter, and I'm sure he'll calm down in a day or two. Assuming you're there that long. Actually, when I said I was sorry, I was referring to the Travellers."

"Don't be sorry on my account." Peter gritted his teeth for a moment as his cup of annoyance ran over. With an effort, he loosened his white-knuckled grip on the steering wheel and continued in a bland voice. "I'll be glad to have this killer imprisoned, where he belongs."

"It's your own family, man. You *are* allowed to be angry about that."

"They are *not* my family. At least not in the way you mean. I was marked from birth as being mahrime. Biologically I may be related to them, but on every other level, they are unconnected to me."

"Except of course for the fact that, like them, you are a Traveller," Dalton pointed out in that same benign voice that hid so well an extremely sharp intelligence. "You know, I never did exactly understand what being mahrime entails. It means unclean, doesn't it? I've seen references to non-Travellers being called mahrime, and assumed it was a way to designate outsiders."

"Yes, although it has a second meaning when applied to one of Traveller blood, like me."

"Ah. Banished, you mean?"

"Disowned would be a better term," Peter said grimly, trying not to think of the years of grief his mother suffered when the love of her life cast her out with a newborn son, alone and without any resources or support. "Travellers don't tolerate anything impure, least of all their own kind. It was fine by them that my father should impregnate a mortal woman, but when she had the audacity to suggest that the family acknowledge me, then all bets were off."

"A harsh policy, for sure," Dalton said, and sneezed wetly. "Still, as it's given the Watch one of its best investigators in this hemisphere, I won't complain." There was a muffled sound of a nose being blown. "Can you get the DNA to me tonight? I'm heading for a small town called

Clampton to follow up on a report of a rogue magician in the area, but I can meet you somewhere within a hundred-mile radius."

"A rogue magician? Rogue in what sense?"

"Selling unauthorized favors. No, not sexual, the magic kind. The committee is concerned that he's not reporting who purchases what from him, and I've been asked to see what I can find."

"Actually—" Peter consulted a map of the area that lay on the seat next to him. "I was in that area earlier today, in a place called Rose Hill. I'm heading back that way now."

"That's where I'm going, as well. I will meet you tonight, then." Dalton sneezed again, muttering obscenities under his breath before adding, "I've risked my health to rendezvous with you, and it may well kill me if I have to stay here much longer. If you get the sample to me this evening, I can take it to the L'au-dela lab in Portland, and be away from this nightmare country."

"I'll be there in the next two hours. I found a spot we can use to rendezvous—it's out of sight, yet close to the camp."

"Do we need to be out of sight?"

"With several Travellers lurking about? Yes. They already know I'm here, but I'd rather not have them seeing us by chance, and one or the other of them is frequently in town."

"Very well. Where is the location?"

Peter told him about a small clearing not far from the Faa camp. "I had to run into Blaine in order to check on some new information the mortal police uncovered, but I should be back in Rose Hill within half an hour."

"You're still dealing with the mortal police?"

"I am so long as they are having a spate of deaths in the vicinity of my murder victims."

"Deaths? What deaths are these? I don't recall you saying anything about other victims." Dalton's voice, although thick, was now sharp with concern.

"That's because the other deaths aren't connected to us. To the Otherworld, that is," Peter explained.

"It's an odd coincidence, don't you think?"

"Yes. That's why I'm keeping in touch with the mortal police. So far as I can tell, whenever a mortal's life is stolen by this Traveller killer, an unrelated mortal suffers a suspicious death."

"And you think the two deaths aren't related?" Dalton was clearly skeptical.

"I thought the subsequent deaths were related at first, but the mortals all died by means other than time theft. One died in a car accident. Another choked to death. The one that happened shortly after this latest murder was stabbed in an alley behind his apartment house. None of them were killed by a member of the Otherworld."

"You are certain of that?"

Peter made a face even though no one could see it. "I have been a member of the Watch for more than forty years. I know when a killer is not mortal."

"Just so, just so." Dalton's interest in the additional murders clearly waned at that reassurance. Peter didn't blame him. They had enough on their respective plates without taking on the woes of the mortal police, as well.

"I'm continuing to monitor the situation, but I've yet to figure out how it's related to our cases. I think it's just a matter of coincidence."

"I suppose that's possible. What information did you get from the police today? Something tangible toward our case?"

"It might be. They found a gas station receipt, and the

address connected to the account is located in Rose Hill. Coupled with the information I had regarding Travellers in that area, I thought it best to return and do a more thorough investigation. It's entirely possible that they are using that town as a temporary base of operations."

"I suppose. Where was the latest victim killed— Yreka? Isn't that in California?"

"Yes, but it's close enough to Rose Hill—about two hours' drive—that it makes those leads viable." Peter's jaw tightened again when he thought of the murder scene he'd recently examined. According to the mortal police records he had covertly accessed, the woman had been in her late eighties. That someone could kill an elderly woman was bad enough, but the thought that it was a Traveller who had killed her enraged him. He might not have any ties to his family, or for that matter any Travellers, but that didn't mean he would turn a blind eye to their crimes. For too long the Travellers had been a world unto themselves, outside the laws of the mortal and immortal worlds. It was time they be brought into the present. It was time they were held accountable for their way of life. "Those bastards stole her life away, Dalton. They just stole it, and left her corpse with nothing."

"They? More than one?" A note of interest crept into Dalton's voice. "Are you—" The sound of another explosive sneeze filled Peter's ear. "Pardon—are you certain it wasn't a solo Traveller?"

"Two men were caught on the security camera outside her apartment."

"Is it possible for more than one Traveller to steal time? I was under the impression that the thefts were always conducted by one individual."

"It's possible," Peter said with grim finality.

"I really must request some of the L'au-dela's records on your people. I feel a sad lack of knowledge about them, and since you are now certain that it is, in fact, a Traveller—or Travellers—who is responsible for this outbreak of deaths along the West Coast, then it would behoove me to familiarize myself with the abilities of such people."

"They're thieves, pure and simple."

"Time thieves, yes. That much I know." Even through the distraction of pain and the electronic buffer caused by the Bluetooth device, Peter could hear the amusement in Dalton's voice. "How is it that you're sure the two men were Travellers? Did you recognize them?"

"No. The security camera was located at an intersection half a block away, and only caught a brief, blurred glimpse of their profiles, and longer shots of the backs of their heads."

"But you know they're Travellers?"

There was a moment of silence before Peter spoke one word. "Yes."

"Ah."

Neither of the two men said more. There was much unspoken speculation, however.

"I believe you told me some time ago that your grandmother was a savant," Dalton finally said, breaking the silence. "At the time, I thought you meant she suffered from a form of autism, but that is not what you meant, was it?"

"Is this important, Dalton?" Peter asked, aware that the ever-present sense of annoyance was now quite evident in his voice, but unable to keep it from tainting his words. "I'm in the car right now, and you know how hard it is for me to concentrate when the damned Bluetooth is giving me a migraine."

"It is often the littlest things that have the biggest impact," his boss said in his usual understated manner, which, until that moment, Peter had thought of as being an asset to Dalton's position. Now it just ruffled his mental feathers, if there was such a thing. "And I'm sorry that you're still having trouble with mobile phones. Did you speak with the healer I recommended?"

"Yes. He wanted to run tests to see why Travellers can't be around certain types of machinery without either destroying them or burning out their own brains with migraines. I don't have time for that. I have a job to do."

A minivan pulled up behind him. Sunil's light stopped wandering up and down the edge of the pullout, and zipped back to the car. He had to admit that Sunil was very considerate when it came to mortals, ensuring his presence went unnoticed by them.

"That was a most exciting experience, Peter-ji!" Sunil announced as he settled back into the car seat, his little light quivering with pleasure. "The falls were excellent, and highly deadly, as the sign warned. Did you know that many people have fallen to their tragic deaths right upon this spot? You should take the time to see it. I am sure that you would be appreciating just how magnificently deadly a sight it is."

Peter didn't follow that train of thought, but knew better than to ask for an explanation.

"Mmhmm." Dalton didn't sound the least bit sympathetic, damn him, and Peter had a nasty suspicion that his boss wasn't going to leave well enough alone, a suspicion that was fully justified when Dalton continued. "You know, I read a study once that discussed the hereditary traits amongst Guardians, and how savants were often found in the same family, but separated by a generation. I wonder if the same can be said for Travellers?"

Peter said nothing, but his fingers tightened on the steering wheel again.

"Shall we being on our way again?" Sunil asked. "It would be very greatly terrible if those mortal children were to peer into your expensive car and notice me sitting here. It cannot help but be most unnerving for them, and would likely cause them to have the terrifying dreams of exacting painfulness."

"Yes, we're leaving now," Peter said, and suited action to word, listening to Dalton continue to speak in his earpiece.

"Guardian savants showed extraordinary abilities, and were able to do things that were beyond the means of ordinary Guardians. It holds that such abilities, were they applied to another type of being, could also be shown by those who are deemed of the savant level of proficiency."

Peter contemplated turning on the radio to drown out his boss's voice, but he was too much of a professional to do that.

Besides, the radio was sure to get nothing but evangelical channels and pass reports this far deep into the mountains, and the pain in his head was bad enough as it was.

"One might almost be willing to speculate that savants of all types of beings would be able to recognize their fellows without even being near to them," Dalton commented blithely. "I wonder how one would go about verifying that?"

"I'll be in Rose Hill before dark," Peter said, ignoring the line of speculation altogether.

"Excellent. Call me when you get to town, and I'll arrange to meet you and pick up the DNA."

"All right. I want to check out the address first. It may be nothing but a red herring, but it's worth looking at."

"I enjoy herrings," Sunil said, apropos of nothing. "When I was visiting my distant cousin in England, where you killed me, Rajesh gave me both herrings and kippers to eat. To be factually honest, I enjoyed the kippers more."

Peter sighed.

"Agreed. Later, perhaps, we can discuss just how it is that you knew those two men were Travellers—"

Peter clicked a button on the Bluetooth device, hanging up the phone, and relishing the cessation of pain in his head.

"Dalton really is the limit," he muttered under his breath.

"I am wondering, the limit of what?"

"It's just an expression," Peter explained.

"Ah. A colloquialism." Sunil pronounced the last word very carefully, his pleasure at learning something new evident in his voice. "He is the limit. I am the limit. You are most respectfully the limit. Yes, I see it now. It is a very good colloquialism, is it not?"

Peter felt the weight of his sins pressing down on him despite the fact that Sunil was apparently happy. "Yes, it is a good expression. However, Dalton is mad if he thinks that I'm going to discuss my talents, such as they are. I haven't spent my entire life trying to get away from the time-thief label to have a lengthy discussion about what it is to be a Traveller."

"And yet, that is exactly what you are, is it?" Sunil said. "For if you were not a Traveller, then I would not be here, and we would not be having this grand adventure together! We really are most fortunate."

Peter sighed again, feeling the Eeyore cloud grow a couple of sizes larger. "You are the only man I know who is happier dead than you were alive."

"That is because my distant cousin Rajesh was a very great man, a Vaishya Vani, you understand, and did not have time for one such as me. Although it is true that he gave me a job at one of his very successful restaurants, for which I was most grateful."

"Sunil, what did I tell you?"

"You have told me a great many things, Peter-ji, all of which I value highly."

"One of those things was that I don't hold with the caste system. No one in the Otherworld does. It doesn't matter that you were born to a lower caste than your snobbish cousin who couldn't be bothered to give his own flesh and blood a better job than dishwasher. You're a valuable person on your own."

"Yes, yes, you have told me this, and I am agreeing," Sunil said quickly, his light bobbing earnestly.

"Good. See that you remember it. I don't want to hear any more about you being unworthy of anything but the utmost respect and honor. There is no such thing as the untouchable caste anymore."

"No, there is not, there is most certainly not, and we Dalits are most extremely grateful about this."

Peter gave up trying to make the Indian understand the idea of self-worth. He had centuries ahead of him in which he could instill that.

The tiny ball of light buzzed around quietly in the seat as they drove.

"I am thinking that I have angered you with my reference to my death. For that, I am most entirely sorry," Sunil said a few minutes later, his voice contrite and subdued. Peter hated the fact that the man whose death he had caused felt obligated to apologize to him.

"There's nothing to be sorry about," he said brusquely. "I'm the one who was responsible."

"It was an accident," Sunil said, and as penance, didn't even comment on the petting zoo sign that loomed up on the horizon. Peter knew that the animus—what mortals would describe as a cross between a soul and a spirit—desperately wanted to see the petting zoo just as he had desperately wanted to see every other point of interest that they'd come across during their stay on the West Coast. To be honest, Sunil's joie de vivre was one of his most endearing traits, if at times somewhat wearing.

"At least you've been saddled with a cheerful person," Dalton had told him when he announced three years ago that thereafter he would be accompanied by a tiny ball of light that had once been a teenage illegal alien in England. "Count your blessings. You could have been stuck with someone much less pleasant."

And for that reason Peter pulled off at the next sign indicating the route to the petting zoo. Instantly, Sunil's light began blinking very fast, a sign he was filled with excitement. "We are going to the zoo of petting animals?"

Peter shook his head. "We can't stay long. And if there are others around—"

"I will stay close to the ground so that no one sees me," Sunil promised, chattering away happily. "The sign informs us that the petting zoo has alpacas! I've never seen an alpaca. Do you think they will try to eat me like that buffalo who tried to do so a few weeks ago when you kindly let me visit the ranch? Its tongue was most amazing. Ah, another sign, what a happy circumstance. Perhaps it warns us that alpacas eat shiny things? *'Please keep your children at your side. Unattended children will be given a shot of espresso and a puppy.'* What a very most amazing sign that is. I wonder what sort of puppy they are giving?"

The sun was setting behind the mountain peaks when Peter arrived back at the small town of Rose Hill. He drove slowly down the street, this time noticing the composition of the town. When he had been here earlier, he hadn't paid much attention, intent as he was on surveillance on his family. That had all gone bust when, while Sunil was off ecstatically chasing a butterfly in the woods, he ran into that redhead with the dogs.

What a bizarre woman she was. Not at all to his taste, with her breezy, flippant way of speaking, and her attempts to pull the wool over his eyes by acting like he was the crazy one, when clearly she was playing some game with him. One that involved populating his person with annoying little balls of fur that had faces only their mothers could love.

A horrible thought struck him. What if she was one of his cousins' wives? He was annoyed by that thought, and then he was annoyed by the fact that it annoyed him. "It doesn't matter who she is," he told himself as he cruised down the main street, idly noting that it contained the usual mom-and-pop businesses, ranging from country diner to a thrift shop, a grocery store, and a motel that was located in what appeared to be a small, renovated church. "She's nothing to me. No, she's something—she's dangerous. She belongs to them."

"Who is dangerous? Who belongs to someone? It is a

woman in the forest you are speaking of? The popsy you said you saw?"

"Yes, the pretty woman in the woods."

"Ah," Sunil said, his light flickering in a manner that indicated great wisdom. "You fancy her, do you not? This is a good thing. You are without a woman, and men such as you should not be without a woman. My mother always said that women bring us much happiness."

"I don't fancy her, and even if I did, it wouldn't matter. She's obviously connected with one of the family."

Which was a pity, because he felt something inside him ease a little when he had run into her in the woods, a sense of something lightening, as if the burden he carried wasn't quite as heavy as it had been.

"Ridiculous," he snorted, then remembered the way she had spoken the same word. She had a lovely voice, light and bubbling like a spring. Just like her personality. He could tell she was one of those light-and-bubbly-personality people like Sunil. He disliked light and bubbly. He had no time for it. His life was one of grim responsibility and darkness.

She did amuse him, though. How long had it been since a woman had genuinely wanted to make him laugh?

"I do not laugh," he told his reflection in the rearview mirror. It looked rather surprised, to be honest. He didn't like that, either, and added it to his list of annoyances. "I am a man who hunts down murderers, even if they are in his own family. I have killed an innocent man, and have had his animus bound to me forever because of my sins. I have nothing to laugh about. I scoff at laughter, and light, happy women with beautiful eyes and breasts and bellies. They are as nothing to me."

"You noticed the popsy's eyes and breasts and belly? This is good," Sunil said, his light nodding with the full wisdom of his twenty years. "It is the way of women that they tempt us with such things, although we must not touch unless so invited. This I have learned."

"I wonder what she was doing with Lenore Faa's pugs," Peter mused, half to himself.

"I do not know the answer to that, not having seen the woman. Or the pugs."

"She must be one of my cousins' wives. There was no sign of a wedding ring on her finger, though. Hmm."

"That is a highly most excellent piece of news. I consider it a sign of good fortune. You can pursue the popsy knowing that you will not be disturbing the happy home life of another."

The honk of a horn behind them ended Peter's musings on the pugged woman. He waved a hand at the truck behind him, obviously impatient because he had stopped in the middle of the street, and pulled over into the parking lot of the church motel. It bore the same address that the Californian police had traced from the gas receipt.

"Right," he told Sunil, pocketing his cell phone, and making sure his gun was tucked into its holster. "Enough mulling over women who thrust pugs on people, and time to focus on the job at hand. You stay in the car until I've seen the lie of the land."

"I am certain that I could be of much help to you," Sunil said hopefully. "Should you need the assistance of one such as me, that is."

It was on the tip of his tongue to refuse the offer of help, but he just didn't have the heart to do so.

"You can come with me, but you have to stay out of

sight, and not speak until I tell you it's safe. Do you understand?"

"Most accurately do I understand!" Sunil bounced happily up and down in the seat until Peter held open the pocket of his jeans. The light flitted over to it and inserted itself, leaving Peter with a slight tingling sensation on his hip bone.

He exited the car, quickly scanning the immediate surroundings. It looked as innocent as could be. The building had clearly seen better days, bearing the usual small-town church shape—steeple up front, a couple of (mildewed) stone steps, and a few pieces of somewhat dismal stained glass visible on either side of double doors from which paint peeled in long, dingy strips.

A sign that alerted potential customers to the joyous possibilities of vacancies lay on the ground, half-covered by a round bush covered in yellow flowers. Peter walked carefully up the slippery steps, and pushed open one of the doors, blinking a couple of times as his eyes accustomed themselves to the sudden gloomy interior.

"Silence now, Sunil."

"I will be the most silent you have ever heard," came the muffled reply from his hip.

In the distance, he heard the faint sound of a buzzer. The interior of the church—now motel—had been divided up into a main passage down what was once the center aisle that led to the altar, with rooms opening off it on either side. At the far end of the passage, an archway opened into a dark, dismal space, above which an equally dark balcony had been added. Peter was about to explore the former when the sound of quick footsteps had him pausing midway down the aisle.

A woman with a halo of curly brown hair restrained by

a brilliant lime green headband suddenly appeared at the balcony, leaning over it to yell, "Hi! You looking for a room? I sure hope you are, because man alive, are you a long drink of water for sore eyes. Or something like that. I never was really good with similes. Or metaphors. Whichever that is. I'm Alison. You *do* want a room, don't you?"

She was nothing like what he expected. She also wasn't a Traveller, which relieved his mind on that regard. "Actually, I'm looking for a friend of mine. He recommended this motel to me, and I wondered if he was here. His name is"—covertly he slid a glance to the slip of paper upon which he'd written down the information from the California police—"Alan Renfrew."

"Really?" Alison's eyes opened wide for a few seconds before she jumped back and scampered along the balcony until it met a circular metal staircase, down which she thundered.

"He is here?" Peter asked, somewhat confused by her response.

"No, the 'really?' was about someone actually recommending this place. Oh, don't get me wrong, it's home and everything, and I'm grateful to have it because the alternative is staying with my mom and stepdad, but it's not quite the Hilton, you know what I mean? And we never, ever get guys like you here."

Peter stiffened, eyeing the woman warily. She reminded him of a friendly puppy, bouncing around with happy abandon. "I don't know whether you expect me to apologize for something, but it appears you do."

"No," she said with a surprisingly wolfish grin. "I was being wildly inappropriate to a potential customer, though, and that's something that Vic would have a hissy over."

"Vic?" Peter ceased being annoyed, and threw himself wholeheartedly into confused. He was tired of being annoyed by everything. Confusion might not be the ideal state to find oneself, but there were worse things that could befall him. Besides, he'd always been rather good at untangling chaos, and this young woman's verbal acrobatics offered him an opportunity to do just that. "Vic is the owner of the motel?"

"You know him? He's not here right now. He's off fishing at Crescent Lake for a few days. He left me in charge. Do you want a single room or a double room? We only have four rooms total, and three are doubles, so I hope it's the latter because there's a Goth in the single and a pair of hikers in one of the doubles."

"A pair of hikers?"

"Yeah, an older guy and a younger one. They said they're father and son, but I don't think they are." She winked at him. "I think they're having a romantic getaway."

"Ah. Just so. And what about the Goth?" Peter leaned his shoulder against the wall marking one of the four rooms. What a bizarre place this was. He felt oddly at home. He wondered if the woman from the forest would like it, as well, then quelled the thought instantly. He didn't care what his cousin's wife thought. She was nothing to him. Less than nothing. As of that moment, she ceased to exist for him.

Her eyes lit up when she smiled. He'd read about such things, but never actually seen it happen. It was as if her whole being glowed with an inner illumination.

"He's a Goth." Alison shrugged. "You know, the people who are dark, and depressing, and mope around thinking black thoughts. They wear black and never crack a smile."

He never smiled. His life was dark and depressing, and mope-worthy. Did the woman in the forest ever mope? He doubted it. She was all sunshine and freckles and warm, silken skin that he bet tasted of wildflowers. "I wouldn't imagine that Goths find a room in a church motel to be particularly pleasing on an aesthetic level, but I could be wrong. However, such a thing begs the question of what a Goth would be doing in a remote town in the middle of nowhere."

Alison giggled, and stuck her hand into her jeans pocket to dig out a set of keys. "I know, right? It's just what I said. I asked him what he was doing here. He said something about having his picture taken in a tree for some Web site, and then went off to be emo somewhere. Your friend isn't here, but I can give you the bridal suite if you like. Not that I hope you have a bride along with you, because I am single and all, but still, you look like you could do with a nice room. It's along here. It's not much of a bridal suite, but it does have a queen-size bed, and its own entrance on the side of the building. It's forty-five bucks a night, breakfast included, pay in advance if you're staying less than three nights."

Peter allowed himself to be escorted to the room in question, noting with not a lot of interest that the room was sparsely furnished for a honeymoon suite. The room itself was small, but had the high-vaulted ceiling of the church to compensate. The furnishings consisted of a bed, two chairs that sat at a chess table, and in a small separate room, an antique claw-footed bathtub. A door with accompanying side panels of stained glass depicting the beheading and subsequent drawing and quartering of a saint were the only other sights to be seen.

"Toilet's just off the TV room," Alison said from the

doorway, gesturing toward the dark area under the balcony. "But you have your own tub, which is nice. I hate knowing someone else's butt has sat in my tub, don't you? I mean, you don't know where that butt has been! Unless, of course, it was a boyfriend's butt. That's totally different."

She grinned at him again.

Peter was no stranger to the admiring looks of women. He was not an extraordinarily modest man, but he was also quite aware that although he was considered by most women to possess all the qualities desirous in appearance—dark hair, pleasant features, eyes that were frequently referred to as "bedroom"—there was little value in the arrangement of his bodily attributes except so much as it allowed him to more easily acquire information from smitten women.

No one had ever looked at him the way the woman in the woods had, though. Her eyes had all but glowed with admiration. It made him feel wonderfully heroic, as if he could scale the highest mountain on her behalf.

"Thank you," he said, accepting the key Alison held out to him. "If you were about to offer to share the tub with me, I must decline."

He certainly wouldn't be saying those words if it was the other woman offering.

No! He refused to countenance such thoughts. She belonged to one of his cousins. That was the end of the subject.

"Damn," Alison said, giving a shrug and a still-friendly smile. "Was worth a try."

"It was. Do you take credit cards?"

"Nope, cash only. There's an ATM at the local store, though. It's on the other side of the street, just beyond the barbershop. I'll hold the room for you, if you like. It's not like we get a ton of visitors here. Most people go up to Crescent Lake. How come your friend told you he was here when he isn't?"

"I would very much like to know that," he said, closing the door of his room. "Thank you, I will use the cash machine shortly." He waited, hoping she'd go away so he could do a little exploring of the hotel. It wasn't that he thought she was outright lying, but experience had taught him never to take anyone's word for something important.

"No problem. Want me to show you around first? That's the breakfast room just beyond us, and above in the balcony is the TV area."

"That's not necessary, no."

He waited, looking at her.

She looked right back at him.

With a mental sigh, he turned and marched out of the motel, warning Sunil that they would be in public before making his way down the street to a small shop that bore neon signs advertising two kinds of beer, as well as fresh sandwiches, and bait. He used the cash machine, pausing briefly to chat with the woman behind the counter to see if she knew anything that might be useful to him, and then emerged into the night to conduct a little reconnoiter of the motel and surrounding area.

Shortly before nine, he reentered the motel and quietly moved to the door of his room. From the room opposite, he could hear the muted thump of a bass line. Obviously the Goth resident was back and listening to some music. From the balcony, the tinny strains of a commercial jingle drifted down to the dark main floor. Alison was most likely watching TV. He took a step toward the breakfast area, now completely in the dark with only the odd shaft of light spilling over from the balcony. He could make out the forms of a couple of small kidney-shaped tables and chairs, and what looked like a sideboard.

There was nothing that he could find that was the least bit suspicious about the motel. He'd discuss his findings—or, rather, lack of them—with Dalton. A glance at his watch showed that it was time to phone him and see if he was in town yet.

"I'll let you out once we're in the room," he whispered to his pocket. It buzzed its acknowledgment.

Wary of making noise so as to attract the attention of the effervescent Alison, he moved quietly to his door, unlocked it, and stepped inside.

Wherein he was promptly stabbed in the side.

FIVE

"I'd feel like a martyr, except I don't really have anything to be martyred over," I told Eloise as we bumped our way down the drive to the family camp. "You are at least running, although your engine dies if I try to go over thirty, or you have to idle for more than forty-five seconds, or you make two left turns in a row, and I'm earning money to get you fixed up right, and Mrs. Faa told the nasty William to get cracking on setting up my little home away from home, so really, all things considered, I'm a pretty lucky girl."

Eloise wheezed and backfired a few times as I rolled her to a stop across from the crescent of RVs. I added getting new brakes to my list of things that needed to be done to restore my beloved car to her former glory, then refused to think about how much more that would add to my bill. "Focus, Kiya. You have a job, albeit a temporary one, with a bunch of adorable little puggies. Who cares if the rest of the family think you're some sort of lesser species of leper? You're not working for them."

"I can assure you that not *all* of the family views you as a leper, lesser or greater," a warm, masculine voice spoke behind me as I crawled out of the window. I jumped, cracked my head on the edge of Eloise's roof, and swore profanely for a few minutes.

"Sorry," Gregory said, wincing in sympathy when I rubbed the back of my head. "I didn't intend to startle you. Are you bleeding? My grandmother has a first aid kit in her caravan, if so."

"No, just bruised." Gingerly, I felt the sore area on my head, quickly dropping my hand when the bruised area protested such a gesture. "What are you doing here?"

He looked slightly taken aback at my brusque question.

"That sounded far more rude than I intended it to be," I said quickly, not wanting to offend him. "You have to forgive me. I just whacked the bejeepers out of my head while a man stared at my ass as I got out of my car, so I'm bound to sound a bit cranky."

He grinned. "How do you know I stared at your ass?"

"I may crawl out of the car butt first so that I can keep the movement from dislodging Eloise's parking brick, but that doesn't mean I'm an idiot. Besides, I felt you looking at it." I pursed my lips and considered the handsome man before me, suddenly beset with the horrible thought that perhaps my butt wasn't watch-worthy. "Oh my god, you didn't, did you? It's because it's so big, isn't it? That's it, I'm getting one of those 'fabulous buns in ten days' DVDs the second I get home."

He laughed and took me by the arm. "As a matter of fact, I did look, although I averted my eyes as soon as you hit your head. I didn't think it right to continue to ogle you while you were writhing in pain."

"Gentlemanly," I agreed, but dug in my heels to stop him from walking me away from the car. "You didn't deny that my butt's too big, though. But we'll let that go. Here, make yourself useful and take this."

I reached through the window into the backseat where the things I'd purchased (after some successful haggling) sat in all their glory.

Gregory looked from me to the car. "My grandmother told me that we were loaning you the extra camping things. Did you purchase more?"

"Just things like food and necessities of life like chocolate and Doritos. Oooh, is that my tent? It looks . . . uh . . ." Lifting out the large, empty plastic paint bucket filled with as many assorted camping items as my advance would purchase, I stopped in front of the rusty green tent that was now erected at the opposite side of the clearing from the RVs.

Gregory's nose wrinkled. He set down the box of canned goods that I had shoved into his arms. "Yes, that's it. You have my profound apologies about it, too. I gather it hasn't been used in some time."

I set down my paint bucket and flinched. "It smells like the tent ran over a skunk."

"My grandmother asked me to give this to you." He held out a bottle of room spray that claimed it could neutralize any odor.

"Thanks. I suppose that once the air roams around and through it, it'll smell nicer."

An expression of discomfort briefly crossed his face. "I only wish I could invite you to stay with me, but as it is, I have to leave shortly to take a videoconference. I may be back later, but even if I am, I'll be rooming with my cousin, and . . . well . . ."

"And I wouldn't be welcome." I made a wry face and moved past him with my armload of camping supplies.

"It's not that. He simply does not have the room. Nor do I think you would be comfortable staying in the RV with him."

I remembered the man who asked me if I was going to drown the pugs, and shook my head. "You're right about that. Don't worry about me, I'll be fine. I haven't camped since . . . well, since I was a little girl. It'll be a new experience, and my foster mom—she's a psychologist, and knows these things—she says that opening up one-self to new experiences is the way to self-enlightenment. Although honestly, I think I'm pretty self-enlightened already, but Carla says that I'm more goofy than enlightened, and won't be able to dissect my true inner being until I take stuff more seriously."

"That sounds almost as unpleasant as this foul tent," Gregory said, nudging it with the toe of his shoe.

"What, enlightenment?" I looked inside and noted the air mattress and pump that had been arranged inside. I wasn't quite sure how I felt about being positioned so far from the others—on the one hand, it was nice to have privacy. William had set up the tent so that it opened to the woods, rather than inward toward the mill center. But on the other hand, I definitely felt like an outsider, suitably far enough away that Mrs. Faa and her family wouldn't get cooties from me. Not that I had them, but they sure made me feel like I did.

Although to be perfectly honest, I wasn't sure what a cootie was.

"No, dissecting your true inner being." He paused for a moment, giving me a curious look. "What are you do-ing?"

"Hmm?" I looked up from where I had been staring at my feet. "Sorry, I was trying to remember if I ever knew what a cootie was. Fleas, do you think? Or lice? Both are icky, but I can't decide which is worse."

He just looked at me for the count of seven, then said slowly, "You are the most bizarre individual I have ever met. And I have a wide circle of acquaintances."

"It's 'cause you look like a male model," I said, nodding. "People are drawn to you. Shallow people, that is, because people with real depth of character look beyond something like a gorgeous face and six-pack and really nice ass. Not that I've noticed your ass."

He opened his mouth to say something, thought better of it, shook his head, and turned to stride away.

I took stock of my new possessions, took a deep, mildewy-skunk-scented breath, and set to work making my own little slice of paradise in a camp full of unfriendlies.

By the time the sun set, I had sprayed the tent with the air freshener that most decidedly did NOT kill all offensive odors, as it claimed, and set up a small wobbly tabletop charcoal grill in a makeshift fire pit, a resin lawn chair and matching table, and two portable camping lanterns with fresh batteries (the latter of which cost more than the former) that did a pretty good job of lighting my little space. As I was making small adjustments to my domain, I received a visit from a barely civil Andrew, who thrust a toilet seat at me, and dragged me off into the woods to see the pit he had, upon William's orders, dug specifically for my use.

"How very kind of you," I said in a frosty tone upon viewing the arrangements. I clutched the toilet seat (still in plastic wrap) to my chest, and fought hard to keep from screaming.

"You will not visit our women's latrines," Andrew said sternly. "You are—"

"Mahrime, I know, thanks so very much for mentioning it. *Again*."

He grunted, ignored my withering sarcasm, and stomped off to go lounge around in expensive RV luxury. I muttered several rude things under my breath as I set up my facilities, and returned to my tent, where I pulled my chair out to the side so I could look pathetically hungry in hopes that someone would offer me a bite of food that was being grilled by two of the women.

They didn't even glance my way. And since Mrs. Faa wasn't around to make people be nice to me, I settled down to develop my campfire cooking skills. Mrs. Faa and her dogs emerged for their dinner, after which I hooked up the little beasties and took them for their prebed constitutional, opting to go down the drive toward the main road rather than get tangled up in the undergrowth. By the time they'd had their walk and been returned to their owner, I was too beat to even make a pretense of conversation with her, and, with a weary smile at Gregory, who was deep in conversation with his cousin Andrew, headed into my tent and spent the next forty minutes pumping up my air mattress. Despite the odiferous surroundings, sleep claimed me the second my head hit my rolled-up sweater that served as a pillow.

Until, that is, my entire tent was shaken by an earthquake, one that had me groggily grunting, "Huh?" before the earthquake manifested itself into a human form. "What on earth?"

The moon was just past full, and although the tent canvas was too thick to let a lot of light in, it gave me enough to make out the fact that a man had entered the tent.

"What— Who the hell are you? And what are you doing here? This is my personal tent, sir, and I—"

"Help me," the man croaked, dropping to his knees. "They want ... kill ..."

Startled, I rolled off my sleeping bag, but before I could even process his dramatic statement, male voices called urgently to one another behind me, out by where the RVs were located.

"Help ..." The man's voice wavered as he swayed.

I don't know what possessed me at that moment. It makes no sense to me now, and it didn't then, but despite that, despite the fact that I had no idea what was going on, or who this mysterious man was, or why he was in my tent, despite all forms of common sense, I flung my sleeping bag to the side, grabbed the stranger by his arms, and more or less dragged him over to the air mattress. He collapsed on it facedown without a sound. I hurriedly arranged his legs so they lay on the mattress, as well, pulled his arms down to his side, then spread my sleeping bag on top of him.

It looked like a sleeping bag oozed over a man-shaped mattress. "Damn," I whispered to myself, then apologized softly. "Sorry, mister, but I hear people, and that means—"

Hurriedly I lay down on top of the sleeping bag/man arrangement, and pretended to snore.

Nearby, a man shouted something in a language I didn't understand. I screwed up my eyes tight, sprawled as best I could to cover as much of the sleeping bag (and man) as possible, and snored even louder.

"Kiya? Kiya, are you all right?"

"Hruh?" I tried to sound groggy and surprised when Gregory stuck his head into my tent. "Whosat?"

"It's me. Gregory Faa. You didn't happen to see a man skulking around here, did you?"

"A man?" I didn't have to work to make my voice sound high and sketchy with shock. "What man?"

"A prowler. We caught him trying to break into my grandmother's RV." Gregory pulled his head back and spoke quietly with one of his cousins who was obviously just outside. He leaned in again and I saw the brief gleam of his teeth in the moonlight. "Sorry to disturb you. Go back to sleep."

"Are you kidding? You think I'm going to be able to sleep knowing there's some strange man running around?" Again, I didn't have to work to sound like I was on the verge of freaking out. I was, and one part of my brain—what Carla calls my superego—told me I was an idiot, and yelled like crazy to tell the very nice, very normal Gregory that there was a strange man lying underneath me who had delusions of paranoia. My id, however, told me that something about the man's claim sounded entirely realistic, and to go with my gut instinct. My ego—the part of the psyche that Carla says is all about realism—simply pointed out that I was probably smothering the man, and needed to get off him pronto before he asphyxiated.

"I will zip up the door to your tent," Gregory said all the while my brain was bickering with my psyche. "If you see anyone, yell and we will be right here."

I said nothing as he zippered up the tent flap—which I had left loose to encourage air to flow—but the second his shadow moved away, I rolled off the man and yanked the sleeping bag off him.

"Mister?" I said softly, poking him in the arm. "Sorry I had to lay on you, but it was the only thing I could think of. You OK? I didn't smother you, did I?"

The man didn't reply. I wanted badly to turn on my camp light to see his face, but knew that would alert Gregory and the others to something being awry. "Hey, you OK?" I asked, and with a stifled grunt, grasped his arm with both hands and heaved, rolling him over onto his back.

He didn't make a sound. In the dim light, I could only see the outline of his face, no details. "Holy carp on rye, I squashed you to death!" I whispered, and put my hand on his chest to feel if he was breathing.

Something warm and wet and sticky smooshed beneath my fingers. I pulled them back and squinted at them. "This had better not be blood, because if it is, and you're dead, that means I laid on top of a dead guy, and that's grounds for a full-fledged freak-out. Hey, you. Wake up. Please wake up."

Wiping my hand on the sleeve of his shirt, I felt along his chest again, almost sobbing with relief when I felt him breathe. "Thank the gods and goddesses and all their little minions," I said in a whisper as I patted the man's face. "Hey. You're not dead. That's good news. But you've been hurt. Was it one of Mrs. Faa's family? Hello?"

I spoke the last word in the man's ear as I continued to pat his face, having a vague memory of black-and-white movies wherein people chafed wrists and patted the faces of women who had fainted. It seemed to work, too, because after a couple of stressful moments during which I envisioned him dying right there before me, he made a moaning noise deep in his chest.

"Shhh," I said softly, gently clasping a hand over his mouth. "Mrs. Faa's family is searching for you, and by the sounds of it, they're not very far away."

What felt like a steel vise clamped on to my wrist, causing me to bite back an exclamation of pain. "Ow! You're hurting me!"

The vise loosened its grip enough for me to reclaim my hand. "Who the hell are you?" he asked in a rough whisper. "And for that matter, where am I?"

"Kiya Mortenson. This is my tent. You staggered into it claiming Mrs. Faa's family was trying to kill you. At least I assume it was them you were referring to. Are you bleeding?"

"Yes. I was stabbed. Twice. The first time was when I entered my motel room. The second when I ran into an ambush outside of Lenore Faa's caravan."

I jerked my hand back from where it was gently feeling his upper torso. "Holy jebus!"

"Did you just say—" Suddenly, the man pushed me back and sat up, his quick intake of breath indicating the truth behind his claim of having been stabbed. "You're the woman who thinks she's Elizabeth Taylor. The one with the bag of dog shit."

"The popsy?"

"Hush!"

I goggled at his silhouette (really all that I could see of him). "What ... who ... was that someone else speaking? Or are you like a ventriloquist or something?"

"No."

"But your voice just sounded different than when you said popsy. And did you just tell yourself to hush? Wait— you're the man who jumped out at me in the woods, aren't you?"

"Yes, I am. What are you doing in a tent? Why aren't you with your husband?"

"What husband?"

"The one you married, obviously. Stop touching my chest. You keep poking the stabbed area."

I jerked my hands back from where I had been trying to gently feel how badly he had been injured. "Sorry. I'm not married, hence no husband."

"What are you doing here, then?"

"I told you—I'm working for Mrs. Faa."

"I know you told me, but I didn't believe you."

How annoying he was. And also, how warm, and how nice smelling he was, too. "Well, thank you very much," I said softly. "I do not lie!"

"Pfft. All people lie."

"I don't. My foster mom taught me that people who lie pay the price in the end. Karma, you know."

"I'm very familiar with karma, thank you. You needn't lecture me on the history of our people."

What the hell? The poor man must be delusional with pain or fever or whatever it is that stab victims get. Blood loss, maybe.

"If you are working for Lenore Faa, what are you do-ing out in the middle of the woods?"

"I'm not in the middle of the woods."

"You're not?"

"No. OK, William set up my tent as far away from the RVs as he could, but still, I'm technically on the mill grounds. Just on the fringes. And I'm here because the family has some weird cleanliness fetish, and evidently I don't meet their standards. What are you doing running around getting stabbed? And what is your name, any-way? I can't go around thinking of you as 'the guy with violet eyes who jumped out at me in the woods,' and while we're on that subject, I never said I thought that I looked like Elizabeth Taylor."

"My name is Peter. You are not a Traveller?"

"Well, not really, no. I was on my way home when my car broke down and Gregory—that's Mrs. Faa's grandson—rescued me. One thing followed another, and I'm taking care of the dogs until I can get my car fixed."

"Gregory," the man named Peter muttered under his breath.

"Yes. He's very nice."

"That's what you think."

"Yes, it is what I think. That's why I said it. I do things like that. It's called polite conversation. You might want to give it a try when you're not busy being stabbed or leaping out at unsuspecting women. Wait a sec." I blinked at him, all shades of surprised. "You know him?"

"I do." The man grunted with pain as he tried to get to his feet, but the tent wasn't big enough to allow him to stand at full height, which I figured must be a couple of inches over six feet. "I must leave."

"Where do you intend on going?"

"There's a spot in the woods where I was to meet—no, that isn't safe. They almost caught me there. It will have to be the motel in Rose Hill."

"What's at the motel? Other than people who stab you. Just why were you stabbed? Was it a burglary? Or something else?"

Peter made a face. "Do you do anything but ask questions?"

"No. Why do you want to go back to the motel so badly if that's where you were stabbed?"

He sighed a long, put-upon sigh. "I wish to return because it's entirely possible that the friend I arranged to meet here, but who may well have been attacked by the same people who stabbed me a second time, might have gone there to find me."

"Dude, you got stabbed there. You can't go back!"

He waved that away just like it didn't matter. "The person or persons who stabbed me were gone when I recovered consciousness. They have no reason to return, especially if they are the same person or persons who attacked me here. Stop holding my arm, and kindly allow me to get up."

I let go of him, not sure what to say. I was appalled that someone had attacked him—twice. And yet he was so calm and cool about the whole thing. If I'd been stabbed, I sure as hell would be making a huge fuss about it!

"Whoa!" Peter weaved violently to one side. Luckily, I caught him before he fell. "You are in no shape to be marching off anywhere, not if you've been stabbed all over the place. Which reminds me, you didn't say who attacked you."

"No, I didn't. It's called not having a conversation. I prefer to do that when I'm busy being stabbed and stumbling around in the dark attempting to escape with my life."

I might have taken offense at his smart-ass answer, but for one, the memory of those violet eyes haunted me, and for another, his words were very breathy and labored. I figured he had about thirty seconds before he passed out again.

"Well, got that one wrong," I murmured as Peter, with an odd little choking noise, keeled over onto his face. I bit my lip as I considered rolling him onto his side to make him more comfortable, but since I didn't know exactly where he had been stabbed, I hesitated to do much that might aggravate the wounds. "And now what am I going to do with you?"

What I wanted very badly to do was to help the man. I shook my head at that notion—I knew nothing about him other than his first name, and that he was most likely a policeman. But if so, where was his backup? His partner? His whatever it was that police had these days?

Maybe he was an undercover cop. It wasn't out of the question that he was nosing around Mrs. Faa's family given that folks in town felt they were a bad sort. Was that why one of her family had attacked him? Or had that happened somewhere else? He said something about a spot in the woods where he had been attacked. "Dammit, you didn't tell me who hurt you. Now I don't know who I can trust to get to help with you. Annoying man."

I spent a good ten minutes trying to figure out what to do. I had just decided to search his pockets for ID, but when I eased my hand into his front pocket, my fingers encountered some sort of object like a joy buzzer. It zapped my fingers, causing me to jerk my hand back.

"Well, that's odd." I squinted at the pocket in question. A faint glow seemed to flicker for a few seconds before fading away. "Must be some sort of anti-pickpocket thingie. OK, think, Kiya. What are you going to do with him?"

After a few minutes of concerted thought, I emerged cautiously from my tent, glancing around the camp in case murderous Faas were standing around with sharp daggers at the ready.

There was no one to be seen. Not even the cars were present, which meant that some of them, at least, had gone somewhere. I must have been so busy talking with Peter that I didn't notice the sound of them leaving.

An idea blossomed in my head, one so bold and audacious that for three minutes I mentally argued with myself over its brilliance (sometimes, I really wish Carla hadn't taught me so much about the inner workings of my brain, because it just seemed to make all those ids and egos and all the other bits and pieces argumentative and unruly), but in the end, I told all the inner voices to shut the hell up, and rolled Peter back onto the mothy sleeping bag.

I had almost made it to Eloise when a soft voice spoke, making me jump for what seemed like the umpteenth time that day.

"Good evening, Kiya. Or perhaps I should say good morning since it's after midnight. What is it you are dragging behind you?"

I dropped the end of the sleeping bag upon which Peter lay unconscious, and spun around, fear causing my heart to feel as if it had leaped into my throat. "Gregory?" It was more of a question than a statement. What on earth was I going to do if he flung himself on the immobile Peter and attacked him? Hurriedly I moved between the two men, blocking the latter with my body. "Er . . . good evening. Morning. Whatever. I thought you were gone with the others."

"My cousins, you mean? The ones who seek the man who attempted to break into my grandmother's caravan?"

"Yes."

"They have gone to search for the interloper."

"Ah. Um . . ." I looked around quickly, wondering if I could find something to use as a weapon in case Gregory tried to attack either me or the wounded Peter.

My id, ego, and superego all screamed at me that I

was insane for even thinking of protecting a man who was clearly not what he appeared.

"Kiya?"

"Hmm?" I tried to adopt an innocent expression, not that much of it would be visible, since I was standing in the moonlit shadows cast by the tall firs and shrubs surrounding the camp.

"What is it you're dragging so stealthily to your car?"

"My sleeping bag. See?" I tipped up one corner to shield Peter, and pulled the edge of the bag around to show Gregory. "It's ... uh ... it's just too mildewy. I figured I'd take it to a cleaner to see if I can get the smell out."

"At one twenty-seven in the morning?" Gregory suddenly jerked to the side to see around me. I jumped sideways, as well, wincing a little when the quick movement caused what sounded like a human-sized body to roll off a sleeping bag and into the shrubs, the resulting dull thunk indicating something very like a head had collided with a tree trunk.

"I hate to be late. See?" I pulled the rest of the now Peter-less sleeping bag around in front of me, using it as a form of downy shield. "Sleeping bag."

Gregory sighed. "What did Peter tell you to make you protect him this way?"

I gawked at him for a minute, then shoved the sleeping bag through Eloise's passenger window, and gestured toward the dark shape that was sprawled in the shrubs. "Did you stab him?" I asked as I stood next to where Gregory squatted over Peter.

"Me? No." The surprise in his voice was quite genuine, I was sure. "He is hounding my family under the auspices of the Watch, but I did not do him physical harm. Not this time, at least."

I had no idea what he was talking about, but I didn't like the sound of any of it. Although at that moment there were more important issues at hand—like getting Peter to a doctor. "Well, he seems to think that someone in your family did. He's been stabbed. Twice."

"I gathered he was harmed when I saw the trail of blood around my grandmother's caravan." With a slight grunt, he hefted Peter up in his arms and turned toward the RVs. "My grandmother has some healing skills—"

"No!" I said quickly, catching him by the arm before he could take Peter away. "We have to get him away, Gregory. He's not safe here."

He looked down on me, the moonlight giving his golden hair an odd, washed-out hue. "Are you implying my grandmother would harm him?"

"No, of course not, but I wouldn't trust your cousin Andrew farther than I can throw a shot put. There's bound to be a doctor or clinic in town, or a phone we can use to call for a paramedic."

"Peter would not want paramedics called," Gregory said, annoyance making his voice brittle. He turned toward the far end of the RV crescent, then paused. "Christos. Andrew has my Jag. We'll have to use your car. I assume it's running?"

"Yes. Mostly. So long as we don't get wild. Here, let me climb in first, and then you can stuff Peter through the window and I'll guide him onto the backseat."

Never having tried to shove an inert six-foot-two-inch-tall man through Eloise's passenger window, and maneuvered him onto her short backseat, I had no idea just how difficult that feat was going to be, but after about fifteen minutes of both Gregory and me swearing, sweating, and occasionally making grimaces of sympathetic pain when Peter's head bashed into the roof, window, or side of the car, we finally got him placed more or less in a fetal position.

"I just hope to god he doesn't die because we had to cram him into the backseat," I said as I gave Eloise's ignition wires a couple of flicks, jumping when the electrical charge zapped my too-close fingers.

"That's not very likely." Gregory, who had climbed into the passenger seat, and taken Eloise's parking brick without comment, stared in disbelief as her engine sputtered to life. "Did you just hot-wire your own car?"

"Yeah. Something's wrong with the part of her ignition where you put in the key. This is the only way to get her going. It's not too bad so long as you don't hold the wires long. All righty, off we go!"

Eloise stalled seventeen times before we finally rolled into the small town of Rose Hill. Since it was the middle of the night, Main Street was silent and empty, the road and sidewalk creepily dark, and spotted every ten yards with jaundiced pools from flickering streetlights.

"Well, this is straight out of a horror movie," I said as we crept down the street. I peered back and forth, looking for signs of a clinic or doctor's office.

"I don't think it's that bad, but it's certainly not where I wish to be at this time of night." Gregory glanced at his watch. "Where do you plan on taking Peter?"

"To a doctor. He's been stabbed," I reminded him, then frowned. "You don't seem to be overly worried about that fact."

"I'm not."

"He could die!" I exclaimed, horrified at Gregory's callousness.

"I told you that wasn't likely." He shot me a curious look with an even more curious half smile. "Peter is not easily killed."

"And you know this how?"

He just shrugged. "We are at the end of the town and I have seen no signs of a doctor. What now?"

"Now I use that phone I saw at the gas station and call 911."

"You seem to delight in making me repeat myself—" he started to say, but I interrupted him.

"Yes, I know you said that Peter wouldn't want an aid unit called, but there's no doctor, and not to beat a dead horse, but *he has been stabbed*!"

"There's some sort of a motel over there," Gregory said, pointing across the street from where I'd coaxed Eloise to park, prepatory to using the gas station's pay phone. "Why don't we dump him there, and since you seem to insist that Peter receive some sort of medical care—which, I assure you, is unlikely to be needed—I will call someone to see to his injuries."

"Call who?" I asked, making a shooing gesture until, with a sigh, he climbed out of the window.

He waited until I followed before answering. "A healer. What are you doing?"

"Peter mentioned something about someone he was meeting at this motel. I'm going to see if the guy is here." I marched resolutely up to the front door of the motel—which had clearly done duty in the past as a small church—and gave the door a shove.

"Someone else is here with him?" Instantly, Gregory

was at my side, suspicion giving his eyes a glint of interest. "Who?"

"Don't know. He just said a friend. Hello?" Lights ran down a long narrow hallway toward a black space at what must have been the nave of the church. "Anyone here?"

"It's almost two o'clock," Gregory said, brushing past me to stride down the aisle toward the yawing blackness. "I doubt if this place runs to a night clerk, but perhaps they have some sort of a register we can check."

"A register?" I trotted after him, feeling a bit unnerved as we approached the dark section that consisted of a cluster of dimly visible chairs and small round bistro tables. There were a couple of night-lights on the walls that cast ovals of blue-white light on the walls and floors. "Why do you care about a register? Peter needs a doctor!"

"Ah. Staircase. Perhaps the office is upstairs." Ignoring my question, Gregory ran up the black wrought-iron metal staircase, the sound of his footsteps echoing eerily enough that, after one quick look around the room, I hurriedly followed him.

"Gregory, what about this doctor person you said you were going to call? Oh, hello. Um. You're not a doctor, are you?"

"No. But I do have a first aid kit." The woman who emerged from a doorway on the second-floor balcony was clad in an oversized T-shirt, and had obviously been sleeping, because not only was her hair mussed up; she also had sleep wrinkles from her pillow crisscrossing one cheek. "Do you want a room? We don't normally take people this late at night, but—"

"You wouldn't be able to let me look at your register,

would you?" Gregory asked with a smile directed at the woman that she'd have to be dead to miss.

I glared at him, and knocked off several sexy-guy points for the fact that he was so blatant with the use of his handsome self.

She blinked at him; then a slow smile spread over her face. She leaned against the doorframe and said, "It's on the laptop, and that's password protected. You want to try to get the password out of me? I'll warn you that I'm *very* security conscious."

"We need a doctor," I said loudly, giving Gregory a hard shove on his back. "Like right now."

"Why?" the woman asked, looking me over before returning her gaze to Gregory.

"Because we have a man in my car who's been stabbed, and he said something about coming here to meet a friend of his."

"A man? What man? Sec." She disappeared into the room for a moment before emerging with a silk kimono pulled on over her sleeping shirt. "I can call 911, but it will take them forever to get up here. We don't have paramedics around here anymore. People voted them out since it raised taxes. Your car out front?"

"Yes." I trotted after the woman as she ran down the metal stairs, following her flapping robe as she hotfooted it down the hallway to the front door. "Is there a doctor in town? Or a nurse? I hate to leave Peter stuck in my car—"

"Peter?" The woman hesitated for a second as she reached the door, casting a curious glance over her shoulder at me. "Tall, dark, and has purple eyes Peter?"

"Yes." I frowned again. Just how did this woman know about his eyes? She was probably one of those women who threw herself at every male-model-worthy man she ran across. Poor Peter. He might be somewhat annoying, but he didn't deserve to be pestered by hussies like this. "His eyes aren't purple, though. They're violet. Like Elizabeth Taylor's eyes, except prettier."

"He's in your car?" She dashed through the door and down the couple of steps to where Eloise sat.

"Yes, but don't move him," I said, ignoring the fact that Peter had been moved several times since he passed out. "He's been grievously injured and ... where is he?"

"I don't know, but he's not here." She tried to open Eloise's door, but that had long since been frozen shut. Abruptly, she spun around and glared at me just as if I'd done something wrong. "Are you trying to pull a fast one on me?"

"A fast what? Look, Peter was in the car. He'd been stabbed, and was unconscious. Gregory had to help me get him—Gregory!"

It suddenly occurred to me that Gregory wasn't there backing up my story to this man-ogler.

"What the—oh no, you don't!" As I ran back up the steps and into the churchish motel, the woman dashed past me and ran hell-bent for leather to the spiral staircase. "Hey, you! I'd better not find you've been into the motel records on the laptop, because that's private property and it's against the law to pry, and I know the sheriff in this—"

Her words stopped before I made it to the top of the stairs. The door to her room was open, light spilling out onto a small wooden desk that sat before it, upon which was a laptop that was indeed turned on.

"That bastard! He went into my room and got the laptop!" She whirled around and jabbed a finger toward me. "And I just bet you were the bait to get me away from it, weren't you?"

"No!" I protested, irritated at any number of facts, not the least of which was that Peter had disappeared (along with Gregory), which left me looking like I was guilty of nefarious intent. "Everything I said is the absolute truth. Peter was stabbed. We stuffed him in my car and brought him to town to find a doctor. I don't know how he got out of my car so fast, since he's a big guy and Eloise's window is small, but evidently he did, and he wandered off somewhere."

"Right, like that's going to happen when he has a perfectly good honeymoon suite here."

I blinked. "He's on his honeymoon?"

"No. It's the best room we have. And I don't care what you say, I know the truth when I see it, and so will Sheriff Al. I'm going to call him right now to come over and grill you about your rotten boyfriend."

I straightened myself up to my full height, squaring my shoulders. "Peter is not my boyfriend. I just lay on him in order to hide him from Gregory's cousins."

"Not Peter!" She shot me a scornful look that raised the hairs on the back of my neck. "He wouldn't be interested in someone like you. It's the other one. I just bet you Al will be able to track him down."

I was rallying a really potent retort when she strode into the bedroom to get her phone. I have occasionally been called a bit naive about some things, but I've never been horribly slow on the uptake, and there was no way I was going to waste the opportunity to get the hell out of Dodge while the motel woman was on the phone.

On my way to the stairs, I paused at the laptop and glanced at the opened spreadsheet that showed the current occupants of the rooms. Sure enough, there was a Peter Moore listed for the honeymoon suite. But it was another name that had me thinking when I ran as quietly as I could down the metal stairs, and out to Eloise. Was it a coincidence that Dalton McKay the allergy sufferer was staying in town, or was he ... my brain stopped when I tried to think of viable reasons he might be there. "It's not like he fell madly in love with you and is stalking you," I said aloud as I released the parking brake, removed the parking brick (needed because the parking brake was frequently as temperamental as Eloise's engine), and hunkered down to flick the ignition wires together. "It's still kind of an odd coincidence nonetheless."

I heard a woman's voice over the roar of Eloise's engine as she came to life, and obligingly drove down the road toward the main highway. Glancing in the rearview mirror, I smiled at the sight of the motel woman doing a little dance of rage in the street, and waved cheerily when she shook her fist at me. "Not the brightest enchilada at the fiesta," I said before spending the rest of the trip back to the Faa camp wondering how I was going to track down Peter.

Just because I wanted to make sure he was all right. Not because his chest held an unholy fascination for me.

My egos rolled their eyes at that qualification. My id started a journal called "I Wouldn't Kick Him Out of Bed for Eating Crackers." And I pondered what the man was up to that people would so viciously attack him.

SIX

"What do you know about anal glands?"

I stared in horror at the tiny woman who sat across the table from me bathed in the bright morning sunshine, and wondered if lack of sleep from my interrupted night had finally, some eight hours later, caught up with me. At least this topic had the benefit of distracting me from wondering where and how I was going to find Peter, a subject that had been uppermost in my mind the last few hours. Right, anal glands. "Um. They're in the behind?"

"Here." Reluctantly, I accepted the pair of thin latex gloves that were thrust at me. "It is time for Jacques to have his anal glands expressed. If you do not do it every two months, he attempts to do so himself by dragging his bottom on the carpet. It is most disconcerting, not to mention unclean."

We both looked at the fat pug who lolled on his back in a patch of sunlight that ran down the interior length of the RV. The morning sun was strong, heralding a warm, pleasant day, but I felt as if dark clouds had suddenly rolled in and started a deluge overhead.

"It's not that I don't want to help Jacques," I protested with careful choice of words, "but I've never ... er ...

expressed anyone before. I don't know how to do it other than, judging by the gloves, you must go . . . inside."

"Ah. Yes." Mrs. Faa rummaged around in a large cloth bag that sat next to her on the suede couch, and emerged with a small object. "Lubricant."

"I wouldn't want to hurt Jacques because I had no practical experience in the matter," I said somewhat desperately. There are many things I am prepared to do in life, but expressing a pug's anal glands isn't one of them. Not unless it was a life-or-death situation. "Besides, I have big hands. See?"

She frowned at my hands. "They *are* large," she admitted.

"Right. And Jacques' little orifice is small. Even lubed up, I don't think he'd enjoy the experience at all." I sure as shooting knew I wouldn't.

"Hmm." She looked at Jacques, then at my hands again, then back to Jacques. "Perhaps it would be wiser to have a veterinary doctor do the expressing. At least until he can teach you how to do it properly, so you won't cause discomfort."

I made a mental note that no matter how much money I might be short when the time of Jacques' next tune-up was upon us, I would quit my job and run far, far away. "Sure thing. Is there a vet in Rose Hill?"

"No." She named a town to the south about fifteen minutes away. "You will take Jacques to the vet there as soon as you can make an appointment. In fact . . ." She paused a moment in thought. "Yes, it has been almost a month. You will also set up appointments at the grooming shop in Rose Hill, since you will be passing through it after the expressing. That way you might get both tasks accomplished easily. You have a mobile phone, yes?"

"I do, but it's always been temperamental, and besides, the battery is about dead, and I don't have the charging cord with me. If you have one . . . ?"

She shook her head. "Electronics do not work well for me. I do without."

"I'm sure I can use a phone in town," I said, making a note on a little notebook that Mrs. Faa had given me to keep track of all the doggy things to be done. "What do they have done at the grooming place? Just a bath, or something else?"

"Bath, brushing, nail trim, ear cleaning, and of course a blueberry facial."

I laughed until I realized that she was serious. "They make blueberry facials for dogs?"

"Of course. It is excellent for removing the stains around their eyes. You will make those appointments for tomorrow afternoon, following Jacques' visit to the veterinary doctor. Since my darlings have had their morning constitutional, they will remain with me for the next three hours. I wish for you to go into town to the post office, where a case of the dogs' special food is awaiting pickup. We will not need that until their suppertime, so you may have until—" She glanced at the clock on the wall behind me. "You may have until two p.m. to do as you like. By then they will want to visit the lake and have a brief swim before supper. My grandsons' wives and their children will likely also be there if the weather is suitably hot; please keep the dogs away from them. The children are much too rowdy for my darlings' safety. That is it, I believe. You may wash your coffee cup at the sink."

I looked down at my list of chores and, seeing nothing there that required further explanation, did as I was ordered. "This really is a gorgeous RV," I commented as I

rinsed out the cup Mrs. Faa had given me with her morning audience. "I can't believe you have water and power
out here in the middle of the woods."

"We use a generator for power, and my grandsons
bring in water regularly," she said grandly. "We stay here
because of the privacy it affords us from the townsfolk.
They do not like us being here, and have attempted to
drive us away."

"I bet that attitude gets old real fast." I dried off the
cup and set it and the saucer back in the cupboard. "I
can't believe in this day and age people have that sort of
prejudice against Gypsies."

"Gypsies?" Mrs. Faa snorted, and with an effort, dis-
lodged her blanket of pugs and got to her feet before
tottering over to a reclining leather chair. Two pugs followed her and leaped onto her lap as soon as she reclined in the chair. The other three reassumed expressions
of bliss as they spread out in the pools of sunshine. "We
are not Gypsies!"

"Oh my god, I'm so sorry! That's politically incorrect,
isn't it? You prefer . . . oh, what's the word . . . Romany,
isn't it?"

She glared at me, her gnarled hand shooting out to
grab my arm, and pulled down my cotton shrug, poking
one finger into the lightning flower on my bicep. "We are
not Romany. We are Travellers, girl, just as you are."

"You are?" I asked, thoroughly confused now.

"Yes." She let go of me, allowing me to straighten up.
Absently, I rubbed my arm where her finger had jabbed
me somewhat painfully.

"OK. I don't get to travel around much, but I am here
and I live somewhere else, so I guess that qualifies me as
a traveler. I won't be getting any frequent-flier miles with

Eloise, but I'd rather have her than be zipping all around the country."

The old lady looked at me like I was a crumpet short of a high tea. "What are you talking about?"

"Traveling."

She opened her mouth to say something, closed it again, then narrowed her eyes at me. "Where is your family?"

"My parents died when I was a little girl. It was an accident, caused by a freak lightning storm that came out of nowhere. Some trees were zapped, and went up in flames, and since it was the middle of a droughty summer, the whole camp went up in a matter of minutes. I don't remember any of it, to be honest. I have a really great foster mom and two foster brothers, but they're all out on the coast."

She glanced at my arm again, then sighed a long, slow sigh. "You do not know, do you?"

"About a lot of things, no, but I have a really big curiosity about stuff, and I like to learn. What is a Traveller if it's not someone who travels around?"

"We are an ancient people, long persecuted for our ways. We seldom settle in one place for long," she answered, her face serene, but she didn't meet my eye.

"That sounds like Gypsies to me. Sorry, Romanies."

"Society often confuses the two, but I assure you we are as different from the Rom as we are from normal mortal beings."

Now, how on earth do you answer a statement like that? I simply smiled, and wondered if she wasn't feeling her age this morning. Just a bit, since she seemed lucid in other respects. "Who exactly is persecuting you?"

"Everyone. Anyone. The Watch, in particular," she answered quickly.

"The Watch?" Peter had used that word. It was an old-fashioned expression for the police, or so I remembered from a history course. "Isn't it a bit odd for the police to be persecuting you? I mean, they have accountability and stuff, don't they?"

"Not the L'au-dela Watch," she said with grim finality. "Our people have borne such persecutions for centuries. We are used to it."

"Doesn't make it right, though," I said, hesitating to ask what I wanted. "You haven't been persecuted lately, have you? I mean, not right here? Say, last night?"

The look she shot me should have skewered me up against the back wall. "Last night?"

"Gregory said that there was a man harassing you last night."

She made a *tch*ing sound in the back of her throat, and picked fretfully at the material of the chair's arm. "The Watch was here last night, and they are always troublesome. Never do they leave us be. They must always poke and prod and dig for some incident with which they can damn us in the eyes of the world. I grow tired of such tactics. We came here to be left in peace, and now the old trouble is starting up again. It is most distressing."

"If there's anything I can do to help," I offered, worried by how agitated she had become. It couldn't be good for her health, and since she was employing me, it behooved me to keep her as chipper as I could. I just wished I knew how to calm her down. "I'd be happy to do what I can. Maybe talk to someone about leaving you alone?"

"Someone?" That razor-edged gaze was on me again.

I lifted my hands helplessly. "Yeah, like . . . I don't

know, maybe a state ombudsman, or something? They're supposed to fight for the average Joe. I mean, someone has to care if the police are harassing you for no good reason."

But there is a very good reason, my ego suddenly pointed out to me. *Peter was stabbed here. Perhaps to keep him from finding out something about your employer?*

I shook my head at the question. Until I could talk to Peter, speculation wasn't going to get me far. Going into town to run errands, however, would suit me just fine — that would give me the opportunity to track down the mysterious Peter and find out just what he was up to. Assuming he hadn't been attacked again . . .

Mrs. Faa sighed again, and waved me away. "It seems easier to let the explanation of what has happened go until another time, Kiya Mortenson. I am tired. You may leave now."

As I was momentarily gripped with a horrible mental vision of Peter lying dead somewhere in the wilds of the Umpqua Forest, it took me a minute to process what she was saying. I wanted badly to ask what exactly had happened last night, but since she was evidently calming down enough to entertain her midmorning nap, I said nothing, and tiptoed out of the RV, relishing the fact that I'd have a few hours to myself once my chores were done.

Gregory's car was gone, I noticed as I left the RV. That didn't surprise me, since it hadn't been present earlier that morning, when I returned to camp after losing both Peter and Gregory. "I'd like to have a word or two with him about leaving me with that deranged motel woman," I grumbled, then made an attempt to organize my thoughts so I'd have the maximum amount of free time. "Run into town, pick up dog food, make appointments for vet and doggy spa day, and then a couple of free hours to find out what happened to Mr. Gorgeous Eyes," I murmured to myself when I hurried across the open space toward my tent. As I passed them, I waved at three of the kids who were sitting in a small plastic wading pool that had been filled with sand. The kids stared at me with the same faintly appalled expression that their mothers wore.

I hurriedly changed into a pair of walking shorts and a light gauze shirt, grabbed my wallet and phone, and was about to leave the tent when a low male voice spoke right outside the tent.

"You have seen him? Alive?"

"*Hsst.* That's the woman's tent."

"She is with Mother and those little monsters. Answer my question—you have seen him with your own eyes?"

"Yes, he survived."

"Then we must see to it that he does not remain that way."

A chill ran down my back as I clutched my wallet. I knew, I just knew, they were talking about Peter.

"I said I would take care of it," the second man snapped. His voice was lower, and harder to pinpoint, but I was pretty sure it was Andrew. Although it did kind of sound like Gregory. . . .

"And yet you failed miserably last night after swearing the same thing." That had to be the ever-sneering William. "If I cannot trust you to do a simple job—"

"I'll do it all right," Man Two snarled, and I jumped when his shadow flickered briefly against the wall of my tent. It had to be Andrew. It was shaped like him. Wasn't it? "He's gone to ground, but I'll find him and take care of it."

"Now. Take care of it now. I don't want him snooping around here again."

A second shape was briefly silhouetted against the tent before melting away, the voices fading, as well.

I unzipped the door to my tent and stuck out my head, thankful once again that the tent opening was faced away from the RVs.

"I'll go into town and find him just as soon as I've taken a little from the woman," drifted back to me as soft as the wind.

"Andrew. Has to be Andrew. Gregory knew where Peter was last night, and he didn't try to kill him then. Of course, I was there, and he might not have wanted a witness. And then Peter disappeared. And Gregory disappeared. Oh, holy hell, it could be him. Crap. Well, whichever one of them it is, all I can say is over my dead body," I whispered, and pulled out my scant supply of cash and sole credit card, all of which I stuffed into my bra. Take a little from me, indeed! Unless he hadn't meant money . . . but no, that didn't make sense. I didn't have anything else Andrew might want. Or Gregory. Damn. I wish I knew which one had been speaking.

I waited until I could hear nothing more, then crawled out of the tent, my mind awhirl.

Across the empty space, Andrew and Gregory stood together. Gregory appeared to be arguing with Andrew, who stood listening with his arms crossed.

Which one had been talking to William? And did it really matter? If I needed any proof that Mrs. Faa's family had been behind the attack to Peter, I had it. The question was, what was I going to do? Go to the police? To Peter?

To Mrs. Faa? Maybe the pugs could do something about it.... I shook my head at that bizarre thought, but before I could ask my inner self—ego, id, and superego—what was up with the odd thought processes, the world seemed to shimmer and shake and spin, making me blind for about three seconds.

When my vision returned, I was stunned to find myself in the middle of washing a cup, the very same cup I'd been drinking out of a few minutes before. Even worse, I was speaking familiar words. "I can't believe in this day and age people have that sort of prejudice against Gypsies."

"Gypsies?"

I spun around and stared at Mrs. Faa as she snorted, gave a grunt, and got to her feet.

What the hell?

"We are not Gypsies!"

I felt the cup start to slip from my fingers, clutched it tightly, and with infinite care dried it off and set it in the cupboard.

"I'm sorry," I said slowly. "You're not a Gypsy or a Romany."

"No, of course I'm not. I'm a Traveller, just as you are." She gestured toward my arm as she made her way over to her recliner, two pugs following.

"This is so utterly bizarre."

"What is? No, Clothilde! We do not lick ourselves there. Come and lie down with Mama."

I looked around the interior of the RV, and wondered if I had gone insane. "Nothing," I murmured.

Once again those dark, piercing eyes studied me. "Where is your family?"

"Dead," I said, not bothering to give the explanation

that I knew I'd just given almost minutes before. "I have a foster mom."

"Tch." Mrs. Faa lay back, closing her eyes, one hand absently stroking the nearest pug. "That tells me much. It is easier to let the explanation go for now. Another time, Kiya Mortenson."

I stared at her for a good eight seconds, then turned on my heel and walked resolutely out of the RV. I passed the kids playing in the sandbox. I didn't wave, but it didn't matter—they still gave me the same look they'd done a few minutes before. I looked at my tent, then down at myself. I was wearing a gauze shirt and walking shorts. My left breast itched. I pulled out my shirt enough to see the tops of a couple of bills poking out from where I'd stuffed them.

"OK, this is too much. Something seriously weird is going on here." I walked resolutely back to Mrs. Faa's door, mentally rehearsing how I was going to ask her if she had just had the biggest case of déjà vu ever, when the masculine rumble of voices had me pausing before I could knock.

I looked over my shoulder to see William, Andrew, and Gregory clustered together near my tent. William snapped something I couldn't hear, and marched off without a look in my direction. Andrew and Gregory continued to talk, although they stopped when I stumbled toward them, both their faces devoid of expression. I watched them for a second or two, trying to make up my mind about which one of them I had overheard, gave it up as a lost cause, and went over to my car instead.

Something odd was going on, something that involved a murder attempt, persecution by the police, and a weird brain attack on me.

"Whatever it is," I told Eloise as I climbed in through her window, "I don't like it. I don't like it one little bit, but I can promise you this—it's going to stop. What on earth?"

Something was digging into my hip as I settled into the driver's seat. I reached into my back pocket and pulled out eight shiny silver dollars. I stared at them in silent disbelief for a few seconds, then carefully tucked them into the pocket on the side of the car door.

I was ready to swear that there were no silver dollars in my shorts when I put them on earlier.

It took me little more than half an hour to drive into Rose Hill, collect the giant cases of expensive dog food, make a couple of calls to arrange for the vet visit and doggy spa appointments (I was assured the blueberry facials were very popular amongst the canine clientele), and pick up a few nonperishable food items to stock my scanty larder.

I had stored the groceries on top of the dog food where it sat on the backseat, and was about to conduct the intricate ritual that was the act of starting Eloise's engine, when a shadow fell over the front window, and a man leaned into the car.

He held a gun, which was pointed at me.

"Where is the vial?" Peter asked, his eyes a flinty shade of violet.

"A vile what?" I asked, looking between the very real black gun and the man about whom I couldn't seem to stop thinking. "Is that real?"

He frowned as I gestured toward the gun. "Of course it's real. You don't think I go around waving toy guns at people, do you?"

"I don't know, perhaps you do. Any man who leaps

out at women in forests, and bleeds all over their air mattresses, and then disappears mysteriously when someone tries to help him, just might be the sort of man who sports a fake gun."

"Come with me," he said imperiously, waggling the gun at me.

"To where?"

"I can't tell you that." He had the nerve to look annoyed by my question. "And since I have a gun—a real gun—and you don't, you will do as I say."

"And if I refuse?" I asked, curious as to what he'd say next. It was odd, my superego said to my ego, that we weren't at all afraid of him despite the fact that he had a gun aimed at us. My id murmured something about his eyes being the eyes of a gentleman, not a madman, but the egos would have nothing to do with that. They bickered back and forth about whether or not it would be wise to continue contact with Peter. I ignored all three and watched with pleasure as an indescribable look crossed his face.

"Then I will force you to come with me," he said finally.

"Let me get this straight," I said, wiggling my fingers against Eloise's red leather steering wheel. "You're attempting to kidnap me."

"Of course I'm not kidnapping you. I'm with the Watch! We do not kidnap. We detain and question."

"And you wish to detain and question me about something vile?"

"A vial. It is an object, one that you removed from me last night while I lay insensible in your tent. You will return it to me now."

"Why? Is it valuable?" I asked, making myself comfortable, greatly enjoying the conversation, bizarre as it was.

"For the love of the saints, woman, will you get out of the car and do as I say?" he all but yelled. I could tell by the way he shifted that he was getting tired of leaning through the window. He suddenly stood up and called loudly, "No, stay in the car. You'll be safer in there."

I didn't see anyone in his car. Maybe he had a dog with him? I searched for signs of a companion, furry or otherwise, but my gaze was caught by the sight of a familiar red car cruising slowly down the main street. Two heads were silhouetted in it, which meant that either Andrew or Gregory was in town to hunt down Peter. Most likely both.

"Now, listen here," Peter started to say as he leaned into the car again.

"Get in the car!" I squawked, taking him off guard by grabbing his shirt and pulling him farther into the car.

"What the hell!" he cried, his voice muffled since I had managed to smash his face up against my chest as I continued to jerk his body in through the window. "Unhand me, you deranged, if lovely, female! I do not care for aggressive women!"

"Get in the car and shut up!" I grabbed the back of his belt and heaved, successfully pulling his legs into the car. Unfortunately, he was sprawled across me, rather than sitting as I had hoped, but as Gregory's car got closer, I managed to shove Peter's head down, flick Eloise's wires, and slam my foot onto her accelerator.

SEVEN

I must have taken Eloise by surprise, too, because the car not only started without her usual dramatics but leaped forward, immediately plowing us into the dark blue sedan that was parked in front of me.

"By the saints!" came a muffled oath from the direction of my thighs, where I had jammed Peter's head.

"Stay down, you fool!" He struggled to sit up, managing to swing his legs around into the area of the car meant for such limbs. I grabbed him by one ear, and pulled his head back down to my lap. "They'll see you!"

"I don't care who sees me. That was my car you just hit!" Peter snarled, and tried to shove away my hand that was holding down his head. "I repeat, unhand me, woman! May I remind you that I am armed?"

I reversed, shot out into traffic (which consisted of a couple of tourists leaving the gas station), and, pulling a U-turn, sped off in the direction opposite the one Andrew and Gregory had come.

"What are you doing? Where are you taking me? By the gods, you're kidnapping me!"

"Turnabout, fair play, etc."

"You cannot kidnap me! I'm with the Watch!" He managed to pry my hand off the back of his neck and sat up, his face red and very, very angry. "I can arrest you for this!"

"Yeah, but you're not going to," I said, not taking my eyes off the road.

"Why the hell wouldn't I? Where's my gun?"

"Under my left foot. Sec, and I'll get it for you."

He waited until I maneuvered around a hairpin turn, then accepted with ill grace the gun I fished out from the footwell. "Right," he said, pointing the gun once more at me. "You're under arrest."

"Safety's on," I said, glancing at him.

He made an annoyed noise and flipped the safety switch. "You will now do as I say. Return us at once to the town so that I might see what sort of damage you did to my rental car."

"No way, José."

I thought his eyes might bug out at that. He ground his teeth for a moment before saying, "You appear to be under the misimpression that you are in charge in this situation. You are not."

"I think I am," I said, giggling to myself. Why, oh why, was I taking such a perverse pleasure in baiting the man? Maybe it was the way his beautiful eyes sparked with ire. Maybe it was because I liked seeing him sputter. Perhaps it was the bossy way he had, or the fact that he smelled wonderful, and I had been possessed with a desire to run my hands over his chest to see how his owies were.

"You are delusional on top of deranged. Pull over. I will drive."

"Look, you seem to be confused about a few things. I am kidnapping you. Yes, I know you can arrest me for that, but since I have a benevolent reason for doing so, you won't."

"What reason could you possibly have for forcing me into this rusted hulk of a car?"

I glared at him for a moment before turning onto a small dirt pullout. "Look, you can insult me all you want, but lay off Eloise. She's a good car. She just needs a little work."

"Thank you for stopping. Now, get out of the vehicle so that I might drive us back to town, whereupon I will have you detained for interfering with an officer of the Watch in the course of his duty." Peter's face was stern and resolute, and for some insane reason, it just made me want to grab his head and kiss the dickens out of him.

I fought hard to keep my hands where they were, ignoring the way he brandished the gun at me. "And just how do you think you're going to do that?"

"Arrest you? Quite easily. As a member of the Watch—"

"No, drive back to town," I interrupted. "Just how do you expect to do that?"

He sighed, and gestured at me again with the gun. "I'm not an imbecile. What is your name? Kiya?"

"Kiya Mortenson, yes. And I never said you were, although if you think you're going to drive Eloise back to town, you're mistaken."

"I assure you that, despite my ancestry, I am the master of every vehicle I meet, even one as . . . eccentric . . . as this," he said with smug self-assuredness that had me smiling to myself.

"You think so? Fine. You get her started, and I'll let you drive us back to town." I put Eloise into neutral, and took my feet off the gas and the brake (both have to be engaged in order to keep her running when she's at a stop). Her engine promptly died.

Silence filled the air around us, broken only occasionally by the sound of a car or logging truck whipping down the road.

Peter ground his teeth at me. Visibly.

I giggled.

"Move," he ordered, putting the gun in a holster under his armpit.

"You forgot to put the safety back on," I pointed out as he struggled to open the passenger door. "And sorry, but you have to go out the window. The door is welded shut."

He snarled something very rude that I thought it best to ignore, put the safety switch back on his gun, and then crawled out of the window.

I followed him out, leaning against the door in order to contemplate the fir trees that encompassed the little pullout.

"Where's the key?"

I shrugged. "I don't remember. Doesn't matter; you can't start her with keys. You have to use the ignition wires."

The look he gave me just made me want to kiss him all the more. I stopped looking at the trees, and watched him as he bent double in his attempt to get the car started. He really was exceptionally handsome. I didn't know if it was the combination of his dark hair and those beautiful violet eyes, or the way the stubble on his jaw seemed to beckon to me.

I reminded myself that not only was he a man who had just been stabbed, but he was also harassing a very nice old woman who paid my wages.

"How come you're annoying Mrs. Faa?" I asked, apropos of the latter.

"I'm not annoying her. How the hell do you start this thing?"

"She says you're annoying her. You were poking around her RV and stuff last night. And evidently her grandson, or grandsons plural, stabbed you. Why did they stab you, Peter? What is this vial you're looking for, and which you think I took, but I didn't? And why can you bend over double like that when you were all bloody and stuff last night?"

"That is a great many questions. I don't feel inclined to tell you the answer to any of them," he told me, sitting up, his face flushed. "How do you start the car? Is there a trick to it?"

"Yes. I don't feel inclined to tell you the answer," I said, watching with interest as he pressed whatever buttons he could find. "What exactly is the Watch?"

He shot me an irritated look. "You're not going to pretend to be innocent, are you? That really annoys me, and I can assure you that I'm about at my limit of annoyance lately, what with having the vial stolen, and being stabbed, and being ambushed in my own motel room."

"Ouch." Just seeing him gave me more pleasure than I really should have acknowledged. There was something about him, though, some sense of need in him, that overrode all the warnings of ego, superego, and even my normally "do whatever makes you happy" id. I had an almost overwhelming urge to help him. It was odd, this urge, and I spent a few minutes trying to analyze just what was behind it.

"Ouch doesn't begin to cover it. Just once I would like a simple, straightforward case, one where I could arrest the guilty, and get on with my life."

"What is it you do when you're not popping out at

women in the woods, or being stabbed?" I couldn't help but ask.

A slight dull red tint rose on his cheeks. He looked even more annoyed than he did a moment before, but I was all that much more intrigued. He was blushing, actually blushing. I couldn't remember the last time I'd seen a man disconcerted by so innocent a question. Now I badly wanted to know more about him.

"What I do with my spare time isn't important," he said in a voice that was both haughty and grumpy.

"That bad, huh? Would it help if I guessed?"

"No. Just tell me how to start this car."

"Let's see," I said, tipping my head to the side as I considered him. That was certainly no strain to my eyes. "Male model?"

"I said it isn't important," he snapped.

"No, I don't think male model. You don't have that Zoolander feeling to you, although I bet you'd do a heck of a Blue Steel."

I swear he rolled his eyes.

"Porn star?"

He shot me a look filled with venom.

"No. Not a porn star. You'd be all—" I made a vague gesture and gave a little shudder. "You'd have that vibe, and I don't feel that from you. Hmm. What else would make a grown man blush?"

"I did not blush. I'm simply hot."

"You can say that again," I said softly, and smiled brightly when he cast a startled glance at me. "Stripper."

This time he really did roll his eyes. "No."

"Clown at children's birthday parties."

"No!" he said louder.

"Door-to-door adult-toy salesman."

"I am ceasing to listen to you. You may babble to your heart's content. It will have no effect on me." He actually started humming a tuneless little hum.

"Professional sperm donor?"

"For the love of the saints, woman!" he exploded. Not literally, of course, although he kind of looked like he wanted to.

"I thought you weren't listening to me?"

"You are the single most irritating woman I have ever met," he said, giving up with trying to get Eloise's wires to cooperate. "And as I said, I am at my limit of annoyance."

"If you'd answer my question, I wouldn't have to keep guessing," I pointed out. "I mean, it's a fairly innocuous question. I'm happy to tell you what I do with my spare time—I like to knit, and design sweaters—but if you have some unsavory secret that you don't want anyone to know—"

"Physics!" he all but bellowed at me. "I'm getting my doctorate in physics."

I blinked at him. "You're embarrassed because you're going to college?"

He sighed, and banged his head on the steering wheel a couple of times. I could have told him that wouldn't help. "I look at least twice as old as all the other students, and no, I'm not embarrassed about it. I'm simply trying to understand the nature of Travellers by exploring their relationship with time on a quantum level. If I can do that, perhaps I can find a way to change them, to make them see that they have so much to offer people, and that to continue with such an exclusionary attitude will sound the death knell of all."

"Whoa, you lost me," I said, making a gesture over my head. "Death knell? Really? I don't think I've ever met a man who's used that phrase in an actual sentence."

He shot me a look. I grinned.

"I'm glad you think that the extinction of our race is amusing."

"I don't. Not that I know what you're talking about, but I don't think the extinction of anything except animal and child abusers is good. You're the second person who's mentioned Travellers to me today, though. You are talking about the not-quite-Gypsy people like Mrs. Faa, yes?"

"I am."

"Well, good luck with your project, whatever it is. I will say that I think it's very cool that you've gone back to school. I'd love to go to art school and learn how to design well, but it's really pricey. Good for you for living your dream."

He grumbled something that sounded even more embarrassed. Clearly, he was a man who didn't take compliments well.

"One last question . . ."

"I find that difficult to believe. You strike me as a woman who is full of questions."

I ignored that bit of snark. "How exactly did you get out of my car last night?"

"I went through the window, since I couldn't get the door open."

"But you were unconscious. And bleeding. You said you'd been stabbed twice."

"I *had* been stabbed twice." He heaved himself over to the passenger seat, then shooed me away so he could exit the car. "Once at my motel room, the second time at the lumber camp. Now it's my turn to ask questions. What is your relationship with Lenore Faa?"

"I've told you twice now—I'm taking care of her pugs. Let me see your chest."

His dark brown eyebrows rose.

I made a little gesture of denial. "You don't have to get that look on your face. I'm not coming on to you."

"Why?" He looked down at himself for a moment. "Do I disgust you?"

"Far from it. You're really ... and your eyes ... I just want to bite ... but that's not why I asked. I want to see how badly you were stabbed."

He watched me for a few seconds, then unbuttoned his shirt to the point where it was tucked into his jeans.

"Oh!" I said, reaching out without thinking to touch his right pectoral. "You have a lightning flower, too."

He stiffened as my fingers trailed down the light tan marking that started at his right shoulder and crossed diagonally down to his breastbone. His skin was warm, much warmer than I imagined, and the little brown hairs on his chest were as soft as silk. My fingertips tingled as I looked into his eyes, suddenly extremely aware that we were standing together in near isolation. The world faded away to nothing, leaving behind just Peter and me in a little pocket of sun-drenched privacy. And I had my hand on his bare chest. His very manly bare chest.

He stiffened at the contact, his pupils dilating to fill those beautiful irises.

"Why are you staring at me?" he asked, and a little thrill went through me when I could feel his voice rumble around his chest beneath my fingers.

"I think my brain has stopped. My ego and superego

are stunned. My id has all sorts of ideas, but she's not usually the best judge of actions in situations like this."

"Your hand is on my chest," he pointed out, sounding just the teeniest bit breathless. Oddly enough, I was suddenly breathless, too.

"Yes, yes, it is. Does that bother you?"

He considered that question for a moment or two. "No." His gaze dropped first to my mouth, then to my breasts, which of course meant my nipples immediately went into full red alert, and hardened themselves into little hussies of breastitude.

"You're doing that on purpose," he accused, his voice now very husky, his gaze glued to my chest.

"I'm not now, nor have I ever been, in control of my nipples. They have a mind of their own." I shivered a little despite the warmth of the day, and the fact that I was standing full in the sunlight with my hand on the chest of a man so hot, his skin felt like it was scorching my flesh.

I tried desperately to think of something that didn't involve me suddenly jumping him and licking that gorgeous chest. I might not be able to control my lustful fantasies, but I was no fool, and despite the attraction I felt toward him, I wasn't about to give in to such desires without knowing a whole lot more answers. With an effort, I swallowed back what felt like a gallon of saliva, and focused on the one thing that wouldn't have me imagining just what the rest of him looked like all bare and glistening in the summer sun. "Were you hurt when you got struck by lightning?"

There emerged from his chest something that sounded like a cross between a growl and an oath. He leaned forward, his breath brushing my lips when he answered, "You know we do not get harmed by lightning."

"I do?" I asked, my brain utterly consumed with the fact that he was so close to me, I could smell his sun-warmed skin. It was a good smell, a sexy smell, one that seemed to wrap around me little spirals of pure eroticism. I shivered again, unable to keep my back from arching so my breasts were thrust forward to brush his chest. I wanted to kiss him more than I wanted anything else at that moment, including Eloise returned to a full working state, and world peace. Not necessarily in that order.

Just as his lower lip brushed mine, he pulled back, his eyes narrowed as he glared down at me. "I told you that I do not appreciate people pretending innocence. It is my job to seek out the truth, and attempts to cover it up will not do you any favors."

"Pretending innocence?" I scrunched up my nose in confusion. "What are you talking about?"

"You asked if I had been hurt when I was marked." To my dismay, he buttoned up his shirt, hiding that lovely, touchable chest from my view. "When you clearly know that to be false."

"When you were struck by lightning, you mean?" I asked, more puzzled than ever. "A lot of people die from it, you know."

"We are not normal people," he said in that same annoyed voice.

He must have realized that I truly did not understand what had irritated him, because he stopped buttoning his shirt and gave me a good, long look, one that didn't have the least little bit of sexual awareness in it. "Or perhaps you are normal . . . no." He shook his head, and continued on slowly. "You are not the same as others, and yet, you do not know what I'm talking about, do you?"

"Not really. I think the fact that I almost kissed you distracted me from the subject."

"*I* almost kissed *you*," he said in that bossy way he had that made me smile to myself. "I did not do so because I thought you were attempting to fool me. But now . . ."

"But now?" I prompted, hoping for a return to that almost-kissing state.

"Now I think you're just ignorant."

"Hey!" I gasped, smacking him on his (delectable and highly lickable) chest. "I am not!"

"Not in the sense you imagine," he said brusquely, finishing up the last of his buttons. "You are not aware of what you truly are. Of what I am. And since I do not have the time to explain it to you now, you will start that devil of a vehicle, and we will return to town."

"Where Mrs. Faa's two grandsons, who I saw driving down Main Street, will finish up the job they started last night."

He snorted. "They do not have the ability to harm me."

"Really? Sure looked like they did last night when you were passed out bleeding all over my air mattress."

"They took me by surprise," he said, waving away that statement. "They will not do so again. And although I appreciate the fact that you sought to remove me from their vicinity—I assume that is why you abducted me so forcibly—I do not need your help or protection. I am a member of the Watch. Should there be any need for help and protection, I will be the one to provide it."

I judged enough time had passed that Andrew and Gregory must have cruised through town and not found Peter. Accordingly, I climbed back into the car, and tried to start her up. "Wow. Do you ever laugh out loud at how arrogant you sound?"

"I am not arrogant. I am simply competent."

I would have answered that outrageous statement, but Eloise was being obstinate. It took eight tries before I could get her engine to start.

"Whew. She's in a testy mood today," I said, sitting up and pulling a U-turn to head back into town.

"Machinery does not like Travellers," Peter said enigmatically. "Electronics specially so. Have you never found that they give you a migraine?"

"It's like you're speaking in English, and yet not. I wonder if there's such a thing as a course in Peter-ese."

"You wouldn't need it if you weren't in denial," he countered.

I gawked at him for a couple of seconds before returning my attention to the road. "I am so not in denial! My foster mom would never let me get away with that. She's a psychologist," I added in explanation. "She totally has me in touch with my ego, superego, and id. All of whom think you might be a few blocks short of a Lego set."

"Foster mother?" He gave me another one of those long, considering looks. I had to admit, I didn't at all mind being the focus of his attention. My breasts, in particular, enjoyed it. "Your parents are deceased?"

"Yes. They died in a forest fire at a park when I was three."

"And did one or both of them have issues with things of a mechanical nature?"

"Mechanical? You mean like farm equipment or something?"

"More like watches. Electronics. Televisions."

"That's a really specific, and yet seriously odd, question." I drove in silence for two minutes before answering. "Carla—my foster mom, who was also my mother's bestie—once told me that my mother could not only *not* wear watches, but she also stopped clocks if she got close to them. I'm kinda the same way, although mostly I just can't wear watches."

"Ah. Your mother was the Traveller, then." He nodded just as if that made sense. "You are a half-breed."

"I beg your—look, buster, you may be Mr. Elizabeth Taylor Eyes, but that doesn't mean you get to insult me!"

"I didn't insult you."

"For your information," I said, breathing loudly through my nose, "the term 'half-breed' is seriously unpolitically correct."

"Bah. That is a mortal conception, and we are not beholden to their beliefs."

I would have stared at him in outright shock, but I didn't want to plow us into another car, so I contented myself with shooting him disbelieving little glances, and saying, "What the hell does that mean?"

"Exactly what it sounds like it means. Pull over there." He gestured as we rolled into town.

"You are not beholden to mortal beliefs?" I repeated, doing as he requested by stopping next to a boarded-up sporting goods store. "I hate to break this to you, Peter, but unless your name is really Clark Kent, you are not a superman. You are mortal."

"As you so erotically pointed out, I am a Traveller. I am not mortal."

"I pointed this out?" Now that we had parked, I could indulge in outright gawking.

"Yes. You put your hand on my chest and invited me to kiss you by looking at me with those big eyes that hold so much promise."

I blinked my big, promising eyes at him. "And because of this, you think you're immortal?"

"Not immortal. I can be killed. I simply have the ability to avoid dying of natural causes. All Travellers can do so. Even you."

"You're nuts."

"And you're in denial. No, do not protest." He put a finger across my lips, froze at the contact, then leaned forward and gave me the kiss that I'd secretly been waiting for since I first laid eyes on him. His mouth was warm on mine, warm and soft and so very wonderful that I wanted to melt into a big old puddle of Kiya right there in full view of everyone on Main Street.

His tongue teased my lips into parting, but before I could really taste him, he pulled back, his eyes so hot I swear they raised the temperature in the car by at least ten degrees.

"That, I'm afraid, will have to be continued another time. If my cousins are in town as you say they are, I have work that must be done now. But first, I have to make sure Sunil is still in the car."

My brain was so bemused by the heat of the kiss—and the overwhelming desire I had to fling myself on Peter and demand he kiss me again—that his words didn't register until he was striding away from the car.

"Hey!" I yelled, clambering out of the car to go after him. "You can't say things like that and walk away. Peter? Peter!"

I stopped after running around the side of the church motel. The yard was empty. He had disappeared, leaving me sexually smoldering, confused, and with at least a hundred questions about what he meant. He didn't think he was mortal? Worse, he didn't believe I was? And cousins? His *cousins* were in town? Andrew and Gregory? But that would mean ... "Holy jebus," I swore softly to myself as I slowly retraced my steps back to Eloise. "Either he's deranged, or he's ... I can't believe this. ... He's Mrs. Faa's *grandson*. Whichever it is, he has a whole lot of questions to answer."

EIGHT

"Dalton McKay."

Peter frowned at his cell phone before putting it back to his ear, ignoring the sharp jab of pain that the action caused. It must have been the frustrating conversation with the delectable Kiya that caused him to think something was awry with his employer. That or the phone was distorting Dalton's voice. "There you are. I've been calling you for the last twelve hours. Where have you been?"

"Peter. My apologies—I was called away briefly."

"Did you get any information from the magician?"

"The magician?" Dalton sounded oddly surprised. "Ah, him. No, I haven't seen him. I don't think he's worth investigating after all."

"Bad lead?"

"Something like that."

"Well, your timing is as bad as ever," Peter said, taking fresh clothing from his suitcase.

"Peter-ji, would it be acceptable to you if I was to explore the most intriguing grounds of this holy place? I will absolutely keep to the plants and shrubs and green growing things that surround it, so that the mortals will not see me and be startled or even frightened."

Peter nodded and opened a window enough for Sunil's tiny ball of light to slip out. He watched for a minute as the animus zipped this way and that across the lawn before disappearing into the cool, dark woods.

"Bad timing? Me?" Dalton gave a short, harsh laugh, but Peter didn't really hear it. He pulled off his shirt and frowned at the mirrored image. The two stab wounds had healed, as he knew they would. Travellers might not have a lot of healing abilities, but they shared a common trait with most other denizens of the Otherworld, and did not suffer physical hurts for long. It was the Traveller mark that he looked at now.

What had Kiya called it? A lightning flower. Hers was on her arm, her soft, smooth, silky arm. He envisioned kissing a line down that arm, then told himself that he really shouldn't be thinking inappropriate things about a woman who was working for Lenore Faa. At least now he knew that she wasn't wed to one of his cousins. That thought had consoled him through the long hours of the morning.

Then again, she did manage to get him away from his murderous cousins, so she couldn't be wholly under their sway. She certainly was intriguing enough to keep his mind from being where it should be: on the murder investigation. He owed it to the victims to stay focused. Why, then, did Kiya keep pushing her way to the front of his mind?

"It's not like she is anything spectacular to look at," he said aloud, sitting on the edge of his bed. "She's just normal. Breasts and legs and arms and a face."

"Who is normal?"

"Hmm?"

"Who are you talking about?"

"No one you know."

"I see. What did you want if not to tell me about this woman?"

Oh, who was he trying to fool? She was gorgeous. She was his ideal personified. She had curves in all the places he liked women to be curved, and she smelled good. Not perfumed, but just . . . good. Attractive. Sensual, even. And her mouth, oh, how he wanted to taste that mouth again. Her lips seemed to hold an unholy attraction for him to the point where even now, just thinking about that mouth was making him aroused.

"Peter?"

"Yes?"

Then there was her mind. He liked that, as well, although if he had to put it up against her curves and mouth, he might have a hard time picking which one he liked better. He smiled to himself, sure that if he told her that, she'd punch him in the arm, and lecture him for being shallow and not looking beneath the surface to what really mattered about a person. Then he'd have to admit that he really did like the way her mind worked, as well as the fact that he never knew exactly what she was going to say or do next, following which he'd make love to her for at least three days straight. Maybe four if she was particularly flexible and had the needed stamina.

"Why did you call me?"

"Oh, hello, Dalton."

Really, it was a good thing that he was an experienced man of the world who could compartmentalize his interest in the gorgeous Kiya—for truly, she was a very beautiful woman, and he'd take umbrage with anyone who said otherwise—and he congratulated himself that he could keep his personal and professional lives separate.

"I really don't have time to waste like this."

What was she doing at that moment? Probably damning him for blithely walking away from her seductive, too-tempting self. If only she knew how hard it had been for him to do so. Then again, what if she was happy to see the back of him? What if she was a whole lot friendlier with his cousins than she had let on? What if they had set her to spy on him? Worse, what if she was playing him along for her own purposes?

His hands fisted as he imagined her and Gregory laughing together about how easy it had been to pull the wool over his eyes.

"Dammit, I'll kill him," he muttered, picturing many ways he'd like to teach Gregory once and for all to stop meddling with him.

"I'd ask who, but you appear to have forgotten I'm on the phone with you, so instead, I'll just hang up."

As for Kiya, he'd like to . . . like to . . . "Hell," he said, slamming down his fist onto his leg. He didn't want to do anything but kiss her. And make love to her. And say outrageous things to her just to see what she'd do in response. And then make love again, just because.

Why hadn't he gotten her cell phone number? By rights, he should call her up that very moment and demand to know what she thought she was doing by spying on him for Gregory. Then he'd lecture her about the wisdom of joining forces with the murderous bunch that was his family, and finally, he'd graciously accept her heartfelt apology for her role in the deception and possible vial theft, and grant her plea to save her from the family. Which of course he'd do, because he was nothing if not a gallant man. Following that, he'd get her into his bed. It was clearly the only way to keep her out of trouble with his cousins. Yes, he would do it. It was for her own good.

Feeling immensely virtuous over the fact that he had decided to save Kiya despite the temptation she posed him, not to mention interruptions to work she was sure to cause, he wrapped up the phone call so he could get on with the saving. No, that wasn't right. First he had to catch the murderers; then he could save Kiya by seducing her. Yes, yes, it was a good plan, a sound plan, a plan that a man could really sink his teeth into. "Sorry, Dalton, I have to go. I want to search a tent for the vial, just in case I'm completely wrong and she is with them after all. Not that I think she is, not really. It's just an extremely slight possibility, and you hired me because I am nothing if not thorough. Also, it would be just like them to hide it in her tent assuming I wouldn't look there because she had nothing to do with them. Yes, the more I think about that, the more it makes sense. I'll see you at the rendezvous spot at nine tonight, as planned."

He clicked off the phone, filled with all kinds of righteousness at his plan.

Half an hour later, washed, dressed, and with his plan in place, he stepped out of the motel and immediately forgot all about his good intentions.

Kiya lounged on a faded lap blanket in the shade of the trees that backed the motel property, a couple of plastic containers of food and some paper plates set on the edge of the blanket. She sat up when she saw him, and waved.

He was instantly hard. This made walking toward her extremely painful, but there was no way on this good, green earth he was going to be able to walk away from her a second time that day. He lurched toward her, praying she wouldn't think he'd suddenly lost the control of one or both legs. "What are you doing here?" he asked, trying to make his voice sound stern and businesslike. To his ears, he sounded just like a happy puppy begging for attention.

"I thought we could have a picnic. Unless you've had lunch? Ouch. That . . . uh . . . looks kind of painful. I hope I didn't interrupt some quality time with the local porn channel?"

He steadfastly ignored her gaze on his bulging fly lest it make matters worse. "There is no television in my room."

"Oh?" A sudden smile spread over her face, warming him to the tips of his toenails. "Are you happy to see me, then?"

He willed his erection away. Or rather, he tried, but it was still painful walking the last couple of steps to her. "I am not here to discuss my penis's inappropriate behavior, and I am certainly not responsible for its method of greeting the sight of you."

"Kind of like how my boobs go all happy when they see you," she said, and instantly, his gaze was on her chest. The lovely little mounds of breasts visible through the opening of her shirt made his mouth water. "They just see you, and whammo! They're fully into their happy place."

With an effort, he dragged his gaze from her breasts. "You will now tell me how you knew to find me here."

One side of her mouth quirked up higher than the other when she smiled. He loved that about her. "I brought you here last night, remember?"

"But how did you know I came here now?"

"Dude, really?" She gave a short laugh. "You got out

of my car half a block from the motel. It doesn't take a rocket scientist to figure out where you went. And last night, that hussy who runs the place told me that there was a separate entrance to your room, so I figured you'd probably go in and out that way rather than risk running into other people staying here. You hungry? I have some fried chicken I bought from the bait shop—which turns out also to be some sort of greasy spoon diner. I picked up a potato salad, and a fruit salad that has a lemonade-based dressing, as well."

He relaxed, and sat down at the edge of the blanket. Of course she hadn't been following him. She hadn't a deceptive bone in her body. Unless . . . unless Gregory or Andrew had followed him, and told her where he was. "No, I am not hungry."

"Man, what is with your face? One minute you have a stony expression that wouldn't be out of place on Mount Rushmore, and the next you look like you're thinking how much you like strawberries."

"I am a man of many moods," he said loftily, absently taking a piece of chicken, and accepting a plate of food from Kiya, who giggled when he did so. "I have many deep thoughts of which I am not allowed to tell you."

"Oh, I can tell you're full of it," she said, giggling even more when he raised his eyebrows. "Deep thoughts, that is. So, tell me about this vial you lost. And why you're pestering Mrs. Faa, even though you say you aren't. And just exactly what happened to you when you got stabbed? Who stabbed you? Why were you stabbed?"

"Are we having luncheon? It looks as if we are. Oooh, very yummy. I am wondering if I am invited. Is this the popsy?"

He stopped enjoying the mouthful of chicken, closing

his eyes for a second in resignation before saying, "Yes, if you like, and yes, although I'm not sure how she feels about the name popsy. Kiya, what do you think of 'popsy' as a nickname?"

"Uh . . ." She blinked, staring at Sunil's light with a somewhat dazed expression. An adorably endearing dazed expression, he amended, wanting to do nothing more than to kiss that stunned look right off her face.

"I'll take that for a 'I don't mind being referred to as popsy at all,' then, shall I?"

"Eh . . ." She blinked again, then pointed. "That's a . . . a light thing."

"Yes, it is. It has a name, and that name is Sunil."

"Greetings," Sunil said cheerily, and bobbed in a way that indicated he was making a Namaste gesture to her. "It is my very great pleasure to meet at last the popsy of my most cherished friend Peter-ji."

Her finger wavered a little. "A *talking* light thing."

"He is an animus, actually, and since I can tell by the way your eyes are bugging out you have never seen one before, yes, he does appear to be a small, golden ball of light the size of a Brussels sprout. He used to be a person. He is now an animus, and he is bound to me. He doesn't, I need not point out, eat actual food, so it's not necessary to offer him lunch."

"This is very true that I am not eating the chicken that Peter-ji is consuming with such relish, but I appreciate the welcome to your picnic most dearly. We have many picnics, Peter-ji and I, although frequently I must keep myself hidden from the view of mortal beings. You are not a mortal being, so I thought it safe to greet you properly, and ascertain your married status on Peter-ji's behalf. What, popsy, is your married status?"

"Single." Kiya stared at the ball as it slowly bobbled in front of her, her mouth opening and closing a few times before she dragged her gaze over to his. "My eyes do not bug out. They widen. In complete and utter disbelief. Can I . . . that's real, isn't it? This isn't some sort of a hocus-pocus trick? Can I touch it?"

"You're not referring to my penis, are you?" he asked with some hope.

The look she gave him quelled all such foolish emotions.

He sighed. "I thought that was the case. You can hold him in your hand, although his energy field tends to make you go numb after five minutes. Sunil?"

"I would be most happy to sit in the beautiful popsy's hand," the animus burbled, and, when Kiya held out her hand, settled on her palm, vibrating in a way that indicated he was greatly enjoying himself.

She poked the golden ball gently with one hesitant forefinger. Sunil giggled. "This . . . no. It can't be real."

"I am. I am very real. I have been real since I was born to my most revered parents some twenty years ago."

Kiya looked even more confused, if that could be said to be possible. "You're a twenty-year-old ball of light?"

"Animus is the word that is most commonly used for us. You see, I was in London working for my very important cousin when Peter-ji came along and—"

"Yes, I think I had better be the one to tell that story," Peter interrupted quickly.

"Ah. Yes. Ah." Sunil bobbled a bit more on Kiya's hand. "I am the third company, am I not? I will go and watch the raccoons mate. They were very interesting, you know. I have never seen them before, and I feel it is my duty that while the Watch has gone to the great and gigantic expense of sending us out here, we should appreciate all the beauty that is around us."

"Just be back in . . ." Peter glanced at the sky. "Say half an hour."

"Very good, I will most assuredly do so." Sunil bounced off Kiya's hand. "And to you I say many good wishes, popsy. We will see each other again, I am much confident."

"You have a twentysomething Indian talking ball of light," Kiya said conversationally after watching Sunil disappear into the shrubs. "That's . . . different."

He sighed, taking another bite of chicken. "I don't have time to explain things to you. It would take too long, and I have far too much to do. Is there more of the fruit salad?"

"Yes, but you're going to be wearing it if you don't answer a few questions," she warned, dragging her gaze from the shrubs to the bowl of fruit. "I'm taking this really well, don't you think?"

"I do. What questions do you have other than how Sunil came to be bound to me?"

"I want to know how—hey! No fair taking away the questions I want answered." She eyed him as if considering what he'd look like with fruit dripping down his head. What a wonderfully unconventional woman she was. No one had ever threatened him with fruit before. He definitely would save her from his family, no matter how deeply she was involved with them.

"I will offer a trade, then," he said slowly, trying to decide how much to reveal to her. Just enough that she could hear the ring of truth, but not so much as to help his family, should she pass the information along. "I will answer some of the questions you have, and then you will answer mine. And give me more fruit salad."

"Deal," she said, handing him the bowl. "You start."

"What are you doing working for Lenore Faa?"

"No, I meant you start by answering my questions."

"Which one?"

She sat back, clasping her knees. "Sunil—"

"No. The subject of how Sunil came to be is off the table."

A hurt look flashed into her eyes. The pain seemed to go straight through him, making him feel like a brute. "I am willing to answer other personal questions, however. Do you wish to know if I sleep naked? Which side of the bed I favor? Boxers or briefs?"

The pain in her eyes changed to amusement. "Of course I want to know the details on all of those questions, but how about we start with the most pressing concern—who stabbed you, why, and how come you're not rolling around in pain now?"

"I don't know who stabbed me," he admitted, finishing the impromptu lunch. "I suspect it was one of my cousins, but I didn't see my attackers either time, so I have no definitive proof."

"So you *are* related to Mrs. Faa?"

"She is my grandmother."

Kiya looked surprised by that, genuinely surprised. He frowned, trying to decide if his family had neglected to tell her that fact, or if she was an exceptionally good actress. "Which means Gregory is your cousin?"

"Yes. As are all my grandmother's other grandsons. I have no siblings."

"But . . ." She picked off a bit of strawberry from her

plate and popped it in her mouth. He watched the movement with avidity, wondering if her lips tasted like the sweet berries. "But that doesn't make sense. Mrs. Faa said something about her family being very tight. Why would your own cousins stab you?"

"I am mahrime," he said simply, and waited to see what she would do with that information.

"You too?" She gave him a smile that he felt right down to his testicles. "They keep saying I am, as well. I take it that means not hip to the family code and all that."

"With regards to mortals, yes. In your case, it means that you are a half-breed. As, I believe I've mentioned, am I."

She frowned, and began to gather up all the leftover containers. "That again? I told you that's not at all politically correct."

"Nonetheless, it's accurate. I have a Traveller father and a mortal mother. I assume your mother was the Traveller, since you were not taken in by family after her death."

"My mother didn't travel around a lot. At least, not that Carla told me," Kiya protested. "And you know, you're kind of overdoing that whole mortal thing."

"What mortal thing?" he couldn't help but ask.

"The thing where you refer to people as mortals, like you aren't one. And yes, I remember that you said you aren't, but that doesn't make any sense. You look perfectly normal to me. Well, the ball of light named Sunil aside."

"Regardless, I am not mortal, nor am I normal. Nor, for that matter, are you."

"I'm as normal as they come, babe," she said blithely. "I really do not have time to sit here and explain what

Travellers are, or why it is I know that you are one," he said sternly, then leaned back against a tree and contemplated her. By the saints, she was captivating. The way the sun gilded her skin, burnishing her hair and warming her body so that her scent, the intoxicating scent of a sun-warmed, sensual woman, reached his nostrils, binding him with little silken cords of desire. "Travellers are an ancient people. They originated in India, and later moved north and west until they were found in every country in Europe. Some migrated to the British Isles and Scandinavia. Others went to the New World with the explorers. My family remained in what is now Romania for several centuries before my grandmother brought us to the United States."

"Uh-huh," she said, disbelief written clearly on her face. "So you're like, what, super-Gypsies? Sorry, super-Romanies?"

"We are not Romany, although many suspect we have common ancestors if you look back far enough, and many facets of Travellers have been used to describe the Rom."

"Such as?"

He looked at her for a moment, trying to gauge whether she was playing him along. Her eyes were as clear as the sun-washed summer sky above them. "Travellers have been persecuted for centuries, as have the Rom. Both are feared and shunned because of their nomadic lifestyles. Even the word 'traveler' in some places means the Romany people. But that is a misnomer, since they do not have the skills that we possess."

"What skills are those?"

"We tend to be migratory, have tight-knit extended family units, shun outsiders, and we are thieves," he said simply. "Time thieves."

Kiya's delicious mouth hung agape for a second or two. "You're kidding me."

"I wish that I was."

"I don't believe it," she said, her face obstinate. "How can you *steal* time?"

"The same way you steal anything else."

She stared at him, her gaze locked to his. Genuine disbelief was clearly readable in her eyes, affirming his suspicion that his family hadn't told her who they—or she—was.

"Prove it," she said finally.

He didn't hesitate; he didn't stop to ponder the repercussions of his actions. He simply pointed to something over her shoulder, and when she turned to look, he stole ten seconds of her time.

"You're kidding me," she said.

"I wish that I was."

"I don't believe it," she said, her face set in an expression of obstinacy. "How can you steal—holy garbanzo beans!"

"No jebus?" He pulled a half-dollar out of his pocket and pressed it into her slack hand, closing her fingers around the coin.

"That was ... I mean, we just said those things ... and then it was happening again. Like super déjà vu." She sucked in a large quantity of air. "Just like what happened this morning!"

He sat up straight. "What happened this morning?"

"That thing that you did. Making me déjà vu. That happened this morning."

He made her describe exactly what happened, grinding his teeth when she did so. "That bastard."

"What bastard?" she asked, suddenly looking down at her hand. "Why did you give me fifty cents?"

"One of them stole your time. Andrew or Gregory, that is."

"What?" Her voice was shrill with panic. Without thinking, he put his arm around her and pulled her tight against his side. "Someone stole my time?"

"It's all right. It sounds like it was only a few minutes."

"But . . . but . . ." She shook her head, and leaned into him, clearly seeking comfort. Unfortunately, his body didn't realize that, and began celebrating the fact that the woman who was beginning to consume his thoughts was pressed against him, all warm and soft and smelling good. Parts of him that were previously warm and soft quickly became otherwise.

She turned her head, her nose brushing against his. "Someone stole my time, Peter. I don't know what to do about this."

It was more than he could resist. He dipped his head toward hers, and allowed his lips to caress that sweet, sweet mouth. Her lips parted on an inhalation of pleasure, inviting him to explore the delights that lay within. It would have taken a stronger man than him to turn down such an offer.

"The raccoons have ceased mating. It was most interesting while it lasted. Did you know that the male— merciful goddess! I am being so embarrassed at disturbing you at the time of your great seduction! I will most very immediately take myself off to see . . . er . . . something. Carry on, Peter-ji."

Peter didn't stop at the interruption. He couldn't. He kissed Kiya gently at first, tentatively, almost hesitantly to make sure she was fully on board with the idea of the kiss, but when she started making little happy noises in the back of her throat, he unleashed his passion, deepening the kiss until his mind and body and, hell, even his soul were caught up in the sweetness that was Kiya.

"Holy hand grenades, do you know how to kiss," Kiya said against his lips as she came up for air. "That was the best kiss ever. My whole body is tingling. However, there's a rock digging into my back, and although I don't mind the fact that we got kind of carried away, we are out in the open where anyone can see us."

It took him a second or two to come to his senses enough to realize that they were lying prone, entwined like lovers, and that poor Kiya was bearing the brunt of his weight.

"If I didn't know better," he grumbled, rolling off her and helping her to sit up, gently massaging her back where she had lain on the rock, "I'd say you have cast a spell over me. But you don't know how to cast glamours, do you?"

"Glamours?" She looked thoughtful, which was so endearing, he just wanted to kiss her again. "That's a word that means something magical, right? I remember seeing it in a book about vampires that I read last summer. I didn't think they were real, though."

"Vampires, or glamours? It doesn't matter—both are real."

Her eyes widened. "Get out of here!"

"Why? Is it Sunil? He won't harm you." He leaped to his feet regardless, swiftly searching the area for the threat that she had obviously seen. There was nothing but a small family of rabbits rustling about in the shrubs.

"I didn't mean get out of here literally, you know," she said, getting up to straighten her shirt. "I meant it like 'you're kidding.' But you aren't kidding, are you?"

"No." He bent to gather up the remains of their picnic, handing Kiya her blanket before proceeding to a trash can in the motel parking lot.

"You know, I think I'm just going to let the idea of vampires and glamours go for right now, because there's only so much my brain can process in a day, and right now it's full of the idea of time theft and Indian balls of light who enjoy watching raccoons go at it. Hey, where are you going?"

"I have work to do," he said, pausing to look back at her. "You may try all you like to distract me with your sweet mouth, and those delicious-looking breasts, and your legs and such, but I won't have any of it. I am a member of the Watch. I am above such things."

So saying that, he marched back, pulled her tight against his chest, and kissed the daylights out of her.

"No, I can see that you are strictly business," she said, laughing against his mouth.

He frowned at her.

She licked the tip of his nose.

"You can't leave me like this," she said, quickly taking his hand and not releasing it when he tried to politely shake her off. "I have oodles of questions, and besides, I want to not distract you again sometime in the very near future."

"You cannot come with me," he said sternly, altering his path and leading her to her car.

"Why? Are you going to a men's room or something?"

"No. I'm going to Lenore Faa's camp, so that I might discuss with Andrew and Gregory the theft of your time."

"Oh, you really can't go there," she said, clasping his hand with both of hers, and digging in her heels.

"Why not?"

"Because of what happened last night. And what I

heard this morning." She paused, thinking. "What exactly did happen last night? You didn't get around to telling me that."

"I didn't tell you because I had no intention of telling you." He tried to pry off her hands. It just made her hold on tighter.

"Nothing like the present to take care of pesky chores," she said cheerily. "Tell me now."

"No."

"I'm not going to let go until you do."

He gave her a haughty look, one filled with manly intent. "Do you seriously believe that you can dictate to me, a member of the Watch?"

She suddenly released his hand, leaning forward into him, teasing his lips with her tongue, while at the same time boldly stroking her hand down his chest. "What if I ask nicely and said please?"

"Do not delude yourself into thinking I can be swayed by physical temptations," he said firmly as he led her over to a small wooden picnic bench that had been chained to a tall fir tree at the edge of the parking lot. "I am made of sterner stuff than that."

"Yes, you are," she agreed, giggling under her breath. "What were you doing at Mrs. Faa's RV last night?"

"I went to confront the family, hoping to save them embarrassment by having the guilty person surrender himself to my custody."

"What guilty person?"

"If I could tell you that, I wouldn't have need of the vial."

"No, I meant what's someone in Mrs. Faa's family guilty of? And just what's in that vial you keep yammering on about?"

He jerked back, giving her a stern look that she utterly disregarded. "I do not yammer! I have never yammered in my life!"

"Uh-huh. What's in the vial?"

"DNA proof that one of the members of Lenore Faa's family is a murderer."

Her eyes widened in alarm. She was silent for a moment before saying, "You're serious, aren't you? I can see you are. But really, Peter—a murderer?"

He nodded, and briefly explained about the murders he had been investigating the last few months. "The latest one finally gave me the evidence I need to pin down the perpetrator of the crimes."

"I can't believe—" She shook her head, her hand on one of his. "I just can't believe that one of them is a murderer. Rude, I agree. Nasty, if you're talking about Andrew. Very cliquish, oh, hell yes. But a murderer? Someone who would take an old lady's life? That's just . . . appalling."

"I am in full agreement. Which is why it's important I retrieve that vial before the DNA is destroyed or damaged."

"So that's why you were at Mrs. Faa's camp last night? You figured one of your cousins took it when they stabbed you?"

"That was one reason why I was there. I had arranged to meet my boss at a rendezvous point near the camp, but before I found him, I was ambushed."

Her face was drawn with worry and concern. That fact warmed him like nothing had in many decades. "And that's when you got stabbed a second time?"

He nodded.

"That's really horrible. I don't know why I think it's

any less evil that your own cousins would stab you, but when you compare that to outright murder ... it's just awful, Peter. You have to stop it."

"I intend to do so." He looked away from her, struggling with himself as to whether he should put into words the feeling that he had battled for so many decades, since the time his beloved mother had died. "It is the twenty-first century. It is time for Travellers to break the bonds of tradition that keep them outside of society. We could do so much together, Kiya—we have powers that could benefit the mortal and immortal worlds alike. But Travellers have never wished to share their skills that way. They've never given back, and the time of taking has to come to an end."

Kiya's gaze was steady on his. "You know what you are?" she asked after a moment's silence, her fingers tightening where she had clasped his hand.

"A man?"

"You're a hero, that's what you are. An honest-to-god hero. If you were in a comic book, you'd be ... I don't know, Timey-Wimey Man or something."

A warm glow began deep inside him at the look of admiration in her eyes. No one had ever admired him before. Fear, yes, that he'd seen in the eyes of the people he tracked. Loathing and hatred and anger were all familiar reactions to his presence. But no one had ever looked at him as if he were a knight in shining armor. Kiya's admiration made him feel simultaneously extremely uncomfortable and just like he really could do anything he set his mind to.

"I wouldn't go that far," he said, basking for another second or two in the shy smile she gave him. "It's common sense, really. By excluding ourselves from the world, Travellers do nothing but create an atmosphere of suspicion and fear. And now, with some members feeling they answer to no law, they are a danger to their own kind."

"Because people will think that all of them are like that? Murderers, I mean?"

He nodded, giving her hand a squeeze before releasing it. "It's why I hope to reason with Lenore Faa after I prove to her that one of her own kin is responsible for such heinous crimes against mortals."

"Good luck with that." She stood in thought for a moment, allowing him to drink in her delicious scent. "Something's bothering me—you keep saying her name like you're not part of that family."

He shrugged. "I'm not. I'm mahrime, as I told you."

"So because your mom wasn't part of the family, that makes you an outcast? That's really heavily incestuous, you know."

"You need only have two parents who are Travellers to be considered part of a family, not parents who are members of the same family. To have a mortal parent is what pollutes your blood and makes you impure to Traveller eyes." He glanced at his watch. "I must leave."

"Hold on there, Bobalooey. I have about a gazillion more questions, not the least of which is why you gave me fifty cents when you stole my time. Not that I mind you doing it, because you were showing me, although I'm really skeeved out about the idea that someone can do that to me without me knowing."

He stood up, pulling out his cell phone to consult notes he had made earlier. "That was payment for the time."

"Huh?"

She looked so adorably confused, he couldn't help but give her one more kiss, a swift one this time because he had work to do. "All Travellers pay for the time they steal, and always in silver. It helps avert the consequences."

"It does?"

She looked even more confused, but hardening his heart—and ignoring the demands of his groin—he walked away from her to see what sort of shape his rental car was in. He'd track down his two cousins and have a chat with them about stealing Kiya's time before demanding that they turn over the murderous member of the family.

But before he did that, he'd take advantage of Kiya being away from the camp to search her tent. Although he hated the idea that she might not be as innocent as he hoped she was, he couldn't rule out the possibility that she might be working for his enemies.

It was enough to send a chill down his spine. He knew exactly how his family would discard Kiya when they were done using her. She'd be lucky to escape with her time—and life—intact.

NINE

"Of all the irritating, arrogant—holy cats, can he kiss!—men I've ever met, you, sir, are the worst," I grumbled aloud as I got into my car. "And if you think you can just walk away from me without answering more than a couple of questions, you can just think again, buster. Eloise, follow!"

I performed the intricate ritual that normally results in Eloise starting up, but after having been so obliging earlier in the day—multiple times, yet—she had evidently felt she'd done her part in granting me happiness. She played coy by pretending to start, then sputtering into silence.

"Dammit, Eloise!" I said, stomping hard on the gas. "Don't you do this to me! We have a man to kiss! Er . . . follow. Although the kissing was really, really nice. Did you see that he got all bulgy when we were going at it out on the lawn? I did. Mmrowr."

A little ball of golden light zipped along the ground, then disappeared into Peter's car just before it drove out of sight.

"At least Sunil didn't get lost in the woods," I groused, peering impotently over Eloise's dashboard. "And seriously, I need some sort of formal recognition that I didn't freak out at the idea of balls of talking light, and Travellers, and glamours and such. At the very least, a big ole herkin' piece of chocolate is in order."

I sighed and straightened up in the seat, cursing myself for forgetting to ask Peter for his cell phone number. A horrible thought struck me then—what if that kiss was an anomaly? What if he didn't want to give me his phone number, didn't want to see me again? Dear god, what if I repulsed him?

Really, my ego said to my superego, *someone has got to stop watching so many reality TV shows. She's gone all drama queen on us.*

Totally, my superego responded. *Any minute now she's going to start saying that no one finds her attractive, and she'll die alone and unloved in a small one-room apartment filled with thirty-nine cats. Which will eat her when she drops dead. And then escape to find better, more loving, non-cat-hoarding homes.*

"For the love of the good green turtles, will you stop!" I told both of them, and bent over with determination to start Eloise.

Turtles are not green, my id said quietly. I threatened to punch her in the gooch, and ignored the other two parts of my psyche when they made rude comments about my state of mind as I got Eloise going, and drove back to the camp.

Seriously, there were days when I wish Carla had been anything but a psychologist.

"You! Girl! Kiya!"

The voice assailed me as I parked Eloise near my tent, and crawled out of the window.

Mrs. Faa was standing at the steps of her RV, her dogs plopped in the shade around her like furry mounds of dough. "Come here. I have something important to discuss with you."

I bit my lip and hurried across the camp, ignoring the strained faces of the women as they bustled their kids out of my path. What had I done to make Mrs. Faa so angry? I didn't have a watch, because they never worked for me longer than an hour or two, but I had checked the time when I was buying the picnic lunch, and I didn't think I was late coming back.

Unless Peter had stolen more time than I thought he did. I gave a shake of my head, amazed that I could process something like Travellers without checking myself in for a mental evaluation. But Peter had seemed so sincere, and when he did that trick of making me déjà vu, it proved that his claim was possible.

"Come here," Mrs. Faa repeated, gesturing toward a couple of Adirondack chairs before turning to the women. "I would speak with her alone."

The two women and the children disappeared into their respective RVs. I caught sight of Mrs. Faa's two dark-haired grandsons, Piers and Arderne. They watched me warily, as if they expected me to suddenly go mad and run amok. One held an ax, while the other was lugging an armful of chopped wood to a stack that sat at the rear of one of the RVs.

Peter's comments about the family being exclusionary came immediately to mind. What I thought was simply a tight-knit family took on a new light.

"Peter's absolutely right. You can't be this isolated and not end up with everyone hating you," I said to myself as I obeyed the royal command and duly walked over to the indicated chair.

Before I could get to the chair, the door to the nearest

RV opened and William stepped out. He glared at me, turned on his heel, and returned to the RV without a word.

I thought a few rude things about him, but kept from voicing any of them as I smiled at Mrs. Faa, and took my seat. "Yes, ma'am?"

"You! Girl! Kiya!"

The voice made me jump when I crawled out of Eloise's window. I cracked my head on the roof and swore as I spun around, rubbing my head and gawking at the elderly woman standing at her RV, surrounded by pugs.

"Come here. I have something important to discuss with you."

"Oh, no, you did not!" I said, outraged as I marched toward William's RV. That bastard just stole my time!

"Kiya! I wish to speak to you!" Mrs. Faa said imperiously.

"Just a minute, please. I have to have a word with your son," I called to her, then stopped before William's RV and banged on the door. "Come out of there, William. I know you're in there!"

The door was flung open. William stood glowering down at me. "How dare you disturb me!"

"How dare you steal my time!" I countered, and gave him the meanest look I could summon, the one Carla called my psychotic-murderer-in-a-straitjacket face. "Don't you deny you did, because I know it was you."

He smiled.

"You! Girl! Kiya!"

Once again, I jumped at the voice shouting at me, and hit my head on the edge of Eloise's window as I crawled through it.

"Oh!" I screamed, my hands fists as I bolted for William's RV.

"Come here. I have something important to discuss with you."

"Yeah, yeah, be there in a sec," I snarled as I yanked open William's door and bellowed inside, "You do that one more time and I'll—"

"You! Girl! Kiya!"

This time, I was ready for it. I ducked my head down and didn't jump at the summons.

"Come here. I have something important to discuss with you."

I stood up and yelled loudly, "I would, but your son keeps stealing my time so I can't. Make him stop and give it all back!"

Mrs. Faa stared at me for a moment before turning slowly to look at William's RV. "He would not dare."

"You think not? I just lived through this moment four times. That . . . rat . . . keeps taking my time. And I don't appreciate it! Here." I marched across the yard, ignoring the women as they hurried the kids out of the way, as well as the two grandsons who appeared at the end of the RV. "I don't need silver dollars. I do need my time back, thank you very much."

She folded her arms across her chest, refusing to take the coins that had appeared in my pocket—as if by magic, I snorted to myself—and pursed her lips, a hard expression on her face. "So. You are not as ignorant as you led me to believe."

"I'm every bit as ignorant as you think I am," I said, still riled up from William's blatant thefts.

She raised one eyebrow.

I cleared my throat. "That came out wrong. What I meant was that I didn't know what Travellers were until today."

"I see. And from whom did you learn the truth?"

I sat down when she gestured toward one of the Adirondack chairs. I opened my mouth to tell her, but something stopped me. If Peter was correct about the family, and one of them was a murderer, did I really want to go blathering on about that fact? What if Mrs. Faa was protecting that person (please, oh please, let it be William who was the murderer)? I wasn't overly concerned about my own safety, but I very much wanted to help Peter.

"Does it really matter?" I finally said, meeting her gaze without the slightest wobble.

She pursed her lips again, her hands moving absently over the hem of her blouse. Around us, the dogs snored loudly in the shade. Birds overhead sang happy little midsummer songs, and called their joy to one another. The wind gusted gentle puffs of pine and campfire scents, mingling in a manner that encouraged you to breathe deeply and give thanks you were alive. It was as idyllic as it possibly could be . . . with the exception of time-stealing bastards lurking behind the curtains of an RV.

"My family is an old one," the mother of one of the bastards said slowly, as if she was having a hard time working out just what she wanted to say to me. "We go back many centuries, many centuries. My husband was a prince, nobility, you understand. I was chosen for his bride because I came from a family of women. No sons, just daughters. This is very lucky amongst Travellers, you see. There are not enough women for our men, never enough daughters born. Even my own sons and grandsons have produced only male children."

I was suddenly aware of the frailty of the old woman across from me, and was unable to stop the surge of compassion that welled up at the sight of her gnarled, spotted hands fretting with her shirt.

"He was a devil, my Piotr," she said with a faint smile. "But a good man, and he loved his family." Her gaze suddenly flickered toward me, the smile fading. "He was caught by the Nazis, rounded up with Romany in Poland because they believed he was one of them. The Nazis treated the Rom horribly. Did you know that? Most people think it was only the Jews who were persecuted by the Nazis, but they were only a part of the devouring. As were many Travellers. The Germans sent Piotr with the Rom to the death camps, and when he tried to escape by the only means possible, he was killed."

"I'm sorry," I said simply, feeling the pain that rolled off her. "I thought—I'm sorry, but I understood that Travellers can't be killed."

"That is untrue. We are not mortal, but we can be destroyed. We can have our lives stripped from us, either by the will of another, or through our own stupidity." She bit off the last few words, one hand gesturing in sharp, angry movements. "Piotr did not need to die. He would have survived the starvation, the deprivations, the cruelties inflicted, where the others who were with him would not. But he was never one to bow down to mortals, and it irked him to be forced to do so."

"How horrible. For everyone. I had no idea that Gypsies were hunted by Nazis, too. What . . . er . . . do you mind if I ask what happened to your husband? You don't have to answer me if it's too painful, but the truth is, I'm still trying to wrap my brain around the idea that there's a group of people who can steal time."

"Steal?" She sat up straight in her chair, or as straight as she could manage. Her chin went up, and I could almost feel the whipcrack of her voice. "We do not steal! We pay for what we take!"

I glanced at the couple of silver dollars that sat on the flat arm of the chair. "Yeah, but in order to buy something, the seller has to want to sell. Otherwise, you're taking away that person's choice."

"Bah," she said, dismissing that argument. "You admit yourself that you do not understand our ways. You may have Traveller blood, but it is clear to me that you have not been brought up properly."

I let that slide, not wanting to argue with her. "Are you saying your husband tried to steal time to get out of the concentration camps?"

"It is our way." Her lips tightened, and her expression changed from one of defensiveness to anger. "Although there are limits. There is always a price to pay for taking time. Always. Sometimes that price can be minor, if you offer enough silver to compensate the shuvani."

"The what?"

She gave a little sigh, shaking her head. "Your family has much to answer for. A shuvani is a spirit, child. There are four spirits that rule us—earth, water, air, and field. We offer silver to placate the earth shuvani when we take time. If it is not enough, then we pay a price in other ways."

"Like what?" I asked, wishing I had a notepad so I could take notes. I never had the best of memories, and now there were all sorts of new things being thrown at me that I just knew I'd forget.

Silence fell. The sun went behind a cloud, leaving me in the shade. The dogs sat up and whined. I shivered, feeling as if someone were walking over my grave. Even the birds stopped singing their happy songs.

"The price depends on the amount of time taken," Mrs. Faa said slowly, her eyes on mine, but now unreadable. "Once, when I was very young and learning the way of things, I did not pay properly for time taken from a girl I met at a small country town. The next day, my favorite hair ribbons were gone. They were scarlet for good luck, and my papa had given them to me to wear on my wedding day. I cried until my mother told me that I must always pay what is owed. Later, when I was a young bride, I forgot that lesson, and once again did not pay the correct amount when I stole time from an elderly man."

"Was something else taken away from you?"

"No." Her gaze was turned inward as she stroked the pug who jumped on her lap. Maureen, I thought it was. "No, I received something instead. The man's dog, the ancestor of my darlings, as a matter of fact. I was obligated to care for the dog no matter how difficult the circumstances. I did it, although Piotr was furious at both my lack of care and the fact that I brought a dog into our home. Most Travellers do not like dogs. They are unclean. My darlings, however, are very clean."

"And your husband?" I asked, almost hating to hear the answer, since a feeling of foreboding seemed to coat everything in despair. "What happened to him?"

"In the death camp he took larger quantities of time," she said, her gaze dropping to her hands. She tucked the dog into her side and smoothed one hand over the other, trying to straighten the bent fingers. "Deliberately. But he had no silver, nothing to use to pay for the time that he took. He told the earth shuvani that he would pay later, once he was free. He said that the mortals he had stripped of time were evil, and their loss would not be mourned."

I waited, dreading what was to come.

"He killed three of them, three evil ones, by stealing enough time to Travel."

I sensed an emphasis on the word that indicated she wasn't talking about merely getting in a car and driving away.

"To Travel requires the most silver of all, since it demands the debt of so much time. Piotr took enough time to Travel back the four months he had been confined at the camp. He intended to avoid being captured at all by doing so."

"You can time travel?" I asked, my mouth ajar for a few seconds.

She made a gesture of dismissal. "The shuvani did not grant Piotr leniency. He took too much without repayment. For that, he lost his own time."

"Good lord. Your time god killed him?"

Her eyes were hooded now. "He killed himself. If he had only waited; he would have survived it. They could not have killed him."

"That's so tragic," I said, reaching out to gently squeeze her hand. "How did you cope with his loss?"

"I had my sons." She took a deep breath. "We are Travellers. We have been persecuted since the time we first opened our eyes and knew the world belonged to us. We survive where others do not."

I wanted to say something to comfort her, but couldn't formulate anything that didn't sound like I was lecturing her. It was very evident, however, that Peter was absolutely right about Travellers—they existed solely for themselves, when they could do so much for people. Imagine being able to time travel and stop atrocities?

There is always a price, my superego pointed out

smugly. *Not to mention paradoxes that are created when you meddle with time.*

"I tell you our history so you can understand that all we desire is to be left in peace. We are not a violent people. We do not look for trouble. That is why we are living here," she said with a wave toward the RVs. "We do not bother others, and we hope that they do not bother us. But of late, we have been the target of the Watch. You understand what the Watch is, yes?"

"The police are the Watch, right?"

"That is a mortal word for it, but it will do—the Watch governs the Otherworld. My grandsons tell me that last night one of the Watch disturbed our camp, attempting to cause mischief or worse. They drove him off, but Gregory feels that you might have seen the man, and have been worried by the contact."

Gregory knew damned well I had, and wasn't worried, at least not in the sense he meant. How very interesting that he hadn't told his grandmother the truth. Briefly, I wondered why, but gave it up when I realized that Mrs. Faa was watching me with obvious expectation.

"I'm more than happy to reassure you that I'm not in the least bit bothered by what happened last night," I said not quite truthfully. Mrs. Faa didn't need to know that the way I was bothered by Peter had much more to do with his abilities to kiss than the fact that he had come to the camp to track down a murderer. "Please don't worry about me with regards to that."

"You *did* see the man, then?"

"Yes, I saw him."

She leaned back, her eyelids drooping, but her eyes were as sharp as ever. "Ah, so you did not tell Gregory the truth when he checked at your tent."

"No, I didn't. I was trying to help the man—Peter, your grandson—after your other grandsons stabbed him. Why, Mrs. Faa, did you allow that? Do you hate him so much?" I was going way over the line of what was polite and respectful, I knew, but I couldn't seem to stop my mouth from asking the questions that had been haunting me. I blame my id for that. It's always been the trouble-maker in my psyche. "I'm sorry if it's rude of me to ask these questions, but what you're saying doesn't really jibe with what Peter says. And I really don't understand how you can tell me how important your family is, when he's a member of it, and yet you treat him like he's the enemy."

"He *is* the enemy. He is with the Watch. Have you not listened to what I have been telling you?" She shook her head in dismay. "Peter Faa is not a member of this family. He is mahrime. He chose to turn his back on us and, indeed, has a personal vendetta against us. He seeks to see us destroyed."

I was lost, not sure what to believe. Sincerity rang in Mrs. Faa's voice, and yet, the same could be said for Peter. Plus, there was that kiss. And the fact that I felt a definite attraction for him. I couldn't be so poor a judge of people that I could enjoy snogging a man who was trying to destroy his family, could I?

It's been known to happen, pointed out my superego.

Not to me, it hadn't.

"That doesn't sound like Peter," I said, looking down at my toes. Something wasn't right, but I didn't know if it was Mrs. Faa, or my own faulty judgment.

"Child, do not allow yourself to be swayed by a hand-some face. Oh, yes," she said when I glanced up in surprise. "I've seen Peter Faa. He is very handsome. It is true that he takes after my Piotr, for whom he was named. He has the same eyes. But he is *not* a member of the family despite this. He rejected us, Kiya. He made the choice to remain with his mother, a mortal, rather than to be brought into the family to learn the ways of our people." Her eyelids flickered down for a few seconds. "Just as you have been isolated from your family, so has he chosen to be from his."

"That's not quite what he says happened." Honestly, who was I supposed to believe? They each said something different, and yet, I heard the ring of truth in both their voices.

Her head snapped back. "You had words with him about us? What exactly did he say?"

"He said that he was mahrime, and that he's tracking down a murderer." I clamped my lips together for a few seconds, damning myself for admitting that last bit. I didn't want to blow his cover and alert the family to the fact that he was on to one of them. On the other hand, what if he was persecuting them unfairly? The family members might not win any awards for hospitality, but they didn't *seem* like murderers.

"He has said that before," she answered, her eyes closing as she leaned back. "My son, Peter's father, has told me that we have long been the target of his persecution."

"Peter doesn't at all strike me as the persecuting type. . . . Wait—his *father*?" I glanced around the camp, wondering who—

"Vilem is the father of Peter Faa."

"Holy great big piles of cow crap!"

Her eyes opened as the exclamation escaped from me. "I mean . . . um . . . wow. William? Are you sure?" She continued to look at me as if I was an idiot, which made me blush with embarrassment. "Sorry. Of course you're sure. It's just that William is so ... and Peter is nice, and ... yeah, there's no way I can end this that's not going to be more insulting, so I'll just stop."

She closed her eyes again and waved a dismissive hand. "You will tell me what it was that Peter Faa said to you."

No, I don't think I will, I thought to myself. My id cheered. Ego and superego were less pleased with that decision.

"I think if you want to know what was said between us, you should ask Peter himself," I said after some minutes' thought. "I'm really not comfortable repeating the conversation."

She waved her hand again. "If he wishes to beg my pardon for spurning his family, and for the persecution of his father and myself, then I am willing to hear him. Otherwise, I have nothing to say."

Obstinate old ... I bit off that thought before it could even really get going, feeling that when it came to my employer, it was better to keep a civil tongue in my mind. So to speak.

"Would you like me to take the dogs for their evening walk now?" I asked, rising and looking as helpful as I could.

"You may take them to the lake. All but Maureen. She is not feeling well, and will remain here with me. My darlings will like to play in the water a bit, and then you will dry them off and bring them home for their supper."

"Aye, aye," I said, saluting, and went off to gather up leashes, poop bags, and the towels that Mrs. Faa had indicated were reserved for the use of the aquatic pugs.

Two hours later, and we returned, although I wondered as I unloaded the dogs if the smell of damp fur would ever leave Eloise. It seemed the predominant note, and one that was reluctant to fade away. "Still, you all had a good time. Especially you, Terrance."

The amorous little pug looked up at me, tongue lolling, as he trotted alongside. He had a smile on his face, blast him.

I knocked on Mrs. Faa's RV door, opened it up to let the dogs scamper up the stairs, and leaned in to call, "The dogs had a great time at the lake, although you might be contacted by a vacationing lawyer about paternity tests and puppy support. Terrance took advantage of me rescuing Jacques from a large bullfrog to seduce the lawyer's fox terrier. I'll get their dinner going now."

I ducked out before Mrs. Faa could respond, hoping I wasn't going to be the one to pay for the puppy support since it was on my watch that Terrance went straying.

It wasn't until the dogs had been fed and had a long après-supper stroll in the woods, and I helped Mrs. Faa brush them all so they'd look nice for their respective anal squeezing and spa treatments, that I returned to my tent.

Someone had been in it.

I stood just inside the door of the tent, my eyes scanning the few things scattered in the tent . . . the air mattress and accompanying foot pump, a duffel bag with the few pieces of clothing I'd brought with me to watch Lily's trees, and a box of nonperishable foodstuffs.

The duffel bag had been shifted slightly from where I'd left it. I knew that because I had been using it as a pillow, and now it was moved slightly off center of the mattress.

"Dammit, I just know it was that creepy William. He probably fondled my underwear." I shuddered as I opened the duffel bag. Luckily, my undergarments weren't on top, so if he had been in my things, at least I didn't feel like I had to burn them. Everything in the bag looked fine, nothing missing, and nothing added. "Not that I'd know what someone would put in there unless they were trying to plant drugs or something on me. And there's no reason to do that, because if Mrs. Faa wanted me to leave, she'd just fire me. Hmm."

The few other possessions I had in the tent had been moved ever so slightly, but otherwise not disturbed. I "Hmm"-ed again, and sat back on my heels in thought until hunger overcame me. I consulted my box of canned goods, thought about how good a nice juicy hamburger would taste, then thought about how much better Peter would taste, and, finally, considered the idea of eating the nice, juicy hamburger on Peter.

I positively drooled at the last thought.

"That does it," I snarled to myself, and gathered up all the silver dollars and half-dollars that had magically appeared in my pockets in payment for my stolen time. "If the man is going to insist on filling my every thought, then he can just feed me. Or let me eat off his lovely warm, muscled chest. Whichever comes first."

It took some coaxing to get Eloise to start—she likes to let her engine rest at least twelve hours—but at last I managed it, and with nary a glare directed at William's RV, I drove into town and went straight to the motel.

Luck favored me in two ways: the honeymoon suite was so marked, and the brazen hussy who ran the place wasn't in sight, although I could hear sounds of a TV from the balcony that overlooked a small dining area.

I tapped on the door to the honeymoon suite, but no one opened the door.

"Hell's toasted bells," I swore to myself as I left the motel. "I guess I can stop feeling noble because I came to see Peter before I went to the hamburger joint."

My stomach growled its unhappiness at such a thought, and I was about to give in and go to the mom-and-pop hamburger place at the other end of town when I remembered the other door into the suite. Unfortunately, it was locked, as well. "Rotten policemen and their safety-conscious selves. Well. Where does that leave me?"

I sat on a white resin lawn chair that was placed next to the window of Peter's room (also locked), and considered my options.

The most obvious option was to break into the room. "Oh, that's not going to work," I told my feet. "Even if I knew how to jimmy a lock—and I don't—I'm just not the breaking-and-entering sort of person."

I could bribe the motel hussy to let me into Peter's room. "I don't have the money to do that, and if I did, I wouldn't give it to her. She'd just use it to seduce innocent men. No. That's not an option. Maybe I could steal a room key from her without her knowing?"

My feet wiggled nervously at that thought. I won't go into what my ego and superego had to say on the idea of me stealing things.

"Hey . . . stealing things." I sat up straight and looked out into the trees. "Peter and Mrs. Faa say I'm a Traveller. Which means I must be able to steal time. If I could locate where the hussy kept her keys, I could steal just enough time from her to get them. Somehow. Maybe."

The more I thought about it, the better I liked the idea. Oh, sure, there was the whole repercussion thing that both Peter and Mrs. Faa had mentioned, but neither Peter nor any of the others who'd taken a few seconds from me had suffered any calamity.

"Oh, money!" I said suddenly, remembering that payment was an important part of the whole process. I scrabbled around in my pocket until I came up with forty-seven cents. "The silver dollars I need for sustenance. I don't know what the going rate for time is these days, but this should cover a couple of seconds, surely."

With my payment tucked away in my shirt pocket, I steeled my nerve.

"It makes sense," I argued to my psyche as I marched around the motel to the entrance. "It'll let me get in contact with Peter—and possibly save him from encountering his murderous family—and yet it won't require me to do anything really reprehensible, like smash a window to get in. Or bash the hussy over the head to take her keys. This way, I'll just take a couple of seconds of time from her when she's looking the other way, and snag the keys."

My egos were yammering away and waving their hands around while going on about what a bad idea that was, but my id approved. I'd always liked her. She saw big-picture things better.

"Just shut up and leave me alone," I told the handwaving egos as I entered the motel. A man was about to reach for the door when I opened it, giving both of us a start. He was about twenty, skinny, and had the pale skin of the die-hard basement-dwelling gamer who seldom saw the light of day. He was also clad all in black, and had dyed black hair, and a thick ring of eyeliner around each eye.

"Sorry?" he said, looking startled.

"No, my fault. I wasn't actually telling you to shut up. Just the voices in my head. Wow. That sounds really bad.

I don't mean it like crazy talking voices. Not voices telling me to kill people. They're actually my ego and super-ego and id, which are all quite sane. Most of the time. Everyone has them, even you."

I tried smiling at the man, but he just looked even more startled, and edged around me to the door. I figured I'd better stop before he ran to the police about the deranged voice-in-head woman wandering the halls of his motel, so I said nothing more.

The Peter-ogling woman wasn't in the darkened area under the balcony, but she did emerge from a room upstairs when I clumped my way up the spiral stairs. The sounds of a TV came from the room, as well as a warm glow that cast a pool of amber light on the small desk I remembered from the previous visit the night before.

"Hi, can I help—oh. It's you." Her eyes narrowed on me. "What do you want?"

I pulled out a key that I had detached from my key chain. It was the key to an apartment that I no longer rented, but which I'd forgotten for two years to remove from the chain. "Good evening. I was here to visit my friend Peter, but he doesn't seem to be in."

A little smile curled the edges of her lips. "Oh? Too bad."

"Yes, isn't it? However, I did find this key lying on the carpet just below us, and wondered if it was one of the housekeeping keys." I held it out.

She frowned at it for a minute, then pulled open a desk drawer and removed a bulky circle of keys. She counted silently until she found one she liked, and then looked up and shook her head. "No, all of my keys are accounted for. I'll put it in the lost and found in case someone dropped their car key."

"Sure thing." I handed over the key, and smiled in a friendly manner when she tucked the keys away back into the drawer. The one that she had stopped at had a dab of red fingernail polish painted on the end to differentiate it from the others, which would make it easy to pick it out from its brothers. "Guess I'll be going, then. Bye."

"Good-bye."

She sat down at the desk. I trotted down the stairs, and slunk into the dark dining area to lurk unseen. After a few minutes, I heard her moving around. "OK," I whispered to myself. "All you have to do is steal a few seconds so that you're sure she's in her room and not out and about, and you can nab the keys. Let's get to it."

I don't know if you've ever tried to steal time before, but I didn't find it at all an easy thing. I crept back up the staircase in my stocking feet, careful not to make it thump and squeak as I did so, and stood hiding in the shadows while the motel woman wandered around in her room, pondering how one went about stealing time.

"How do you steal time?" I remembered asking Peter.

"Just like you steal anything else," had been the answer. And then he distracted me, and whammo, it was stolen.

The door to the woman's room was ajar, no doubt so she could hear anyone who wanted a room or needed assistance. I jerked back when she headed toward the door in her circuit around the room, but luckily, she didn't do more than glance out the door before returning to the room's interior. Still, she wasn't settled as she had been before I marched loudly up the stairs to give her my key, and I worried that she might pop out and see me were I merely to steal the keys.

Feeling carefully in my pocket, I fingered one of the two pennies that was part of the time payment, and swiftly threw it over her head so that it hit the wall beyond her, opposite the door.

She turned to look at what made the noise, and took a few steps in that direction. I took a deep breath, closed my eyes, and imagined myself lifting a handful of nothingness from her. Only that nothingness was really time.

The TV began the same commercial that I had heard a few seconds before. I didn't wait to do a little dance of success; instead, I clung to the walls, then the balcony railing until I was past her door and at the little desk. Thirty seconds later I was hotfooting it down the stairs. Thirty-two seconds later I was bolting back up the stairs—silently and stealthily—to deposit the forty-six cents on the reception table, and a minute after that, I let myself into Peter's honeymoon suite.

TEN

I wilted against the door to Peter's room as I closed it behind me, my heart racing like crazy, but a strange sense of elation filling me.

I had stolen time! "I am so good at this," I told the room, which was dark and empty of handsome violet-eyed men. "Boy howdy, that could get to be addicting. I can see why people get into trouble doing it. Well, now. That's done. What next?"

I turned on the light nearest the bed and looked around the room.

"Why, oh, why didn't I get your cell phone number?" I asked, and plopped myself down on the end of the bed. Any hope that Peter might have left a handy "How to contact me in an emergency" list lying around was dashed.

"Great. He's probably back at the camp harassing Andrew and Gregory. Or Mrs. Faa." I gnawed on a hangnail as I considered my options. "One, I can stay here in hopes he's just out getting some dinner. Downside is I may starve to death waiting for him. Two, I can go back to camp and see if he made good his threat. Downside: Eloise won't want to come back to town if he's not, and I don't really want a can of spaghetti for dinner. Three, I can find a way to call him and tell him that I need to talk to him. Downside of that is . . . hmm. No real downside, except I will have to come up with something to tell him that would be worth his while to return here. Plus, I don't know how to get his number. Hmm again. I guess I wait."

Something on my head tickled. I scratched it, and with the absent thought that I needed to wash my hair came the realization that I was in a motel room. "One with running hot water!" I ran for the door to the little room attached to the main room, and sighed at the sight of a bathtub. "A bath. Dear god, how I've missed you. I wonder if Peter would mind if I had a quick soak?"

I gnawed my fingernail a bit more, and then decided to throw caution to the wind. The worst he could do was yell at me, and at least I'd have had a bath and washed my hair in something other than a bucket filled with cold water.

The water was as hot as I could stand it, and I sighed with bliss as I sank into it, mentally rehearsing any number of apologies that I'd offer if Peter came into the room while I was still bathing. Luckily, I didn't need to use any of them. A half hour of wonderful soak time later, I utilized the complimentary hair dryer, tidied up the towels I had used, and was dressed, feeling much more human.

"So. Now I wait. Unless I can think of something . . . ow. What the hell?"

Something was wrong with my mouth. All of a sudden my lips felt sore and hot and tight, as if a bee had stung them. I touched my upper lip, and dashed to the mirror, horrified by the massive protuberance that I had felt.

"Oh mah goh," I said as my tongue joined my lips in swelling up to a hideous, repulsively shiny red state. "Whah happen? What ih goin' on?"

Was it the soap? The water? Something in the tub?

Behind me, in the main room, the door closed with a solid thunk.

"Freeze!" a masculine voice called out from behind me. I spun around to find Peter standing in the doorway in a classic shooter's stance, his gun pointed at me. He blinked twice at the sight of me.

"Who is the intruder? Is it one of your cousins come to stab you again? I will fling myself into their eyes so that you might arrest—oooh. It is the popsy. With bulbous lips. Something is not right here, Peter-ji." The golden ball of light that was Sunil bobbed in front of my face.

"Peher!" I wailed, ignoring Sunil's tuts of sympathy, tears spilling down my cheeks to my massive, bulging lips. "Something wrong wif me!"

"By the saints," he swore, putting away the gun and stepping into the room to examine my mouth closer. "Were you stung by an insect?"

"No! It jush happen. Mahe it stoh!"

"I had a cousin who was most decidedly allergic to peanuts. Perhaps the popsy is the same way?" Sunil continued to bob in front of me until I glared at him.

"Are you allergic to anything? Nuts? Milk? Have you eaten anything?" Peter asked, leaning forward to peer at my poor, abused lips.

I stamped my foot. "No, no, no! Jush happen!"

He shook his head. "Then I don't know. What were you doing when it got this way?"

"Sittin' on your beh." I pointed to his bed. "I had a bah, too. Sorry bouh thah, buh it was thoo good tho mith."

He glanced at the bed, then moved around me and got a washcloth, which he soaked in cold water. "Here.

Hold this on your mouth. I'll go fetch some ice from Alison."

"Thath huthy? No thanh you." I held the cold cloth to my mouth, which I admit did make it feel a little bit better. Peter examined his bed briefly, then the bathtub.

"I don't see any foreign substance present in either the bed or the tub. Sit down. I'll be back in a minute with some ice."

"I shall stay here and guard the popsy," Sunil declared.

Peter paused at the door, one eyebrow cocked. "I thought we discussed the idea of you keeping surveillance on the motel from the outside?"

There was a pause; then Sunil said, "It is that I am changing my mind, popsy. I will not be guarding you. Instead, Peter-ji has given me a very excellent job to watch the comings and goings of the motel. You are understanding that I am his partner in all things, and must put our investigation before pleasure time, is it not?"

"Yeth. I unnerthan." I sat in the armchair next to the bed, so miserable that I didn't say a thing about the subtle way Peter got rid of his light buddy, let alone argue with him over the idea of asking a favor of the motel hussy. Instead, I thanked my stars that although my tongue had swollen up, it wasn't so bad that it blocked my airflow. Peter returned shortly with a small bowl of ice, which he put inside the wet washcloth before handing it back to me.

He sat on the edge of the bed and gestured toward me. "All right. Start from the beginning."

"Whah beginnin'?" I asked from behind the ice pressed to my hot, swollen rolls of flesh that had replaced my lips.

"The beginning of whatever it is you did to get like that."

I glared silently at him.

He sighed and scooted back on the bed until he was leaning against the headboard, ankles crossed, and his arms over his chest. "Start at what it is you're doing here in my room. How did you get in?"

It took some time to tell the tale of just why I had felt it necessary to break in. I wasn't able to articulate very clearly my plan of offering up some tidbit of important news vital to his well-being, leaving him to guess the details.

"You wanted to see me?"

I nodded.

"Because you had something to tell me?"

I nodded again, and shifted the ice to the opposite corner of my mouth. It felt so good, I sighed in relief.

"Something about my family?"

"Mrs. Faa noh happy wif you."

"I'm well aware of that, but thank you for coming into town to tell me." He considered my miserable self for a minute. "You couldn't have left that in a note?"

I shook my head, and pulled out my cell phone. "Wanted to geh your nuher."

"Ah. Oddly enough, I have wanted the same thing. Here. Allow me." He took my phone and quickly maneuvered its intricacies to make a new entry in the phone book for himself, then repeated the process with his own phone. I accepted it back happily, my lips trying to form a smile of gratitude, but screaming instead. Hurriedly, I put the ice back on my mouth. "Your battery is almost dead."

"I knoh."

"That explains what you're doing here, but not how you got into my room." He was silent for a moment. "I find it difficult to believe that Alison let you in. She has . . . desires . . . that she's made all too clear."

"I knew ih! I knew she wath a huthy!" I said loudly, and thought of several things I'd like to say to her when I had my lips back.

"Therefore, you must have gained access to my room by some other means. Some illegal means."

I batted my eyelashes and tried to look innocent.

"How did you get into my room, Kiya?"

"Can't talk. Mouf hurths."

"I'll get you a tablet of paper and you can write it out," he said, making like he was going to get up.

"Jeeth. Tho puthy. I thtole time, all wigh? I'm a Twaveller, tho I thtole time."

He bolted upright. "You what?"

"You hearh me."

"For the love of the saints, woman!" He leaped to his feet and began pacing in front of me, his hands drawing undefined shapes in the air. "Are you insane or just stupid?"

"Hey!"

He ignored my exclamation, rounding on me, his hands on his hips. "You do not steal time, do I make myself clear?"

"I juth dih."

"And you can see the consequences of such an idiotic act," he snapped.

I blinked, and removed the ice to touch my lips. They were still swollen, and now chilled, but I thought the swelling had gone down some. "Thith? My mouf?"

"Yes, that, your mouth. Now you see exactly why you

shouldn't steal time. You have no experience doing so—
I thank all the gods for that small miracle—and clearly,
you have no idea how to do so without suffering a karmic whiplash. I just hope this experience has taught you
a valuable lesson."

"You're juth bein' obnoshush," I told him.

"What?"

"Obnoshush!"

"I can't understand you. Are you saying that you're
nauseous?"

"Argh!"

A half hour later, the solid application of ice while
steadfastly ignoring the rude, albeit annoyingly sexy,
man, and my mouth and tongue had shrunk down to a
level where I looked less like I'd been whacked in the
face with a two-by-four, and more like a too-frequent
visitor to a lip-plumping doctor.

Peter emerged from the bathroom, where he had clos-
eted himself and his phone so he could make a call in
private. He stopped in front of where I was sitting on his
bed. "Are you calmed down now?"

"Yes, but only because my lips are in working order
again."

He stared at them for a moment, causing heat to grow
from my belly and spread out. "Ah. I see. Yes. Much better. They look very . . . pink. And soft. And . . . yes."

"Thank you for getting me the ice. I'm sorry I threw
the bowl at your head, but you were beyond tolerable."

"On the contrary, I am the very personification of rea-
sonableness," he countered, sitting on the edge of the
bed opposite me. "Are you prepared to discuss the facts
of your crime with me in a less emotional manner?"

I straightened my shoulders. "Crime? What crime? I

didn't break into your room, you know. I happened to have a key."

"The crime I'm referring to is the theft of Alison's time. At least, I assume it was Alison whose time you stole."

"Oh. That." I squirmed a bit uncomfortably. "I would like to say in my defense that you're the one who told me I'm a Traveller. I had no idea about that until you explained it. So really, you're to blame for the whole thing."

He looked charmingly outraged. "I am in no way responsible for your reckless and illegal acts! I am a member—"

"—of the Watch, I know, you've told me that like ten times now," I interrupted, taking the sting out of it by scooting over to sit next to him. I patted his knee in what I hoped he'd interpret as a friendly manner, rather than an "I really want to get you naked and lick all over you" way. Which, of course, it was, but I didn't need him to know that. Unless he wanted to be licked. Hmm. I eyed him. He was back to looking all stiff and unyielding, his lovely eyes glittering with ire. No licking on the horizon, alas.

"And because of that, I did not incite you to commit a heinous and morally reprehensible act."

"Hey, now," I said, turning so I could face him. My knee brushed his thigh. We both stopped and looked down to where my leg was pressed against his.

"You have really nice thighs. I like the bulgy muscle parts of them," I said without thinking. As soon as the words were spoken, I clapped a (careful) hand over my mouth.

"You haven't seen them," he said, an interesting parade of emotions crossing his face. I particularly enjoyed the one that had him looking all seductive and sleepy-eyed. "How can you possibly judge them if you haven't seen them?"

I pulled my hand from my mouth. "I'm sorry. That wasn't me that said something so utterly and completely out of line. It was my id. She makes me say things like that. Please forgive her and go back to looking annoyed so I can explain that I'm really not to blame about the whole time-theft thing."

He looked again at my leg, his fingers flexing before his gaze went briefly to my breasts, and then back to my face.

My id encouraged me to fling myself on him. The egos were rolling their respective eyes at such a thought.

"I . . . you really are the oddest woman I've ever met."

"And you've met a lot of odd ones, right?" I said hopefully.

He shook his head. "Not really, no. May I return the compliment and say that you have very nice thighs, too, before we continue on to the part of the conversation where we discuss your punishment?"

I sat up straighter, still very much aware of my knee pressed against his deliciously muscled thigh. "Oh no, we are not going there. I do not like men who tell me what to do or think or when to eat, or any of that bullcrap. That's totally abusive behavior, and besides, I am not into kinky sex."

He looked startled. "Who said anything about abuse or sex, kinky or otherwise?"

"You did!" He continued to look startled. "Didn't you? Wait . . . what do you mean by punishment if not bondage sex?"

"I don't care for that sort of thing, either, although I

will admit to having a fantasy right now wherein you—"
He suddenly stopped talking, his eyes—a lovely smoky
amethyst—widening as he realized what he was saying.

"It's your id," I consoled, and thought about patting
his leg again, but felt it was better not to tempt myself.
"They make you say the most embarrassing things, don't
they? Although Carla once told me it was better to have
a tongue that ran away with you, so to speak, than to
keep everything bottled up inside you. She said that
she'd never met a psychopath who was a chatterbox
about every last thing they were thinking. I've always
taken comfort from that."

"You took comfort from the fact that you aren't a psychopath?"

"Yes. I think that's an important trait in people, being
connected with others. I mean, if I was a psychopath, I
wouldn't like your thighs so much." I couldn't help but
glance down at his leg, and from there to his fly, the latter
of which was looking pretty strained. "That looks painful."

"My leg?"

"Your penis. You don't mind if I say penis, do I? Some
men don't like women to just come right out and say the
word when they haven't first been introduced to the part
in question, but you strike me as a man who doesn't hold
to conventional standards. I mean, you are a time thief."

"I am not a thief, and no, I don't mind if you say the
word penis. I would happily reciprocate with a mention
of your vagina, if it would put you at ease."

"Oh, I'm quite at ease," I said, leaning back slightly
so as to be able to drink in all of him. There was something about him, a heady sense of danger that simmered
with a sensual awareness of him on a fundamental level.

He was mysterious, and different, a man who could manipulate time, a man who wasn't mortal, and I knew I should be running as far away from him as Eloise would carry me.

And yet, I didn't run. I decided it was his eyes that kept me sitting on the bed next to him, soaking in the exciting thought that he was just as aroused as I was. That he was as sexually interested in me as I was in him was obvious.... What was less obvious was the loneliness that I saw shadowed in his eyes. There was pain in there, as well, an acknowledgment that he was on the outside of life looking in. And it was that sense of wistfulness, that neediness, that called out to me.

I wanted him on a physical level because I'd have to be dead to do otherwise, but it was that lost, lonely man beneath the handsome covering that made me shiver with desire.

"Cold?" he asked.

"Not just yet. Maybe later," I answered, my mind filled with all sorts of erotic pictures. Like Peter spread-eagle, naked, and welcoming my attentions.

"That doesn't make any sense."

Or perhaps he should be wet and naked. I glanced at the claw-foot bathtub apparent through the tiny room that contained only the tub and a sink, and wondered if he was at all interested in taking a bubble bath. I pursed my lips at the thought of spreading soap over his sleek, wet flesh. "Thanks."

"You're not really listening to me, are you?"

Then again, that session outside on the picnic blanket was pretty wild. I had a sudden yearning to give him a massage—a sensual massage—out there under the light of the moon, the cool, pine-scented breezes encouraging the warmth of body-to-body contact. Especially as enhanced by massage oil.

"What is it exactly that you're thinking about?"

"Sliding around on your well-oiled body," I answered without thinking, the mental vision of doing just that commanding every last bit of my attention.

"Kiya," Peter said, his voice somewhat strangled.

A hint of something being wrong snapped me out of my reverie. "Yes?"

"Against my better judgment, I must ask that you leave this room immediately."

I gawked at him, outright gawked, all the happy dreams of molesting him with massage oil dying a sad and cruel death. My cheeks went red-hot as I stammered out, "You want me to leave?"

"If you do not leave right now," he said, his face rigid and unmoving, "it is quite likely that I will take advantage of the sacred trust placed in me by the Otherworld Watch by doing lascivious things to your delicious thighs. And breasts. And mouth, assuming it's no longer painful. There are other parts, as well, that would come under my scrutiny, but since I am a gentleman, and gentlemen do not go into details of a personal nature with women they've known for such a short amount of time, I will desist from listing exactly what I plan to do to those parts. Instead, I encourage you to leave so you do not have to witness my moral downfall."

I stared at him, my mind exploding in a wild celebration of joy and desire that left me momentarily speechless.

"You have"—he consulted a clock—"exactly eight seconds before I can no longer restrain myself. Do I make myself clear?"

I blinked a couple of times, not because it helped the thought processes, but because I honestly couldn't think of anything else to do that didn't involve shredding the clothes right off his wonderfully warm, hard body.

"Kiya? Do you understand what I'm saying?"

I nodded.

"You have four seconds left. Leave now if you are intending to escape me slaking my not-insubstantial lust upon your fair and tempting self."

I blinked again. There really didn't seem to be much else to do, to be honest.

"Three," he counted down, his gaze on the clock. "Two."

"One," I said just a fraction of a second before I pounced. My action, not expected by him, resulted in us lying in a heap on the bed, Peter solid and warm and smelling oh-so wonderfully good beneath me. "You don't happen to have any massage oil, do you? The kind that gets warm? Because I can think of a lot of places on you that I'd like to use it."

"I am the man," he answered, moaning slightly when I sat up on his thighs and slid my hands into his shirt in order to caress that glorious chest of his. "If there is any usage of massage oil—and no, sadly, I had not thought to bring some with me, but I will rectify that oversight at the earliest convenient moment—then I will be the one to use it first. You may use it only after I've had my way with you. How is your bra fastened? It refuses to come off."

While he spoke, he had been busy removing my shirt, his hands wonderfully warm on my breasts. I stopped stroking his pectoral muscles long enough to undo the hook on the front of my bra, doing a little moaning of my own when his hands cupped my breasts.

"You are so soft," he murmured, his fingers doing

things to what I had previously thought of as mundane breasts until I arched back, thrusting myself into his hands, glorying in the feel of him. "Soft and warm and begging to be tasted."

"Tasting is good," I said breathlessly. He pulled me forward and slightly up so that his mouth could capture one suddenly needful breast. "Tasting is wonderful. Tasting is to be commended. Oh lordy, yes, right there. Do that thing with your tongue again. Wait. You need your pants off."

"Yes, yes, I do," he agreed, but refused to release me so I could take them off. What followed no doubt would have looked to a witness like an awkward tangle of arms and legs and jeans and breasts as I struggled to get his clothing off at the same time he tried to remove mine, lavish attention to my breasts, and touch me with what felt like molten fingers of pure sexual rapture.

"You're supposed to be a magical person," I said at one point, my voice muffled since my hair had somehow become tangled around one of his shirt buttons, leaving the shirt draped around my head while I tried simultaneously to work free my hair and pull off his remaining shoe so I could shuck his pants. He was likewise trying to remove my jeans, and continue to molest my breasts in a way that left me utterly witless. "Why can't you just make our clothes disappear so we can be naked together? Get with the program, magic man!"

"We are Travellers, not magicians," he grumbled around my other breast, paying it due homage because it had complained of being left out of the fun. "We can't make things disappear."

"Time," I gasped, finally getting my hair untangled from his shirt. I flung it onto the ground, growled at the sight of his now-naked chest, and jerked the jeans right off his body, like a waiter pulling a tablecloth out from under a full set of dishes.

"What about it?" he asked, trying to pull my torso back in range of his mouth at the same time his hands were busy removing my underwear.

"What about what? Holy jebus, man!" His underwear had come off with the jeans. I stared in wonder at the magnificent sight that greeted my eyes. "You are like . . . woof! That's . . . impressive."

"What is?" he asked, his words obscured by my breast, which was once again quite happily in his mouth. I squirmed in pleasure and tried to twist in such a way that I could reach his very impressive penis, and yet continue to allow him to do all those wonderful things he was doing to me.

"Huh? Oh, your penis."

"Ah. Thank you." He looked modest for a moment. "I don't have any complaints about it, although I will admit that around you it has been a bit less than comfortable. I trust that it won't pose a problem later?"

"Later?" I stopped nipping at his collarbone, glancing back at where his penis saluted me with a jaunty little bob. "In what way would it pose a problem? Wait a minute, just what are you planning on doing with it? I told you that I'm not into anything kinky! No back-door action! No weird foot fetish stuff! No mushroom stamping!"

"I don't plan on . . . what the hell is mushroom stamping?"

I squinted at him. "You don't need to know."

Those glorious violet eyes looked heavenward for a couple of seconds. "You referenced my size, Kiya. I was simply trying to ascertain, without saying it in so many words because, as I've mentioned, I am a gentleman, and we do not discuss things like lady parts unless it is absolutely necessary, which I've yet to find it to be unless the lady in question was indisposed, and then it's not so much a discussion of her parts, but of her general sense of disinterest. . . . Where was I?"

"Lady parts?" I asked hopefully, gesturing to mine.

"Ah. Yes. Very nice."

"Thank you. I trimmed last night in your honor. Well, to be honest, I was going to trim anyway, because there's nothing more off-putting than having your pubes running rampant in your pants, but you probably don't want that mental picture, so we'll just go back to whatever it is you were saying."

He took a deep breath. I much appreciated what it did to his chest and gave his nearer nipple a little lick in gratitude. "I was trying to ask you if you anticipated any trouble with your comfort in accommodating such a size."

I eyed the penis in question. It bobbed again. "You're not obscenely made. Not like porn-star quality, which is good because there is such a thing as too much. No, you're just beefy, and that's fine. I don't anticipate any problem. Does that ease your mind?"

"Infinitely so." He returned to kissing a hot, wet path back to my first breast, which made it incredibly happy. "I love your breasts. They are just the perfect size for my hands and mouth. I would like to see them covered in the massage oil that I don't yet have."

"I would like that, as well. Whoa, you are really, really hard, aren't you?" I struggled to get one hand back in order to touch his genitals, but it was a difficult position to hold. "And hot. Really hot. You don't have a fever down there, do you? An infection or something?"

He released my breast with a wet popping noise, and leveled an outraged look at me. "Are you saying that I look like I have a venereal disease?"

"No! Of course not! I would never! It's just that your penis is really hot. Is that normal?"

His brows lowered. "It is perfectly normal. You are simply consumed with lust and thus can't differentiate between a normal penis temperature and that of one that is infected. Now cease moving around so that I can lick your belly. I wish to admire your job of trimming, and plan on taking in the scenery on the way down there."

I giggled, allowing him to pull me up even higher. "I like how you talk. It's part formal, part old-world. And you get bonus points for doing more than grunting right now. Most men don't like to talk during sex."

"This isn't sex. This is foreplay. And I was born in a small village in Romania, so much of my linguistic pattern comes from there."

"I thought you said your mom was—oh merciful heavens, yes! Your thumb! Do that again!—I thought she was American?"

His fingers, which had preceded his mouth, had done an intricate little dance in my aforementioned lady parts, leaving me cross-eyed and twitching with all sorts of wonderful emotions.

"I said she was mortal, and she was. Will you cease attempting to escape my hold? I wish to do wicked things to you with my tongue."

"Oh, I'm totally on board with that, but I want you to feel the love, too."

He stopped kissing my belly and looked up at me with round eyes.

"So to speak," I added, bending backward to wrap my fingers around his penis. As I said, it wasn't a comfortable position, but I was determined that he have his share of the fun, too. "I am nothing if not a thoughtful lover," I informed him.

"I can tell that you are," he said, and for a few seconds, his eyes crossed, as well, as I started up a rhythm that I felt he'd enjoy. "However, at this moment, I'm more interested in driving you wild with desire."

"You're succeeding," I gasped when he flipped me over onto my back, and nipped at my hip before continuing his tour to regions southward. "Peter, I—no, seriously, that is the best thing I've ever felt in my life—I don't think I'm going to last much longer."

"Then, my easily aroused beauty, I believe we have come to the part of the evening where I ask you if you prefer that I use a condom."

"I would, yes. It's not that I'm not using something myself, but I just think until we know each other better that it would be a good idea."

He gave my belly button a lick and a kiss, rolled off me, and padded over to where his duffel bag was sitting on a small table.

"You have the nicest butt I've ever seen on a man," I said conversationally.

"And you've seen a lot of men's asses?" he asked, parroting my comment earlier.

"No, actually, I haven't. Just a couple in person, but you know, there are such things as pictures and movies, and I have a pretty good idea of what the general male populace sits on, and you, sir, have a very nice specimen."

"I will be happy to return the compliment," he said, handing me a condom package.

"Oooh. I get to put it on you?"

"I thought it might help you resolve yourself to my beefiness," he said pleasantly, but that was basically the last coherent thing he said for the next sixty seconds. He moaned, he groaned, he muttered things in a language I didn't understand, he clutched huge handfuls of the sheet, and writhed in absolute pleasure as I worked the condom down the length of him.

"Was it good for you?" I asked, laughing, as he panted beneath me.

He opened both of his eyes and glared at me.

"You did that on purpose."

"Did what?" I batted my lashes in innocence.

He growled, flipped me onto the side of the bed, and, before I knew it, had me spread-eagle, and was looming above me. "You made that the best condom application ever performed."

"Well, I don't want to appear immodest, but I did try to make it a memorable experience since I know most men don't like wearing them, and I wanted to show my appreciation for the fact that you offered, which was really niiiiiiiiiiiii! Peter!"

Suddenly, he was there, beefy-filled condom and all, thrusting inside me in a manner that left me as the incoherent one. The way he moved was pure magic, and if I didn't know better, I'd say he had been gifted with some supernatural sex powers, because it wasn't more than a few minutes before I was shattering into the most intense orgasm I'd ever experienced.

Luckily for all my overly sensitive parts, he was just as quick off the mark as I was, and I dug my fingers into the thick muscles of his behind as he arched his back, and gave himself up to his own moment of rapture.

"You're fast," I told him some minutes later, when I could think again. I was grateful that my egos and id were so sated by the experience that they didn't have a thing to say other than to weakly demand that we do it again.

He opened one eye to look at where I was draped across his still-heaving and damp chest, my legs tangled around his, my chin resting on my hands. His hands moved to my butt, where he squeezed a cheek. "That is not a nice thing to say, woman."

"I didn't mean it as an insult." I kissed his collarbone. His hands stopped squeezing my butt and switched to gentle little swirls, instead. "Honestly, I'm glad you're fast, because evidently with you I'm fast, too, although I don't remember being that way with other men. So, it's kind of nice that we're both a little excitable, and don't waste time getting to the brass ring."

"Any other woman in the world would complain that I didn't spend enough time ensuring her pleasure," he grumbled, closing his eyes again. "But not you."

"Nope, not me. Am I staying the night?" I asked, not sure whether he wanted me to. "Or would you prefer I take off?"

"You're staying here, where I know you're safe," he said, pulling the blankets over us and switching off the bedside light.

I relaxed into him, feeling warm and comfortable, and emotionally engaged on a level that I hadn't been for many years.

He would be very easy to fall in love with, my id said with a happy sigh. *We should do that.*

Let's just take this one step at a time, the ego told us all. *There's no sense in rushing into something.*

Just because he smells nice, and is fabulous at sex, and has a wicked sense of humor that for some reason he doesn't seem to want people to know about, doesn't mean that he's the man for us, my superego agreed.

Perhaps not, I told my inner voices. *But it's sure starting to look like he is.*

ELEVEN

"It's too bad that tub isn't big enough for two. You'd think they'd have that for a honeymoon suite," I commented the next morning as I gave myself up to the luxury of a second hot bath in as many days. "When will your little light friend be back?"

"Not until I let him know it's safe to return. He'll be very aware of the fact that you did not leave last night."

"I feel bad about making him stay out all night by himself," I said, uncomfortable at the pang of guilt that soured an otherwise wonderful memory of the hours we'd just spent.

"Don't. Sunil loves surveillance. He enjoys seeing who goes where and with whom. He'll be back bristling with information about what he saw all night."

"Sounds like you know him well. Are you ready to tell me how you guys got connected?"

"No." Peter was dressing in the main room, but he popped his head around the door to answer me, paused zipping up his pants when he saw me soaping up my breasts, and before you could say "Two people in a tub" there was a splash, and he was kneeling between my calves, buck naked.

"Let me help you with that," he ordered, taking the

washcloth away from me and using his hands to spread the soapy bubbles around my breasts. "Move your legs aside."

"If I move my legs any more—," I said, pulling them up so he had more room. There really wasn't anywhere comfortable to put them other than to let them dangle over the sides of the tub. "I'm going to be very exposed, and—hoobah! Peter! Holy jebus, you're massive!"

"I thought the word was 'beefy'? By the saints, woman, if you tighten those muscles any more, you're going to squeeze it off."

He lunged forward, a tiny tidal wave of water washing over my chest as our bodies met in the manner that guaranteed a happy, if untidy, bath for both of us. Almost immediately, the wet, soapy friction of his body moving against mine sent me to the stars and back again.

"I swear," I panted a few minutes later, my legs wrapped around his hips, his body slumped on mine as we both tried to catch our breath from the fast and furious lovemaking, "you're getting faster. But damn. It's so good, I can't complain."

"I've asked you not to tell me I was fast. Men don't like to hear that. We like to hear that we've pleasured our women to the tips of their delicate little toes and back again. We like to hear that we're manly men who could break concrete with our penises if we so chose. We want to know that we drive you to the very borders of sanity with the intense amount of pleasure we bring you. And if we are swift doing so because our women have hair-trigger responses, then fine, but we would appreciate the emphasis to lie on our skill, and not our speed."

I pinched his adorable, wet butt. He pulled his head

up from where he had been panting on my neck, and suddenly grinned at me, his hair mussed and damp from the inevitable splashing, his eyes smoky from our activities. It was a grin that melted my heart, and I didn't need to hear my egos warning me that I was going to be a goner if I didn't separate myself from this adorable, needy, wonderful man.

"You're damned good, and you know it," I said once I recovered from that grin.

He gave me a sloppy kiss, and climbed out of the tub, leaving me to sigh in sated pleasure as I watched him dry off. "I expect better than just 'damned good,' but that will have to wait for another time. I have things to do today, and I assume you are expected back at Lenore Faa's caravan."

"How come you call her by her full name, and not Grandma or Nana or any of the other normal grandmother names?" I asked as I got out of the tub, my legs a bit wobbly from all the unexpected muscle usage.

"Would you call a woman who refuses to acknowledge you 'grandmother' even if she was that person?"

I patted myself dry with the only other towel, and shook out the clothing I'd worn the night before. "I suppose that would sting a little. What is it you have to do today?"

"Meet with Dalton."

I froze in the act of pulling on my jeans, hopping to the door on one leg to ask, "Who?"

"My boss. We had arranged to meet last night, but he wasn't at our rendezvous point. I was supposed to give him the DNA evidence I collected at the crime scene, but that's been stolen." He gave me a long look.

"Don't you even think it, Peter," I warned, suddenly hurt that he could imagine I'd do something so heinous as to take his important evidence.

His eyes glittered for a moment before his shoulders slumped. "I don't think you took it. Not now. I admit I was a bit suspicious at first, what with you being a Traveller, and in Lenore Faa's camp, but that was before I knew you."

"Before you knew I was honest and aboveboard, and would never do such a thing?"

"Before I knew you had no idea what you really were."

I glared at him. He was in the middle of putting on his shoes and missed it, drat it all.

"Well, if you want to be pedantic, we don't really know each other," I said slowly as I finished dressing. "I mean, not deep down knowing, do we?"

"I know you're not a thief," he said, then corrected himself. "Not a thief of anything but time."

I touched my lips briefly. "Yeah, well, lesson learned there, trust me. I'm not going to be stealing anything, especially not time. That karma thing is nasty."

"It can be," he agreed.

"How do you get around it?"

"I don't steal time."

"Never?"

"Never."

"Did you used to in the past, but you gave it up for Lent or something?"

His expression turned to granite. "Those days are well past me. It's the present that matters now."

Judging by the closed expression on his face, he wasn't

planning on expounding on the subject. I wondered what it was that made him stiffen up. It had to be something serious.

I weighed my innate curiosity and desire to know about him with the desire to not force confidences, and opted to go with the latter. He'd tell me in his own good time. And if that didn't occur naturally in the next couple of days, I'd see that it had a helping hand.

"Give Dalton my best," I said, gathering up my things preparatory to heading out. "I hope his allergies are better."

Peter looked at me like I was a three-headed llama.

I smiled, and briefly explained how I knew him. "Small world, huh?" I concluded.

"Evidently." Peter slid his gun into its holster, watching me for a few seconds before he added, "I don't suppose if I asked you to give up the job taking care of Lenore Faa's dogs, you'd do so."

I paused in the act of combing my hair, turning from the mirror to look at him. "Not unless you had a really good reason why I should. She's paying me the money I need to get Eloise running properly. I don't have a job, and the weather isn't bad for camping, so it's a win-win situation."

"And if I gave you the money you needed?"

I set down my comb. "I wouldn't take it. Peter, are you trying to say something but don't want to come right out and say it? Because if you're having postcoitus regrets, and want me out of the area—"

"Christos, no," he exclaimed, making an aborted gesture. "I don't like you in that camp. My cousins are ruthless, and they've already stolen time from you."

"Tiny bits. Just a few seconds here and there. Not that I like it at all, and I made a big stink when your . . . er . . . William is your father, isn't he?"

Peter's lips tightened until they were a thin, unhappy line.

"Yeah, I don't like him, either. Apologies about saying that about your dad, but he really rubs me the wrong way. Anyway, when he tried pulling that crap on me yesterday afternoon, I made a big deal about it to your grandma, and she stopped it. So I'm not worried about him stealing more."

"I, on the other hand, am quite worried about your well-being." He stared at me.

I stared back at him.

"So, you're not trying to get me out of the area?" I asked, my frail little id forcing me into clarification of that all-important point.

"No."

"OK. Good." I gave him a dazzling smile. All was right in my world again.

He ignored it, frowning at me. "I will be the one leaving this region once I have the proof of the murderers."

It was as if the sun turned to lead. I didn't want him leaving. I wanted him right there, where we could explore the possibility of a relationship, and have fabulous — if very quick — sex in the bed, and the bathtub, and possibly outside, assuming we found a private enough location. I wanted him where I could watch his eyes, and wait for another of those brain-melting grins, and where I could reach out and touch the lightning flower that trailed down his chest.

I just wanted him, period.

"How long do you expect that to take?" I heard a flat, lifeless voice ask, and was momentarily startled to find it came from my mouth.

His gaze met mine, then flickered away before I could pinpoint the emotion in it. "I need that vial. I can't prove anything without it. I will have to find a way to search the camp without my cousins knowing I'm doing so."

It would be wrong to wish that vial a million miles away. Someone had been murdered, and the person who committed that crime had to pay. Still, I couldn't help making a wee little wish that it took Peter a bit of time to find the proof.

I felt so guilty by that desire that my mouth opened up and said, "Would you like me to help you?"

"Search the camp?" he asked, shaking his head. "It's too dangerous."

"I could help you get into the camp so you can search it," I said slowly, not feeling in the least bit threatened by Mrs. Faa's family, but knowing that helping Peter solve the case was the right thing to do, even if it did make me feel as if all the joy had gone out of life.

He looked thoughtful. "How would you do that?"

"We could smuggle you into my tent, and then wait until everyone was asleep. My tent opens to the woods, not the camp itself, so no one would see if you if it was dark, and you slipped in from the trees."

"And how would I search the caravans if everyone was asleep inside them?" His voice was neutral, but I saw a hint of warmth in his eyes.

I gave a half shrug. "I don't know. I haven't thought much about it."

"Kiya." He took my hands in his, and turned them, pressing a kiss to each palm. The heat of his mouth made me give a little shiver of pleasure. "What's wrong? All of a sudden you sound as if you've lost your best friend."

I looked at our hands, and said nothing. What could I say? That I didn't want him to leave? That I thought we might be on the edge of having something wonderful together? Every explanation that my brain came up with sounded trite and unrealistic, like dialogue from a badly written TV show.

Real people didn't tell the man they met a few days ago that they thought they were about to fall in love with him. Real people didn't beg that very same man not to walk out of their lives, leaving them alone and lonely again.

Real people didn't act needy, no matter how vulnerable they suddenly felt.

"I have to go," I said after several seconds of awkward silence. Reluctantly, I pulled my hands from his. "I have an anal-gland squeezing appointment that I'll get hell if I miss."

"Please tell me that appointment is for one of Lenore Faa's dogs," he said as I collected my purse and started for the door. Humor was rich in his voice, making my knees wobble a little as I walked.

"Would you still love me if I said it was for me?" I heard my id asking, and, horrified, I slapped my hand over my mouth.

Peter looked surprised, and opened his mouth to answer.

"Oh my god, I didn't just say that," I said quickly, before he could speak. "You did not hear that, OK? It's my id, I can't take her anywhere!"

"Kiya," he started to say, but I just could not take what I knew he was going to say next.

"Seriously, pretend that never happened. My mouth says stuff all the time that I don't authorize. It's really embarrassing, and I'm going to go sit in my car and try desperately to remove the last few seconds from my memory. Bye. Thanks for the baths. And . . . the other. In bed. It was fun. Bye."

I dashed out of the room before I dropped dead of embarrassment, running smack-dab into the motel hussy named Alison. She squawked something at me, but my brain had had as much mortification as I could stand. I pushed past her and ran to my car. I heard Peter behind me, followed by Alison's seductive tones, and knew that she had snagged him.

Not even that kept me from running away in shame. I chastised myself both verbally and mentally the whole time I drove back to the camp, and continued a short while later while taking the pugs for their morning walk.

"Is something amiss with you?" Mrs. Faa asked when I returned. She watched me measure out the dogs' food, keeping an eye that I matched the correct tiny can of dog food to the small bowls containing varying amounts of dried food. "No, the lamb and rice belongs to Maureen. She cannot tolerate chicken. You look flushed. Are you ill?"

"I'm perfectly fine," I lied, and switched cans before opening them and dumping the contents into the appropriate bowls.

She gave a little snort of disbelief, but returned to her RV after giving me an envelope with money for the vet and the dog groomer.

The anal-gland squeezing was not an experience I wish soon to relive, although I was pleased that I managed to escape the vet teaching me how by gasping at the clock on the wall and exclaiming that I had to run or we'd be late for the spa day. I bustled the newly squeezed Jacques out, along with his compatriots, and into the back of Eloise. By the time I returned to Rose Hill, and dropped the dogs off at their grooming appointment, I had worked through the worst of my embarrassment, and decided on a policy wherein I would disclaim all knowledge of what I had said should Peter bring it up again.

"Like he's going to do that," I muttered to myself, pausing outside the grooming shop to look up and down the street. "Men hate talking about relationship stuff. Especially if you don't really have a relationship beyond a highly erotic night and morning. Hey."

I shaded my eyes against the sun to better see a block away where a familiar-looking man got out of a car and stood in front of the church motel.

"Hey!" I said, this time in a shout, and waved my arm when the man's head turned to see the source of the noise. "Dalton! I was just talking about you!"

He watched without moving as I jogged toward him, a hesitant smile on his face.

"How are you feeling?"

"Me? Just fine, thank you."

"Good. It's odd seeing you when I was just talking to Peter about you. I didn't realize you were his boss."

"And I didn't realize you knew Peter," Dalton said with another smile. "What a very odd coincidence. Have you known him long?"

"No, just since I ran into him outside my employer's camp. So, are you staying here?" I asked, nodding toward the motel.

His smile grew broader. "I am. I was about to go inside. Would you care to come in so we can have a cozy chat?"

"Sure, I've got a bit of time. Have you seen Peter this morning? I think he was looking for you."

"No, I haven't. I'm sure I'll see him later, though. This way." He unlocked and held open a door right next to the front entrance. It was dim inside, the sunlight not able to penetrate the thick curtains on the windows. As I entered the darkened room, I stumbled over something large that was lying in the inky shadow cast by the bed.

"Whoops. Sorry, I tripped over your bag or something—oh my god! That's a body! Holy shiznit, Dalton, there's a body in your room!"

My mind shrieked at me to run far, far away, but I had trodden on the body, causing it to roll onto its front. The police would freak out if they knew I had disturbed a crime scene. Without thinking, I reached out and rolled the body back the way it had been before I tripped over it, my brain coming to a grinding halt at the face attached to the body.

"This . . . it's . . . it can't be." The face was the same one I'd seen just seconds before. It was Dalton. I stared down at him, trying to resolve what it was I was seeing. "What exactly—"

Pain burst into being along the back right side of my head. It didn't last long, but that was only because blackness claimed me, swallowing me up and leaving me completely insensible.

The world as I knew it swam for a few seconds, then settled down into a more-or-less well-behaved manner. Except for the light. That was wrong. I blinked, and shaded my hand against the sun, noticing as I did so a familiar man standing in the gravel parking lot at the side of the motel. "Hey!" I called, waving at him. "Dalton! I—"

Horrified, I dropped my hand. "No," I whispered to myself, and then dived into the doorway next to me when Dalton looked in my direction. My head suddenly swam with pain. I clutched my forehead and held my breath against the wave of nausea that followed my unwise movement for a few seconds before exhaling slowly when the pain dimmed down to a bearable level. "Oh my god, one of them must be around!"

"One of who?" a woman at the counter asked. Carefully, so as not to aggravate my aching head, I glanced around. I'd leaped into the small café that was Rose Hill's morning coffee spot. Several older people seated at small plastic tables watched me with evident concern. I tried to smile, gave it up when a couple of the old people looked horrified, and released my hold on my head.

"Sorry, just talking to myself." I straightened up and tried to look like I hadn't just had time stolen from me. "Um . . . can I get a coffee and bagel to go, please? And maybe a piece of that berry pie. I think I'm in shock. Are those chocolate muffins? I'll take one of them, too. Chocolate always makes you feel better."

"Mmhm," the waitress said, not meeting my eye.

I lurked at the window while the woman packaged up my order. There weren't very many people out on the street—the general population of Rose Hill didn't seem to be too inclined to stroll around on the two blocks that made up their little community—but those who were going to or from cars were not familiar to me.

Somewhere out there was one of Mrs. Faa's family. And one of them had stolen time from me. *Again.* The bastard.

I gritted my teeth, not in pain, but in frustration. I hated the helplessness this whole time theft left me feeling.

After a quick check to make sure the road was clear, I took my food and coffee, and walked as smoothly as I could over to my car, where I managed to hit my head three times climbing into the front seat.

"Son of a sea biscuit!" I swore the third time, slumped into the seat and holding my head again. "I do not know why I have such a massive headache. I didn't have one the ... other ... time. ..."

A vision rose in my mind's eye as I spoke, a vision of a darkened room, and twins, two identical twins. And something very, very wrong ...

"What on earth?" I murmured, then remembered that Carla had once told me to clear my mind of all troubles in order to concentrate when something I wanted to remember was just beyond my mental reach. "Right. A little meditative thinking never hurt anyone ... ow! Oh, holy hand grenade!"

When I leaned my head back against the headrest, a red wave of pain washed down over me, threatening to make me pass out. I focused on keeping the wave from swamping me, breathing in and out in the prescribed manner of one who is fighting to retain consciousness. A few minutes later, I lifted a shaky hand to gently feel the back of my head. My fingers came away sticky and red.

"Ow?" I said to my fingers. "What happened?"

My fingers didn't answer me, and to be honest, I was thankful for that, because it meant that I hadn't suffered any brain damage—noticeable, at least—from the injury to my head.

"Right. Whichever one of those rat bastards hit me on

the head when they stole my time is seriously going to get what's coming to them," I growled. "Now. I just have to focus on what I was doing before they stole my time, and then I will tell Peter, and he will beat the living daylights out of whoever it was. And I will help him."

It took another five minutes or so before my brain was calm enough that I could relax, and focus on what had happened. That same mental image of a darkened room containing something sinister rose before me. "I was with someone," I told Eloise, my eyes screwed up with the effort of remembering. "Someone I was talking to. I went into the room and . . ."

If the top of my head lifted off and let the sunshine into my brain, it wouldn't have been less startling than the flood of memory returning. As if a switch flipped, I remembered kneeling next to the body of Dalton McKay.

"But it was Dalton who let me into the room," I said, staring blindly ahead as my skin crawled in the very best horror movie way. "We had been walking together. And talking. Which means he was alive. Unless . . . oh, merciful mangrove trees, what if he was a zombie!"

My flesh didn't just crawl at that thought—it all but leaped around in horror. I scrabbled through my purse for my phone to call Peter, praying I had enough battery power to tell him I'd been in contact with a zombie, and demand some sort of a cure for the rampant zombieism that was sure to affect me. Just as my fingers closed around the phone, it rang, making me jump in the seat so hard that I banged my sore head on the roof.

"Ow. Hello? Ow."

"Kiya? It's Peter. I wanted to tell you—"

"Peter! Oh, thank the good, green earth. I was about to call you. I've been with a zombie!"

"—that I have reconsidered . . . you *what*?"

"Been with a zombie! Been with a zombie! What's confusing about 'I've been with a zombie'? It's pretty straightforward, really. There was a zombie, and I was with him, and I think he may have touched me, although I can't really remember, because when one of your bastard family members stole my time, they also whacked me on the back of the head and it's bleeding and everything, and oh my god maybe it was the zombie who chomped on me! I thought that brains thing was just a joke! OH MY GOD, Peter! A zombie tried to eat my brains!"

"Kiya, I don't . . . a *zombie*?"

"Yes, yes, a zombie!" Quickly I rolled up the open windows lest the brain-muncher decide to come after me again. "The walking undead. Really, Peter, I don't see why you are having such a problem understanding this. It shakes my faith in you a little, it really does. I was hoping you'd be the sort of man who, upon hearing that his lover has been mauled by a flesh-consuming atrocity of nature, would rush to be at her side to comfort her, check her flesh wounds, and speed her to the nearest zombie immunization office so that she doesn't end up ripping off his limbs because she's a mite peckish."

"Kiya—"

"Great, now I'm trapped in my car and it's getting hot because I had to roll up the windows. That or I'm already getting feverish from the zombie virus."

"Kiya!" Peter said loudly, making my head hurt worse.

"What?" I snapped, somewhat crankily, to be true, but I felt a certain amount of crankiness was justified after a zombie attack.

"Be quiet a minute and let me speak. First of all, there is no such thing as a zombie virus."

I had puffed myself up at the way he had told me to more or less shut up, but at his words, my outraged deflated. "There isn't?"

"No."

"But there are zombies."

"In a manner of speaking, yes. They are called revenants, though, and they are not the monsters made popular by mortals. Most revenants are perfectly normal, and you'd be hard put to tell them from anyone else."

"Do they eat human flesh?" I asked, wincing when I touched the back of my head again.

"They can, but most of them are strict vegetarians so as to avoid temptation. So unless you've come across a rogue revenant who's gone off his diet, I'd say the chances are extremely slim that someone tried to eat your brains. I'm more concerned about what you said concerning my cousins. Did you lose time again?"

"Yes," I said, both relieved and feeling somewhat pouty. At least I didn't have to worry about becoming a brain-slurper myself. "One of them must have hit me on the head if it wasn't the zombie."

"Tell me exactly what happened."

"Well, I got done dropping off the pugs at their spa—what?"

"Nothing. I just snorted disgustingly."

"Don't be such a hater. Those puggies are adorable, and besides, the doggy spa really is just a bath and brushing. And blueberry facials, but we won't go into that. Anyway, I was walking to my car and I saw Dalton."

"Dalton? Dalton McKay? The Dalton I work for?"

"Yes. He's the zombie!"

"He's *what*?"

I explained how I had met Dalton and gone into the motel with him.

"Dalton had a motel room? That doesn't make sense. He didn't tell me he was staying there."

"Well, he is. Only when I got into his room, I stumbled over him, and he was lying dead on the floor!"

"Who was dead on the floor?"

I sighed. "I have an open head wound, and have had time stolen from me, not to mention having suffered from a huge zombie scare. If you could please pay attention, I'd appreciate it."

"I am paying attention, and I'm sorry you've been hurt. I would, in fact, rush to your side and whisk you off to the nearest zombie immunization center, or in this case healer, but as you don't seem to be in too much distress, I'd like to get the facts straight first. Who was lying dead on the floor?"

"Dalton." I couldn't help but smile to myself at the fact that Peter said he'd rush me to the zombie center. A man who would do that wasn't a man who would just walk away from a woman. Would he?

"I thought you said Dalton was the revenant?"

"He was. Is. Whichever tense is appropriate for one who was a person, but is now a zombie. Man, that's confusing. Is there a nonmortal grammar book I can read about how to refer to zombies?"

"So you walked into Dalton's motel room with Dalton behind you, and stumbled over his body?"

I stopped wondering about grammar, and paused to consider what he said. "Yes."

"Don't you think that's a bit odd?"

"Well . . . I just assumed that when you're a zombie,

your original body is stuffed somewhere," I said lamely. "That's not how it works?"

"No."

"How am I supposed to know these things!" I wanted to wail, but knew my head wasn't up to it. "A couple of days ago, I thought I was a perfectly normal person."

"One who has been struck by lightning twice, and not only survived, but bears the physical marks exclusive to Travellers."

"Yeah, well, that was a bit odd, but I didn't realize just how odd until I met you."

"Are you sure it was Dalton who was dead?"

"Fairly so, yes. Oh, Peter, I'm sorry, I didn't even break that to you nicely. In all that zombie scare business, I forgot that he was your boss. Did you know him well?"

"Yes." There was silence as Peter obviously chewed over the sad news. "One of the two Daltons you saw was not real. The question is, which one?"

"I don't know, but I am very sorry that he's dead. He seemed like a nice guy, even as swollen with hives as he was."

"Mmm. Where are you now?"

I told him.

"And you don't see any Travellers around town?"

"Not that I can see, no." Sweat was snaking its way down my back from the building heat in the car. I gave in and rolled down the windows, alert to any sudden attempt on my brain by a rogue zombie. "I was going to go visit the lake that I take the pugs to, since I have a few hours before I have to pick them up, but maybe I shouldn't. Maybe you need me to show you where I saw the body."

"I think it's better if you were out of this, Kiya," Peter said after another few seconds' silence. "If one of my cousins actually committed physical assault on you, then I don't want you anywhere around them."

"That makes me feel all warm and fuzzy, but you know, I'm not some shy, delicate little flower who can't defend herself. I took a self-defense class. I have pepper spray in my purse, and I know how to bring down an attacker with nothing more than a set of keys."

"I'm sure you are well able to take care of yourself, but you will allow me to be an expert on the lengths my family can and will go to in order to protect themselves." His voice went from its normal deliciously deep, sexy tones to hard and flinty. "Go to the lake and enjoy your afternoon. I will see you this evening."

My toes curled with happiness. "You will?"

"Yes. I was calling to tell you that I'd reconsidered your offer of help accessing Lenore Faa's camp, and will meet you at your tent when the sun sets."

The idea of him in my tent had my full approval. "What are you going to do about Dalton's body? The inert one, not the zombie one? Are you going to call the police?"

"There is only one Dalton, Kiya. I don't know which one is real, but there is only one of him. And as for the body, I *am* the police. I will head back to Rose Hill and check out the motel room."

"Should I meet you there?"

"No. I want you well away from there. I'd prefer you were well out of the area, period, but I gather you don't want to do that."

I squashed down the little pang of pain at the thought that he wanted me gone, telling my id and egos that he was just concerned for my safety, in a very manly-man sort of way that had me simultaneously sighing in happiness, and the tiniest bit irritated that he didn't think I could take care of myself. "I have a job to do, and I intend to do it."

"As do I. I will see you this evening. Call me if anything else occurs. Oh, and Kiya . . ."

"Yes?" I held my breath, hoping he'd say something romantic about the thought of spending the night in the tent with me.

"Don't mention this to Lenore Faa."

"Why? Are you ashamed of the fact that you're going to spend the night with me?" I couldn't help but ask.

"What? No, I meant don't mention Dalton's body. I don't give a damn what she thinks about you and me."

I didn't quite know how to feel about that statement, so rather than respond with a flip comment, I simply said I'd be at my tent by nine that night, and hung up. Part of me wanted to go to the motel and help him investigate what happened to Dalton, but the other part of me, the one that was still silently screaming in my head that it had touched a zombie, and stepped on a corpse, was too wigged out to do anything but want a strong bath in a tub filled with disinfectant.

Instead, I drove back to the camp, smiling to myself the whole way with thoughts of the evening to come.

TWELVE

"Peter."

"Dalton." Peter considered the man in front of him. He looked perfectly normal, absolutely healthy, and not the least bit like a revenant. "I'm delighted to see that the reports of your death are grossly exaggerated."

Dalton's eyebrows rose. "As am I. Who reported me dead?"

"No one you know." He thought for a moment. "Or rather, yes, you do know her. At least, you've met her."

"Who is that?"

"Kiya Mortenson. She says she saw you at the local doctor's office."

"Ah, did she, now?" Dalton looked thoughtful. "Kiya? Yes, I believe I do remember her. Pretty girl with red blond hair."

"That's her." Peter was a bit surprised that Dalton hadn't recognized her as a fellow Traveller. Normally, his boss was much more prescient than that, but perhaps his illness had affected him more than he knew.

"And she reported me as dead?"

"She says she stumbled over your body at the local motel."

"Gracious me. She was mistaken, naturally."

"Naturally," Peter agreed. "She appeared to think that you were a revenant, and attempted to eat her brains, as well, but I put that down to more the fact that she's still a bit flustered over finding out she's a Traveller than to any lack of mental cognizance."

"Indeed." For a moment, Dalton sounded genuinely shocked.

"Evidently, she was orphaned at an early age, and raised by mortals."

"You have much in common with her, then."

Peter relaxed at that statement. There was a moment when he wasn't sure, when Kiya's experience with the body fed him all sorts of outlandish ideas of Dalton not being what he seemed, but that moment passed. "I've sent Sunil off to keep a covert eye on her."

"That sounds like a very good idea."

"I thought so. If it wasn't your body she stumbled over, then it must have been someone else's. That leaves the question of whether it was you who escorted her into your motel room."

"My motel room?" Dalton shook his head, and gestured toward the small dark rental car parked on the edge of the road. "In the local town here, you mean? It definitely wasn't me. Not only did I *not* escort any young woman to my room, I don't actually have a room here. I drove in this evening from Glenville. That's a good hour's drive away."

The fact that they were parked at the entrance to the lumber camp made Peter nervous that they would be seen before he was ready to confront his family, but Dalton had suggested that spot to meet at. He'd just hurry things along so he could get back to Kiya. Er . . . work. Yes, work first, then Kiya. "If it wasn't you, then there is an impostor running around pretending to be you. Could be it's one of the family trying to throw me off the track."

"What purpose would that serve?" Dalton asked, shaking his head and answering before Peter could respond. "They don't know for certain that you suspect them, do they?"

"I imagine that after knocking me out, stabbing me, stealing the vial, and stabbing me a second time that yes, they have a pretty fair idea that I suspect one or more members of my family is responsible for the murders."

"What would they hope to prove by such a tactic?" Dalton asked, apparently not at all surprised that the vial had been stolen, not to mention that he, Peter, had been stabbed twice. "It doesn't make any sense."

"Neither does murdering mortals, but they've done that enough to draw the attention of not just the Watch but the mortal police, as well."

"And yet despite the evidence that you said was stolen, there are no other signs that this family is behind the acts." Dalton eyed him in a way that made Peter vaguely uncomfortable. "Where is the punishment meted out on them? Where is proof of the price paid for such great thefts? Has any calamity bestruck the family?"

Peter looked out into the woods, toward where Lenore Faa's camp was situated. He knew better than anyone just how heavy the penalty could be for stealing time, and yet, as Dalton pointed out, where was proof that someone in his family had done likewise? It was the one thing that had kept him from descending upon the camp with a small army of Watch members. "I don't know why the punishment hasn't manifested itself on whoever it is who's killing the mortals, but I intend to find that out. Tonight."

"Far be it from me to discourage you, but I think you have to ask yourself whether you are not pursuing circumstantial evidence solely to persecute the family," Dalton replied, his voice a gentle rebuff that sat ill with Peter. "Only you can answer that, but given the lack of evidence, I will not be able to bring the full forces of the Watch down upon them."

"You'll have the evidence," Peter said grimly, his fingers curling into fists. "I'll get back not only the DNA, but I'll find out just what they are doing to bypass being punished for the crimes they've committed."

Dalton shook his head, and turned toward his car. "You do as you must. Let me know what you find out."

"I will." Peter watched as his supervisor got into his car. "Although it's a hell of a lot easier if we can just talk on the phone as we did before."

"My phone is no longer secure."

"It's not? In what way?"

"I lost it for a few hours. The chip could have been cloned."

"That sounds highly unlikely, Dalton—"

"Nonetheless, I must insist that we meet in person rather than rely on a phone that might be compromised. You may call to tell me you wish to meet, but do not reveal any other information on the phone."

Little warning bells went off in Peter's head, but he didn't know how to address his boss's bizarre line of thinking. Perhaps it was related to another investigation Dalton was heading up? He mentally shook his head and simply said, "Do you want to meet at the rendezvous spot we arranged the day you came into Rose Hill, or this one?"

"This one. The other one is less convenient since it's

farther from the road," Dalton said, starting up the car. "Call me when you know more, and good luck."

With a wave, Dalton drove off, leaving Peter to stare moodily at nothing in particular. "Something is not right there, but I'll be damned if I can put my finger on just what it is."

The thought of Kiya drove that worry out of his mind: Kiya, warm and lying in his bed earlier that day. Kiya, warmer and soapy in the tub. Kiya saying outrageous things about zombies, and making him want to drop everything and rush to her side to defend her, not that he thought she'd let him do much defending. She seemed to him the type of woman who'd bash him on the head if he got too overprotective. He smiled at that thought, a smile that turned into a wolfish grin when he contemplated all those hours he'd have to spend in her tent waiting for his family to fall asleep so he could search for the vial.

He very much looked forward to those hours.

With that thought uppermost on his mind, and an accompanying tightness around the fly of his pants, he moved his car to a secure (and hidden) location, and then spent half an hour stealthily making his way through the woods to the outer fringes of the camp, where he found Sunil hiding behind a large man-sized fern.

"Where's Kiya?" he asked in a whisper.

"They are all dining, the popsy included. She is well and not harmed. I have watched over her extremely diligently as you asked. When I first arrived here some time ago, she was in her tent doing what appeared to be calisthenics. Then she went into the gleaming metal trailer in the center, and emerged with five pug dogs. She took them for a walk in the forest. I followed with extreme stealth. After the walk, she returned to her tent briefly, then went to make use of a latrine, and—"

"That's fine," he interrupted. "I don't need to hear a minute-by-minute summary. Did any of my cousins go near her?"

"Not that I saw, no, and I was concealed very definitely outside her tent opening."

"Thanks for watching over her," he said stiffly.

"What would you like for me to do now?" Sunil asked eagerly. "Shall I remain with you so to see that no one stabs you? I am most distraught that I was not being here earlier when you were attacked. I should not have given in to my desires to see the bats emerge from the nearby caves, which the tourist brochure calls a magnificent testament to nature."

Peter was facing a dilemma. He had a very clear mental image of just how he planned on enjoying the next few hours with Kiya, but at the same time, he didn't wish to hurt Sunil's feelings by telling him he was in the way. What he needed was a job that Sunil could do while he spent those enjoyable hours with Kiya.

Guilt reminded him that he was responsible for Sunil's happiness. Above all else, above his own pleasures, above even Kiya's enjoyment, he was bound to ensure Sunil was at all times fulfilled. "You could remain with me," he answered slowly, keeping any inflection of regret from his voice. "I am always grateful for your assistance. However—" He grabbed the first idea that came to him. "If you wanted to be of real help to me—"

"You know that I do!" Sunil said excitedly, his light shimmering. "I am your partner! I will investigate while you guard the popsy!"

He wished Sunil had a form other than light so he could assess his expression. "Dalton mentioned something about a magician being in the area and handing out magic without authorization. He said later that the investigation didn't pan out, but I've been thinking that it's a little too coincidental that there's a magician in the same location as this family. If you could—"

"I will go this instant!" Sunil announced, and zipped off into the woods, returning almost the same moment to ask, "Where is it I am going?"

Peter gave what information he could recall about the magician, relieved to find a solution that would benefit both his need to be with Kiya and Sunil's obvious desire to be helpful. Given Dalton's comments, he didn't expect Sunil would find anything untoward, but it wouldn't hurt to be able to cross off the coincidence of the magician.

"I will return in the morning, then, yes?" Sunil asked before departing, a note of male comradery in his voice. "I am thinking that you and the popsy will be busy until then."

"Morning will be fine. If you need me earlier than that, I'll be here." He couldn't help but grin at Sunil when the latter sped off into the night whistling softly to himself. Peter had been aware of the background rumble of voices, but the obvious sounds of a meal in progress had kept him from worrying about Kiya's well-being. Now, however, the sounds of forks on plates had ceased, replaced with voices. He pulled down one of the fern fronds to peer out at the clearing.

"And I'm telling you that I didn't hit anyone on their head," Andrew was saying loudly, his voice as obnoxious as the rest of him.

Peter frowned at his cousin, his gaze shifting along the

line of people who sat at two picnic tables littered with food items and plates. He was a bit surprised to see the family dining with Kiya present, since those who were mahrime were considered too unclean to be present at a meal. And yet, there sat Kiya at Lenore Faa's side, two of those blasted little pugs on her lap.

"And if that gadjo says otherwise, then she is a liar!"

"Gadjo! I am so not a gadjo!" Kiya snapped, standing up and pointing a pug at Andrew. "You take that back!"

The pug growled.

"You don't even know what a gadjo is," Andrew sneered, slamming down a can of beer.

"I don't have to know the meaning of the word. The way you say it makes it clear that it's an insult," Kiya answered, and sat back down, murmuring softly to the pugs when they continued to growl at Andrew.

"It means someone who is not a Traveller," Gregory said wearily. "That is all. It's not an insult per se, although to be brutally honest, I think it's time we stop using it. That sort of mentality doesn't work these days."

Peter eyed his cousin at the same time that Kiya shot a startled glance across the table. What was this? Gregory speaking out against Traveller traditions? That was interesting . . . and perhaps should be investigated further. Assuming, of course, that he wouldn't be arresting Gregory for the murders. "Enough of this squabbling." With a wave of her hand, Lenore Faa addressed the table as a whole. "Piers, Arderne, take the women and children to the lake."

One of his cousins—he thought it was Arderne— glanced worriedly at his wife. "It's late, puridaj. The water will be cold, and the little ones might take ill there."

"Then do not let them in the water. There are playthings there, are there not?" Lenore Faa pinned back her grandson with a look that brooked no argument. "They can play. It is not so dark that they cannot see."

To Peter's intense surprise, one of the women—probably Arderne's wife—clutched her toddler to her chest and rose, declaring, "I will not go. I will not risk seeing a martiya. It would bring bad luck on my son."

"Do as you are told," Lenore Faa told Arderne, and without another word, he and Piers hustled their respective wives and children off to a minivan.

"What's a martiya?" Peter heard Kiya ask Gregory.

He leaned toward her to whisper the answer. Instantly, every hair on the back of Peter's neck stood on end. Without thought for his plans, or safety, or even common sense, he shoved aside the sagebrush and marched out into the clearing. "*Martiya* is the word for spirit of the night, Kiya. They are feared by most Travellers."

"You dare come here!" William leaped to his feet, his face suffused with color.

"Peter!" Kiya squealed at the same time, hurriedly shoving her lapful of pugs onto Lenore Faa before dashing over to him.

"Somehow, I had a feeling you'd show up here and stir things up," was all Gregory said, but the amusement in his voice had Peter looking closely at him. Just as soon as possible, he'd have a little chat with his cousin.

"It will be the last time he does so," Andrew spat, rising to his feet and stalking toward Peter. "We warned you before that there would be no tolerance of your attempts to smear our name."

"Don't you even think of stabbing him again," Kiya said, standing in front of him and spreading her arms.

Peter was touched by the gesture. No one had ever tried to protect him, not since the death of his mother some eighty years before. And to think that Kiya, his Kiya, his delightfully quirky, naive little Kiya, should be the first person to do so warmed him to the depths of his being. He wanted to simultaneously kiss her, punch Andrew in the face, and point out to his grandmother that not everyone thought he was an outcast.

He settled on gently moving Kiya to the side. "No one is going to be stabbed," he said firmly, sharing a look among all his male relatives.

"Damn straight you're not," Kiya agreed, and before he knew it, the world shifted infinitesimally.

"It will be the last time he does so," Andrew spat, rising to his feet. Before he could move toward Peter, Kiya hefted a large pot that contained the remains of spaghetti, and bashed it over the back of Andrew's head.

"There. That'll teach you, you time-stealing bas—" She shot a look toward Lenore Faa. "Er . . . rat fink."

William shouted an obscenity. "Did you see what she did, Mama? She stole time from him!"

Gregory, looking more than a little surprised, got to his feet and went over to squat next to his cousin.

Peter sighed. "Kiya, we've had the discussion before about the wrongness of stealing time, did we not?"

"Yes, but this was totally justified. He was going to stab you again. Or worse. I just know he was. I had to stop him."

"Regardless, you know full well what can happen when you do it."

Kiya's fingers went to her mouth briefly before her eyes widened. "Oh no, I forgot to pay him. Let me see what I have. . . ." She grabbed a purse that was hung across the back of her chair, and dug through a wallet. "I've got a couple of quarters and some dimes. . . . No, wait, there's my mad money. Thirteen dollars." She picked aside strands of spaghetti noodles that were splattered across Andrew's head and torso, and tucked the bills into the front of his shirt before shooting a worried glance at Peter. "That should be enough, right?"

He hadn't the heart to remind her that Travellers always paid such debts in silver. "It is more than enough," he said, pulling out some silver dollars, and, tossing them onto the still prone form of his cousin, returned the paper money to Kiya. "But I will pay, since you acted in my defense."

She beamed at him, and he seriously considered scooping her up in his arms and driving to town with her so that he could make love to her in the bathtub again. And the bed. And possibly the floor if he couldn't make it to the bed or the tub.

"Kiya Mortenson." The voice that spoke the words held a wallop of power in it that Peter knew Kiya would be unable to ignore. He had a difficult time himself not responding to it, but inexperienced as she was with Lenore Faa, and Travellers in general, Kiya would be putty in her hands.

To his intense pleasure, Kiya twined her fingers through his before turning to face her employer. "Yes, ma'am?"

"I will thank you if, in the future, you can refrain from assaulting my grandsons. Rehor, is he gravely injured?"

"No," Gregory answered, taking a napkin to wipe the red spaghetti sauce that dripped with faux gore down Andrew's face. "He's just unconscious. I am confused, however, by what just happened. It appears as if Kiya took Andrew's time, and yet that isn't possible." He looked up at Peter. "You must have done it."

"I did not."

"Then that would mean that Kiya..." Gregory stopped, his gaze speculative on her.

Without thinking, Peter put an arm around Kiya and pulled her tight against him. Hopefully, the look on his face was enough to warn his cousin about even thinking of upsetting her.

Gregory appeared to have enough wits about him to read the expression accurately, for other than looking sidelong at his grandmother, he said nothing, just remained kneeling at Andrew's side.

William, however, had no such wisdom. He slammed down a bottle of whisky that he'd been hitting pretty hard, and got to his feet, weaving as he did so. With a swagger that was more than half stagger, he shoved out his chin, and started forward. "This is intol—"

Peter's fist shot out and sent William flying backward a good eight feet.

"Don't say it. I'll check him," Gregory told Lenore Faa as he rose and—with an unreadable look at Peter—went over to see what state the now-unconscious William was in.

"Nice one," Kiya told him softly.

Not softly enough, evidently, for Lenore Faa, with a sudden boil of pugs around her feet, got painfully out of her chair, and pointed a finger at him. "You are not welcome here, son of Vilem, yet you continue to blight us. What is it you want?"

Kiya stiffened against him, but wisely said nothing.

Peter gave a long look to the woman who once he had hoped would take him in and love him as his mother had. "I'm here to spend the night with Kiya. Do you object?"

"Holy jebus, Peter, you did not just say that!" Kiya spun around and stared at him with her mouth slightly ajar.

He put a finger beneath her chin and closed her mouth before bending down and giving her a swift kiss. It was sweet, far sweeter than he remembered, and it took all his strength to not give in and claim her mouth as it begged to be claimed. "I did, you know."

"Did what?" she asked breathily, her eyes misty with desire.

Oh, how he loved that he could distract her so much with just one kiss. He indulged in a little smug satisfaction about that point before her nearness to him demanded that he give in and kiss her once more.

He was about to do so when Lenore Faa cleared her throat in a meaningful manner, and said, "What Kiya does with her personal time is not any of my business. However, while she stays here, in my charge, I do feel obligated to see to her protection. It is for that reason that I repeat to you that you are not welcome here."

Peter looked down at Kiya, who had stopped staring up at him and was now looking in surprise at the old woman.

"Whoa, now," she said, taking a step away from Peter. He didn't like that, and pulled her back to his side. "With all due respect, I'm not in your charge. I'm not in anyone's charge but my own. My foster mom is very big on people taking responsibility for themselves, and I'm not about to mess up my ego and superego and id just because you have an issue with Peter. Which, I have to say, is just really not right, because he's a perfectly nice man, and he doesn't intend on hurting you or anyone who doesn't deserve it. Do you, Peter?"

She looked up at him with big eyes filled with trust and admiration, and at that exact moment, all the anger, all the pain, all the decades of anguish for being deprived of a family, melted away into nothing. Kiya wanted reassurance that he wasn't a vindictive, vengeful monster, and by the gods, he would move the stars themselves in order to justify her belief in him.

He looked over to Lenore Faa. "I am here to find a murderer. Nothing more."

"What murderer?"

With an eye on the two unconscious men, he explained about the trail of murders that had appeared over the course of the last year.

"That can have nothing to do with us," Lenore Faa said dismissively when he was finished.

"I know Travellers when I see them," he said, giving her a long look. To his surprise, her gaze dropped, her fingers moving restlessly over the material of her dress. "And it was Travellers who were caught on film leaving the building of the latest victim, even if we couldn't identify them. The DNA I took from the mortal police will prove which one of this family was behind the murders."

"Proof that you claim was conveniently stolen," the old woman muttered.

"By someone in this camp," he pointed out.

"You have no proof of that! Rehor, escort this man out of our camp."

Gregory slowly got to his feet. "Puridaj, if he has video of someone in the family—"

"He cannot. It is impossible. Everyone was here, with me, during the time he mentioned." The old woman's jaw set in a manner that indicated she would brook no objection.

Kiya stirred. "I know it's hard to hear that someone in your family is doing something so horrible, but I think you should give Peter a chance to prove his points. Maybe if you saw the video, or if you could see the lab report of the DNA—"

"Be quiet," Lenore Faa snapped, making Kiya bristle.

Peter almost smiled watching her try to keep a civil tongue in her head. He knew it had to be a struggle not to tell the old windbag what she thought.

"I'm proud of you," he told her sotto voce.

She slid a glance up at him. "For not telling your grandma that she's a stubborn old besom?"

"Yes. And also for using the word 'besom' in a sentence. It's almost, but not quite, as good as 'death knell.'"

"I will not have this family torn apart because this mahrime one wishes vengeance against us," Lenore Faa continued, but was interrupted when Gregory turned to Peter.

"I'd like to see your proof."

"Because you want to destroy it?" Peter couldn't help but ask.

"No." Gregory took a deep breath, and ignored his grandmother's outraged gasp when he continued. "Because if someone in this family is killing mortals, they must pay for their crime."

"Rehor!"

"We cannot ignore him, puridaj. Peter is with the Watch," Gregory said, facing Lenore Faa.

A grim smile twisted her lips. "And you have ever wanted to join them, have you not? I told you a century ago, and I will tell you now—Travellers keep unto themselves. We do not work for others. We have never been lackeys or slaves, and I will not let you degrade us now by becoming just that."

"Whoa!" Kiya's spine stiffened. "Peter isn't a lackey or a slave just because he's a woo-woo cop!"

Lenore Faa blinked, while Gregory, with a puzzled look, asked, "Woo-woo cop?"

She waggled her fingers at him. "You know, woo-woo like supernatural. 'Cause you guys are not natural. That sort of thing."

"There is nothing unnatural about us," Lenore snapped, giving Kiya a sour look. "And you will stay out of this. It is not a situation that concerns you, your lust for Peter Faa aside."

"Hey, you're the one who told me I'm just like you," Kiya answered with a blithe disregard that made Peter want to kiss her again.

"This arguing is doing no good," Peter said, putting a halt to what would appear to be a useless debate. "Facts are facts, and if you would turn over to me the vial that was stolen from me two nights ago, I will prove my accusations."

"I have no vial," Mrs. Faa said, and looked away.

"Then you won't mind if I search the compound," he said smoothly.

"I most certainly will mind!" She got shakily to her feet, clearly done with the conversation.

"Let me talk to her," Gregory said quietly, watching as his grandmother set down the pugs and snatched up her cane. "I might be able to reason with her. Sometimes I can."

Peter considered his cousin a minute, then nodded. "Kiya says you helped her drag me out of here when I was stabbed."

"I did."

"Why?"

Gregory gave a little half smile, most of it pointed toward Kiya, which just made Peter's arm tighten around her. "Let's just say that I have my own reasons."

"Like what?" Kiya asked, but before Gregory could answer, Lenore Faa interrupted them.

"And the girl?" she asked, gesturing toward Kiya. "What is your interest in her?"

Peter raised an eyebrow. "That, madame, is between us."

Kiya gave him an approving smile that sent waves of heat rippling down his body. Once again, he thought seriously of simply scooping her up in his arms and taking her back to his motel room, but the realization that once he got her in his bed, he wouldn't want to leave for a long time, days, possibly years, had him scrapping that plan.

"I do appreciate your concern," Kiya was telling Lenore Faa. "But I assure you—whoa! Peter!"

He gave in to temptation. He just couldn't stop himself. He scooped her up into his arms and, with a quelling look at his cousin Gregory, carried her over to her tent, where he stooped and deposited her inside.

"I don't expect to be disturbed," he said loudly over the top of the tent before entering it.

"OK, you get ten out of ten for playing nice with your grandmother, but that he-man stuff had better be used pretty sparingly from here on out, because I'm not the sort of woman who is a doormat. You can't make decisions for me about when and where and how we indulge in nooky-time."

"How is your head?" he asked, deliberately interrupting her lecture.

"I don't mind a little bit of manliness, like you putting

your arm around me to let your grandmother know you're not asking, 'How high?' when she says, 'Jump!' but that doesn't mean—hmm? Oh. It's fine now. It only hurts if I smack it on the roof of my car. Speaking of my head, and the amazing things it can do, where's your friend?"

"What does Sunil have to do with your head?" he couldn't keep from asking.

"I believed in him. Thus, my id and ego and superego are all clearly balanced."

"Ah. Sunil is off doing a little job for me. With luck, he won't be back until morning." He stooped down and knelt next to where she was sitting on a flimsy-looking air mattress. "I should tell you that I met with Dalton within the last hour."

"The zombie?" she gasped.

"He's not a revenant. He's perfectly fine." Peter ignored the twinge of doubt regarding the sense of something not being quite right with regard to Dalton. "Which means that someone must have wanted you to think he was dead, and for that purpose either manufactured something that looked like his body or . . ."

"Or?" she prodded, blinking owlishly in the gloom at him.

He turned on one of her camp lights. "Or someone made an actual body resemble him."

"The body I saw was definitely real," she said with a little shudder. "It was squishy. And . . . ugh. Corpselike. Where did you see Dalton?"

"At the entrance to this camp, as a matter of fact. He had no idea why someone would want to make you think he was dead. Do you?"

Kiya shook her head, and patted the air mattress. "This is much more comfy than kneeling on the ground."

He looked at the bed. "The sleeping bag smells like a skunk."

"I know. I think Andrew did it on purpose. I've tried all sorts of deodorizers on it, but it still has a bit of a pong, doesn't it? You get used to it, though. You do know what everyone thinks is going on in here, don't you?"

"Why do you think I let them know I was here?" he asked, moving over to sit on the end of the air mattress. A faint odor of a long-deceased skunk wafted to his nose. He ignored it, focusing on the lovely scent that Kiya seemed to produce naturally. It reminded him of a lazy day spent sunning on a rock, surrounded by a cool, deep stream. She smelled fresh, and clean, and like the sun-warmed rocks.

"That, my good sir, is an excellent question. I don't know. I thought we were going to be all stealthy and stuff and sneak around trying to see which of your cousins—which I'm sure must be the obnoxious Andrew—is the guilty party. How you can be related to him and William is beyond me."

"I assure you that I hold no feelings of fondness, familial or otherwise, toward either of them."

"Good, because they are both seriously dillwads. Andrew especially."

Peter stopped imagining Kiya naked on a rock next to a stream. "Dillwads?"

"Yeah. I was going to say asshats, but I didn't know if you'd be offended by that or not. Are you?"

"Offended? No. Profanities don't disturb me."

"No, are you going to make love to me before we scout out the cousins for vial-theftage?"

That certainly had been his plan. In fact, it's all he had been able to think about ever since he got close to Kiya.

But he was a man who was in control of all his natures, base or otherwise, and he wasn't about to let a need to glory in the delights that she had to offer sway him from the work he knew had to be done.

"Peter?"

"No. I admit that I had intended to earlier, because it was all I could think of, but now that Lenore Faa and Gregory Faa think that is exactly what we are doing, I don't feel in the mood. I dislike being expected to act in a certain manner."

"Then I guess you shouldn't have carried me off to the tent in the best impression I've seen in a long time of a man about to ravish a woman," she said drily. He thought there was a hint of a smile in her voice, but her expression was one of placidity, and nothing more.

Dammit, he didn't like her placid. He wanted her all soft and yielding, and with that smoky, misty look to her eyes that told him that he had pleasured her like no one had ever pleasured her before.

"I did that to make a point," he said nobly, trying very hard not to look at her. If he could just sit there and think of things that weren't Kiya, he could make it the two or three hours that would be needed for the family to go to sleep. He simply had to focus on not seeing her, and he'd be fine.

"So, you act in a manner that gives a very obvious impression, and then you're all bent out of shape when people accept that impression?"

Her voice was going to be a problem. There was a lilting tone to it, as if she was secretly laughing at the sheer joy of being alive, that called to him on a fundamental level. He considered asking her to sit there, out of the range of his vision, without saying a word, but knew in the way of a man who was informed about women that should he do so, she would hit him on the head with something heavy. Or possibly stab him.

The sad fact was that he wanted her weaving a spell of fascination by means of her voice and her delectable body. He wanted to be there with her in the close, slightly skunk-scented confines of her musty tent. She brought him a sense of belonging, as if it wasn't just him against the world, alone and unloved.

He wanted her right where she was, at his side, tempting him, driving him insane, making him laugh at the way her thoughts leaped around, and, most of all, making him feel as if at long last he had a home.

That home was Kiya.

"Marry me."

The words surprised them both, but at least he had a warning of the directions of his thoughts. He mulled over what he had said, decided it made sense—Kiya was the woman with whom he wanted to spend the rest of his life—and adopted an expression of a man who knew what he wanted, and expected others to fall into the plan.

Kiya gawked at him, her mouth once again ajar. "What did you say?"

"Marry me. I said marry me."

She continued to stare at him for the count of eleven. "Are you out of your ever-lovin' mind?" she finally got out.

"I am a member of the Watch," he pointed out. "They do not let those of feeble minds into such positions, so the answer is no, I am not out of my mind, ever-lovin' or otherwise. Will you marry me?"

She whomped him on the arm with a rolled-up duffel bag. "You can't ask someone you just met to marry you!"

"Why not?"

"Because you don't know anything about me! I don't know anything about you! It's just . . . you don't do that, Peter!"

"I don't see why not. It makes perfect sense to me. You enjoy my company. I enjoy yours. I wish to spend a great deal of time with you, and since my mother raised me to hold women in honorable esteem, the solution to such a situation is a marriage. That would also be appropriate should you become pregnant."

He didn't think it was possible, but her eyes widened even more. "You met me, what, three days ago?"

"Two, I believe."

"And now you're talking about kids?" She sucked in a huge amount of air. He was surprised the side of the tent didn't bow inward.

"They aren't high on my priority list at the moment, no. We have plenty of time, given that our lives can span centuries. Just out of curiosity, how old are you? You appear to be in your late twenties."

"Thirty-two, actually. But thank you." She looked pleased for a few seconds before she returned to looking outraged and shocked, and wholly beddable.

"We both have ample time to be together before we begin a family. I merely mentioned the possibility should such a situation arise."

"But—" She hit him on the arm again. "We don't know each other!"

"I am happy to answer any questions you have about me."

"And then there's the other thing."

His brow wrinkled. The only thing he could think of at the moment was in his pants and growing more and more demanding that it have its share of time with Kiya. "What thing? My penis? Do you have an objection to it? I know you said it was beefy, but I believe we fit together rather nicely."

"No, not your penis," she said, casting a glance toward his lap.

Instantly, he was fully aroused.

"Wow," she said, her gaze fixed on his groin. "You really are bulgy. I like that in a man."

"I don't share," he said primly. "And I don't expect my woman—wife or otherwise—to have cause to look to another man."

"Oh, I wasn't saying I wanted to fool around," she said with a smile that filled him with warmth, and light, and a desperate need to lick every inch of her body. "I was actually referring to . . . you know . . . love."

She said the word almost in apology. He stopped imagining himself doing all those things to her that he so desperately wanted to do, and considered what she said. "Love is not something I have much experience with."

"You've been in love before, haven't you?" she asked gently.

"I loved my mother," he answered, meeting her gaze. "You would have liked her. She was a strong woman in her way. She died about eighty years ago."

"I'm so sorry." Without hesitating, Kiya was there at his side, pressed against him, one arm around him as she offered him comfort. No one had ever comforted him before. He relished the sensation, and pulled her closer. "I know what it's like to lose your parents. I wasn't talking about that kind of love, though. How many girlfriends . . . no, I can't ask that. How about this: how many times have you been in love? Really in love? The deep, all-consuming sort of love where all you do is think about the other person, and want to be with them day and night, and seem kind of empty inside without them sort of love."

He looked at her, anger driving away all the lovely warm feelings she had brought him. "I have never felt that way about any woman." Other than Kiya, that is. *Was* he in love with her? He gave a mental headshake and focused on what was at that moment of prime importance. "Just how many times have you been in love with other men?"

She wrinkled her nose as she thought. "I think . . . yeah, three times. Well, one was when I was sixteen, so that doesn't really count, because all teenage girls are desperately head-over-heels in love at some point or other. Twice. We'll go with twice."

"Who were they?" It was all he could do to keep from growling the words. The idea that Kiya, his Kiya, the delightful, effervescent Kiya who made him feel like he could do anything, had felt the same way about other men filled him with a fury the likes of which he had never known. Fury and jealousy, but the latter was a petty emotion, and thus did not deserve to be acknowledged. "I want their names. And addresses. What state are they living in? Never mind, just their names will do. I will find them."

Kiya started laughing. "You are so sweet to pretend to be so jealous that you would demand to know about my former boyfriends. I can't tell you how warm and fuzzy that's made me feel. Thank you, Peter, for acting like an idiot just to let me know you care."

Idiot? She thought he was acting like an idiot? He wasn't, but clearly she didn't understand his need to have her acknowledge that *he* was the one she loved, not those others. His mind didn't even shy away from the word *love*. Just because he had never been in love with a woman didn't mean that she shouldn't be madly and wildly in love with him. Starting right that minute.

"I do care," he said, deciding that now was not the time to press her for details of former lovers. He'd wait until he was in a better position to act upon the information. "I enjoy your company greatly. You interest me. I like the way your mind works. It's different from other women. Your body gives me immense pleasure, as well."

She snuggled into him, and patted his leg, careful to avoid the bulging area of his pants. "I like you, too, Peter. A lot. And I like you for your brain, as well, you know. Although, holy hell, man, you have a chest that could make a nun forsake her vows. And the ass of a god. We won't go into what your nether regions are—"

"Beefy," he said with complacence.

"—but I will second your opinion about the pleasure to be had from our rompy time. If they had Olympics in sex, you'd definitely be a gold medal winner."

"Then you will marry me." It was a statement, not a question, a fact he hoped would escape Kiya.

"I didn't say that." She kissed his jaw. "I'm not in any rush, Peter. I agree that we have something going on between us, and I think it might be something that should be permanent, but it's too soon for me to tell for sure."

"I can tell. You should trust me to be the judge of whether or not we are ready to progress," he said loftily, knowing she wasn't going to stand for it, but unable to keep from teasing her.

"You are so asking for it, buster," she said, laughing and elbowing him in the side.

A horrible thought occurred to him then. "There's not another man to whom you are tied?"

"No, and I ought to punish you for even thinking I'd get together with you if I was interested in someone else, but I'm going to let it go because, for one, I can see by your expression that you're actually worried about that, and for another, I'm about twelve seconds away from ripping off all your clothes and having my way with you. And I can't do that if I'm busy being mad at you."

"Twelve seconds?" He looked at his watch. "Do you want me to count down the last five seconds?"

She laughed again and moved away from him, pulling her shirt over her head as she did so. "I think what I like the most about you is your sense of humor. You never fail to make me laugh. I want you naked, Peter. Even with everyone in the camp knowing what we're doing, I want you right this very second."

He was never one to turn down a reasonable request from a woman, he mused as he stripped himself of his clothing, and even though he had already informed Kiya that he would not, in fact, be making love to her, he decided that it would be churlish to deny her when she so obviously needed him.

Yes. It was for her benefit that he would do this. He would prove to her once and for all that she was meant to be with him for the rest of their time on earth.

THIRTEEN

"Remove your clothing, and lie back so that I might touch you."

I dragged my gaze up from where I'd been ogling Peter's bare chest and arms and all the rest of him—and the rest of him was well worth the time spent ogling—and looked at his expression to decide if he was actually serious in thinking he could order me around like that, or if he was so aroused that he just sounded bossy and arrogant.

"You, sir, are nuts if you think I'm going to respond to commands," I told him, deciding he was being high-handed. As if demanding that I marry him weren't enough, now he seemed to think he could direct our lovemaking. "I'm all for sharing experiences, and letting the other person have their fun time, and whatnot, but I am not a doormat, Peter, sexually or otherwise. You can't just tell me to lie back and get naked and expect me to do it. Even if I did, I'd be so annoyed that I wouldn't enjoy anything you did to me, and I gather that is the point of you being so incredibly pigheaded that you think you can become Mr. Lovemaking Bossy Pants."

"I don't remember you speaking this much last night," he said somewhat thoughtfully. "You moaned, yes. You groaned, as well. And at one point, you hummed a happy little song of sexual completeness, but you did not chatter on and on when I was trying to provide you with intense pleasure. Are you suddenly shy? Does the fact that my family are all around us bother you? Is the presence of Lenore Faa causing you to have second thoughts about the rightness of our sexual joining?"

I stopped wriggling out of my pants (I wasn't aware that I was, in fact, complying with his demand to strip until that moment), and glared at him. "You didn't just tell me that I talk too much! You couldn't. Not even you, a man who claims to never have been in love with a sexual partner, would be so downright stupid as to tell the woman he was about to pleasure to the very tips of her toes that she talked too much. You didn't just say that, did you, Peter?"

"No," he said gravely. "I like the fact that you feel comfortable telling me everything you think. I enjoy seeing how your mind works. However, there is a time and a place for narration, and this is a time for you to be lying naked on that foul sleeping bag, so that I might do all the things to you that I've wanted to do to you since I saw you in the forest."

I was about to protest, but the thought that he had been as attracted to me as I had been to him eased my annoyance. Instead of telling him that there was no time where communication was not a good thing, I removed my pants, socks, and underwear. "Right." I lolled back on the sheet I had bought, and looked expectantly at him. "I'm naked and lying down. What exactly is on your list of things that you wish to do to me?"

"I know what I'd like to do to you, but it doesn't matter if you're naked or not," a voice said from beyond the confines of the tent. "Except so much as it makes the beating more effective."

"Eep!" I stared at Peter for a moment, my face burning with the knowledge that Andrew—it had to be Andrew—was standing just outside the tent listening to us. But what did I expect? Any man who would bash a woman on the head from whom he had just stolen time was not a man who would afford privacy where it was due.

Peter looked just as shocked as I was, an expression that quickly changed to one of fury. He dropped my ankle, which he had picked up prefatory, I was guessing, to kissing his way up my leg, and spun around on his knees, clearly about to exit the tent and confront his cousin.

"Peter! Stop!" I hissed, grabbing at his foot.

He pushed back the flap of the tent, pausing to glance back at me. "Why?"

"You're naked," I pointed out, gesturing toward his torso.

"Andrew Faa will just have to bear the sight of my nudity," he said with mingled anger and dignity, and left the tent.

I hurriedly pulled on the nearest thing at hand (Peter's shirt), and grabbed his jeans before scrambling out of the tent. I crawled out and stood up, turning to find Peter striding over to where his cousin stood, while not twenty feet away, two women and assorted children stood like stone statues next to their minivan.

In unison, their heads swiveled from the sight of naked Peter to me, struggling to button up his shirt so my boobs weren't hanging out. "Oh," I said, freezing at the sight of the wives and kids. From around the far side of the van, the two other cousins emerged, both of them stopping to stare at Peter and me. "Um. Hi. We ... uh ... weren't just doing what you think we were doing in the tent."

"It seems to me pretty clear that you were," Gregory said from where he sat, his chair rocked back to lean against Mrs. Faa's RV. "Not that I eavesdropped, you understand, but you weren't being very quiet."

My blush cranked up to a level that I had previously thought impossible. "Great," I told Peter. "Everyone here knows we were about to go off to boink-land."

One of the wives squeaked and, grabbing two of the littlest kids, hustled them off to their RV. The second wife did likewise, casting an appalled look over her shoulder at me.

"I'm so sorry," I called to them both, waving Peter's jeans toward him. "I didn't mean to say that in front of the little ones. But I did tell him to put his pants on before he left the tent, so that part isn't my fault."

"Do not speak to the women!" Andrew spat, little flecks of spittle accompanying the words. "You are not fit to be in their presence!"

"I've had enough of you tonight," Peter snarled, heading to where Andrew stood in the center of the clearing. "If you ever again threaten Kiya, even obliquely, I will see to it that you spend the rest of your blighted life regretting it."

"Peter," I whispered loudly, glancing worriedly over at Mrs. Faa's RV. Thus far, she hadn't emerged, and I wanted to keep it that way. I had a feeling I was in enough trouble with her, and didn't need to add another scene to the balance.

"I'll say whatever I want to say," Andrew replied to Peter, his eyes narrowing. "You are nothing to us, son of a mortal. Less than nothing. Take your whore and leave our camp."

"Oh!" I gasped, my worry and concern that Peter might do something to cause problems evaporating in the face of that untoward insult. "I am not a whore! I admit that we had no idea that we could be overheard so easily while we were in the tent, but that doesn't give you the right to call me names! In fact, since I know you won't take it back, I'll just make sure you don't even say it!"

Peter turned his head toward me. "Kiya—"

One of the wives squeaked just as she had before I reset time a few seconds, and grabbed her kids, rushing them to their RV. The second followed after giving me a speaking look. "Sorry," I called, digging through the pockets of Peter's jeans to look for some money to throw at Andrew.

"Kiya!" Peter, en route to confront Andrew, stopped to turn a stern look upon me. "What did I tell you about doing this?"

"He called me a whore! I'm not going to stand for that. Where's your wallet?" I said, going from pocket to pocket.

"I will take care of him. Stay out of this. I have no money in my pants—it's in my wallet, which is in your tent."

Without a word, Gregory settled the chair on the ground, stood up, and reached into his own pocket before walking a few steps over to me and handing me a handful of silver coins.

"Thank you," I said, smiling at him before throwing a couple of the silver dollars at Andrew's feet. "Now, let's get a few things straight here, Mr. Potty Mouth. One—"

Andrew looked aghast at the coins at his feet. He stared at them as if he couldn't believe they were there; then his gaze touched on me, anger quickly replacing the confusion. "Take your whore and leave!" he thundered, interrupting me.

"Hey! You're not supposed to be able to do that. Fine! This is war now!"

"No, it is not." Peter grabbed my arm just as I stole a few more seconds from Andrew.

The wives squeaked. The kids were hustled.

"Ha! Take that!" I couldn't help but tell Andrew.

He looked confused. "Take what?"

I stuck my hand in Peter's pockets again, then remembered he had no money in them. Without a word, Gregory handed me a couple more coins, which I threw at Andrew's head just as Peter walked over to me (again) and, taking my arm, hauled me backward toward the tent.

"What the hell?" Andrew yelled, ducking to avoid being struck by the coins.

Peter ignored him, gently pushing me to the tent. "That was uncalled-for."

"What was?" I asked, trying to appear innocent.

"You stole time from him."

"Yes, but he called me a whore. Twice. Wait just a minute." I would have stopped, but I was conscious that if either of the women had looked out the window of her respective RV, she'd get another eyeful of Peter. I waited until we got back inside the tent to ask, "How do you know that I stole time? Everything was reset when I did it, wasn't it?"

"In a manner of speaking. It's possible to steal time from Travellers, but only very small quantities. The greater the amount of time you try to take, the higher the chances are that you will fail."

"So you can't take big chunks of time from other Travellers? Damn." There went my plans to have Peter steal time enough to make Andrew an infant again. If he wanted to act like a big ole baby, then he could just be one.

"I didn't say that. I said that if you try to take a large amount of time, you have a higher chance to fail."

"Fail meaning you don't get the time?"

"Fail meaning you risk killing the Traveller or yourself." His voice was grim, but his expression was grimmer. "Kiya, I know that you have not been exposed to Travellers before, but you need to listen to me when I tell you not to steal time. It is not only morally wrong; it is dangerous. I thought you learned that fact."

"Yes, but doesn't the intent have something to do with that? Mrs. Faa said that it was the shuvani person that you had to appease when it came to paying for the debt, right? So if you do take time from someone bad, isn't it easier to get away with it than if you do what I did with that motel hussy, and steal time solely for your own benefit?"

"What do you think you just did with Andrew?"

I plumped down on the sleeping bag. "He had it coming. The rat."

"I agree that he was acting inappropriately, but I was attempting to deal with the situation in a manner that won't have karmic repercussions on either of us," Peter grumbled.

"Yes. Stark naked." I shot a look at his groin, which was now quiescent. "In full view of your cousins-in-law.

I have to say, I don't mind that you aren't an overly modest person, but I really don't like you parading around in front of other women while naked. Nothing good can come of that."

He zipped closed the flap of the tent and gestured toward the mattress and sleeping bag. "Your jealousy is gratifying to my ego, but unnecessary, I assure you. I don't particularly care what my cousins' wives think of me. Would you please lie back down so that we can recommence?"

"You're crazy if you think we're going to continue." I pointed to the back wall of the tent, which faced the compound. "Not when someone could be lurking just outside listening to us."

"Then we will have to be quiet, won't we?" he said, picking up my ankle.

I narrowed my eyes at him. "Was that another dig about me talking too much?"

"No. It was a hint that I am so desperate to make love to you that not even my annoying family can stop me. Lie back, please."

In the end, I let him have his way. I liked to think it was because I was altruistic and caring, and obviously the man needed a sexual release, but my id and egos have never let me lie to myself, and they weren't about to start now.

Peter started kissing his way up my leg, murmuring words that caressed almost as much as his mouth, his hands stroking my flesh in a way that had me whipped into a frenzy in no time. I writhed, I squirmed, I stroked and touched and teased him just as much as he stroked and touched and teased me. I kept my moans to a whispered level, and by the time his mouth had moved up to very sensitive ground, I was more or less one giant blob of orgasmic Kiya.

"Please," I begged when he lifted his head to gently bite my hip.

"Please what?" he asked, his voice soft and husky at the same time.

"Please do whatever else you want, because I really like your list so far," I managed to get out.

He chuckled against my belly, then moved upward, catching my legs under his arms as he did so. "My list is long and varied, my fair beauty, and I plan on enacting every single item on it. But for now, this will have to do."

"Condom?" I gasped as he nudged forward into me.

He paused, looking down at me with eyes so beautiful, they made me want to dive into their violet depths. "Do I need one? We are going to be married."

"Possibly. Maybe. I don't know. Oh, hell, no, we don't need one. I'm on birth control, and I assume you don't have any diseases, and I don't either, so—hooyah!"

He took my breath away with his thrust forward, making me want to shout with the glory of the feeling of him so deep inside me, but I remembered in time that we were being quiet, and bit his shoulder instead. He groaned when I dug my fingers into his wonderful behind, pulling my legs up higher in order to accommodate him all that much better.

"Please tell me you are close," he groaned into my neck, his hips working a rhythm that had me seeing not just stars but entire galaxies filled with planets, moons, and several asteroid belts. "I don't think I'm going to be able to last much longer. I'm trying, I'm really trying to not give in to your heat, and your muscles that grip me so tightly, but by the saints, if you move like that again, it will be all over."

I crossed my legs around his hips, and made the little swiveling move that had him rising back, his eyes blazing with passion. "Finish it," I demanded, and pulled him down again so I could kiss the orgasmic yell right out of his mouth.

He did. Oh, how he finished it. I felt just like I'd been struck by lightning again, my entire body tingling with static electricity. Which explained why, when I recovered from the orgasm to end all orgasms and opened my eyes, I found that we were both bathed in a blue white aura of moving, snapping lines of . . . I didn't know what. Electricity?

I froze, unsure of what had happened, and whether it was dangerous. "Um. Peter?"

"Do not ask me to speak now, woman," he mumbled into my neck, his chest heaving on mine as he fought to catch his breath. "You have exhausted me. I am depleted of energy. You have worn me out to the point where I may well die of sexual gratification. Speaking is not possible. Breathing barely so. I will lie here and recover, and when I've done so, say a week from now, then I will be able to talk to you again."

I watched little tendrils of electricity snake out down the length of his back, snapping and crackling in the air. Tentatively, I lifted my hand from where it was still clutching his butt, and pursed my lips at the sight of little blue-white fingers of electricity curling and lashing in the air. "Huh. It doesn't seem to hurt."

"I should hope not. I may be beefy, but I don't think I'm anything out of the ordinary so far as that goes." He lifted his head from my neck, and for a moment, I saw a flash of something in his eyes.

"Holy shit, Peter! You have lightning in your eyes!"

He started to say something, but then his eyes (thankfully back to their normal appearance) widened and he pulled back a bit to look down at me. "I could have sworn . . . what on earth are you doing?"

"Lying here?" I asked, putting a hand to my face to see if my lips had blown back up or something like that.

"You have . . . there is something emitting from you."

"From you, too," I pointed out, nodding toward his torso. He disengaged from me, rolling off to stare down at first his body, then mine. "It's just like we're in one of those plasma balls they have at the science museum, huh?"

"I've heard of this, but never seen it in person." He examined his hand. Slowly, I was aware that the tingling sensation was fading, and with it the light show faded, as well.

"What is it?" I asked, feeling a vague sense of regret. The odd electrical effect hadn't been unpleasant—if a bit visually startling—and had left me missing the tingling sensation. "Was it some form of lightning? Because you had lightning in your eyes there for a second."

"So did you. It's an effect called *porrav*, which is an old word that the Travellers took from . . . I don't know where. Probably from the Romany or some other Indo-Aryan group a few millennia ago. Regardless, to Travellers, it means to open up. The term is used when two Travellers, bound together, open themselves up to the elements."

"You're kidding me." I looked at his chest, had a moment wherein I went off to the land of wanting to kiss and lick it, and with an effort recalled what we were talking about. "So when we get down and boogie, we, what, turn into lightning rods?"

He scratched his chest, then shrugged. "I don't know much about what the actual form of energy is that we manifest. I'm told it's fairly rare, and that only couples who are attuned to both each other and the elements can conjure it up. I imagine it has something to do with our ability to channel lightning, yes, although on a much smaller level."

I stopped him when he reached for his clothing. "Wait a second—we channel lightning? Like . . . *channel* it? How is that possible?"

"We are Travellers. Why do you think you've harnessed lightning twice, and bear the mark of the Traveller?" He touched the lightning flower on my upper arm. "It is your nature to control lightning, just as you can steal time. It is what we are, Kiya."

"I didn't harness anything," I argued, absently watching as he donned his clothing. "I was struck by lightning. Wham, bang, pow, knocked-on-your-ass sort of struck."

"That is because you were not raised to know how to control the lightning that is attracted to you." He handed me my shirt and bra. "I will teach you what I can, but I am far from an expert on the subject. We will find someone better versed in the art to help you, if you like, so that the next time you attract lightning, you are not harmed."

"I wasn't harmed, just kind of discombobulated—wait, next time? There's going to be a next time?" I shook my head, having a hard time absorbing this strange new world into which I'd been thrust. "And what about that poorab thing? Is that going to happen again?

Because I have to tell you, Peter, if it is, I want to film us. Not for kinky sex reasons, but because we were like living plasma balls! It was really cool, if a bit weird, and I'd like to see it happen where I'm not so out of my head from the fabulous sex that I can't focus on anything but how wonderful you are."

He smiled. "And yet I prefer that you stay thinking that. The word is *porrav*, by the way."

I whomped him lightly on the arm, and quickly got into my clothing. "Of course you want me thinking you're superfabulous at nooky; you're a man. That's all you guys normally think of." I held up my hand to stop his protest. "Most of you, anyway. I know you can think beyond your penis. So what do we do now?"

He finished tying his shoelace, and sat down on the mattress, his arms resting on his knees. "We wait for the family to go to sleep."

"OK." I scooted over next to him, and put my hand possessively on his thigh. My fingers tingled, and not the porrav sort of way. "Speaking of that—"

"Speaking of what?"

"Porrav."

"I didn't realize we were speaking of it."

"Hush. I'm thinking aloud. Where was ... oh yes. Speaking of porrav, why is it that we, two people who aren't full-blooded Travellers, can do the sparkly plasma thing? If it's that rare, I mean."

He looked vaguely uncomfortable before making a little gesture of defeat with the hand nearest me. "So far as the rest of the world—the Otherworld, that is, the part of the world where immortal beings reside—so far as they are concerned, we are Travellers. Our mortal blood is discounted due to the Traveller parent. It is only within the Traveller society that we are viewed as tainted, stained by our brush with mortal life, and unfit to truly be a part of the family."

"So, if you marry outside of the Travellers, you're ousted out of the family?" I asked, feel incredibly sad for some reason. "William wasn't, and I assume he . . . er . . . was fooling around with your mom."

"But he didn't marry her. Travellers can, in very rare circumstances, marry outside the group, but the spouse is always considered mahrime, and often the children of their union are, as well. It's only by integrating them at birth that they are later accepted."

"And your dad didn't do that. Oh, Peter, I'm so sorry."

He waved away my sympathy, but put both arms around me and hoisted me onto his lap, where he rested his cheek against my hair. "William could have brought me into the family, and made a case for them to include me since—well, I am a bit different from other Travellers. But he did not. He and Lenore Faa spurned my mother's pleas to have me recognized as a member, leaving us with nothing."

I snuggled into him, relishing the scent and feel of him, and feeling even more of my resistance to his outlandish idea of marriage fading away. He didn't say it in so many words, but I knew instinctively that marriage to him was the real deal. It would be an all-or-none sort of thing, no "let's try it out for a little bit and if it doesn't work, there's always divorce." Binding myself to Peter would mean a lifetime. Which brought up another thought. "So, you guys really are immortal, then? You said that you don't die of disease and stuff, but what about old age?"

He shook his head. "Travellers do not die of normal causes, because they steal time."

"I don't . . . nope, I don't understand it. How are the two things related?"

"What happened when you stole time from Andrew?" he asked, his breath ruffling my hair. It was all I could do to keep from slipping my hands inside his shirt to stroke that gorgeous chest.

"Oh, to hell with it, I'm going to." I suited action to words, and pulled up his shirt until I could slide my hands under it. His skin was so warm, it felt like heated satin. "When I stole Andrew's time, I put him back a couple of seconds, like a reset."

"That's not all you did. You added his time to your life. Your life span is now what it would be, plus the two or three seconds you stole from Andrew."

"It might be more like twelve, after adding all of them up," I admitted.

He pulled back to give me a look that I disregarded, saying, "I paid him. Or rather, Gregory did, because your wallet was in here."

"Kiya, not that I condone stealing time, but if you ever do it again, you must pay for it in silver. Anything else is not acceptable."

"Really? Why?"

"It is just the way things are done," he said with another half shrug before tightening his arms around me.

"So Travellers are immortal because they don't die of normal stuff like old age, but you have to steal time to keep going past your normal life span?" I asked, trying to get a handle on the obscure idea. "That assumes that you buy into the whole fate theory of each person having a specific amount of time allotted to them, and nothing you can do will change that. I don't believe in that, Peter. I believe each person makes their own fate."

"As do I. It helps to think of time as a physical object rather than a dimension." He reached into his jacket pocket and pulled out a couple of silver dollars. "Imagine that this coin is a piece of time. It is mine because it is in my possession. The number of coins I have at any given time is not a set figure—some days I have more coins, some days I have less. It is a fluid number that I influence by whether or not I spend the coins."

"I'm with you so far," I said, eyeing the silver dollars. "What happens when I steal the time from you?"

He looked to the side, the coins still in his hand, clearly offering them to me. I took one, and he looked back at me. "Now I have one less coin, and you have one coin more than what you had a moment ago. To Travellers, time works the same way. We take it from the person who has it, and it is added to our possessions. In that example, it's added to our time, the time that we hold and exist within."

"It's a bit too metaphysical for me," I told him, putting the coin back in his palm. "I'm willing to accept that you steal time to stay alive . . . unless . . ." I eyed him. "You told me that you don't steal time."

"I don't."

"Then how do you stay alive? Wait, maybe I should be asking you this: how old are you?"

"One hundred and three."

I slid off his lap, too startled to speak for a few seconds. "You aren't!"

"I am. I was born in 1910."

"But . . . but . . ." I waved a hand up and down his body. "You're gorgeous! You're male-supermodel gorgeous! You can't be a hundred years old! Especially not if you don't steal time."

"I do not steal time; I purchase it. From a troll who runs a home for unwed poltergeists."

I rubbed my forehead. "I think my brain just exploded. Yup, my id fainted with an overload of information. My ego is staggering around with a bottle of whisky in his hand."

"And your superego?" Peter asked with a smile that melted me into a big puddle of Kiya goo.

"He's running up and down the hallways of my mind with his arms waving in the air. I think he's gone mental, if you know what I mean, and no, no pun is intended."

"I'm sorry if I've overwhelmed you, Kiya, but these are the facts of what it is to be a Traveller."

"You buy time? How is that different from stealing it and paying for it?" I asked, still rubbing my head.

"The troll from whom I purchase time is willing to give it to me. He is immortal. He would rather trade some of the time he possesses for money, which he uses to—"

"Take care of pregnant poltergeists, gotcha." My mind skittered away from the idea of lusty ghosts. "So that's how you live, and how you expect me to live, too? By purchasing time from folks who have too much of it?"

"I do not want you stealing time. You are too new to it. I will provide time enough for both of us," he said with a finality that rubbed me the wrong way.

"You also said that what was in the past didn't matter. Which makes me think that was a really nice way of saying you used to steal time but don't anymore. Would that be true?"

He didn't say anything for a few seconds, but an interesting parade of expressions passed over his face: guilt, anger, pain, and finally resignation.

"I suppose you should know the worst about me if you are going to marry me," he said, his shoulders slumping.

I didn't point out that I hadn't agreed to marry him; I just put an interested expression on my face and sat back to listen.

"Sunil was bound to me a few years ago. It was my punishment for his death."

FOURTEEN

My jaw dropped at Peter's bald statement. Since I've been jaw-dropping a lot in the last few days, I quickly sucked it back up to where it belonged, and asked, "You killed someone? Sunil? You stole all of his life?"

"In a manner of speaking. I—"

"You great big ass!"

He looked taken aback, as well he might, but I was too incensed to apologize for calling him names. "Here I was feeling like dirt because you're all shiny and clean and pure and don't steal time, and yet you killed someone nice! You don't even have Hitler for an excuse."

"Hitler?" he asked, looking adorably confused. "What does he have to do—oh, Piotr Faa?"

"That's right." I pinched his arm. "How could you do that, Peter? How could you kill someone? Especially someone as nice as Sunil?"

"It was an accident," he said quickly, and once again, that parade of guilt and anger and pain trooped across his handsome face. "I didn't actually steal so much of his time that he died. It was an . . . er . . . odd circumstance."

"Tell me about it," I said, crossing my arms over my chest more to keep from touching him than to show just how annoyed I was. I felt absolutely certain that Peter wasn't at all like his cousins, and if he had done what he had said, there must be some extenuating circumstances.

"I can't. If I tell you what happened, you'll loathe me—as, I admit, I am due—and then you won't marry me, and I'll end up spending my days in a haze of unfulfilled need and want, and will make all sorts of bad choices, ending, no doubt, with the acceptance of the many offers Alison has been making to me every chance she has."

I glowered. "Did you just threaten me with that motel strumpet?"

"No. I would never do that." His expression was absolutely stone-cold sober, but there was a twinkle in his eyes that made me feel giddy.

"Good, because I absolutely will not tolerate any such threats. If I promise to not loathe you, will you tell me?"

"Yes," he said, his tone resigned. "But I will hold you to that promise." He pulled me up to his side, his body warm and solid against mine. I oozed into him, ignoring my superego when it told me I should be ashamed to be cuddling with a self-professed murderer. Peter wasn't bad, I told my inner voices. He couldn't be bad. He felt much too right to be anything but an honorable man.

Famous last words, my superego snarked.

I put him in the corner of my mind on a time-out, and donned my most understanding expression.

"A few years ago I was working a job in London. As you surmised, at the time I was no different from any other Traveller, and took small amounts of time here and there, as a matter of course. It was automatic—a few seconds here, a few there, with no one the wiser, unless the donor noticed a few extra coins in his or her pocket. One day, I was on a street corner, and absently took about thirty seconds from the man next to me. I started across the street, but in a horrible quirk of fate, that thirty seconds cost the man his life. Because I took it from him, he was still on the street corner when a drunk driver careened around a car and ran him down where he stood on the sidewalk."

"I don't understand. Wouldn't the driver have gone back thirty seconds, too?"

"If he had been close enough to have been affected by the time theft, yes. But he wasn't. He was speeding down the street at a distance that left him untouched by the theft."

I put both arms around Peter, responding not to the words but to the very real pain and regret in his voice.

"You must understand this, Kiya, because it is something we Travellers have to live with every time we steal from mortals—you never know how that time you take might have been used. In this case, that ten seconds that I stole was the time Sunil would have used to cross the street, and be out of the way of the drunken driver."

"How awful for you both," I said, pressing a kiss to his neck. "Poor Sunil. Poor you. You didn't know that something as ingrained in you as breathing would result in the death of another."

He grimaced. "I deserve the punishment. No one forced me to take his time—I simply acted as all Travellers act, and was cursed for my actions."

"I can see that this is why you're so adamant that I don't steal time, and I understand what you're saying about weighing the consequences of doing so—is the person in a position where they might be harmed from the loss of time?—but surely that doesn't mean we can't ever do it. I mean—think of the possibilities, Peter! Think of all the genocide that could be avoided! The abuse of people and animals by monstrous individuals—we can stop them. We can make the world a better place. Don't you see? This isn't a curse—it's a gift, a wonderful, precious gift."

He eyed me warily, all hints of humor gone from his face. "What you're talking about is the act of a god, Kiya, and we are far from those ethereal beings. We were never meant to hold the sort of power that you are describing. That's why the shuvani hold us accountable for every second taken."

"But surely if the motive is for the common good—"

"Define common good."

I shook my head. "Now is not the time for a philosophical discussion of what is good and what is evil. I simply want you to see that just because you had a tragic, horrible experience doesn't mean that we can't use this ability for good."

"You're right," he said wearily, letting his arm drop from around me.

I beamed at him, relieved and not a little bit surprised that he so quickly agreed with my point of view. My pleasure was dashed a few seconds later when he continued.

"This is not the time for a philosophical discussion of the moral bounds that are stretched by all Travellers. I am on the hunt for a murderer, and that's where my focus must now lie."

I was about to argue my point further, but before I could get the words out, the sound of angry voices from the RVs caught our attention. We listened intently for a few seconds.

"That sounds like Andrew," I whispered, jerking when

car lights suddenly flashed on the canvas of the tent. The sound of a car starting and pulling out with a squeal of brakes and a spray of dirt and gravel immediately followed. "Who was he yelling at? We're both in here."

"It sounded like William. Ah, yes." The angry muttering of William could be heard all the way across the campground as he, too, got into a car and slammed his foot on the accelerator, leaving with a loud roar of the engine.

"Wow. They must have had one heck of a fight. I wonder what it was about."

"I don't know. Stay here." Peter ducked and exited the tent.

I gave the tent flap a dirty look, scrambled into my shoes, and followed him, saying, when he stopped to glare over his shoulder at me, "I so do not take orders. Besides, I want to help search their RVs now that they're gone."

"When we are married, you will respect my requests and do as I say."

I glanced at him to see if he was serious. The way he peeked at me from the corner of his eye told me he was waiting to see what sort of outraged reaction I'd have to that load of crap. "I have news for you, Buster Brown— no woman will ever marry you if you expect that sort of subservient existence. Certainly I won't."

"Hrmph. Why?" Peter asked, gesturing me to the fringes of the camp, where the shadows were the deepest.

"Because that's the most sexist, moronic, unrealistic attitude—"

"No, why do you wish to search the RVs?"

I nudged his shoulder as I crept silently behind him,

careful to keep my volume to a whisper. "So we can find the stolen evidence, of course."

The sun had long since set, but the moon hadn't risen yet, which left the clearing dark and somewhat creepy, what with the hulks of partially destroyed buildings lurking around the edges. Faint little glows of light could be seen alongside the RVs, but they did little to lighten the area. The entire lumber mill looked exactly what it was—a ghost camp, once a thriving, bustling place of industry, and now devoid of all but the memory of those times.

And a handful of immortal time thieves.

"I'm so glad ghosts don't exist," I muttered under my breath, more to bolster my spirits than to initiate a discussion.

"Why do you think they don't?" Peter asked, skirting the first RV.

I stopped for a moment to stare at the back of his head. He must have felt the stare, because he turned back and held out his hand for me. I rushed to accept it, taking great comfort in the warmth and strength of his fingers.

"Kiya, ghosts are not the frightening entities that the mortals so delight in. They are simply the spirits of people who have died, but who haven't gone on to the next plane of existence."

"That sounds pretty frightening to me, but I don't have time right now to be either worried or scared over the idea of real ghosts. What are you doing if not searching for the evidence?"

"Trying to locate the vial. I think that's Andrew's caravan. If I tell you to stay outside while I search, will you do it?"

"Not on your tintype." I clutched the back of his shirt so he couldn't escape me. "And isn't searching for the vial the same thing as finding the missing evidence?"

"No." Evidently Andrew had taken the time to lock his RV. Peter pulled out a small black case and, with a quick glance around the crescent of RVs, bent over the lock on the door.

"I don't see the difference."

"That's because you are assuming that the two are the same thing."

"Now you're really confusing me. Why aren't they the same thing?"

A faint noise from Mrs. Faa's RV had me spinning around, crouched and prepared to hide behind the nearest piece of lawn furniture.

"False alarm," I whispered to Peter. "I'd better stand guard, though, just in case someone looks out their window or decides to take a late-night stroll through the forest."

The faint whooshing sound of the door opening had me turning back to the RV.

"Stay here," Peter said, mounting the stairs.

"In your dreams, immortal boy."

Peter didn't even bother sighing; he simply entered the RV with me on his heels. Carefully, so as not to make any noise, I closed the door behind us, blinking like crazy when all light was shut out of the RV. "Where are you? I can't see—ah, thank you."

The penlight that Peter switched on didn't illuminate the inside of the motor home much, but it did calm an imminent case of the heebie-jeebies that I felt crawling up my back. "So. Search time. I've never done this before, but I've seen it on TV, so it can't be too hard. I can take the left side, and you can do the right, OK? I just need to know what this vial looks like."

"It looks like this," Peter said, standing up from where he had been squatting in front of a small refrigerator. In his hand was a long glass tube, like a test tube, but stoppered and encased in some sort of thin foam wrap.

"Do you mean it just looks like that, or it *is* that?"

"This is the vial." He flashed the penlight onto it. A label was clearly visible, along with some handwriting that I took to be Peter's.

"Well, hell," I said, disappointed despite the relief of knowing he had the vial back. "I was kind of looking forward to searching. I've never done it before, and although I know it's reprehensible doing it in the first place, we have justice and stuff on our side, so I figured that karmically speaking, it was OK. I guess that means we're done, right?"

"For the moment." To my surprise, Peter set down the vial and continued to flick the penlight around the interior.

"What are you looking for now?"

"Evidence."

I pointed to the vial, even though I knew he couldn't see me doing so. "Isn't that it?"

"I'm looking for evidence that Andrew is involved in something else." He moved down the aisle, his light sweeping back and forth in front of him.

"Another murder?"

"No. I know he's involved in those."

I stopped, my hands on my hips. "OK, I've been the ignorant sidekick to your brilliant master detective for long enough. Spill with exactly what it is you're doing."

He disappeared into a room that I assumed was the

bedroom. I went to the door of it, and watched as he systematically searched through the built-in dresser. At last, he turned to face me, his expression one of profound frustration. "I don't know what it is I'm looking for. I just have a feeling that he's involved in something, and I had hoped that I'd find proof of it."

"Something connected to this murder?"

"Yes." He hesitated, obviously loath to tell me what it was. I waited silently to see what he'd do, feeling it was important to know now, before our relationship had gone too far, whether he was a man who would value me for more than just our sexual compatibility. "The thought had crossed my mind that Andrew might somehow be involved with the body that you saw earlier."

"Dalton's body?"

"The one made to resemble his body, yes."

I watched him closely. That wasn't the sum total of what he was thinking. "Or?" I prompted.

The penlight moved. I could see Peter's jaw tightening. "Or Dalton's body. I don't know which it is, now. I thought I did earlier, but the more I think about the meeting I had with Dalton, the more I'm convinced that something wasn't . . . right."

"How so?" I put my hand on his arm when he left the bedroom. "Peter, I'm not just being nosy, I really want to help you. I'm not stupid, and I do notice things—most of the time—and what's more important, I'm the one who saw the body and the Dalton zombie."

"Revenant, not that he is one."

"Let me help," I said. "If you want for us to have a life together, you're going to have to resolve yourself to the idea that I want to share more than just your bed."

He took my hand and kissed my knuckles. "I'm not

trying to frustrate you, sweetheart. I'm just—other than having Sunil bound to me, I've never really had a partner, especially not one romantically linked to me, and it takes some getting used to."

I smiled and slid my hand down to pinch his adorable behind. "Are you trying to tell me that you were a virgin before that night at your motel?"

"I said I didn't have a partner, not that I'd never had sex. Come. Andrew could be back at any time, and I'd rather not he see us in his caravan."

"You forgot the vial," I told Peter when he followed me down the stairs.

He made an annoyed noise.

"Honestly," I said as I dashed back inside, and retrieved the precious object. "It's like you don't care about it."

No one was present outside, and we made it back to the tent without anyone knowing what we'd been up to.

"OK, that was fun," I said as I tucked the vial into my purse. "I've never done anything like that before. I can see why you like being a police detective. Do you have to go through special paranormal police school to be part of the Watch?"

"Yes." Peter stood outside the tent for a moment before he reached in and, taking my hand, pulled me out.

"Where are we going? My purse is inside—"

"We're going somewhere we can talk privately. One that doesn't smell of skunk."

"Are you sure you're not taking me off to seduce me under the midsummer moon?" My fingers tightened around his, and I gave myself up to thoughts of just what I'd like to do to him under the moonlight.

"I hadn't intended on doing that, but I am nothing if

not a considerate man, and I will naturally oblige your lustful desires." Once we were beyond view of the camp, he adjusted the penlight so that its beam broadened, making it possible to see obstacles before us.

"Maybe later," I laughed, warmth filling me as he squeezed my hand. "After you tell me what you're thinking."

"Right now I'm thinking about your breasts, and belly, and how much I like it when you tighten your muscles around me."

"That is the result of years of Kegels. My foster mother always said I'd bless the day I started doing them, but I always thought she meant I'd have awesome bladder muscles when I am an old lady. I guess this is just as good. Our incredible sex life aside, now that you're resolved to the idea of sharing your thoughts with me—"

"That, my fair little squab, is going to take more than a few minutes," he interrupted, stopping before a small clearing that consisted of an official forest notice posted to a tree. The light of the flashlight made it possible to see that next to the sign were a couple of low, smooth rocks that were just the right height for sitting. He led me over to one, taking a seat opposite me.

I giggled at the squab reference, and continued. "Now that you're OK with the idea of telling me what's going on, why doesn't the vial matter to you any longer? What did you mean by saying that finding the evidence and finding the vial weren't the same thing? And why do you think Andrew of all people was involved with whatever is going on with your boss?"

"Do you always ask this many questions?" Peter asked. "If so, I may have to reconsider the proposal I made earlier."

"Smart aleck." I nudged him with the toe of my sandal. He took my foot and began to absently rub the top of it.

"To answer your first question, the whole thing was too easy. Or too convenient, if you will."

I thought about that for a moment or two. "You mean that it was convenient that Andrew drove off in a huff?"

"Partially that, yes. Particularly so when he did it after I announced I was spending the evening with you."

"You think he meant for us to search his RV? He locked it up, though."

"Anyone with rudimentary lock-picking skills could have opened his door. Yes, I think exactly that—I think he put the vial where it would be easily found, and then made himself scarce while I was in the area. He must have known I'd take advantage of his absence to search his caravan."

Something puzzled me. "Why would he want you to have the vial? That doesn't make any—oh!" Enlightenment struck me. "It isn't the same vial!"

"No, it's my vial."

"He took the evidence?"

Peter nodded. "I'm fairly certain that examination of the DNA in this vial will result in a different profile than what would have been gained from my evidence."

"That sneaky bastard." I stood up, flexing my fingers. "Well, there's just one thing to do! We have to steal enough time to set the clock back to before Andrew took your vial, and—"

"No."

"—then we can prove . . . why not? You're not still going on about how wrong it is to steal time, are you? Because I agree that doing it when it's for your own gain, like me taking that motel hussy's time, is very bad juju, but doing it for a righteous cause isn't the same. I mean, I haven't been zapped at all for taking Andrew's time this evening."

"That's because you limited yourself to taking just a few seconds. Had you tried for anything longer, even so relatively short a time as five minutes, you would be in a very different situation. Not that I think you have the ability to take that much time from a Traveller, but you have to stop thinking of reasons to justify stealing time, Kiya. There is no justification for it. It is simply wrong, and if you continue, you will find yourself in a dire situation sooner rather than later."

"I understand what you're saying, and I agree that stealing is totally wrong, but there has to be situations—"

"No." He released my foot, leaving it (and me) feeling sad and lonely. "What you are experiencing is normal, sweetheart. You just found out you have a tremendous ability, one that can do seemingly miraculous things, and you want to use that skill. But every time you do so, you risk more than you can possibly know."

"If it's that horrible an ability, then how do other Travellers do it and not suffer?" I asked, trying not to make my scoffing obvious. I didn't want to hurt his feelings, but I had an idea that because he didn't believe there were any circumstances where stealing time might be justified, he was painting all Travellers who used their talents in a darker light than was necessary. "Your family looks pretty hale and hearty. They all have expensive RVs, and none of them have a job, so clearly they are prosperous and healthy and happy. Where's all the downside that you're talking about?"

"You don't know what truly goes on in someone's life

until you have walked in their shoes," Peter said all righteously and quasi-pious.

"True, but I can also see that none of them are being punished with the equivalent of Sunil, or suffering karmic whiplash, or however you want to describe it. They must be doing something right if the stealing spirit you have to appease isn't smiting them with boils or a plague of locusts or diarrhea."

"Now you're being flip," he said, his brows pulling together.

"And you're being a stick-in-the-mud," I answered, and immediately regretted it. I held up my hand to stop his objection. "No, that was uncalled-for. I apologize, Peter. You have a very good reason to warn me about the consequences of our actions, and I assure you that I don't want anything horrible happening again like the Gigantic Lip Episode. I just think that maybe you are erring just a smidgen too much on the side of caution here."

"Until that moment when you stare down into the lifeless face of the mortal who your actions killed—and I fervently hope that situation is one you never endure— you cannot know just how high a price you risk paying. I don't know why we have seen no signs of the terrible sins that have been committed by someone in this family, but I will find out who it is, and how they've avoided the judgment of the shuvani."

I nodded as graciously as I could, keeping my opinion behind my teeth. There was no sense in arguing the point with him—he'd made up his mind on the matter, and nothing I had to say would alter that. A change of subject was obviously in order. "Now maybe you can tell me what's up with Andrew and your boss. What does one have to do with the other?"

"I don't know for certain," Peter said, rubbing his thumb on his chin. I had to give my id a moment to swoon over Peter's chin and jaw and neck and other nibble-worthy parts of his head before she let me focus again. "But something struck me as slightly off when I met Dalton earlier this evening."

"The easy way to find out is to, you know—" I wiggled my fingers in the air. "Do the time reset thing."

He gave me a weary look.

"Sorry. Won't mention it again." I thought for a minute about what he'd said, allowing the night sounds of the forest—slight breeze rustling through the trees, owls talking to one another, the faint squeak of some rodent or night bird—to calm my mind so I could focus on the tangle of speculation that seemed to surround us. "Why did Dalton seem off to you tonight? Not what was wrong, because if you knew that, then you wouldn't be sitting here trying to puzzle it out. But something must have started you thinking that way. Was it anything in particular?"

"Not really, no. It was just a sense that . . . I was seeing only part of the picture, and was missing something important. But I'll be damned if I know what."

"Carla—my foster mom—used to help me whenever I'd lose my house keys by walking me through what I'd been doing before. Let's do that. Describe exactly what happened when you met with him. And you can stop with the skeptical expression, because Carla is really smart, and she never, ever failed to get me to remember where my keys were."

One side of Peter's mouth curled up into a rueful half smile. It was almost more than I could bear, but I knew full well that if I gave in to the temptation and sat on his lap to kiss the smile, we wouldn't end up talking over the situation with Andrew and Dalton.

"I met with him just off the highway, where the drive to the lumber mill starts. He was already there, pulled off the road and standing next to his car, when I arrived."

I closed my eyes so I could better visualize the scene. Eloise had died at that turn off the road enough that I was very familiar with the location. It was unremarkable in every sense, consisting of a pothole-marked dirt road, lined on either side with a dense thicket of fir trees and shrubs. Cars and logging trucks whizzed by on the main road with a speed that usually caused a mini vortex of wind at the entrance, kicking up the dust, and causing the fronds of the sagebrush to whip around. There was no wildlife there, though, since the highway was just a few feet away, and nothing other than the chain and sign I'd seen when I first arrived to mark that the lumber camp was there.

"I pulled up, and went to talk to him. He seemed perfectly normal. He looked like he normally does, and sounded fine, but there was something . . . off."

"What did you talk about?" I asked, my eyes still closed.

Peter related a conversation that appeared to be innocuous enough. He hesitated for a few seconds, then hurried over a section that sounded familiar.

"So Dalton thinks you're persecuting your family?" I asked, opening my eyes to watch him. His face was shuttered, absolutely devoid of expression.

"He's wrong. I'm not." The defiance was in his voice.

"I know he's wrong," I said simply, smiling at him. "You're not a vindictive person. You're going after your family because you think one of them is a murderer, not because they abandoned you."

"I know one or more of them is a murderer, yes," he said, his face relaxing as the tension left his shoulders. "And thank you for believing me."

"And what else did Dalton have to say?"

"Nothing beyond that he'd await the results of my search."

"That's so odd," I mused, running through the scene again in my head. "Do you think that maybe someone else has been talking to him? Or convinced him that you're . . . I don't know, incompetent to conduct the investigation? Maybe someone is bad-mouthing you to him?"

"I doubt it. He would come to me with any accusations that had been made against me."

"Hmm." I closed my eyes again. "Let's go over it once more. You turned off the highway, and he was at the entrance of the camp rather than your normal meeting point."

"He claimed it was faster to meet there, and it was."

"Yes, but is that out of character?" Time seemed to come to a halt as I mentally set the scene. Peter arriving in his blue car. Dalton standing beside his car, waiting for Peter. Darkness around them, pierced occasionally by the lights of passing vehicles. "I'm afraid I'm no help at all. It sounds like everything was perfectly normal."

"Obviously something isn't normal if there are two Daltons, albeit one of which is apparently deceased."

"Maybe we're tackling this the wrong way. Maybe instead of wondering what's wrong with Dalton, we should be asking ourselves what's wrong with the body I saw. What happened to it, for one?" I looked up at him. "Do you think it's back at the motel?"

"Hmm. You might have something there." He clasped

my hand and started off at a lope, forcing me to run after him. "I don't know what happened to the corpse, but we can find out quickly enough if it's at the motel."

"Hold up, I can't run that fast!" He slowed down, allowing me to catch up, the light from his flashlight swinging in wide arcs before us. When we reached the rutted drive to the lumber camp, he turned left, and would have started toward the highway if I hadn't stopped him. "Wait a sec, Peter."

"We don't have time to fuss with your car," he called after me when I dashed past Eloise to the tent. "Mine is quicker, not to mention infinitely more reliable."

"I just want to get my purse. The vial is in it, and I don't want to leave it where anyone could . . . oh. Hello."

A shape loomed up out of the darkness of my tent, and resolved itself into a man.

Andrew held my purse in one hand, and the vial in the other.

"Mother pus-bucket," I swore, looking around wildly for Peter. I could tell by the expression on Andrew's face that he was in a rage, and I had no doubt whatsoever who the focus of that rage would be. I took a deep breath to warn Peter, but before I could get any words out, a hand clamped down over my mouth, jerking me backward. As I flailed helplessly against the person restraining me, a second man emerged from the tent, joining the first. My eyes widened at the sight of him a second before blackness exploded painfully in my head, and once again I fell into nothing.

FIFTEEN

They had her in Andrew's caravan.

Peter watched from the blackness of the forest as Andrew and William emerged from the former's caravan, carefully locking the door behind them. They proceeded to William's motor home, and entered it without a word spoken between them.

He smiled to himself, a grim smile, the smile of a man whose woman had been abducted, if not before that very man's eyes, then behind his back while he was waiting for said woman to grab her purse. It was a smile that boded ill for anyone who came between him and the woman who he now admitted consumed his every waking thought. And probably most of his sleeping ones, not that he knew what his mind did while he slept, since he didn't hold conversations with it the way Kiya did with hers.

That trait was one that so charmed him—that and her openness, and her warmth and kindness, and her plump, silken breasts. Those in particular charmed him, but he reminded himself that he was an erudite man, and not one who thought about his woman's breasts, and how warm they felt, how soft they were, how delightfully they fit into his hands. Men of his ilk did not get erections just thinking about the breasts of their women, not while those women were at that very moment being held captive.

He adjusted his bulging crotch, and ordered his brain to cease thinking about Kiya lying sated and drowsy in his bed, and instead to focus on how he was going to get her out of Andrew's caravan without bringing the ire of Lenore Faa down onto their respective heads.

"Not that I should care if she is angry at Kiya," he growled softly to himself as he shifted his position, remaining hidden by the darkness and the trees. "Lenore Faa's opinion does not matter to me."

But Kiya's did, and he knew she'd be more than a little distraught if he forced her to give up her work for the old woman.

He didn't have to like it, however.

Peter waited and watched, expecting movement, his gaze locked on William's caravan. Just as he was about to chance being seen going after Kiya, the two men emerged, and banged on Lenore Faa's door. He was too far away to catch what was said, but when she opened her door at last, her expression was plain enough—she was not happy.

William and Andrew mounted the stairs after she grudgingly gave them permission. This time, Peter didn't wait to see what would happen. It would probably take William and Andrew at least five minutes to say whatever it was they had to say to Lenore Faa, and in that time, he could retrieve Kiya, and spirit her away to safety.

A mental stopwatch started as he dashed around the front of the caravan to the door. Thirty seconds to open the door. Another ten to make his way down the length of the dark interior. Five to peel off the duct tape that had been placed across Kiya's mouth, and another forty-seven to cut the tape wound around her ankles and wrists.

Thirty-two more seconds were spent in kissing her, after which time an alarm went off in his head.

"Hush," he told her when she started spitting indignant threats toward Andrew. "We'll verbally castrate him later. First we have to get out of here."

"It's not going to be such a verbal castration if I have my way," she grumbled, and started forward. Peter ran into her when she stopped suddenly.

"Kiya, we don't have time—"

Lights flooded the interior of the caravan.

"You see?" William's voice was high and fat, filled with satisfaction as he heaved the slight form of Lenore Faa up the stairs. He pointed dramatically at them. "I told you he was here, stealing from us, and that the woman was helping him. Now you have to believe me. Now you must call a kris."

"What's a kris?" Kiya asked him in a whisper. He moved forward, pulling her back to his side while watching his father closely. Behind Lenore Faa, Andrew glowered.

"It's another word for a tribunal," Peter said calmly. He didn't want Kiya to be any more frightened than she was, and could tell by the way her hand sought his that she was more worried than she let on. "It is called by Travellers to judge other Travellers."

"You see we do you the honor of considering your blood," William snarled before turning back to his mother. "You must admit that we cannot delay punishment any longer. He has taken from us that which was most dear, and he must pay the price. Both he and the woman, for she is clearly working for him."

"OK, one, you're a bastard," Kiya said before he could stop her. "And two, I am not working for Peter. I'm helping him find a murderer, yes, and happily so because people who kill other people by sucking up all their time are just asshats. Big, gigantic, sombrero-sized asshats. Who should be locked up. Yes, I'm looking at you, Andrew."

"Kiya," Peter said with an obvious warning in his voice that he had a pretty good suspicion she'd just ignore.

She did, and spoke firmly to William. "What's more, how dare you talk to your own son like that! Peter has never done anything to you, not that I can say the same about a baby-abandoning father!"

"That is enough," he said firmly, giving her waist a meaningful squeeze. "Arguing with him will do no good." He lifted his head to address the man who had severed all ties with his mother. "If you have something to say, you will say it to me. Kiya is not involved in any of my activities."

"Then why did we find this in her purse?" Andrew shoved his arm past his silent grandmother. In his hand was the vial. "It is proof, puridaj. The woman was going to plant this proof upon one of us so that he might call in the Watch and have us all arrested. Call the kris!"

"You must call the kris," William repeated, his eyes intent on his mother. "To delay is to let him damn us. We must be finished with this threat once and for all."

"Or," Kiya said, elbowing Peter when he tried to restrain her, "you could listen to the truth. Which is that Andrew, who is a—" She bit off the word, grinding her teeth for a moment before continuing. "Andrew stole Peter's vial with evidence of who the murderer was. He also probably stabbed him, since no one else really has a motive for that. Do they?"

She glanced up at him.

"I imagine there are quite a number of people who'd like to stab me, but none of them are in this region that I know of." He met his grandmother's gaze, and addressed her when he said, "We have not stolen from you or your family, Lenore Faa. We sought and reclaimed only what was mine—the vial that Andrew holds. They stole it from me and planted it here, in this caravan, using it as bait for which they hoped to trap us."

"I hate to mention this," Kiya said softly, "but I think the trap worked."

"Appearances can be deceiving," he answered before addressing the old woman again. "As for the other charges that William Faa lays at our feet, they are ridiculous. Kiya is not working for me, and I have not sought the downfall of this family, nor have I stolen any valuable object from it."

"You do not consider my nephew's life valuable?" William gasped, holding tight to Lenore Faa's arm. "Did you hear that? He does not consider the life of Gregory valuable. Does this not prove what I have said? Does this not validate our complaints—the complaints of all the family—against this man? He seeks to destroy us! Do not give him the means to do that."

"What's this about Gregory?" Kiya asked him.

"Do not act as if you had no hand stealing Gregory's time!" Andrew screamed, shoving aside the old woman in his haste to get at them. "We know the truth! Gregory is gone, and it is you and the whore who killed him!"

"Whore?" Kiya rolled up her sleeves. "Oh, you did not just say that again. No, not even you, the man who kept stealing my time, and probably hit me on the head so I thought zombies were after my brains, not even you would be so stupid as to use the word 'whore' in reference to me a third time. Because not only is that insulting to your grandmother—it shows that you have a tiny little penis and are compensating for that fact by slandering others in a pathetic attempt to pretend that your gentleman's personal wang is an outie, and not an innie. Which it most likely is."

Andrew sucked in approximately half the existing air in the caravan.

"IN ADDITION TO WHICH," Kiya finished loudly, forestalling the inevitable explosion, "Peter would never steal anyone's time, let alone that of his own cousin, because he learned that lesson with the tragic situation with Sunil. Not, I should point out, that it was his fault a drunk driver mowed down Sunil. So if you are implying that he killed Gregory by taking all his time—the very act that Peter is in the process of investigating, although obviously not concerning Gregory, since he was very much alive a little bit ago when I saw him coming out of my tent *right behind you*—then you are not only at a deficit in the penis department, but in brains, as well! And you can just take back that whore slur before I show you what a really pissed-off half-Traveller woman of *great virtue* does in response to such slander!"

"Of all the outrageous statements coming out of their mouths, the word 'whore' is what you fixate on?" Peter asked Kiya, unable to keep from smiling just a little. How she delighted him. Not only did she surprise him with almost every word out of that deliciously sweet mouth; she actually stood up for him. In front of his family. He had definitely made the right choice in selecting her for his bride. If only she'd acknowledge that fact, they could get on with the business of being deliriously happy together.

"The woman is deranged!" Andrew told his grandmother. "How can you tolerate her presence? Do you not see what a threat she poses to the others? Do you care about your own family so little that you would tolerate an obviously insane slut like her to contaminate the very air we breathe?"

"Insane slut!"

Peter had to physically keep Kiya from attacking Andrew, and even then, he might not have been able to stop her from getting to him if Lenore Faa hadn't spoken at that moment.

"That will be enough, Andrew. Kiya Mortenson, cease flailing your arms. Peter has enough common sense to not allow you the freedom to act upon your ill-conceived desires."

"Just let me have a few minutes alone with him in a small room," Kiya begged. "Just me and a rubber hose. Or maybe a baseball bat. A sheep gelding device would work, too, not that I think that he has much to—"

"Kiya!" Peter gave her another squeeze. She grumbled, but relaxed into his side. Pleased, he gave her a quick smile before fixing his gaze on the old woman, who shrugged off William's hold and hobbled forward to stand before Kiya and him.

"You have left me no choice but to agree to the kris," Lenore Faa told him.

Peter met her gaze without flinching, an odd feeling of empowerment stealing over him. He tried to pinpoint just why he felt that way, and was startled to realize that Kiya was responsible. She was warm pressed against him, a delicate presence that nonetheless made him feel both extremely protective and astonishingly in control of the situation. He was half-inclined to examine this strange sensation more deeply, but recoiled in horror when he realized that such actions might qualify him for the label of "self-aware, sensitive man."

"You have been caught red-handed, as the mortals say."

Then there was the matter of this kris that Lenore Faa threatened to hold. But even in the face of such a situation—one fraught with danger, if his memory of the history of Travellers was accurate—even in the face of that, he was calm.

"And now I'm told that it isn't just our property that you have stolen, but the life of a most-beloved grandson."

"That is utter bull, and you know it," Kiya snapped. "Gregory is no more dead than I am, not unless someone offed him in the last few minutes, because he was perfectly hale and hearty when I saw him coming out of my tent."

His arm tightened around her. How she delighted him. Look at how irritated she was now, talking back to the woman who not only employed her but held a great deal of power. But his Kiya did not let that scare her. No, she was as brave as she was smart. She would give him strong, intelligent children.

"When was this?" the old woman asked.

He just wouldn't mention to her the fact that their children would be born full-blooded Travellers. She might balk a bit at the idea of children who could control time.

"A little bit ago." Kiya touched the side of her head.

"Someone bashed me on the head—again, which I can tell you I don't appreciate in the least. It'll be a miracle if I don't suffer some sort of permanent brain trauma. My poor id will be all mixed up with my superego, who she dislikes intensely because my superego tries to tell the others what to do, and my ego will think he's an id, which is ridiculous, because he's not in the least bit idlike."

The thought of making those children was an absorbing one, but regretfully not suitable for the moment. He made a promise to himself that he'd trot out the idea later, when he could act upon his whims.

He became aware that Lenore Faa and the two others were staring at Kiya as if she'd just said something outrageous. He searched his memory of what it was she had been saying. Something about her inner voices?

She gave a little embarrassed cough. "Anyway, Gregory was fine just before I was knocked out, and since it's still night, that can't have been that long ago."

Peter looked down at her, anger gripping him in a red-hot vise. "Someone *struck* you?"

"Weren't you paying attention? I mentioned that ages ago. Well, almost a minute ago." She squinted up at him. "Why do you have that confused look? Were you daydreaming while we're being falsely charged with offing your male-model cousin?"

"I wasn't daydreaming. I never daydream. I wouldn't know how to daydream if I wanted to. I was merely thinking about our children," he told her calmly. Zen, that was the word to describe his mental state. Other than the fury over the idea of someone striking her. He was Zen with a side of fury.

She looked startled. "What children?"

"The ones we're going to have. Don't worry about

training them—I will help with the process. Who struck you?"

"We're going to have children?"

"Kiya," he said sternly, giving her his best frown. "Please keep your mind on the situation at hand. Who was it who hit you?"

She rubbed her head. "You're the one who brought up kids. And you bet you're going to help with the potty training. I don't know for certain who whomped me on the brain, but I'm willing to bet it was him." She pointed at William.

Peter turned his eyes to the man who was his father, and for the first time in his life seriously considered using his abilities to harm another person.

"Oh, no," Kiya told him, clearly reading his expression accurately. "If I can't, you can't. It's only fair. And besides, he's your father."

"If he was the one who struck you, then it matters little who he is." The fury in him grew with the thought of his family taking out their ire at him on the soft, warm, wholly unique, and utterly precious woman at his side.

She was his, the woman with whom he had decided to spend his life, the woman who gave him immense pleasure, and a sense of belonging. If his family thought they could harm her, then they must be taught otherwise.

The choking, sputtering noise brought him back from the mental vacation he took to a place of unlimited fury. William's face was turning a deep purplish red. He was mildly startled to find that he was holding his father by the throat, the latter's feet dangling a good ten inches off the ground.

He wasn't surprised to find Kiya at his side, fending off Andrew so that he could better throttle his father.

"Put Vilem down!" thundered Lenore Faa.

Peter released his father, not, he told himself, because the old lady ordered him to do so, but because he was an officer of the L'au-dela, and thus charged with protecting and defending citizens of the Otherworld and mortal world. Vengeance had no part in his life.

"Not unless you never touch Kiya again," he growled at the man who lay gasping at his feet. "She is mine."

"Whoa, now, Carl the Caveman!"

"You harm her at the risk of your life," he added, ignoring Kiya when she turned an exasperated look on him.

Andrew snarled threats in Besh, the language Travellers used when they wished to exclude outsiders.

"Hey! None of that," Kiya said, turning back to Andrew. "Didn't you hear your grandma? She said knock it off. And don't give me that look, you tiny-premised little twerp. I may not know what you said to Peter, but I can tell it was nasty just by the way you said it."

Peter couldn't help himself. Kiya was just so irresistible, so perfect. Despite the anger at his father, despite the worry about the loss of the evidence—and he was fairly certain that by now it had been destroyed—despite the pain of knowing he had failed Dalton, he was unable to keep the laughter inside. It just seemed to bubble out of him as he pulled Kiya into an embrace and soundly kissed her.

"Thank you," he said quietly.

Her startled expression melded into one of pink-cheeked pleasure. She slid a quick glance at Lenore Faa, then asked him, "For what?"

"For making my life infinitely better."

"Oh, Peter." She gave his lower lip a little bite. "If you

keep saying things like that, I really will have to marry you."

"That is my intention. Just as soon as I wrap up this case, I will take you home and make you mindless with pleasure."

"Oooh," she said, "that sounds fabulous. Where do you live?"

"Paris."

Her eyebrows rose. "The one in France?"

"Yes. It is just an apartment, but it consists of the entire top floor of an eighteenth-century house. I think you'll like it."

"Paris," she cooed, giving him a sultry look. "I've always wanted to go there."

"If you are quite finished?" The whipcrack voice cut through all pleasurable thoughts that Peter was at that moment indulging.

He turned with Kiya to face Lenore Faa. She gestured toward William, who had gotten to his feet, his face still red, and hatred in his eyes. "Where is Gregory?"

"Gone." William stopped rubbing his neck, obviously forcing his voice into one containing the bare minimum of civility. "He said he was going to confront this one and the woman about their plans to make trouble for us with the Watch. That was more than an hour ago. His car is still here, and he was not seen leaving the camp. We have looked for him, but can't find him. He does not answer his phone." William leveled him with a look that would have dropped an elephant. "He *was* seen going to the woman's tent a little bit ago."

"Andrew! Search for your cousin."

"He's not here—"

"I gave you an order. See to it." Lenore Faa turned to

her son. "Wake the others. I want this area scoured for Rehor."

"It will do no good. He's gone—"

"Do as I say!"

"And if he's not found?" William asked, gesturing toward Kiya and him. "Will you hold them accountable for what they've done to him?"

"I feel obligated to state at this point that we have done nothing illegal, to Gregory or anyone else," Peter said, his Kiya Zen once again firmly in place.

The old woman was silent for a few seconds, her gaze—oddly—on Kiya. "Yes," she said finally, the words weighing down on him like heavy iron chains. "If Rehor is not found, before the sun rises, we will hold the kris."

"And until then?" William asked as she turned and hobbled toward the door. He jerked his head toward Kiya. "What of the mahrime ones?"

"Do as you will." Peter braced himself for the attack that he was sure William would make, but Lenore Faa's voice snapped like a whip around them all.

"Understand me, Vilem, I want no harm to come to them. I hold you solely responsible for their welfare."

William said several obscene things under his breath, but Peter relaxed slightly when he realized that his father's hands were tied. Not literally, of course. That honor belonged to him.

"I hope you realize that as a member of the Watch, I am trained in any number of ways to escape confinement," he told William a short time later as the man who had sired him bound his hands tightly behind his back with a roll of duct tape.

"Then I shall see to it that you have ample opportunity of practicing your so-called skills," William said in a taunting tone of voice before adding another layer of duct tape to Peter's wrists, bound behind his back. Already the circulation was being cut off to his hands, the adhesive on the tape pulling painfully on the skin. "And just because I'm tired of hearing your lies . . ."

William ripped off another hunk of tape and slapped it over Peter's mouth.

He quickly repeated the process with Kiya's hands, shoving her down onto the couch, but leaving her mouth unbound.

"If you move out of this caravan," he told Kiya, gesturing at her with Peter's own gun, "I'll shoot you both. Him first."

He expected his future wife to have something to say about that, and she didn't let him down. "You really are the lowest thing I can possibly think of," she told William, her eyes narrow and glittering with fury. "You're like a donkey-porking, pedophilic, prejudicial, genocidal dictator who has an abnormal interest in dressing up in women's underwear!"

William spat at her feet, and left the caravan, the door slamming behind him.

"What a horrible man. I can't believe his sperm was responsible for you. You're nothing at all like him, and I don't mean just in personality. Andrew looks more like him than you do. And I'm sorry to say this, Peter, but he's not very bright." Skirting the spittle, Kiya moved over to the small kitchen area and spun around, her fingers groping blindly for a knife. "It obviously didn't occur to him that I could just cut that tape right off you."

He made an encouraging nodding gesture, hoping she'd take the tape from his mouth first.

"Dammit, where is the . . ." She turned back to face

the counter, then swore. "Who the hell doesn't have a knife in their kitchen? Maybe they're in a drawer. I'll try opening a few."

Five minutes later, panting slightly from the effort of rummaging through William's caravan with her hands bound behind her, she stood before him. "That bastard deliberately took all the knives out of his trailer. Which is just more proof that he set us up." She looked forlorn. "Hold me!"

He gave her a look.

"Well, do the best you can," she amended, sitting so she was straddling his legs. She leaned forward the better to rest her head on his shoulder. It was an awkward pose for them both—her knee was in the process of squashing his left testicle—but he did what he could to please her, nuzzling her head in a manner that he hoped was both erotic and yet comforting.

"You know, this could be fun," she murmured, kissing his neck before gently biting his earlobe.

Even with the pain from the crushed testicle, he was very aware of her scent and warmth and the nearness of her plump breasts, but until she removed the tape from his mouth, he couldn't tell her that now was not the time to try to distract him with kisses and nibbles, and by the gods, did she just bite his nipple?

His eyes crossed.

"Mmm. You seem to like it, too, judging by Mr. Happy down there. I wonder if I could lock the RV door with my hands behind my back? If so, I could take care of that little problem you have in your pants."

His eyebrows rose in outrage.

"Sorry. Beefy problem." She gave his earlobe another nibble. He was about to demand—just how, he wasn't quite sure—that she cease teasing him and impale herself on his penis when a soft whooshing noise heralded an arrival.

"Peter-ji! Are you being in here? I have been looking—oh la la la! What is this going on? Popsy! What have you done to Peter-ji?"

Sunil buzzed in an irritated fashion around Kiya's face. She looked from the ball of light to the door. "How did . . . ? That was closed. . . . How did you open the door?"

"If I am telling you all my secrets now, then we will have nothing to discuss later," Sunil answered, zipping over to blink in front of his eyes. "Peter-ji, nod twice if this is some sort of kinky sex sport. Once if you are properly bound by villains."

Peter rolled his eyes, but nodded. Once.

"Very well then. Popsy, you must be vacating Peter-ji's lap so that I might free you both."

Kiya seemed to be having some trouble getting over the fact that Sunil had entered the caravan, for suspicion was evident in her face. "I demand that you tell me how you opened that door when you don't have hands, let alone a whatchacallit . . . corporeal body."

"Peter-ji, please be telling her that we do not have time for this. It was only by the very most amazing luck that I returned to tell you about the magician, and for that reason was seeing through the windows that very nasty man bind you with electrician's tape."

"It's duct tape, actually," Kiya remarked as she got off his lap. His left testicle breathed a sigh of relief. "And while we're on the subject of you not having any hands, how do you expect to free us?"

Sunil bobbed in front of his face for a second before

flinging himself to the side, taking the duct tape with him.

"Bloody hell!" The words exploded out of Peter's mouth as the abused nerve endings signaled their discomfort to his brain.

"Oooh, look, the electrician's duct tape took some of your whiskers with it," Sunil said, obviously examining the tape where it now lay on the floor.

"That hurt like sin itself," Peter said once he had control over the pain. "Be careful with my hands. My fingers have already gone numb."

"I will indeed be careful. And while I'm being careful, I will be telling you what I found at the house of the magician you sent me to investigate, no?"

"Oh my god! Why didn't you tell me your hands were hurting?" Kiya gave him an anguished look, moving impotently back and forth in front of him.

"Really?" he asked, wanting simultaneously to laugh at her silly statement, kiss the concern off her face, and yell obscenities over his smarting mouth and upper lip.

"Yes, I will really tell you what I determined with much stealth and no little cunning. The magician did not wish to reveal his secrets, but he could not keep them from me," Sunil said from behind him. "I have never met anyone who was frightened of me before. Evidently magicians do not like animi. It was a very much interesting experience. All I had to do was threaten to haunt him instead of you, and he talked so much I could barely keep up with his confession."

Peter was too busy being entertained by Kiya to pay him much attention.

"What do you mean 'really' . . . ? Oh, I see. All right, despite the fact that you couldn't tell me, I like your hands. They're part of your arms, and you have really nice arms. What is he doing back there? I can't see behind you. Don't hurt his fingers, Sunil! Or any other part of him."

"The magician was admitting most hastily that he had sold several favors without authorization or documentation, including recently one glamour, and over the last year eighteen whipping boys."

Peter didn't think it was possible to be warmed any further by Kiya's concern, but he was. She fretted in front of him while Sunil carefully worked the tape off his wrists, the former lamenting loudly both the fact that she couldn't help him and that William had tied him up too tight. Could she be any more ideal? Mentally, he shook his head. Even her unrealistic demand that Sunil relinquish his place to her so she could be the one to free him was perfect.

That thought triggered another. No person was perfect, not really. For him to feel that way might be an indicator that he was in love with her.

"But what was very much intriguing was that the magician said the man he had sold the glamour and the whipping boys to was a Traveller. He also hinted dark doings about a member of the Watch. I knew that must be a threat against you, my most favored and excellent friend. Thus it was that the moment I heard that admission, I rushed straight here so that we might arrest the perp. That is the correct word, yes? Perp? I heard it on the television show I watched through the window last night while you and the popsy were being intimate with sexual good loving."

Peter examined Kiya from the tips of her shoes to the crown of her strawberry blond head. He'd never been in love with a woman, so he wasn't quite sure what that emotion felt like. Was this mixture of protectiveness, possession, and red-hot desire that left him burning with the need to be with her the emotion so commonly referred to as love? He didn't know, and at that moment, he didn't particularly care. Call it love, lust, or simply meant-to-be, Kiya was his, and he wanted her in his life forever.

"In addition, there was a second Traveller with the one who committed the illegal purchases. The magician would not speak much of him, but I have the feeling that it was he who was behind the other purchases."

"Stop fussing, woman. It's annoying," he said simply to give her something other than his hands on which to focus. "Sunil isn't hurting me, and despite your insistence that he doesn't have hands, he's doing just fine removing the tape."

"Annoying!"

He smiled to himself at the outraged look on her face as she marched over to him and stepped hard on his toes.

"I was expressing my concern about your well-being, you great big lout!"

"Why were you doing that?" he inquired conversationally. "Are you in love with me?"

"Right now I want to smack you upside the head for that annoying comment," she snapped.

"Go ahead. My hands are tied. I can't stop you."

She straightened her shoulders and looked down her nose at him. "I am not the sort of person who takes advantage of a bound man."

With a wry look, he glanced down at his crotch, which, thankfully, had ceased its attempt to burst through his fly.

She colored. He loved that he could make her blush,

and thought of several ways to do just that when they were finally alone.

"Well, I don't take advantage in the sense you meant. Sunil, are you done yet? I think we need to be getting out of here before the others come back."

"I am almost finished. This last bit here is tricky, is it not? Peter-ji, will you be calling others from the Watch in for the arrest? I do not wish to appear like a coward, but I will admit to being concerned about you taking on two Travellers with only the popsy and me to assist."

Peter had opened his mouth to tell Kiya that he had absolutely no intention of running away when Sunil's words penetrated the dense haze of fascination that Kiya had woven around him. "What are you talking about?"

The tape gave way on his wrists, allowing him to (painfully) rip off the bonds. It was both a relief to bring his hands forward to flex his fingers and agony a few seconds later when feeling returned to them. He gritted his teeth and ignored the pain long enough to remove the tape from Kiya's wrists.

"Ouchie. That was beginning to hurt, although William obviously didn't tie me up as tight as you," she said, rubbing her wrists.

"I am speaking to you about what I found at the magician's house."

"What magician?" Kiya asked, kneeling and taking first one of his hands, then the second in her own in order to massage them. Peter didn't have the heart to tell her that she was just making the pins and needles, not to mention the abrasions caused by the tape, hurt worse.

"There's a magician in this area who Dalton has been investigating. Did you find him?" he asked Sunil as the latter's light bobbed around the caravan.

"I was just telling you about it," Sunil said cheerfully, then proceeded to summarize his findings.

"Holy jebus," Peter said softly, considering this information.

"I don't understand. You mentioned a glamour before, but who's this whipping boy? And why would Travellers care about them? Nice appropriation of my favorite swearwords, too."

Kiya pressed a little kiss on the top of his hands. He felt something inside him melting away, leaving him with a warm glow that permeated every cell in his body.

"A whipping boy." He dragged his mind from the wonders of this new emotion to what Sunil had said. "A glamour I can understand—they can be used for many things. But what purpose would a Traveller have for . . . ahhh."

Kiya pointed a finger at him. "You've just had an aha moment, haven't you?"

"I believe the word that Peter-ji was saying was 'ahhh,' not 'aha,'" Sunil corrected her.

"Look at his face," she told the animus. "He knows something and he's not spilling. And he'd better, because if he thinks I'm going to marry a man who doesn't share when he's figured out something that's missed me, he can think again."

"You are getting married?" Sunil buzzed close to his ear and said softly, "Peter-ji, far be it from me to be telling you how to manage your relationships with popsies—"

"Popsy, singular," Kiya said. "There are no popsies plural in his life."

Peter grinned at her. "Just one popsy."

"—but you have not known her very long. Please be

forgiving me for speaking of you as if you were not an honorable woman, but Peter-ji is my friend, and to him I owe my loyalty and advice wherever I can offer it."

"I think it's kind of sweet, actually. That you value Peter so much, that is, not that you're trying to warn him off me. We got off the subject, though. What did you aha about?"

"The whipping boys." He stood up, flexed his shoulders a few times to make sure the blood had returned to circulating as per normal, then held out a still tingling hand for Kiya. "And now it's time to arrest a murderer."

SIXTEEN

They were waiting for us when we left the RV. All of Peter's family: Mrs. Faa, the pugs, the wives and grandsons—even the kids—were parked at a kiddie table where they made sleepy efforts to utilize the crayons and paper before them. It had to be around six in the morning, and yet those poor children had been dragged out of bed and forced to color while the adults stood clustered around Mrs. Faa's chair.

"Well, that doesn't look good," I said sotto voce when they turned, en masse, to glare at us. "Everyone is there but Gregory. That rotter. I swear to you that I saw him right before I was bashed on the head, which means either he's purposely hiding to make us look bad, or he's staying out of our sight so the family can pretend we've done something drastic to him."

"I don't think either of those propositions are correct," Peter answered.

I twined my fingers around his. Behind us, the tiny ball of light that was Sunil whisked back and forth, careful to keep hidden behind us. "You don't think Gregory is guilty? How can you say that? He was in my tent right alongside Andrew."

"I think Gregory is guilty of nothing more than bad

judgment. In fact, I'm beginning to believe he might be the only one in this family who sees things as they really are." Peter's fingers tightened around mine as he marched over to his family.

William stepped forward angrily, but Andrew put a hand on his arm. "I should have used more tape," the former growled.

"It wouldn't have mattered. We have a secret weapon. Oh, you little darlings!" The pugs, who had been clustered around and on Mrs. Faa, scrambled over to frolic around our feet. Clothilde put her paws on Peter's legs until he absently picked her up, releasing my hand so he could stroke her.

"You're a shameless hussy," I told Clothilde. She rolled her bulging eyes back in bliss as Peter's fingers massaged her neck. I bent to pick up Jacques (who was examining my shoe with a familiar glint in his eye) and Frau Blucher, feeling that no one would attack a woman who was holding two adorable puggies.

"What weapon?" Andrew asked.

"It wouldn't be secret if we told you," Peter answered. I gave him a pug-paw high five. "Andrew Faa, I come in the name of the L'au-dela Watch to arrest you for the murders of the mortals Mandy Tallweaver, Shelley Boyse, Antoinette Ducaste, and Melville Wickham. You should know that I am authorized to use force to bring you to a place of confinement, and any statement you make in my presence will be duly furnished to the proper authorities. Are you willing to come with me without resistance?"

Andrew said some things that I won't repeat here, because my foster mom raised me to be a lady.

"Do you talk to your mother with that mouth?" I

asked, tucking Jacques under my arm so I could cover Frau Blucher's ears.

He ignored me. One side of Peter's mouth twitched, however, which made me feel he approved . . . or at least appreciated the humor of the situation.

"No, I will not come with you to be arrested on your trumped-up charges! Further, I refuse to allow your persecutions of my family to continue. Puridaj, it is time for the kris. I stand before you in the form of krisatora. Do you so accept me?

"I stand before you as krisatora, as well," William said, his eyes narrowed and glittering with an unholy light. "Do you so accept me?"

I leaned against Peter. "What's—"

"Krisatora is one who takes the position of judge at a kris. Tradition demands that there are three, and it is they who make the judgment of guilt or innocence."

I glared at both men. "Oh, like you're going to be impartial judges. Right, if those two rat finks get to be krisajudges, I get to be one, too."

"Krisatora," Peter corrected.

"You can't be a krisatora," Andrew snapped.

"Why not?"

"Because this kris is to judge you and Peter Faa!" William answered for him. He turned to Mrs. Faa. "Do you accept us?

"Yes," she said slowly, her gaze dropping when Peter and I both looked at her. "Yes, I accept you as krisatora."

"There, you see?" I smiled my best "beat you at your own game" smile at the men. "She accepted me."

Andrew snorted. "That acceptance did not include you."

"Actually, I believe it did. Lenore Faa did not differentiate between those who stated they were willing to judge the kris." Peter looked at me with interest. "You are about to officiate over your first kris."

"Go, me." I gave him a warm smile, then without asking took my place at one of the empty picnic tables, setting down the dogs before me. "Right, let's get this kangaroo trial under way. I have a man to molest, and I want to do so before the pugs need to do their morning walkies."

"Puridaj!" Andrew turned to his grandmother, clearly pleading for her to take action.

My smile turned to a cheeky grin when the old lady lifted a hand and said in a clear, forceful voice, "Cease complaining, and get on with it."

"Right, I'll chair, shall I?" I bent to the side to pick up a large rock that would make a good gavel, and rapped a couple of times on the top of the table, which made the pugs bark. "First order of business: is Peter guilty of doing something bad to Gregory? I say no. Votes? I'll take your lack of response as a proxy vote for me, which means hurrah, Peter is innocent. I hereby declare this kris finito."

"It does not work that way," Andrew snarled. "Puridaj, you must realize this is intolerable."

"Very well." Mrs. Faa gave him an unreadable look. "We will conclude the kris, and I will allow Peter Faa to take you into custody. You may plead your case to the Watch."

"That's one for team us," I told Peter before sending a little smile Mrs. Faa's way. It seemed to me that her heart wasn't in the condemnation of Peter.

"Perhaps," was all he said, but I could tell he was annoyed. He had that look in his eye like he wanted to punch his dad and cousin, but he was pretty good on the self-control front, and simply stood, relaxed and apparently bored by the whole thing.

"Peter Faa, do you deny stealing that which belonged to the family? Do you deny stealing the time of Gregory Faa until he was left without any time, thus rendering him deceased? Do you deny attempting to make the Watch believe that this family was behind the murder of mortals?" William asked in a voice that was fat with grandiosity.

"I do so deny those charges," Peter answered with a formality that seemed to be inherent to the proceedings.

I sat up a bit straighter and arranged the pugs so that they looked more suited to my sudden role of dignified judge. "I second that denial. That makes two no votes. And since you guys only have two votes, that means we'll have to go to a tiebreaker. As head krisatora judge, I will perform that by saying not guilty. That gives us a three to two majority."

"You already voted," Andrew argued, jabbing his finger toward me. "You can't vote twice!"

"Sure I can. That first vote was from me the person who was charged with these so-called crimes. The second vote was my official judge vote."

"You have just one vote," Andrew said, frowning.

"She has no votes whatsoever! She isn't a member of this family, and thus she is not able to sit as krisatora!" William snapped, shooting his nephew an irate look.

"And yet, it would appear that I'm doing just that." My placid smile was a winner in this situation—it appeared to give Andrew some sort of apoplectic fit.

While he was sputtering with anger, William turned to

where the other men and their families stood. "Piers Faa, do you bear witness to the fact that Peter Faa broke into our caravans, has done away with Gregory, and has long persecuted this family for no reason?"

"I do so witness," Piers answered. The bastard.

"Where's your proof? You have no proof, do you? You can't just say he's guilty and then expect me to believe that, because hello! Life doesn't work that way. No proof, no conviction. Them's the rules." I crossed my arms as Jacques barked at William.

Mrs. Faa commanded him to be silent. Jacques, that is, not William, which was a shame when you thought about it.

"Arderne Faa, do you bear witness to the fact Peter Faa committed those acts which I have just stated?" William ignored me to ask the other grandson.

He didn't even glance our way, just bowed his head, and said in a soft voice that he stood witness to our crimes.

"It's a good thing I believe in karma getting people who lie for their own good," I told Arderne. "Because otherwise, you'd be in a world of hurt right now."

His eyes widened.

"Kiya," Peter warned, his voice a low rumble.

"What, a judge isn't allowed to threaten a witness?" I asked, all innocence.

"No. Furthermore, you are not helping our case by being so flippant."

I gave him a long, level look. He didn't look particularly worried, but all of a sudden, a little spurt of fear gripped me. "I apologize," I said mostly to Mrs. Faa, but spilling a little of the apology onto the other men who stood with her. "I didn't mean to belittle the importance

of your family traditions. Carry on with your mudslin—
er—evidence."

"It is the judgment of this kris that Peter Faa and the
female Kiya Mortenson are found guilty of crimes
against the family—"

"Wait a minute!" I interrupted, standing up. The pugs
not on the table instantly swarmed to my feet and began
yapping. "Don't we get to present evidence of our innocence? Clothilde, really, right there? There's a perfectly
good bush not ten feet away—hold on, everyone. Let me
take care of that."

"Does anyone else find it even remotely farcical that
the kris is being interrupted because one of those at-
tending took a dump next to a krisatora?" Peter asked,
his lips twitching.

I waved the pooper-scooper at the stony expression
on the faces of the others before putting it to its intended
use. "I think you and I are the only ones who see the
humor in the situation." A little light blinked on and off
rapidly from the cover of a fern. "And Sunil."

"What evidence do you have to present?" William
asked in an officious tone of voice as I returned to my
seat. Instantly, I was swarmed with pugs. I cuddled as
many of them as I could, feeling that if I had them in my
arms, I was less likely to punch William on the schnozz
as he deserved. While I might have given in to that temptation had I been on my own, it was clear that Peter
needed to maintain his authority, and my natural ten-
dency to lip off might well undermine that.

"For one, I saw Gregory alive before one of you
coshed me on the brain."

"What proof do you have of that?" Andrew said with
a sneer in his voice. "You have none, do you?"

"William said Gregory was in my tent!"

"I must have been mistaken," the older man demured. The urge to punch him grew even stronger.

"You lying . . . Fine! You want to play that way? What proof do you have that Gregory wasn't with you?" I countered.

Andrew pointed to his cousins. "Arderne and Piers have both testified that Gregory has not been seen since before the sun set."

"Yeah, but they're lying, just like William—"

"You have no proof!" William bellowed, totally ignoring the fact that he was caught in his own web of falsehoods. "Therefore, your evidence is not allowed. It is the decision of this kris that the mahrime Traveller Peter Faa and mahrime Traveller Kiya Mortenson are guilty of the aforementioned crimes of theft and, as such, will be subject to the course of punishment decided upon by the family of Gregory Faa. As the eldest male of the family, I demand an eye-for-eye justice."

That had a particularly grim sound to it. I was just about to inform William that I was not going to stand by while he railroaded Peter and me for something we didn't do when Peter spoke up at last.

"As a member of the Watch of the L'au-dela, I am sworn to uphold the laws governing both mortal and immortal beings, and for that reason, and that reason alone, I have allowed this kris to proceed. However, your summation process is faulty and does not adhere to the precepts governing the Otherworld, so I am forced to reject your sentence."

"Yeah!" I said, standing up with the intention of taking my armload of pugs over to Peter in order to show our unified front. "We reject your sentence."

I got two steps before Andrew was on me. Or rather, behind me, a wickedly sharp dagger that I hadn't known he possessed pressed to the side of my throat.

"You do not seem to understand," he said, his breath puffing annoyingly on my face. I thought of telling him to get a breath mint, but my ego reminded me that I was being good for Peter's sake. "The judgment of the kris has been made: an eye for an eye will be exacted for the crimes you committed."

"We will, however, allow you to pick which one of you will pay the price," William put in, moving over to take the gun that Peter had pulled when Andrew whipped out his knife. "We are not, after all, without decency."

Reluctantly, with his eyes on me, Peter allowed his father to take his gun.

"A bigger load of bull I've never heard," I snarled, trying to figure out if there was any way I could knock Andrew and his nasty blade away from me, so that Peter could snatch back his gun, but Andrew, the bastard, must have read my mind, because he twisted one of my arms up behind my back the better to hold me securely, sending a cascade of pugs to the ground. Luckily, they landed in the sandbox.

"You bastard!" I yelled as the pugs scampered back to their mom. "You could have hurt them!"

Peter turned to his grandmother, his eyes flashing with that strange light that I'd seen once before. "Lenore Faa, you have heard my charges against your grandson. You know what steps the L'au-dela will take should you harm me. What I don't think you know is what I will do should you allow Kiya to be harmed in any way."

The old lady had been silent through most of the mockery of a trial, her gaze on her gnarled hands as they petted a pug, her lined face absent of any emotion. She looked up at Peter now, her expression unreadable. "Do you claim her as wife, then?"

"I do."

"Yeah, well, we're still working that out," I piped in, giving Peter a look that told him I was aware of the gravity of the situation, but that I was not one to be pushed into anything, especially something so important as marriage. He returned it with a look that told me to stop sending him meaning-filled looks when he was busy trying to save our asses. I batted my lashes at him. He pursed his lips and turned back to Mrs. Faa.

"She will be my wife."

"You do not know who her family is. She is mahrime, unacknowledged and unwanted by them," Mrs. Faa pointed out.

"So is Peter, and I think he's pretty damned wonderful," I said, bristling a little. Terrance left Mrs. Faa and tried to mate with a stuffed toy dropped by one of the kids. "And as the saying goes, mahrime is all in the mind."

She shot me a curious look.

"I just made it up. It sounds good. I like it," I said somewhat defensively. "You guys take that whole pureblood thing way too far. Didn't you ever hear that diversity was good for bloodlines?"

"I don't care who her family was. I don't care that she's mahrime like me. I simply want her."

"He loves me," I told Mrs. Faa, giving Peter a bright smile.

He looked faintly startled. "I didn't say that."

"You don't have to. What man would declare in front of his grandma and annoyingly irritating dad, and rest of the family, that he wants to marry a woman without him being in love with her? It's OK. I know how guys are; I won't make you say the words in front of them. But boy, when we're alone, we're going to have a long, long talk."

"You can have that talk now," Andrew said, shoving me forward toward William's RV. "But if I were you, I'd make it about which one of you is going to be sacrificing his or her life, because if you don't decide, we will." He gave my arm a jerk. "And I know who I will pick."

Peter was on him in a flash, but alas, Andrew was expecting it, and yanked me in front of him to serve as a shield.

"Aren't you going to stop this?" I demanded of Mrs. Faa.

She sat still for a few seconds, then slowly turned to look at me. "The kris has spoken. It is out of my hands."

"You're willing to sit there and let your family kill me or your own grandson?" I asked in disbelief. "Are you a *monster*?"

"You will cease speaking to her," Andrew said, yanking my arm until tears started in my eyes.

Peter snarled something in a language that wasn't English. Andrew answered in kind, then turned and shoved me into the RV. I whacked my shin on the stairs as I fell forward, but strong hands and stronger arms were there picking me up before I could get the first curse out of my mouth.

The door was slammed behind us. I stood on one leg, rubbing my shin, leaning into Peter as he asked, "Are you all right? Did he hurt you?"

"Yes, and not really. I just tripped and smacked my shin. Peter, what are we going to do? They have your gun. Can Sunil get it from them, do you think?"

"Not for another twelve hours or so." He frowned and sat down, pulling me onto his lap.

"Why twelve hours?"

"That's how long it takes to recharge his physical energy. He used up most, if not all, of it when he undid the tape on my wrists. Animi have limited abilities to interact in the physical world, and it takes them some time to recover when they do. No, the best we can hope from him is that he eavesdrops and lets us know what they're planning."

"I think it's pretty clear what they're planning," I said, wrapping my arms around him, offering what comfort I could, but also seeking it for the horrible sick feeling in the pit of my stomach. "They want to kill one of us to pay for something we didn't do. Not that I think Gregory is dead in the first place. He has to be in it, Peter. He has to be just as guilty as Andrew. He's hiding so that William can tell your grandmother that we killed Gregory. And dammit, I don't think there's a thing we can do to stop them."

"I'm not going to let them harm you," he said, squeezing me, and pressing a kiss to my neck where Andrew had held the knife.

"Likewise, but how are we going to stop them? They have your gun, and at least one knife, and I'm willing to bet if push comes to shove, your cousins will stop any attack you make on William or Andrew."

"There's Dalton," he said slowly.

"Call him and tell him to bring a great big horde of paranormal policemen," I instructed, sliding off his lap so he could dig his cell phone out of his pocket.

Peter hit the button for Dalton, but shook his head a minute later and turned off the phone. "Voice mail. That's not like him. He normally answers no matter what the time of day."

"Well, then, we'll just have to keep trying." I paced up

and down the narrow aisle, trying to prod my brain into a solution for our dilemma. "We'll have to stall them if they try to force us into giving an answer. Sooner or later Dalton will pick up, and then we'll get help. How long do you think they'll give us—"

A pounding on the door interrupted me, followed by a voice yelling, "You have five more minutes, then we'll decide for you."

"I have got to learn to keep my questions to myself," I grumbled. "OK. We have to calm down."

"I'm perfectly calm," Peter said, watching me pace back and forth in front of him.

"So am I." I glared at my hands. "Except for my hands. Look, they're actually wringing each other. I've never even seen hand-wringing except where it's mentioned in books, and now I'm doing it. Do you see what they've driven me to? We have to get out of here, Peter. Maybe we can slip out of a window or something without them seeing us."

"They'll simply come after us. No." He stood up. "I have to end this now. I will have to take Andrew into custody, and deal with William somehow."

I had visions of the bleeding, unconscious Peter lying on my air mattress, and fear unlike anything I've known gripped me. I grabbed his arms to stop him from leaving. "They'll kill you, Peter! Oh, don't get that offended look like I'm impugning your manhood or something like that—I know under normal circumstances that you can take them down, but we're unarmed, and they aren't. They've already stabbed you twice—what makes you think they won't finish off the job now that they've decided one of us has to die? Oh, god, Peter." The last three words were spoken on a sob. "I don't want you to die."

"Because you love me?" he said, a little smile twitching one side of his mouth.

I punched him in the arm, then leaned into him, breathing in his scent, that wonderfully woodsy scent. "I'm just used to you and your magnificent beefy penis, that's all."

He held me close, long enough for me to cry a couple of silent tears onto his collar. "I'll find a way out, sweetheart. Don't worry."

"We're a team, you annoying timey-wimey Travelling man," I sniffled.

"We are not Doctor Who. Travellers seldom time travel. Even for savants, it's too risky."

"Stop being so pedan—" I stopped and pulled away from him. "What did you say?"

"I said we seldom time travel because it's too risky." His gaze narrowed suspiciously. "Why are you looking happy all of a sudden?"

"Savants? Like the brilliant people who can do math or play piano without ever learning kind of savants?"

"More or less. With regards to Travellers, it simply means we are . . . more."

"We? You're one?"

"I am."

"More what?"

"Just *more*."

"Like extra-oomph powers? You're a super Traveller?"

"We do not have any more powers. We are just more . . . I suppose *focused* would be a good word."

I pinched his arm. "You're a super-focused Traveller savant and you didn't tell me?"

He made a little face. "I didn't think it was important."

"Don't you see? That's the answer, Peter!"

He said nothing for the count of three; then his eyes widened in understanding. "No," he said, shaking his head. "No, it is not the answer. Kiya, you are unlearned in the ways of Travellers, and you do not understand what you are saying."

"Mrs. Faa said that you can time travel, and that if you take enough time, you can actually zap back in time. You're a savant! That means you can do it more easily than others. You just said you were more focused and stuff. All you have to do is take enough time to go back to when your cousins stole your vial, and make sure they don't do it. Then you can turn it in to the authorities, and this whole mess with Gregory will be avoided."

"No, Kiya. It's not possible."

"Why isn't it possible?"

He gripped my arms and gave me a gentle shake before kissing me on my forehead. "Because the only person close enough for me to take enough time from in order to Travel is you. And I will not do that."

"Because of the shuvani being pissed like she was at your grandpa?" I gave him a little headshake. "This isn't like that. He took the Nazis' time without their permission. I will give you mine, so it's no different from your troll selling you time."

"That is not the only reason. The amount of time I'd have to take in order to go back four days is too much."

It was my turn to shake him. "But I'm willing to give up four days of my time. So long as you come find me after you turn the vial over to Dalton, that is."

Sadness filled his eyes. "It's not the taking of time itself that poses the risk. The shuvani frowns on Travellers using their skills to Travel. One way they keep us from zipping back and forth through time is to create the potential risk of death."

"To who? The Traveller or the donator?"

"Either. Both."

I looked at Peter, my heart sinking. Someone pounded on the door again. "One minute left!"

"Are you willing to take that risk?" I asked him.

"No." His thumb brushed first my cheek, then my lower lip. "You are too precious to me."

I turned my face to kiss his palm. "I don't think we have any other way. If we leave this RV, your family is going to kill one of us, and it's obvious your grandmother isn't going to stop them."

"I will not risk your life," he said, his face set in an obstinate expression.

"You don't know for certain that the shuvani will punish you. Peter, we have to take this chance. Dalton is out of reach. Sunil can't help us. They are armed, and we aren't. If you can think of a cunning plan to get us out of this, speak now, because otherwise, I think you're going to have to go back in time four days and get us out of this fix."

He didn't like it. I could tell he really did not like it, but he had to admit that we were stuck between a rock and a hard place, and there was just nothing else we could do.

"If I am responsible for your death—," he started to say, his fingers biting into my arms.

I bit the end of his nose. "I promise I'll come back as a ghost and haunt you mercilessly. Peter . . ."

"You love me," he said, nodding as he made that statement.

"Dammit, I wanted to say it!" I pinched his side, then

leaned into him, my mouth brushing his. "I really think I do love you, you know. I don't know when it happened, but it did. I love your gorgeous Elizabeth Taylor eyes, and your wonderful chest with the lightning flower, and your ass and Mr. Beefy, and your sense of humor, and the way you pretend you're all business but really aren't. I love you, Peter Faa, and when this is done, I am going to marry you and make you the happiest man who ever lived. Now tell me you love me."

"What makes you think I do?"

I stepped on his foot.

"Ow!" He laughed, then kissed me swiftly. "I will tell you I love you when this nightmare is over." He looked at me long and hard. "Kiya—"

"No." I put my fingers over his mouth. "It'll be OK. We'll both be OK because the shuvani will realize we're just trying to put things right and bring a murderer to justice."

"That doesn't concern the shuvani in the least," he said behind my fingers.

I replaced them with my mouth. "Do it," I whispered against his lips. "Take the time you need from me to Travel back four days. I give it to you freely. Do it now, Peter."

His tongue swept into my mouth, tasting, claiming, and twining around my own until my body tingled as if I were holding a live wire. I opened my eyes as the kiss ended, and saw lightning in his violet eyes. The blue white light in them blinded me, consuming me, until I fell headlong into it, and was no more.

SEVENTEEN

"You know that saying about lightning never strikes twice in the same place? Well, I'm the living proof that it's totally false." I blinked in surprise at the words, then stood up and cheered. "He did it! And I'm alive! Woohoo!"

"Who did what? Aaaa . . . aaaa—"

"—choo," I finished for Dalton. I looked around the walk-in clinic's small reception area, nodding when it appeared to be exactly the same as I remembered it.

Dalton was the same, as well. His nose was red, his eyes were swollen and weepy, and he was covered in hives.

"Man, you really are suffering, aren't you?" I said in commiseration with his misery.

"Does it show?" He tried to crack a smile, but failed.

"Don't worry, Dalton, the doctor will have you de-hived in no time."

His eyes, red and running, looked startled. "I'm sorry, but do we know each other?"

I bit my lip, realizing I'd slipped up. "Urm . . . yeah. We met a little bit ago."

"I don't remember—achoo—telling you my name."

"You did, though," I said, crossing my fingers at the slight aberration from the truth. He had told me his name . . . but that was in the previous version of this day. "You told me you were Dalton McKay at the same time I told you I was Kiya Mortenson."

"Kiya. What a very pretty name. Would you mind handing me that box of tissue, Kiya? I appear not only to be forgetful of meeting lovely women, but I've also gone through my supply of tissues."

I handed him the box and winced in sympathy when he sneezed again, mentally trying to run over anything of importance we had said to each other. Peter had never mentioned it, but I had a horrible feeling that if I did something different this time, it might affect the future in some ghastly, unimaginable way. "You'll feel better soon," was all I could think to say.

"I hope so. I want to get away from the vicious plant life of this area."

"Yeah, you might want to stay out of the forest, since it's loaded with mountain sagebrush."

He gave me another startled glance.

I smiled in what I hoped was a reassuring manner. "You told me you were allergic to the sagebrush at the same time we exchanged names."

He shook his head. "I don't remember—I suppose it's the allergy medicine I took earlier in hopes it would make the suffering bearable. No doubt it's muddled my brain."

"We can't have you muddled," I said carefully, gently patting a spot on his arm that was free of hives. "I'm sure you have lots of important things to do here."

"Yes, I do."

"You just might want to rearrange any scheduled

meetings you made in the woods to a less-sagebrushy area. Somewhere that isn't—"

The thought struck me like the bolt of lightning that had left the mark on my skin. I stared at Dalton, feeling little tingles of electricity going up and down my arms.

Dalton had been in the woods. He had met Peter there the evening that we had been caught in William's RV. But he hadn't been affected by the sagebrush. I cast my mind back to the entrance of the lumber camp, where Peter said that Dalton had met him. Yes, it was lined with sagebrush, long arms of which brushed against Eloise's side every time I drove in or out.

"Holy jebus!" I shouted, standing up. No allergy medicine in the world worked so fast or so well that an allergic person would stand near a known allergen shortly after starting treatment. Which meant the man who had stood next to the sagebrush while he talked to Peter wasn't Dalton. I had to tell him immediately. Sometime between now and four nights from now, Dalton would be killed, and someone would take his place.

I twirled around, ready to bolt, but where was I going? I had no idea where Peter had been while I was at the doctor's office. What I needed was a way to contact him and warn him.

Like a cell phone.

I pulled out my phone, but the number that Peter had put in it wasn't there. *Of course it isn't,* my ego pointed out to me in a smug voice that I could have done without. *That meeting hasn't happened yet.*

"Peter!" I shouted again, and grabbed Dalton's arm, heedless of the poor man's hives. He squawked. I released it and apologized. "Sorry, didn't mean to make you itch worse. What's Peter's phone number?"

He reared back like I had struck him. "I beg your pardon?"

"Peter's number. Peter Faa. I need it. Desperately. I have to tell him that the you he met wasn't really you, and that the body I found *was* you. I'm so sorry about that. I didn't mean to step on you, but if you would just give me Peter's cell number, I can call him and we can figure out when you were killed, and thus keep it from happening again."

Dalton's expression went from startled to completely blank. I realized with hindsight that I had gone about getting information the wrong way—he was a professional detective, or whatever they had in the Watch, and I had just mentioned one of the men working for him without any warning.

"I'm afraid I don't know what you're talking about," he said stiffly, or as stiffly as he could, given his runny nose, eyes, and hives. "I would, however, like to know just who you are, and what sort of glamour you're using on me. I've heard that there's a magician in this area who is doling out unauthorized magic, and if you do not have the correct paperwork for whatever deceptive magic you are using, I'm afraid that I will have to bring you before the committee to face charges."

"I'm not the one using a glamour. Andrew was." The second big thought hit me then, causing me to gasp, literally gasp in realization. "That's what he wanted it for! Don't you see? Andrew was pretending to be you. Somehow, he found out about Peter working with you, and he did whatever it is you do to appear like someone else, and whammo! He was you. But he couldn't be you if you were still here, so he had to off you."

Dalton pulled out his phone and, with a wary eye on me, spoke into it softly.

I wrung my hands, ignoring my id when she warned me that such a dramatic gesture was becoming a habit. "We have to find Andrew and stop him from getting that glamour. And killing you. That's really important. Oh, don't you see that I have to talk to Peter? He'll understand all of this. At least I hope he will. He should, because he said that people who were in close proximity when the time theft was conducted would remember what happened during the lost time. Oh man, what if he was wrong? What if I have to seduce him all over again?"

"That's it," Dalton said, getting to his feet, and immediately sneezing. "I am authorized by the L'au-dela to place you under—"

"Gah!" I yelled at him, realizing that nothing I could say would get him to give me Peter's phone number. "Fine, I'll go find him the hard way. But if you're killed because I've spent two days trying to find him, don't come whining to me!"

His expression was priceless, but not one that I had time to stay and enjoy. I dashed out of the doctor's office—there was no need to stay, since I knew the lightning strike had not harmed me—and begged, pleaded, and cajoled Eloise to start.

What had Peter been doing before I had seen him in the woods, that first day when I was walking the pugs? "I don't think he ever told me," I said aloud as I drove down the winding mountain road toward Rose Hill. "But I bet I know someone who was completely aware of where Peter was, and what he was doing."

I gritted my teeth as I drove the roads, aware of the

logging trucks that rumbled so ominously toward me, and careful to keep Eloise from being driven onto the side of the road again. Because I hadn't waited at the doctor's office as I had done the first time, I knew Gregory wasn't right behind me on the road, but chances were fair that his cousin was at the family's camp.

The lumber mill was just as I remembered it, from the mildewy sign on a chain across the track leading up to the mill proper, to the shiny RVs, the handful of children and women, and the shrill yapping of the pugs as Mrs. Faa hobbled forward.

"Andrew!" I yelled as I crawled out of the window of my car. "Where's Andrew?"

"Who are you?" asked one of the grandsons—to be honest, I couldn't tell Piers from Arderne. "What are you doing here? What do you want with Andrew?"

"Mrs. Faa, this is very important. I know you don't give a damn what happens to me, or Peter for that matter, but an innocent man's life is at stake, not to mention all the people who Andrew has killed."

She stiffened up, but the pugs gamboled and frolicked around my feet. "What family are you from? You are mahrime."

"Yes, I am, not that I appreciate you greeting me with that statement, although I guess I did just greet you with the news that I knew Andrew is the one behind all the murders that Peter is investigating."

"Peter?" she asked, her eyes narrowing. "You are a friend of Peter Faa?"

"I'm going to marry him," I told her. "And you don't remember this, because Peter used up a bunch of my time to Travel back four days, but I used to work for you.

I took care of the pugs. Terrance, you'll get slivers in your naughty bits if you try to get it on with that log."

Mrs. Faa was silent for a moment. I couldn't tell if she was stunned or angry, or what—her wrinkled face seemed to be slack and devoid of any emotion. "Peter Faa . . . Travelled?"

"Yeah. And your shuvani person evidently decided it was OK, because my lips are perfectly fine, and I'm not dead and all. Look, I know this is a shock, but it really is important that I find Peter before it's too late. Before Andrew—"

"Before Andrew what?" came a low, mean voice behind me.

I spun around to face the man himself. "Before you kill Dalton McKay. Oh, don't look so surprised—I know it was you who killed him and used the glamour you got from some magician to pretend you were Dalton. I'm sure your plan all along was to get the evidence from Peter so he couldn't turn you in, but it's over, do you hear me? I know what you were doing."

The world twisted for the space between a second.

"What family are you from? You are mahrime."

I looked at Mrs. Faa, then turned around and ran at the man who lurked at the far edge of his RV. "You do that again, and I'll see to it that you never steal time again!" I bellowed at Andrew.

But it wasn't Andrew who stood there. It was William, and he caught me as I flung myself forward, intending to beat the snot out of him, or at least subdue him until Peter showed up to accost me in the woods. He swung at me, sending me flying until I slammed into the side of the RV. I hit it hard enough that my vision went black for a few seconds, but I did hear William order someone to fetch a rope.

Groggily, I tried to rally my wits, but my body didn't seem to want to respond to my wishes. Before my vision could clear, I felt a harsh, scratchy object wrapped around my neck, following which I was jerked to my feet.

"Get the children in the caravans," someone ordered, at the same time I was dragged backward. My eyes slowly began to focus, the blurred colorful shape before me resolving itself into Andrew's face as he followed the person hauling me. Behind him, Mrs. Faa stood, her expression black.

"You can't hang the girl," she said. "She has done no crime."

"She's dangerous," William growled. "I told you Peter Faa is trying to make trouble for us. She's obviously working with him."

"Peter's innocent," I choked out, struggling to pull the rope around my neck slack enough that I could take a proper breath. "It's Andrew who is the murderer. Mrs. Faa, help me."

She shook her head, but at the same time said loudly, "Vilem, I forbid this. She is a Traveller, although she is mahrime. We do not kill our own kind."

"A Traveller?" William stopped for a couple of seconds as he looked down on me. "You are sure?"

"Yes."

He hesitated, then with a grunt slammed me up against a tree trunk, throwing the rope up and over a couple of branches. "It matters not. She is mahrime. The loss of her kind will not harm us."

I didn't wait for him to string me up; I grabbed the rope with both hands, and bolted.

Smack-dab into Andrew.

Andrew threw a left hook that caught me under my chin, making my head snap back with an ugly sound. I was dazed, dimly aware only of the extreme pain in my head, and growing pressure on my windpipe. My id, ego, and superego all screamed at me to get a grip before it was too late, but when I finally did manage to clear my head, it was to find myself being hoisted up by the rope around my neck. I kicked and fought and tried desperately to get my fingers between the rope and my flesh, but the black spots that had appeared began to grow and leak into one another. I realized that I would asphyxiate if something wasn't done in the next few seconds.

"Peter," I croaked, tears filling my eyes at the thought of never seeing him again, never feeling his warmth, never watching him trying to be all business, and failing miserably. I wanted him more than I wanted anything else, and just hoped that whoever was in charge of such things would allow my ghostly form to be assigned to him the way Sunil was. "Although not as a ball of light," I said in a voice that was inaudible to all but me. "Something with a proper body, please."

The inky spots merged together, then grew lighter and lighter until they dazzled me, setting my body alight with electricity and making me feel as if I were floating on a warm, delicious cloud.

One that smelled like the woods. Woods that murmured the most wonderful words in my ears, and pressed steamy kisses all over my face and neck. Woods that had hands and arms and a chest that I snuggled happily into.

A chest? Arms? Hands? *What the hell, mind?* I asked the egos and id.

Wake up, you ninny! You're not dead!

I opened my eyes to see two beautiful eyes of the purest violet, their color shaded with concern and fear.

"Peter?" My voice was rough and harsh and as soon as I spoke the word, feeling flooded back to me in the form of a pounding headache, and a burning sensation around my neck. With shaky hands I reached up to touch his head. "Is that really you? Am I alive?"

"It's me. And you are very much alive."

"I am here, too." A little light bobbled around over Peter's shoulder.

I gazed into Peter's eyes, not seeing any of the love I wanted to see. "Oh no, you don't remember me, do you? I'm going to have to seduce you all over again!"

The lines around those glorious eyes crinkled as he laughed, and gently, as if I were made of glass, he hugged me and kissed me. "I very much remember you, my darling Kiya, but if you wish to seduce me, it would be rude of me to refuse."

Now his face was full of all the love I expected. "I love you so much. I thought I was going to die, though."

His expression changed like quicksilver as he looked over my shoulder. I sat up, astonished to see Gregory sitting over the bodies of both William and Andrew. "You almost were killed. If I hadn't stopped to find Gregory, I'd have been here much earlier and would have kept them from attacking you."

"You stopped to get Gregory? Why? To make him admit he was hiding from us?"

"He wasn't hiding, love. That hasn't happened yet, remember? Not that I think he was hiding from us even then. But today—the day you first arrived—Gregory was just arriving in town. I'm very much afraid that all of your suspicions as to his guilt are false."

"Well, hell!" I said, struggling to my feet with Peter's able assistance.

"Thanks," Gregory said, giving me a wry smile. "I take it you're the woman who Peter says I met a few days ago. Nice to meet you . . . again."

"I'm sorry, that was rude of me. It's just that . . . I had it all worked out that Andrew had you pretending to be gone so he could blame us. And now I'm wrong and Peter was right all along."

"Not so right as all that," Peter said, assisting me to the nearest picnic table. "It turns out that Andrew wasn't the one committing the murders—William was. Andrew was working for him at covering his tracks, and put him in contact with the magician who set William up with the whipping boys, but he himself didn't have a hand in the murders."

Mrs. Faa sat in the chair, her gaze watchful, but her expression as unreadable as ever. At a gesture from her, the pugs swarmed me. I picked up two of them to cuddle, suddenly exhausted at the near-death experience. "Oh, Peter," I said, snuggling my face into a pug. "I'm so sorry that it was your own father who turned out to be the murderer. A cousin was bad enough, but a father—"

"Not a father."

We all turned to look at Gregory. He was looking at his grandmother. "Puridaj, you must tell them."

"There is no reason to do so," Mrs. Faa said, her hands on the cane before her.

"There is every reason to tell Peter who his father really was," Gregory argued. "If you do not, then I will."

She shot him a dark look. "You would betray our family to outsiders?"

Gregory took a deep breath, and to my utter surprise

walked over to Peter and held out his hand. "I have long wanted to tell you how much I've admired and envied the work you do for the Watch. I am honored to call you cousin."

Gravely, Peter shook his hand. "There is always room in the Watch for people who wish to see justice served."

"No!" Mrs. Faa struggled to her feet. "I will not have it! It was bad enough that Tobar left me to be with that mortal woman, left the family, left all that he was raised to honor and cherish. I will not lose another member to the gadjos!"

"Who's Tobar?" I asked Peter.

He shook his head. "I have no idea."

"Tobar is your father," Gregory said, assisting Mrs. Faa when she stumbled, helping her back to the chair. "Tell them, puridaj."

She seemed to sink into herself for a few minutes before finally saying, in a very small voice, "Vilem is not your father. You are the son of my oldest son, Tobar. He mated with a mortal woman, and died before you were born." Pain twisted her face as she continued. "Tobar was very dear to me. He wished to marry the mortal, but I refused. I would not have him bring that shame on the family. He said hurtful things about not wanting to live the life of a Traveller if it meant cutting off everything else. I forbade him to continue. He did not heed me, and left the family for the woman. He did not return."

"Oh, Peter," I said, squishing a pug between us as I hugged him.

"He died?" he asked, watching Mrs. Faa closely.

It was Gregory who answered, however. "Shortly before your mother gave birth to you, he died in an industrial accident, or so I was told."

"Why did you tell Peter that William was his dad if he wasn't? I'm sorry, but it was clear from the first moment that there was no love lost between the two of them, and from what Peter has said, his mom wasn't treated very well by you guys." I frowned at her, not able to understand how a woman could be so cruel to her own son and grandson.

She turned away for a moment. "Tobar was my firstborn. He wished to live outside the family, to be a part of his woman's family, to work for mortals. We could not have that shame brought to us. When I heard that my son had been killed, I did what had to be done—I could not let the mahrime child be a part of the family, and yet he bore the blood of my Tobar. I commanded Vilem to take responsibility for both the woman and the child."

"He didn't take responsibility for us. He did everything to avoid us." Peter's voice was as hard as flint. I set down the pugs and slid an arm around his waist. He pulled me closer until his heat sank into me, giving me strength and comfort. "He couldn't have been less of a father if he tried."

Mrs. Faa closed her eyes. "I do not know what is right or wrong anymore. At the time of Tobar's leaving, I did not suffer any such indecision. Life was simpler then. Now . . ." She waved a hand. "Now it is not so clear. I know only that I do not want shame brought into this family."

"Your son killed people," I couldn't help but say.

"And for that, he must pay," she agreed, which surprised me. Her eyes flashed to Peter. "You may consider me a foolish old woman, but I do not condone murder, not of mortals or Travellers. What Vilem did was an abomination. He has brought shame to the name of Faa.

You will take him away to your Watch and they will banish him so that he can harm us no more."

"They will most certainly banish him to the Akasha," Peter said mildly, but I knew he had to be hurt by his grandmother's actions in the past. But what mattered was the here and now. "And most likely Andrew will be charged as an accessory."

Her face crumpled. "Then he must pay for his actions."

"And what about Peter?" I asked, wanting to make everything right, but not sure how to go about doing so. "Now you know he wasn't persecuting you—will you accept him into your family at last?"

"Kiya," Peter said with an obvious warning in his voice. "I don't need her forgiveness, or her acceptance."

"No, but it would be nice for our kids to have some family other than my foster mom," I pointed out.

Mrs. Faa was silent, her gaze now directed down to her hands.

"Puridaj?" Gregory asked, kneeling before her, taking her hands in his. "It is long past the time when you must let go of the old ways. We are not the same as we have been. The world is not the same place."

Peter looked with speculation at his cousin.

"What?" I asked him in a whisper.

"*What* what?"

"What are you looking at Gregory like that for?"

"I think he wants to break free of Traveller bonds and work for people, instead of taking from them."

I smiled at him, and couldn't stop kissing him very quickly. "I think you and Gregory could be the start of a very good thing. You could form a company that specializes in stealing time from bad people and giving it to good people. Just imagine what the two of you could do! You could take down dictators, and psychopaths, and people who punch babies and hurt animals, and give their time to all the good people out there who need more time to benefit the world."

He gave me an amused glance. "We really are going to have to have another talk about why stealing is bad."

"Puridaj?" Gregory repeated the word.

Mrs. Faa said nothing, but she withdrew her hands from his.

Gregory looked sadly at her for a moment or two, then stood up. Without turning to Peter, he asked, "Can you give me information about joining the Watch?"

"I can. I will also give you a personal reference. My boss will be delighted to have another Traveller investigating crimes."

"I'll give you a recommendation also," I told him, feeling all warm and fuzzy. "Not that mine will count as much as Peter's, but now that I know you're a good guy, I'm happy to back you."

"Thank you," Gregory said with a slight hint of a smile in his voice.

My happy feeling lasted until I looked down at Mrs. Faa. "I'm sorry, but I'm going to have to give you my resignation. Much as I adore the pugs, I find that I can't work for you any longer."

She made a dismissive gesture. "This is a black day for the family. I have lost a son and two grandsons."

"Only if you wish to lose them," I told her. "Well, OK, I'd want to lose William and Andrew, but not Gregory and Peter."

She got to her feet on her own, smacking Gregory on the shin with the cane when he tried to assist her. "I am going to have my rest. Peter Faa, you will remove Vilem and Andrew before I return."

He made her a little bow, his beautiful eyes unreadable.

She paused at the bottom of the steps to the RV, the dogs swarming past her up the steps. For a moment she hesitated, then turned slightly toward us. "I regret my decision to have Vilem take charge of you. Upon consideration, I believe you would have brought honor to the family."

"It's not too late," I said, taking a step toward her. "He can still be a part of the family."

She was silent for a full minute before she said simply, "We shall see," and climbed the stairs, closing the door behind her.

"What an obstinate old battle-ax," I said aloud before realizing that Gregory might not appreciate that sentiment. "Sorry—I didn't mean that in a rude way. But she's . . ."

"An obstinate old battle-ax," Gregory said, his lips twisting into a wry smile. He added, his eyes on Peter, "I've never heard her apologize for anything, however. I think this bodes well, cousin."

"I do not need Lenore Faa in my life," Peter said, his arm tightening around me. "Not now."

I smiled up at him. "That's awfully romantic, but like I said, I'd really rather that our kids have a family. Neither one of us grew up with one, and it would be a nice change, don't you think?"

"We'll see," he answered, parroting his grandmother.

Gregory looked past us to where the two prone men lay. "I should have been around here more, but business kept me away for much of the year. I had no idea that

William was causing deaths, or that Andrew was covering up for him. I simply thought they were running an illegal business, and doing business with a magician for that purpose."

"It's hard to explain away the whipping boys," Peter pointed out.

"Yes, but I didn't know about them." Gregory shook his head. "They would have made me much more suspicious had I known. They couldn't have kept them here, or I would have seen them on my periodic visits. And puridaj would never have tolerated that. She is many things, but she would not tolerate William being in possession of such powerful magic."

"The whipping boys," Peter said thoughtfully, then snapped his fingers. "The motel room!"

"What motel room?" Gregory asked, at the same time as I said, "You mean Dalton's room? The one where his body was, that is?"

"Yes. The woman who runs the hotel told me there were two gay hikers staying there, but it could well be that the two men were William and Andrew."

"Why would they need a motel room when they have fancy RVs?" The light dawned just as the last word left my mouth. "Oh, you mean they holed up their magic stuff there?"

He nodded. "It makes sense that they'd need somewhere close by to store the whipping boys, but away from detection by Lenore Faa or other family members."

"Plus, it makes for a good hidey-hole should they ever want to lie low from the cops," I added.

"That's entirely possible. No doubt that was behind their thinking in using the motel address on any records the mortal police could check, such as the receipt I acquired."

"So, what exactly *is* a whipping boy?" I asked Peter. "I mean, I know what the normal definition is, but I suspect there's some woo-woo explanation that I'm totally missing."

"They're actually very close, only the whipping boy I'm referring to is a magical effect. It allows the user to transfer the guilt from a crime to another. I suspect—given that there have been no other experiences of karmic whiplash, as you call it, on Otherworld members in the area—that William was using it on mortals, transferring his responsibility for taking the life of mortals to whoever was nearest at hand."

"But wouldn't that person then be punished by your shuvani person?"

"Yes." Peter's fingers tightened into a fist. "That's why there were all those deaths of apparently unrelated mortals." He explained briefly that whenever a Traveller-related death had occurred, not long after a mortal died of an unknown cause.

"That's just so heinous," I said, feeling suddenly cold.

"It's beyond heinous."

"It's also the perfect crime, so far as the Otherworld is concerned," Gregory said. "By transferring the guilt to a mortal, William was absolved, and the mortal ultimately punished by the shuvani had no link to William."

"That's why we never had so much as a hint that a Traveller was involved in those collateral deaths," Peter agreed. "I should have known the circumstances were too coincidental, though."

"I don't see how you could without knowing about the whipping boys," Gregory commented mildly, then nodded toward his uncle and cousin. "What do you want done with them? They should be coming around soon."

Peter pulled out a couple of thin plastic ties. "Bind their hands with these and dump them in the back of my car. Dalton is on his way here now with a couple of members of the Watch. They'll be taken into custody and tried for their crimes. Along with the magician who sold Andrew the glamour and whipping boys."

Gregory took the ties. I twined my fingers through Peter's while William and Andrew were restrained and hauled over to Peter's car. Sunil said something about overseeing the maneuver, and followed Gregory.

"Wrap up another case for Detective Elizabeth Taylor Eyes. Um. Speaking of Dalton . . . did he mention anything about me?"

One side of Peter's mouth twitched. "As a matter of fact, he gave me an earful about the deranged woman he met at a doctor's office, and how she kept going on about him dying, and other impossible things. Just what did you say to him?"

I waved it away. "I'll tell you later. But you do owe me something."

He pulled me up against his chest, his breath hot on my mouth. "My thanks? A kiss? A session with Mr. Beefy?"

I giggled, and nipped his lower lip. "You have to tell me you love me. In front of witnesses."

"I love you in front of witnesses," he duly repeated, his lovely eyes dancing with amusement.

"Peter!"

He laughed. "Very well, my demanding one. I love you body and soul, heart and head, breath and . . . and . . ."

"Butt. Thank you." I looked over to where Mrs. Faa's RV sat. "You know, I think I'm going to break the cycle."

"What cycle?" Peter asked.

"This whole Traveller thing. You're absolutely right that it's bad, and it's time we helped it stop." I marched over to the RV, and flung open the door, leaning in to yell into it, "I'm going to marry your grandson, Mrs. Faa. Just so you know. And if you are mean to any children we happen to have, I will personally . . . I will . . . well, I don't know what I'd do, because I don't believe in beating up old people, but you can just bet your silver dollars that it won't be pleasant. You got that?"

Silence greeted me. I was about to close the door when she said, "Peter Faa bears my blood, as well as my Piotr's. I will go forth to the Scarboro faire in two months' time, and I will announce that he is a member of the family."

"Good!" I said, slamming shut the door. I got a bit misty-eyed as I looked at Peter. "Your grandma loves you. Deep down, she loves you. Way, way, way deep down. I don't suppose you'd like to go give her a kiss and tell her you forgive her?"

He looked down at me in horror. "Kiya—"

"Too soon? I kinda thought so. It's OK, we'll take baby steps. Her acknowledging you is a start. We'll work on developing affection, and forgiving old hurts."

He sighed, pulling me into a kiss. "I will put up with your machinations only because I want you happy, and I know how much you want a family. And because you'll make my life a living hell if I don't."

"You got that right," I said, nipping his lower lip before kissing him as he deserved to be kissed.

He pinched my behind, then went off to help Gregory

stuff the two men into the minivan Gregory had appropriated from his cousins. I stood watching Peter and Gregory working together, feeling that the future held more wonder than I ever imagined it could.

"Peter-ji is all right now, popsy?" a voice asked at my shoulder.

"Yes, he's all right. We've just acquired a family," I told Sunil's light blob, smiling and stepping forward when Peter gestured for me. "And a very, very bright future."

EPILOGUE

"So?"

Kiya met him at the door of his apartment. Her hair was pulled back in a businesslike ponytail. Peter disliked businesslike hair, especially on his warm, delicious wife of three months. In her arms was a soft towel, and snuggled into the towel was a tiny, wet, wiggling potato.

"Is that a puppy?" he asked, squinting at it. "Or a larva?"

Her nostrils flared in that delightful way she had. "Of course it's a puppy! It's number two, actually. April is doing just fine, although she has another puppy to go. Speaking of which, I'd better get back to her and make sure that she and Dumas are OK."

"Dumas?" he asked, following her as she hurried to one of the spare bedrooms, which April, the rescue pug he'd given Kiya for her birthday, had claimed as her boudoir. They hadn't known when they adopted the little pug that she was pregnant, but Kiya had taken that news in stride.

"That's what I named puppy number one. I thought we'd name this little girl Lenore, after your grandma. Do you think she'd like that? Mrs. Faa, not the puppy. And what did the Watch overlord thingie say?"

Kiya knelt by the wooden whelping box she'd managed to borrow from a dog rescue organization, gently placing the small squirming larva next to the fawn and black pug. April's curled tail thumped a few times as he knelt next to her, groaning as he rubbed her tiny little black ears. "They said yes."

"Now you see, April, Daddy is home, and you can stop fretting and just have that last puppy that the vet says you have in there, so that we can get you cleaned up and made more comfy." Kiya froze for a second, and looked up at him, an expression of mingled surprise and joy on her face. "They said yes?"

"They did." He touched the two minute puppies with a finger, guiding the smaller of the two to April's teat. The puppy grunted in happiness.

"They really said yes? They're going to reinstate Sunil?"

"Resurrect him is more appropriate a term. The L'audela committee and head of the Watch authorized the funds to hire a necromancer to locate and resurrect Sunil's remains in recognition for his assistance in the capture of a serial mortal-murderer."

She clasped her hands for a second, then, with a stifled yell of joy, threw herself on him and kissed his nose and chin and left cheek before he finally got her positioned properly so that she was kissing his mouth. "So he's going to be a ghost?"

"No. He'll be a lich, but one who is not bound to anyone."

"A free-range lich!" She kissed him again, then asked, just as he knew she would, "What's a lich?"

He laughed, filled with more happiness than he thought possible. "Kind of a revenant. One that doesn't crave flesh, though."

"Woot! He'll be so happy. Have you told him yet?" Kiya glowed with happiness, the soft look of admiration in her eyes warming him more than anything else in the world.

"Not yet. I thought I'd wait until he's back from his visit to Versailles."

She glanced down at the dog. "Well, that should only be a few more hours. April should have her last puppy soon, and then Mr. Afraid of Blood and Birthing Juices can come home."

"This also means that Sunil will be able to testify at William's and Andrew's trials next month," he told her, settling with her on his lap, one hand still petting the pug's head. "Animi are excluded from testimony, since they are bound to an individual, and thus their testimony could be rendered false by command of the person to whom they are bound, but an unbound lich is able to appear before the committee and testify as needed."

"Ha! That means Sunil can tell the jury about all the stuff that he overheard William saying. And what he heard from the magician. This is awesome, Peter! With Gregory, you, and now Sunil testifying, they won't have a chance to get off. Did you see Gregory at the Watch place?"

"I did. He sends his regards. He starts training next month. Dalton said that if all goes well, he will be able to shadow me in about two months."

"The Faa cousins, defenders of the universe," Kiya said, obviously pleased by that thought. "You know, if you guys ever wanted to go freelance, you could make a detective agency or something."

"Actually, we talked about something like that."

Her eyes opened wide. "You're going to become a private eye? Won't Dalton be pissed?"

"We talked about joining forces to bring the Travellers into the twenty-first century." He looked out the window at the late-summer sunlight. The world did seem to be a brighter place now that Kiya filled his life. But there were still dark things out there, battles yet to be won. And for the first time in his life, he wasn't going to have to face them alone. "We're going to talk to the rest of our cousins. Others have to feel as we do. If we can band together, perhaps we can change the Traveller society, one family at a time."

"You really are a hero," Kiya said with one of those admiring looks that made him feel like a superman. "Everything turned out just perfect! Gregory will join the Watch and help you make Travellers less asshatty, Sunil will have his body back, Dalton is alive again, Mrs. Faa is going to tell all the other Travellers that we're not stinky and untouchable, and your uncle and bastard cousin will get what they have coming to them."

She leaned back against him, a solid presence that gave him more pleasure than he had ever thought possible.

"Yes," he said into her hair, giving himself up to the wonder that was this new life. "Everything is perfect."

TRAVELLERS

From the *Otherworld Encyclopedia*, your source to all things
beyond the mortal world

The Travellers are a mortal race that possesses immortal
abilities. They live predominately in Europe, the Americas, and Australasia, and can trace their ancestry back to
500 AD.

TERMINOLOGY

Travellers are most often confused by the mortal world
as being Romany (and thus frequently given the exonym
of *Gypsies*), but that is a misconception that in part owes
its origins to the shared term "Traveller" as a descriptor
for both groups. We shall henceforth refer to the mortal
beings as "Romani" and "Rom" in order to avoid any
confusion.

Although it is unknown at what point the Travellers
began to refer to themselves by that name, they have long
claimed that the term is used to distinguish themselves
from indigenous peoples, since their sense of cultural
identity is strong, and thus it is very important to delin-

eate which people were members of their societal struc-
ture (Travellers), and which were outsiders (gadjos).

There is speculation that classifying individuals has
less to do with culture and more to do with identifying
suitable prey, but modern-day Travellers dismiss this
idea.

ORIGINS

While it is true that Travellers and the Rom share an
origin in the Indian subcontinent around 500 AD, the
two peoples separated early in their respective develop-
ments. Where the Romany people spread out from India
to Europe, western Asia, and northern Africa, the Travellers migrated in waves toward eastern and central Europe. It is believed that by 800 AD, the Travellers had
completed their separation from the Romany peoples, in
large part due to the Travellers' discovery of abilities
concerning the manipulation of time.

Certainly by 900 AD there are mentions in early Otherworld journals of *"travaillour theofs"* being prosecuted
for thefts committed upon various members of the newly
formed L'au-dela, as seen in this translation of an entry
by the Dresden Watch dated 28 January 909:

> *The lord Albert Camus did bring charge of
> full thievery unto Mercallus Dickon, travail-
> lour, and did rightly so demand the penalty
> for loss of time worth three marks. Master
> Dickon was found guilty and sentenced to
> flogging, but escaped he with his skin intact
> before said punishment could be enacted.*

SOCIETY AND TRADITIONAL CULTURE

One reason why many mortals confuse Travellers with Romany people is the similarity of their mobile lifestyle. Travellers seldom settled in any one location until recent times, preferring instead a nomadic life, one in which they were not bound to any land or country.

This insistence on retaining autonomy naturally has led to strong familial ties, to the point where *gadjos*— outsiders, or nonfamily—are excluded from all but the most trivial of matters.

This sense of familial containment is frequently accompanied by ostracism by both mortals and immortals alike, the former because of their incorrect belief that Travellers are Gypsies, and the latter because of an awareness of the Travellers' abilities. Outright persecution against all Travellers within the Otherworld is a thing of the past, but recent records of the L'au-dela Watch indicate that a higher percentage of Travellers are convicted of theft than any other ethnic group within the Otherworld.

With regard to their culture itself, Travellers favor the color red, as it is perceived of being the color of luck. The concept of luck is most vital to Travellers, since they believe it influences their temporal abilities in either a positive or negative capacity. As the traditional Traveller proverb says, "All I need is good luck. With luck I would not mind sitting on two horses at once that were walking on a bent road." Scholars have long debated what such a confusing proverb means, with theories varying from a reference to the long-suspected Traveller ability to be at two places at once via time manipulation, to the more commonplace belief that this proverb, like all other known Traveller proverbs, is an inside joke intended to confuse and bewilder outsiders.

Travellers have an almost dragonlike fondness for gold, although they hold little value for other precious metals, feeling that anything but gold is unlucky. They are also reportedly believers in a unique form of karma, and believe that to take time from another without paying for it will result in much bad luck, the degree of which varies depending upon the quantity of time taken. The payment for time is usually made in silver, not gold, as silver is considered suitable only for gadjos.

TIME MANIPULATIONS

Travellers have long been thought of as "time thieves," but that term is considered by most Travellers as a misnomer. The Travellers claim that their ability to extract amounts of time from willing or unwilling targets is not so much a theft as it is a manipulation, a rechanneling of existing time from one individual to another, conducted on a subatomic level. Although most victims of such manipulations refer to the phenomenon as having "lost time," in fact the time is not lost; it is simply gained by the Traveller, who may then use it in any number of ways.

How Travellers first gained the ability to steal time is a subject of much debate, but common Traveller lore indicates that it was a power granted to them by a deity or demigod in appreciation for some unnamed act. Consideration has been given to the aptitude of savant Travellers (so-called because of their ability to acquire more than just a fleeting moment of time here or there, as is common with most Travellers), which manifests itself in the capacity to harness and utilize electrostatic energy, namely lightning, and to a lesser extent small static charges.

There is no evidence that Travellers utilize static energy surrounding them in order to steal time, although it is rumored that all savant Travellers bear "lightning flowers" branded into their skin. Better known to scientists as a Lichtenberg figure, this phenomenon is created when lightning strikes a human, the current of which leaves a feathery reddish pattern along the skin as it discharges. Although the subsequent markings on mortals are in general of a temporary nature, they are permanent for Travellers, frequently bringing attention to the fact that the Traveller is not what he appears. This "branding" has long been viewed as a viable method of distinguishing a Traveller when he attempts to fool his persecutors into believing he is a mere mortal.

Because of the clannish nature of Travellers, scientific proof of the connection between lightning and time theft has yet to be made. Only the Travellers know for sure whether a correlation exists, and if so, to what extent the two things are related.

GLOSSARY

animus: That essence of a being that can live on after the death of the body. In the case of Sunil, his life force (more or less his soul) was bound to Peter by the Shuvani in punishment for wrongful death. Animuses can take many different forms, but Sunil's naturally sunny nature resulted in his form as a ball of golden light.

gadjo: A Traveller (and Romany) word for outsiders, people who do not share their heritage. It can be merely a descriptive word to indicate someone outside the family, or an insult, depending on the speaker's intent.

kris: A Traveller tribunal called when judgment is needed to be brought against other Travellers. They are officiated by three krisatora, who make a final decision as to the fate of the accused individual.

krisatora: Three individuals of Traveller blood who preside over a kris.

L'au-dela: The formal name for the Otherworld, the society of people who live beyond mortal laws.

L'au-dela Watch: The police force of the Otherworld, the Watch is responsible for keeping the peace among mortals and immortal beings, as well as protecting the mortal world from abuses by members of the Otherworld.

lich: A person who was resurrected from the dead, a lich looks like a normal person, aside from his black irises. Most liches are bound to the individual who holds their soul.

Lichtenberg figure: The pattern made by an electrical discharge through a soft medium.

Lightning flower: The name for a Lichtenberg figure when made on a human being. The pattern is of a delicate, feathery nature, and is also referred to as a *lightning tree*. The pattern is most likely caused by the rupture of capillaries as the current passes through. Although lightning flowers are temporary for mortals, they are a permanent brand on Travellers.

mahrime: A Traveller (and Romany) word for those who are deemed unclean. For Travellers, this can mean one who has impure blood (i.e. one non-Traveller parent) or someone who has no Traveller blood whatsoever.

martiya: A spirit of the night. Travellers, like their Romany cousins, have a great dislike for ghosts, and will go out of their way to avoid them.

pollution, idea of: The idea of pollution from outside sources is very important to Traveller society. They fear having their inner body polluted by outer influences, and for that reason avoid contact with non-Travellers. They also believe cats and dogs are polluted (because they lick their outer body, bringing the dirt into their clean inner self), which is why Travellers seldom have pets living in their homes.

porrav: A Traveller word with Indo-Aryan roots, it literally means "to open up" or "blossom." In Traveller culture, it refers to the joining of a man and woman, and their shared abilities mingling to form something greater than the parts.

puridaj: A respectful way to refer to a Traveller grandmother.

Rehor: an Eastern European version of the name Gregory.

Rom, Roma, Romany: Words describing an ethnic group most commonly referred to as Gypsies. Travellers and the Roma may share a common ancestor since they share a few traits and words. Like the Travellers, the Romany were frequently persecuted for being outsiders.

shuvani: Spirits who hold Travellers accountable for their actions. There are four flavors of shuvani: earth, water, air, and field. A shuvani can be friendly or unkind, depending on his or her nature, but all are charged with punishing Travellers who abuse their abilities.

Travellers: A group of mortal people who possess immortal abilities, can steal time, and have an affinity with lightning.

Vilem: An Eastern European version of the name William.